LAWRENCE BLOCK

This special signed
edition is limited to
750 numbered copies.

This is copy  **724** .

PLAYING GAMES

PLAYING GAMES

Edited by

Lawrence Block

Subterranean Press 2023

First Edition

ISBN
978-1-64524-090-7

Subterranean Press
PO Box 190106
Burton, MI 48519

subterraneanpress.com

Manufactured in the United States of America

Table of Contents

Shut Up and Deal (an introduction)

By Lawrence Block

Anthologism, the last refuge of the over-the-hill writer, is largely the business of persuading talented writers to make time in their already burdensome work schedules, time they can spend writing a story for your anthology. You can't offer them much in the way of compensation, as there's not much money to go around. But they'll be in good company, you can assure them. And, best of all, won't the story be fun to write?

Hmm. The writers whose stories constitute *Playing Games* are indeed in good company, and their contributions read as though they were fun to write. (But never assume. How a story reads doesn't always reflect what it was like to write it. Some painfully dark work will turn out to have flowed almost effortlessly from psyche to page; other writing, light and effervescent and apparently spontaneous, will have been agony for the author.)

Besides the requisite arm-twisting, my job calls for me to come up with a theme. It's possible, as Neil Gaiman and Al Sarrantonio demonstrated in *Stories,* to have an anthology without a theme—but it's easier to generate ideas from writers and enthusiasm from readers if there's a unifying element.

But you have to choose your theme carefully. You don't want everyone writing essentially the same story, do you?

My previous anthology, *Collectibles,* worked well; every story touched upon a different sort of object of desire. And I thought *Collectibles* would be my final anthology—and then, God save the mark, I Had An Idea.

"Pick a game," I urged in my invitational email. And I listed a couple of dozen games, just as an example, and each writer picked a suggested or unlisted game, and the stories came in, and you can see for yourself how very nicely it all worked out.

◎

NOBODY PICKED CHESS.

Now that surprised me, though perhaps it shouldn't have. Around the time *Playing Games* was taking shape, *The Queen's Gambit* was making waves as Scott Frank's brilliant miniseries on Netflix, and sending a whole generation of new readers to the outstanding and endlessly rereadable Walter Tevis novel that inspired it. While chess has turned up in no end of stories over the years, sitting across the metaphorical 64-square board from Mr. Tevis might seem daunting right about now.

When I was a boy, chess was my game. I remember the occasion when I was introduced to the fundamentals. I must have been nine or ten years old, something like that. It was after a family dinner at my grandparents' house on Hertel Avenue in Buffalo, and one of my two uncles—I'm not sure which one—set up the board and told me the names of the pieces and how they moved. (My mother had two brothers, Hi and Jerry Nathan, and either of them could have taught me the game. I rather think it was Hi, because he was a stamp collector, and I remember how he explained the way the knight moved: "From one corner to the other of a block of six stamps." That made perfect sense to me.)

I was no Beth Harmon, but I was good enough to beat most of the kids I played with—until I became friendly with David Krantz, who beat me most of the time. At Bennett High I joined the chess club, and some faculty member organized a chess team, and we competed in an unofficial interschool league. (It was a remarkable enterprise in that Buffalo at the time consisted of an approximately equal number of public and parochial schools, and never the twain did meet; in baseball and football and basketball, the Catholic schools competed in their league, the public schools in theirs. But our chess league of ten or a dozen schools was sufficiently ecumenical to include Canisius and St. Joe's.)

I played on the chess team my junior and senior years. A team consisted of five players, and they were ranked—First Board, Second Board, Third Board, Fourth Board, and Fifth Board. That way the putative best player on our team would be matched with the best opposing player. I was Fifth Board my junior year, Fourth Board my senior year. My fellows were Floyd Lippa, Richard Polakoff, Dave Krantz, and Bob Stalder, and my senior year we beat our arch-rival, Kensington, and won the city championship. While our victory did get announced at a school assembly, I don't think anybody paid much attention. God knows it didn't get any of us laid...

Never mind.

◎

GAMES PLAYED A big role in my parents' social life. My mother played mahjong with the same women every Monday afternoon for years on end. What they mostly did, it seems to me, was talk about other people, and I was frequently within hearing range, and if I'd had the sense to pay close attention instead of tuning them out I'd have had enough material to get in the ring with John O'Hara.

My parents played contract bridge, as did most of the couples in their social circle. A typical dinner party would consist of eight or a dozen at table, followed by two or three tables of bridge for the rest of the evening. Less formally, they'd get together with another couple for an evening at the bridge table. On an evening at home, or to kill an idle hour, they'd often play Two-handed Pinochle, a game I often played with one or the other of them. I played Casino with my father, gin rummy with my cousin Peter Nathan, and, in high school, played a lot of poker and blackjack with friends.

My Uncle Jerry, whose collection of elephants I detailed in the introduction to *Collectibles,* reinvented himself a couple of times. After years partnered with Hi in Atlas Plastics, he launched a career as a promoter of jazz and rock concerts. Then an interest in backgammon became a passion, and he became a student of the game who morphed into a teacher of the game.

◎

AH, MEMORY LANE. All these empty houses, just waiting for an HGTV show to flip them. Two years ago, Lynne and I were stuck for weeks in Newberry, South Carolina, with a nonfunctional TV; we took to playing a few hands of gin rummy of an evening. It didn't really take. Then the cable company finally hooked us up, and we haven't looked at the cards since.

Never mind. You're on your own now, so do what you will. Deal the cards, set up the checkerboard, haul out the Scrabble set.

And, somewhere along the way, read these stories.

Seek and You Will Find

By Patricia Abbott

"Remember Jerry Baker always insisting on waiting until after Memorial Day," Ruth said, slamming the car door. She was dressed in grass-stained overalls and rubber mocs. A faded yellow visor advertising Circuit City partially obscured her eyes. "Retirement's made me less risk-averse," she added, yanking on a pair of buckskin gardening gloves pulled from her pocket. She opened her purse, removed a bottle of sunscreen, and smeared the center of her face with it. "Do you need some?"

Kitty, wearing stylishly wide-legged cropped jeans and a jaunty hat woven with a grosgrain ribbon, resisted laughing at the spotty coverage. Her bare hands, newly manicured, were already encased in medical gloves. She beeped the car lock and said, "Let's go. This place will be teeming with customers in an hour."

"You remember him, don't you? 'America's Master Gardener.'"

"Jerry Who?" Kitty said, grabbing a cart. Its squeaky wheels drowned out her friend's reply.

The women concentrated on the aisles of late spring perennials, hoping to get a week or two of color in their gardens before the blooms were spent.

"Someone should be pinching these back," Ruth said, dealing with one offender with practiced fingers. "Look how leggy they are. I was hoping for a few bleeding hearts, but it may be too late."

"Speaking of leggy," Kitty said, nodding toward a man who seemed to be trying to hide beneath a table of annuals. Chin almost resting on his knees, he reminded her of an insect. Maybe a grasshopper or a katydid, not that she could tell them apart. Sunglasses sliding down her nose, she took a closer look. He was forty-five perhaps, with an explosion of silver hair sprouting from the crown. Despite the chill air, he wore lime bike shorts, a sleeveless red tee, and dirty flip-flops of an indeterminate color. He was as colorful as the plants he crouched among but menacing somehow. Maybe it was the tattoos.

Ruth glanced up from the tray of Johnson's Blues. "Sorry, Kit. Didn't catch that."

"That guy over there. He's been chasing a kid around. Nearly knocked over a display of Fiskars when we first came in." A blank look met her: Ruth was laser-focused on the plants. "Then he ran down a stock boy by the roses," Kitty continued, peering into Ruth's pollen-glazed eyes. "How could you miss it, Rooty-toot? A girl was straddling his shoulders as he galloped past. He had to duck or take her head off on the door frame."

A nod. "Always hated hide and seek if that's what he's up to. I was terrified no one would look for me, so I jumped out too early." She shrugged. "Anyway, I missed the little drama but you've given me a vivid play-by-play." Ruth held a plant up. "Look at this poor baby. Over-watered. What kind of help are they hiring this year?" She looked toward the service counter.

Kitty nodded. "Hide and seek, yes. I never came out of my hidey hole even when the game was over. Afraid of being tricked into giving myself away and getting tagged. Or was that Tag?" Ruth shrugged. "Anyway, I remember hiding on a deep shelf in my grandmother's linen closet—well, my closet now—until everyone grew frantic that I'd stepped into the looking glass or through the back of a wardrobe. I was very good at waiting them out. Of course, my mother was probably hoping for an Edward Eager conclusion. Remember his books?"

"*Half Magic?*"

"Right. They kept calling me and calling…oh, look, Ruth, now he's under the table of Lenten roses."

Head bobbing, neck tensile, muttering, the man begged for attention. Perhaps he looked more like a bird than an insect, Kitty thought. A flamingo, a heron?

"That dusty pink is breathtaking. It's a shame to be planting early spring perennials in May, but you can't pass up such great plants. I always mean to order them online in winter, but I never…"

The raucous laughter of the man filled the greenhouse. "Well, is it so odd for a father to play tag with his kid?" Ruth wondered aloud. "Poised like a praying mantis though, isn't he? And when did people start tattooing their faces? I thought we had an agreement about leaving faces unmarked." A tiny dragonfly, exquisitely inked, hovered on his left cheek. Twitching almost. Was he playing up a tic?

"A praying mantis. That's it. I've been trying to place it. Although, perhaps in this case, a preying mantis." Kitty brightened at her cleverness. "Get it. E instead of A. The kid's hiding in the bathroom, I think. He's probably ready to leap out when she comes through the door. When did tattoos became so popular?"

"And big ones. No tasteful butterflies or tributes to 'Mother.' There's a good chance he'll overturn that table with those scissoring legs. He's practically animated." Ruth put down the plant, looking ready to take action now that the stock seemed at risk. "Why did they choose a garden center for their reindeer games?"

"Probably tripped up by the word nursery." Looking around, Kitty spotted an open spot on a table and began emptying her bag. Coming up with her cell phone, she crammed the rest back in.

"See that flap on the front of your purse," Ruth said, pointing. "That's where you're supposed to keep the phone. Oh, you're not calling the police, Kitty, are you? For goodness sake."

"I'm taking a picture."

"Really. Of Grasshopper under the table?"

"Ha! From *Kung Fu,* right," Kitty said. "Yes Master Po, because maybe he's kidnapped her. There's something off about him. Something sinister. If you'd been watching more closely, you'd know what I mean. I can't remember Bill ever chasing Sarah around like that."

Of course, Bill hadn't been much of a game-player. Especially anything athletic. The most you could hope for was that he'd read his daughter something enriching. *Ivanhoe* perhaps.

"You seem awfully interested in him. It's not going to turn into one of your things, is it? Something you obsess over for days. I doubt Grasshopper would've brought her here if he was up to no good," Ruth continued. "Look, as long as you have a phone out, could you snap a picture of that display?" Ruth pointed to an arrangement of annuals in shades of lavender, bright pink, and orange. "I have a ter-racotta planter begging for something dramatic, and I'll never get the right combination. Remember the year I planted the entire garden in white? Pretty in its way, but I regretted it later. So unimaginative."

"Sort of magical at night though. Glowy. Is that a word?"

"If they can use the word flowy on *Project Runway,* it is."

The door to the restroom opened and a skinny girl of about ten sauntered out, her face expressionless. The man leaped from under the table and the girl delivered the requisite scream. It was unconvincing, a set piece, but the man seemed pleased and looked around for interest.

"He expects us to applaud, doesn't he?" Kitty said. "Can you imagine him chasing after you? Poor kid." She shivered. "Although really he's more comical than scary." She thought for a moment. "Maybe he's rehearsing for a kid's party?"

Ruth picked up a pot of lavender. "Oh, my God, just smell this. So delicate. Perfumers never get it right."

Kitty watched a minute longer, her interest waning as the man and child darted among the tiers of hostas, finally disappearing into the evergreens. The shrieks subsided or were lost in the foliage, and eventually the women's attention returned to their plant selection. Thirty minutes later, they loaded their purchases into Kitty's sedan.

"My Jeep would've come in handy today." Ruth slammed the trunk shut. "Sorry it's in the shop. I hope we don't make too much of a mess. Or me anyway." About to open the door, she peeked inside. "My car wasn't this clean when I pulled out of the dealer's lot." She scraped her feet on the macadam, dislodging mud and leaves.

"Well, it's only a few months old," Kitty said, almost apologetically. How in the world had Ruth gotten so muddy, she wondered, looking down at her own spotless shoes. All that scooting about in the shrubberies probably. And grooming plants she'd no intention of buying. "Never mind, Bill will clean it up. He loves getting out his little vacuum. Men and their gadgets. Look, there they are again," Kitty said, staring as the man and the girl got into a battered Ford across the lot. The girl carried a large white lily, which nearly obscured her thin face.

"Mother's Day? It's not for two weeks yet. That plant will last about twenty-four hours. Why don't the clerks clue them in?"

"The lily she's hugging to death has probably been sitting around since Easter." Ruth looked again to make sure their new purchases were secure. She'd asked the clerk for twine and spent a few minutes constructing a snare. Her Jeep conveniently had one, a net gate that stretched across the back. But in a sedan like Kitty's, the plants would tumble about. Bill would probably be furious if dirt was strewn everywhere. She didn't like having him upset with her even if she rarely ran into him.

Kitty, letting Ruth fashion the plant trappings, took note of the license plate on the Focus—a specialty plate that read 2FAST4U. Seconds later, the man sped out, spraying gravel on an older man pushing a baby stroller. Both women gasped, but fortunately his passenger was a large holly bush.

"Well, you can't say his plate didn't warn us," Kitty said. "Mind if we stop at the resale shop, Ruth? I promised Ava I'd pick up a few Beanie Babies. They sell them for a buck or two there." A few minutes later, they found a parking spot outside of Second Helpings.

"The Beanies are in back near the dressing rooms," Kitty said, pushing through the garments. Hawaiian shirts, concert tees, and cargo pants filled rack after rack. "Bill has dozens of this sort of T-shirt squirreled away somewhere. Hard to picture him at a Lou Reed performance now." She thought about picking one up as a joke but he'd probably look at her with his usual disdain.

The odor of stale perfume assaulted them as they sped through the Better Dresses aisle.

"I paid $18.50 to dry clean my winter coat last week and that was from just a spritz or two of scent at Christmas." Ruth sighed. "Another collective decision we agreed to, I guess. No more perfume."

"Only among academic types. They have more rules than regular folks." A straw hat attracted Kitty's attention and she pulled off the one she was wearing to try it. Too small. Was her head growing along with her feet?

As they passed the makeshift dressing rooms, the girl they'd seen at the plant center shot out wearing a very adult dress. It was a surreal moment that startled both women as dramatically as a gunshot. The dress was a deep royal blue with spaghetti straps. The girl bunched the gaping top with a fist, embarrassed when she noticed the women watching. Her eyes were slits as she slid past them to the desilvered mirror where she appeared and disappeared as if they were looking at her through a kaleidoscope. As she examined herself, her back straightened, her chest rose, even her face hardened and you could see how she'd look in a decade or even two.

A purplish bruise necklaced her collarbone. Kitty winced, imagining angry fingers on that delicate neck.

"Too young for dances," Ruth said, under her breath. "Is he dressing her up for his own pleasure?"

"Oh, for Pete's sake. I hope not. And you accuse me of being gruesome."

Could it be a tattoo and not a bruise? Kitty would've loved to put on her glasses, but the search through her purse would be too obvious. Where was he anyway? She looked around, finding him on a large green plastic frog, not ten feet behind her, his hairy legs draping it. The sudden proximity gave her the hiccups. The Princess and the Frog, was that the one?

"Except for the lack of a chest, the dress almost fits her," Ruth whispered. "She's too old for dress-up, too young for dances, and it's not Halloween."

"Do you see that bruise?" Kitty whispered back, moving further away from the frog.

"What? Oh, damn. I thought it was a necklace."

"Put on your glasses, girl."

The man sprung up. "You look like a million bucks, Sweetie. Knew that dress would be perfect."

The girl hunched her shoulders. "This dress smells like fish. Something icky anyway. We should put it back. I look stupid."

Putting a hand on the girl's nearly bare back, he patted it. "Nah, you look great. Get dressed, kiddo, and we'll hit the road. That plant's probably suffocating out there."

The girl sniffed. "We should've gotten a new lily from the other cart."

"Nah, she likes white lilies best."

White lilies are an Easter thing, Kitty thought. Probably giving them away by now.

The kid slipped behind the curtains, and the man sat down on the frog. He pretended the frog was bucking, his feet hammering the floor. A flip-flop flew off and he got up to retrieve it. "I remember when Tiffany liked those things," he said, nodding toward the Beanie Babies as he bent over and nabbed it with his pinkie. "Couple of years back. She must've had fifty of 'em lined up on her bed."

"Thunderbolt," Kitty said to Ruth, reading the tag on a brown and white horse. "I think Ava's after this one. She's crazy about horses."

"Girls always go for the studs," the man said, snickering. "We probably have ole' Thunderbolt at home. Let me see." He grabbed the horse before Kitty could react. Up close, his tattoos seemed as overwhelming as his odor, which wasn't cologne. "I'm not sure. Maybe it was another one."

"Tiffany's your daughter?"

Ruth fidgeted beside her. Kitty's abrupt interactions with strangers made her nervous because there was no telling where it might lead. During the last election, Kitty asked strangers who they'd voted for much to her friend's alarm. And when their response, if it came, didn't please her, she'd make a snide remark or frown. Ruth would never think to start a conversation with a strange man in a store. If strangers talked to her, especially men, she pretended hearing issues.

"You know how it is," the man said. He handed the horse back to Kitty as if she had foisted it off on him.

On their way across the parking lot, Kitty took a picture of his license plate.

"Who are you, Jessica Fletcher?" Ruth said, getting into the passenger's seat and fastening her belt. Her knees throbbed, promising rain. It'd be perfect if she could get the flowers into the ground and take advantage of it. "Remember her?"

"Of course, I remember. Sunday nights."

"Cabot Cove, right? When's the last time you saw an older woman in a leading role?" Ruth wondered if *Murder She Wrote* was still in reruns on one of the two hundred stations she paid for. "Of course, we were practically girls then. And Jessica seemed elderly."

"Young mothers anyway. I wonder if I should call Sarah to make sure Ava doesn't have this one." Kitty looked at the tag again. "Thunderbolt."

"You're stalling, Kit. Please don't tell me you're going to follow him. First you point out how sleazy he is and then you sidle up to him. Remember those poison pen letters you tried to track down…"

"Of course I won't follow him," Kitty interrupted her, thinking that a little community concern was not out of line. "I've heard about road rage often enough to be cautious." She paused. "There's that woman on *Law and Order.*"

"What? Oh, right. Two female leads actually."

After a few minutes, the man and child emerged, blinking in the midday light. The man opened the rear door of his car and placed the dress, now in a dry-cleaning bag, on the back hook. A moment later, they sped away, the plate, 2FAST4U, disappearing around the corner before Kitty could react.

"She didn't seem scared. He's probably her mother's boyfriend," Ruth said.

"There he was in plain sight, caressing her back. Did you catch that at least?" Ruth was the most unobservant woman on the planet, Kitty thought. Except when it came to flowers. She could spot bulbs before they were a half-inch out of the ground.

"Caressing is too strong a word," Ruth said. "Sure, he's a bit odd, but my nephew, a physicist at the university in Iowa, plays Extreme Frisbee—or something like that—collects tin whistle toys from the 1920s, and, and, oh right, only eats food that grows above the ground and doesn't have a face. Younger people today feel free to be eccentric."

"I'm not talking about odd hobbies, Ruth."

"Playing hide and seek at a plant center isn't a crime. I'm sure kids do it all the time."

"He's not a kid. And she's too old for hide and seek. And too young for that dress." Kitty was growing angrier by the minute. Why didn't Ruth see the danger? She remembered the phrase 'stranger danger' from the eighties. But this was no stranger. He obviously had access to the girl. Grooming her, that was the term now unless the grooming phase was already over. "She hated wearing that dress. I have this sickening image of him dressing her up in that gown and— doing—I don't even know what." Both women shuddered.

When they pulled up at her house, Ruth said, "Look, maybe you're right, but what can we do? I don't think you have the pull or know-how to run his plates."

Tired of the subject, Kitty got out and helped Ruth unload her plants on the driveway. The wind had picked up and the sheets of pink plastic the nursery gave them blew across the lawn. "Maybe we can wrap him in a few of these and bury him among the day lilies," Ruth joked, pulling a sheet off a prickly bush. "He'd probably make good fertilizer. Smelled ripe enough." When Kitty said nothing, she added, "I don't suppose you could just let it go, Kit-Kat?" Kitty shrugged.

Kitty made the ten-minute drive home. Her grandparents had built the Tudor-style house in the late twenties before the market collapsed. Some of her grandmother's rose bushes, or the hardier of their descendants, struggled to hang on. But only a few of the original trees remained. The elms, once framing the property, were long gone. So many blights in the century. Kitty's mother let the garden go to seed during her decades as its disinterested mistress. But now Kitty had the time and ambition to bring it back. Yellowing photos of the original garden, plasticined into an album in the nineteen-seventies, guided her project.

There were also many photos taken inside the house over its history. Plank flooring, rugs, wall to wall, and eventually bare floors again. Dark furniture gave way to blond and then a Danish look. Walls covered with flocked paper with predatory vines and enormous flowers prevailed for decades. And, in one photo, stern-looking birds stood on guard. Falcons perhaps?

Even the closet where she'd hidden as a kid had been thickly papered when they moved in. She steamed it off in the nineties, needing constant breaks from the claustrophobia and near asphyxiation the job induced. Beneath the wallpaper, at the back of the large shelf, she'd found a little door.

So her mother had sort of gotten it right with her ideas of secret kingdoms. There was a door, just not one to another world. When she pried it open, it was dusty inside. The only things she found were the remains of mice or perhaps bats, a few girly magazines, and a flashlight, its battery dead probably for decades. What man sneaked up here to look at these *Cavaliers?* It had to be Bill or her father. How on earth had any live thing worked its way into this space? She thought about sealing it up, but perhaps the entrance to what was hardly more than a crawl space had a purpose? Ventilation? Access to the mechanical systems? She meant to ask Bill but never did. In fact, she never told him of its existence. Of course, if the magazines were his...

She was glad to have that wallpaper gone. Sarah had cried, always hating anything to be changed. But Bill sighed with relief, admitting, "I expected those vines to ensnare me one night."

Peonies, that was it. She'd forgotten to pick a plant or two up at the nursery. Such an odd but gorgeous flower. Did ants really uncover the blooms? That tattooed man at the nursery had been so distracting that she'd also forgotten to get more mulch and fertilizer. It'd been a strange and unfulfilling day after she'd looked forward to it for weeks. Was Ruth right about the man? Was it all in her head? Was she mistaking playfulness for malevolence?

There were at least four troublesome things to dwell on. No, five. His inappropriate behavior at the nursery, the bruises on the girl's neck, the erotic dress he made the kid parade around in, the way he put his hand on her back, and the comment about girls liking "studs." He said "studs" with particular emphasis—like he was one and wanted you to notice. She trembled, realizing with embarrassment that this was all a bit exciting to her. Obviously, it had been too long since...too long since something.

Later, she planted the flowers on both sides of the house, being careful to add new soil, starter fertilizer, and water. A proper beginning was important in the Midwest. She'd already double-dug the ground, a task that would soon be too much for her. Some days she felt sixty, but other days not so much. Usually gardening took her mind off whatever was bothering her, but not today. What could she do about that man? In all likelihood, she'd never run into him again. The only evidence of anything irregular were the photographs on her cell phone of him hiding under the Lenten roses, and the one of his license plate. As Ruth said, she'd no way to run a license plate. Most people seemed to have a cop in the family. She did have a cousin who sold car insurance for AAA. Maybe he had access to plate numbers. Should she call him? Her family members had a way of saying, "Oh, Kitty," like she made this stuff up. Like she wanted to notice things.

Running inside as the rain began, she slipped her gardening shoes off at the door, leaving her gloves there too. She took her cell phone upstairs to the computer in Bill's study and was ready to print the two shots, but there was no photography paper. Bill seemed to have lost his interest in printing things. A record of their 2016 trip to Yellowstone only existed on the picture app on her cell phone. It was time for him to join her in retirement. Then they could do some of the things they'd talked about for years. Or talked about years ago, more like it. He seemed to have no interest in travel now. Unless it was a tour of golf courses or baseball parks, and that would probably be with one of his buddies.

She texted Ruth the photo of the flower arrangement she'd wanted for reference, giggling to herself as she remembered Ruth's white garden. In the midst of all the white that year, a few rogue cone flowers had poked through. Ruth hadn't had the heart to disturb them so they remained till frost, large pink eyes peeking out. It was especially eerie at dusk, the women agreed. The white was long gone, but the pink flowers were still there, coming up each year in increasing numbers.

On an impulse, Kitty delayed starting dinner to look up the website of the police station on Willis Street, the one closest to the nursery. She found the name of the Chief of Police, located his email address, composed a message telling him about her two worrisome encounters with the tattooed man, attached both pictures, and pushed SEND. How easily she accomplished this compared to what was necessary to get attention for some troublesome issues in the past. Luckily, it was not one of the police stations she'd contacted before.

No one would take her warning seriously, of course. It'd be just like the last time. Silence from above. Apathy on the ground. She made herself a drink. It wasn't even four o'clock and she usually waited for Bill to come home from the office, but who'd tell. And who cared?

◎

TEN DAYS LATER, Kitty was reading in a shady spot in the backyard when she heard something stir. She turned around, expecting to find a rabbit or squirrel, and saw it was him—the tattooed man. He came leaping out from behind an overgrown crab myrtle. All that jumping. Were there springs on his shoes?

"Mrs. Gartland? Katherine Gartland?"

How had he learned her name?

"Mrs. Gartland?" he repeated, raising his voice as if she might have a hearing problem. "I want to talk to you for a minute. I knocked on the front door but...hey, hey, you don't need to be afraid."

Kitty was shaking badly. "I should call the police." She waved her cell phone in the air. "And look, my neighbors are home." She nodded toward the car in the driveway next door. "That's their Subaru."

"Calling the cops doesn't always fix things."

"I have 911 on automatic dial," she told him. "So keep your distance." She was wielding the phone as if it were a gun, she realized.

"I won't move." Throwing his hands in the air, he smiled at her as if this was a game. Maybe it was for him. His eyes glinted with humor, which then gave way to something else.

"So what is it? Why are you here?"

He sighed, lowering his arms. "I just wanted to tell you something. You really screwed up."

"I beg your pardon."

"Fucked up, setting the cops on me. You picked the wrong person to bounce out of that house. It's Sally who goes off on her." Kitty's face must have been blank because he explained it. "It's Tiff's mother, Sally, who roughs her up. Sally's the one, get it?"

"Why would I believe that?"

"See these pictures, Katherine. Do they look like the record of a scary guy?" He pulled up the photo app on his phone and passed it to her. It was full of photos of him with the girl and a woman: at Christmas, building a snowman, at an amusement park, licking ice cream cones at a beach. A rollicking, frolicking family. Did she believe it?

"Anyone can look harmless at times."

"Look, I kept Tiffany away from Sal as much as I could, but now—well now that social services worker came roaring into the house like I'd been caught—what's that word—infragrante."

"In flagrante," she whispered. The photos went on and on. She couldn't stop looking. Was taking this many pictures normal? She had a slim album's worth of Sarah's entire childhood. Her voice deepened. "I only have your word that you weren't the perpetrator of some heinous act."

"There you go again. Why do you talk like that? Or think like that? Just because I was playing tag?"

"Hide and seek. What about that blue dress you bought her? Totally inappropriate for a kid."

"It was for a school play." He slapped his forehead. "You even remember the color? You think I'm a loony, but you're the one."

Was she the one? A school play was possible. "How did you find me? Did the social worker tell you who filed the complaint?" This was unconscionable if it were true.

"Nah. I took a picture of your plate when I saw you at the thrift shop. Thought you might have followed us there. You were hanging around, watching us. Sitting out in the parking lot too. You gave me the creeps. I had the number run at some place that advertised online. After the bureaucrat showed up it seemed like a good idea to know where you lived. Cost me some money, but I wanted to come by and tell you, you got it ass-backwards."

"Bureaucrat?"

"Social worker, you know. Thanks to your nosy-parkering you threw Tiff into the hands of her crazy-ass mother. Right now, Sal's probably beating the crap out of her. She always blames the kid for anything bad." He paused. "Sally doesn't like to be without a man— if you get my meaning."

Kitty sank back into the chair. "Maybe I can tell whoever it is that I got it wrong. Misinterpreted things"

He paused. "See, that's not gonna work, Katherine, because I do have a record. Not for messing with kids though. Sold a little dope way back when. Teenage stuff. Stole a few cars for joy rides. A few bad checks." He paused. "Never nothing with kids. They're not my jam." He laughed at his use of the term.

"What can I do to fix it?" She'd grown cold with fear at the thought of Tiffany alone with that mother. Why hadn't she looked at the flowers instead of watching a game of hide and seek?

"The best thing is to wait it out, Kathy. Sally will be more than ready to welcome me back in a few weeks. There's no restraining order issued. Just her being pissed. Throwing my clothes out the window, bringing the neighbors outside when she screeched at me like a barn owl. You know the drill."

At that moment, the sprinkler system came on. A surge of water hit her square in the nose. It was painful and Kitty jumped up, looking around for the remote to shut it off.

Probably on the kitchen counter. "Just wait while I get the... thingy," she said, running toward the back door.

He laughed, saying he didn't mind a little water. "We're best buds now, right, Kathy?"

"It's Kitty. If what you're saying's the truth... Just give me a..." She pushed the sliding door open, nearly tripping over the raised threshold. Inside the kitchen, reaching for the remote, she felt or sensed his breath on her neck. A feeling from long ago arose...a sensation no longer familiar.

"Hey, Kit," he said when she turned around. "Nice place you got here." She followed his eyes as he surveyed the room. "I dig these old Victorians. Real craftsmanship." Then he stepped closer and tapped her lightly on the shoulder. "How good are you at hiding? Or would you rather seek?"

His hand on her shoulder seem to electrify it. "What? You're joking?"

"Do I sound like I'm joking?" He rubbed his hands together. "You owe me, right? Now that you put Tiff out of service, the least you can do is give me a game."

"Give you a what? Hey, I'm an old lady." Annoyingly, she heard a note of flirtatiousness in her voice. Was she flirting with him?

"The easier to catch you then, my dear."

She paused, heart pounding, and looked around. Forty-some years ago, she played hide and seek in this house and found the perfect place. Was she agile enough to climb onto that closet shelf? He'd never look there. Could she outsmart him? She remembered scraping at that wallpaper, finding that secret door. Its purpose was finally coming into focus.

He began counting, his voice growing more faint as she moved through the house. She hadn't felt this light on her feet in years. Nimble almost. She stifled a giggle. Seconds later, she scrambled inside the closet and onto the shelf. Her head wasn't too big to pass through the opening, although her backside proved troublesome. Ass backwards, he'd said. She'd got it ass backwards all right. Almost laughing, she rolled onto her side and slid through, swallowing the little frissons of pain that came with her effort. The door, which must have used a spring of some kind, swung shut. There it was again, a feeling she'd almost forgotten. She swallowed a trill of excitement and prepared to wait. She was very good at that.

The thing was though, she didn't know if she wanted to beat him at his game, to force him to give up, to turn away and follow his footsteps back through her house and out into the yard. Hear the slap, slap, slap of flip-flops growing fainter.

Or did she want to be found, to have him with his shock of white hair and insect-like legs discover her? Reaching into the little room. Perhaps even dragging her out feet first. She could hear him now. Hear the slap, slap, slap of flip-flops growing closer.

Game Over

By Charles Ardai

Lyle certainly wasn't rich, but he wasn't poor either, not so much so that he couldn't blow the change from his slice of pizza (*Anna coke? And a coke, yeah*) on two games of Zaxxon, or one each of Joust and Defender, or if those had too many coins already lined up on the edges of their screens, holding other people's places, maybe a game of Tapper with the sliding glassware and shaken cans of Budweiser, or Pengo, where it was giant cubes of ice that slid around, or Zookeeper, where you literally were shitting bricks to keep the animals in their pen. Two shiny quarters. Or two dull quarters, or two quarters caked with the grime of decades, whatever Nino happened to scoop out of the cash register's sliding change tray before slamming it shut. The only thing Lyle couldn't spend was two dimes and a nickel. But no one had seen either a dime or a nickel come out of Nino's cash register since at least seventh grade.

If there were any new games, and once every week or so there were, Lyle might forgo his beverage, ask for the whole second dollar in quarters, and spread the coins around. There were four machines lined up against the back wall and one on its own facing sideways against the column between the two rear booths, so having five quarters meant you could get a taste of each. Unless Kyle Johnson was playing Zaxxon, in which case, good luck. You might as well double up on Elevator Action or Jungle Hunt or whatever else there was, cause Kyle Johnson could make a quarter *last*. Which was just as well, since he sometimes didn't have but the one.

Lyle and Kyle, Kyle and Lyle. It was just a fucking rhyme, but from nursery school it had yoked them together, fated to be best friends or worst enemies or something else but never strangers. Partners for science experiments, partners in gym class, side by side in detention when it came to that. They learned magic tricks together, they shoplifted Hostess fruit pies together, they watched M*A*S*H and Benny Hill re-runs on their separate TV sets in their separate apartments in two different boroughs, but on the phone together the whole time, hours at a time, so that no one could call the Johnson home between the hours of 7:30 p.m. and 9 and get anything but a busy signal. (Lyle's family had two phone lines, one in the living room and one in his grandmother's bedroom, so it was just his grandmother that no one could phone between 7:30 and 9.)

Kyle had no grandmother; no grandfather, either; no uncles, no aunts, no siblings, no pets, and only one parent cause sometime around the Bicentennial his dad had vamoosed on his mom, leaving no income too, which is why just the one quarter, etc.

Lyle envied him sometimes, not because he wished his own dad would vamoose, he loved his dad, he loved everyone that lived in his crammed apartment, they were family, but crammed it was, and crammed with people who wanted to know where he was going and what he was doing every minute of every day, even if it was just stopping at Nino's after school to play a couple arcade games with his friend. Kyle, meanwhile, could come home when he wanted to. Whenever it was, it was bound to be earlier than his mom, since her shift at the Jennings Hall Senior Citizen Housing Facility of East Williamsburg kept her out till well past her teenage son's bedtime, meaning their interactions (since she also slept late, to make up for those late bedtimes) were mostly limited to weekends and the handwritten notes she packed with the foil-wrapped sandwiches for his lunch.

Lyle also envied him the sandwiches, which were surprisingly good.

Most of the envy flowed the other way, though. Not because Lyle wasn't generous with what he had; more, really, because he was. More than once he'd offered a slice or a soda or whatever, only to be met with a sidelong glare that lived in the halfway territory between embarrassed and offended. Lyle learned to do it via bank shots, like: *Man, I can't finish this, you want the rest or should I just throw it out?* Or: *Damn, you better play my last life, man, I didn't realize it's so late, I gotta get home.* Kyle'd take stuff from him that way, rather than let it go to waste. But then only.

Lyle wanted to do something nice when Kyle's birthday came round, but knowing the bank shot that would be required he schemed for weeks, racking his brain when he should've been studying, and finally he went to the Chase Manhattan branch where his mom had opened a passbook savings account for him at the age of nine, filled out a withdrawal slip with one of the chained-down ballpoint pens, and exchanged it for an orange paper tube containing ten dollars in quarters, heavy enough that if you put it in a sock and slugged someone with it, you'd knock him clear into next Tuesday. But Lyle didn't slug anyone with it, of course. What he did was this: he took it to the payphone at 94th and Lex, one block from school, the one with the missing coin-return door flap. He unfolded the crimped ends of the paper tube, carefully extracted the stack of quarters, and jammed the whole stack up in there like he was administering a suppository. They didn't all fit, of course, and they didn't all stay— some spilled out onto the sidewalk. But he got most of them in and wedged in firmly. Then he scotch-taped the sign he'd prepared at home with the words OUT OF ORDER in big letters, as different from his usual handwriting as he could make them, over the front of the phone. He picked up the stray quarters that had rolled this way and that and headed to the courtyard where Kyle was hammering a Spaldeen against the concrete wall.

You ready to go?

Sure.

And off they went, slouching and loafing, joshing and jostling, apparently aimless, but wending their way past the loaded payphone, which it took three tries to get Kyle to notice.

It's out of order, man!

You never know.

Fingering the coin-return slot of payphones they passed was a habit; rarely a productive one, but every kid in Manhattan knew you'd occasionally get lucky, which used to mean a dime but these days meant a quarter. And a quarter was a game of Galaxian or Pole Position or Missile Command, so why not? Didn't cost anything to try.

And when Kyle lifted up the OUT OF ORDER sign on this phone, he didn't even have to stick a finger in. He couldn't have if he'd wanted to. He had to scrape at the wedged-in stack with a fingernail before it tumbled loose, and when it did, the jackpot flowed like he'd rung up three cherries in Atlantic City.

Holy shit! Get over here! What the hell...?

Must really've been out of order. Lyle said this with a straight face while Kyle scooped his jacket under the falling coins.

For the second time in an hour, Lyle bent to pick up stray quarters from the same patch of sidewalk. He held them out to his friend, who didn't have a free hand to take them with.

What the hell, Kyle said again, shaking his head slowly from side to side, no sign in his expression that he suspected for a moment that his friend had anything at all to do with this windfall.

We should split it.

Nah, man, you're the one that found it.

Only cause you told me to look.

I didn't know!

Yeah but still.

Anyway it's your birthday, man. Treat yourself.

Nino's wasn't full yet, courtesy of them both having skipped sixth period. It was just them and the old man, who was wiping down the counter with a rag, and Manny moving dough in and out of the refrigerator, in and out of the oven.

They walked in like gunfighters, Kyle's pockets ringing as each step landed. He brought out a double handful and spread quarters on the counter.

What you boys want?

Two slices.

Anna coke?

Two cokes.

Every machine was calling, every screen flickering its busy come-on, even the joysticks lit up, some of them.

Nino was picking up quarters one by one. *What'd you do, knock over a parking meter?*

Ah, man. Lyle saw the way it landed and wished Nino had kept his fat mouth shut.

Kyle'd flinched like someone had put a hand on his arm. When Lyle did put a hand on his arm he shook it off roughly. Without saying anything he turned and walked out the way they'd come in.

What? Nino wanted to know. *What?*

Outside on the sidewalk Kyle dug a fist deep into each jacket pocket and came out swinging, quarters going everywhere, caroming off parked cars and landing in the gutter, rolling edge-up down the bus lane and decorating the soil of the scrawny fenced-off tree in front of the Chinese place next door. You could hear the racket even from inside, even over the sound of the machines begging for quarters, begging *play me, play me, play me.*

◎

MANNY SAW THE coins go flying. He saw everything through his plate glass window, every day something else. The job wasn't much, the pay was shit, you came home every night with your shoulders aching, all those guys creaming themselves over photos of Schwarzenegger's arms in the Conan movie ought to try stretching dough after dough after dough all day long, but at least he had his window on the world and the chance to watch life unfold before him. Dogs going by on leashes, little children, the M-103 passing on its way downtown. Sometimes somebody'd be filming a movie out there, or a commercial. Mornings, the truck arrived with the new coin-ops, dollied from truck to sidewalk, long power cords draped over their cabinets and hanging down in front of their screens. Three p.m., you got the kids from all the schools, laughing, shoving, turning in at the door and clawing crumpled bills out of their jeans. Paying Nino's rent, paying Manny's rent. You went home exhausted, crumbs of mozzarella under your fingernails, hungry for anything that wasn't pizza or video games, but you got to see the world along the way.

First time he'd ever seen someone throw money in the street, though.

It wasn't right. Even if it was only quarters. Four quarters make a dollar. Every cash box in every game ended the day stuffed with quarters, nothing but twenty-five cents apiece, not enough to buy anything in this fucking city anymore where even a loose cigarette cost twice that, but you stack up enough of them—and Manny had seen how they stacked, how they filled a canvas bag, how heavy a few thousand of them were that way, when the men who dollied the coin-ops in each week emptied the cash boxes at week's end—you stack up enough and, shit, it's money after all. A guy could pay off some bills with the quarters the school kids jammed one by one in Zookeeper and Pengo and Zaxxon.

There was one key that opened all the cash boxes, the same key for every game, not like the padlock key he used when opening the metal window shutter each morning or a door key or even a mail-box key, it was a stubby thing like you used when servicing Coke machines or those vending machines with the coils that turned and dropped your Doritos to the bottom. Barely looked like a key at all. But it was one all the same, and the men who serviced the machines each had one on the key ring hanging from their belts. Without a key like that, the only way into the cash boxes was a screwdriver backed up by a hammer, and maybe even that wouldn't work. But the thing was, you could buy a key like that down on Canal Street, same as you could buy pretty much anything down on Canal Street, maybe not out front from the plastic bins that lined the sidewalks (though you'd be surprised what you saw there sometimes) but certainly if you went in the back and explained what it was you were looking for. So Manny had one of those keys now, only he'd been nervous about using it, cause who would be blamed if some of the weekly take went missing? Him or Nino. There were only the two of them there.

He looked out the window, at the boy breathing heavily after his brief explosion, the back of his windbreaker tight across his shoulders, hands still clenched but down by his sides now. The other kid had joined him out there, was picking up some of the coins, but the first one, the one who'd thrown them, clearly wanted to be anywhere else and there were still some coins lying in the gutter when they'd walked away.

Not so many that they'd add up to much, even though four of them made a dollar. But the thing was, the kid had thrown them, and that meant he'd handled them, and that meant they were worth a lot more than twenty-five cents apiece.

◎

NO ONE WOULD'VE said Ramirez looked like a cop, even when he'd been in the uniform people had thought it was a put-on, like a kid dressing up in his older brother's clothes. But the fact was, he'd flown through the academy with honors—honors!—and now that he wasn't in the uniform anymore it didn't matter so much that he had a baby face or stood only five-six even with lifts in his regulation shoes. You weren't supposed to look like a cop when you worked plainclothes (though most of his fellow plainclothes officers did, they'd look like cops till their dying day, in their nursing homes and in their coffins they'd be spotted for what they were). You were supposed to be able to develop empathy with the people you policed, they really drilled that into you, empathy, like Mayor Koch was going to head to Harlem and break bread with Al Sharpton, or like Ramirez could empathize with a kid who went to school on Park Avenue. I mean, sure, it was a free public school up near East Harlem, but *near* ain't *in*, and the sort of free public school you got anywhere on Park Avenue was worlds away from the sort Ramirez grew up going to. This one was supposedly for "talented and gifted youth." Right. Empathy only went so far when you were caught busting into a Pac-Man machine like any crackhead thirty blocks north.

Zaxxon, the kid mumbled. And when Ramirez looked at him, the kid explained: *Not Pac-Man.*

Like Ramirez fucking cared what the name was, which motherfucking Atari bleep-bloop-blap coin game he'd ripped off, and anyway hadn't there been three or four of them?

Five. Nino's has five.

Which was true, he had eyes, he could count, but only some had been broken into, the coin boxes empty when the owner phoned the precinct, a handful of quarters littering the floor where the thief had dropped them in his hurry out the door. Quarters with fingerprints on them, partials anyway, and what do you know, those fingerprints were in the system cause of a shoplifting charge not two years earlier. Thirteen-year-old boosting Playboys from the local stationery store, not just one copy to jerk off to but a whole stack to resell to his horny classmates. Empathy my ass.

Why didn't you knock 'em all off, Ramirez wanted to know, and the kid sat there and sassed him right back, *I didn't knock any of them off*, which was so obviously a lie Ramirez didn't even bother saying so, he just barreled on: *You run out of time? Heard someone coming? Or you just had to get to class?*

I didn't rob the machines, the kid insisted. *It wasn't me.*

Which, I mean, come on. They had the kid's prints. And the mom—single mom, surprise, surprise—couldn't swear to when her latchkey kid came or went. And the owner had told Ramirez the story of the handfuls of quarters the kid had tried to pay for his pizza with, which while not evidence of any wrongdoing was *highly suggestive,* like the training manuals said. You make a habit of robbing arcade games, you pay for lots of shit with quarters.

They were sitting in the assistant principal's office, the boy on one side of a bare wooden table, Ramirez on the other, the assistant principal standing just outside the door with his secretary, the both of them pretending not to be listening to every single word. The other kid, the little fat Asian kid, sitting behind a closed door, waiting his turn.

The boys were missing fourth period Social Studies so that they could get an education in the law instead.

So here's where we are. You can give back what you took and Mr. Santangelo won't press charges. You'll just have to pay for the smashed padlock from the front gate. And not in quarters.

The kid spread his hands, palms up. *I can't give back what I never took.*

And that's where it was still, twenty minutes later, when Ramirez said fuck it, got out of the uncomfortable metal chair, and headed to the door, stopping only to aim an index finger and a look like a hanging judge at Kyle Johnson. *You can make things easy on yourself, or you can keep right on lying your way into a jail cell, it's entirely up to you.* To that, the boy had no answer. Which, of course. Park Avenue or Lenox Avenue or the projects of the South Bronx, no one ever had an answer. Ramirez didn't have any answers. He just had a job to do, that's all.

◎

WHY'D YOU SAY I broke into your games?

Lyle had told him it was a bad idea, but Kyle had a head of steam on him, remnants from the day before, stirred up fresh by that cop hammering at them both, in front of Mr. Pourmontain too, like they were criminals. Lyle, of course, could account for every minute, from when he came home, well before Nino's locked up for the night, to when he arrived at school the following morning. His dad, his mom, his brother, his other brother, no shortage of family members to tell Officer Ramirez where Lyle had been when the pizzeria was being broken into. Eating dinner, putting on his benzoyl peroxide, sleeping in the bottom bunk of his bunkbed; eating breakfast, brushing his teeth, dropped off at school on his father's way to work. Lyle was golden. But he still got questioned, and not gently either. Only in his case it was, *Why do you think your friend did it? Did he admit it to you? You understand withholding information from a police officer is a crime, right?*

With Kyle taking his turn behind the closed door, Lyle had explained about the payphone, the birthday present, had even dug out of his pocket the crumpled remnant of the orange coin wrapper, offered to go home and get his bankbook and prove the ten-dollar withdrawal. But Ramirez had told him not to bother. Maybe that explained about the handfuls of quarters on the counter but it didn't mean jack shit when it came to exonerating the Johnson kid for Criminal Trespass, Burglary in the Third Degree, Larceny in the Third Degree, the whole laundry list they could throw at him.

Why'd you say I broke into your games, man?

Ramirez had stalked out after interview number two, and Mr. Pourmontain had sent them back to class, but once safely in the stairwell, they'd headed down instead of up and then out instead of in, and now here they were on Lexington and 92nd, with Nino behind the counter and Manny at his post in the window, ladling red sauce in widening circles.

I didn't tell nobody nothing, the old man was saying. *I don't want no trouble.*

The police just came to my school, man! They pulled us out of class, they questioned us, they accused us—

I didn't tell them nothing! Except they asked had we seen anyone acting strange.

Jesus. 'Acting strange'?

Nino shrugged, half a hint of an apology crossing his creased features. He didn't want trouble. He didn't want to make trouble. He just wanted to sell his pizza and take his cut when people played his arcade games. That's all. But the cop had asked, and he'd answered.

What you tell them? This black kid came in with a pile of quarters, got mad when you asked did he steal them?

I didn't ask if you stole them, I made a joke!

Jesus. Kyle turned to Lyle, not to ask him anything, not to tell him anything, just to have somewhere else to look. *You really did me good.* He turned back to Nino. *You know that? You really— I mean, for what? How much money we talking about, anyway? From Zaxxon there. How much? Is it really enough to ruin a person's life over?*

Nino said: *Coupla thousand bucks.*

Really?

Yeah. Couple, maybe five thousand. All the machines. Yeah.

Seriously?

Not every kid plays for half an hour on one quarter.

Yeah, okay, but—

Lot of kids come in here and play. It adds up.

Shit.

It's not even my money, most of it. I get a cut, sure, but most of it, there's people who gotta get paid. They don't care somebody broke in. They want their money.

I didn't do it, man, I didn't do it. I didn't. I swear.

Lyle was tugging at his sleeve and, looking up, Kyle could see why. Through the big plate glass window, Ramirez was walking toward them from across the avenue.

◎

INTIMIDATE? LIKE HELL he'd 'attempted to intimidate.' And calling skipping class 'truancy' was a joke. Anyway, hadn't Lyle skipped class too? But that cop had been looking for an excuse and he'd given him one. And now, Jesus Christ, he was in it. There weren't bars on the door, but it was a cell all the same. They'd made him fill out forms with his hands in cuffs. When the phone at home rang and rang, as of course he'd known it would, they'd asked for his mother's number at work, and he'd refused to give it. She didn't need that. Hearing that he'd been arrested.

But of course it was just a matter of time. It's not like they were going to just turn him loose. Without a parent into whose care to release him, it was their responsibility to keep him in custody until such time as blah blah blah. Court schedule currently full. Sure it was.

He sat on one of the wooden benches, behind a door that had no knob or handle and a window whose glass was so small and thick and clouded you could barely see through it.

They took his shoelaces, made him lift his shirt to show was he wearing a belt. He wasn't. But the drawstring of his sweatpants amounted to the same thing, didn't it, and they let him keep that. The whole thing was half-assed like that. They put him in a room for adolescent offenders because supposedly the room for juveniles was full. Two older teens sat whispering with each other on the bench across the room and a third had nodded off on the floor. The one on the floor had bruises on his neck and his breath rattled each time he inhaled, like there was something in his lungs.

Kyle fought hard not to panic, not to cry. All his life had been about staying out of places like this, or at least he'd thought it had been. Only maybe all his life he'd been heading right for this very place and just didn't realize it. Maybe there was no steering clear of the places you're meant to wind up. How had years of playing Zaxxon and Defender and Battlezone and Centipede not taught him that? However good you get at playing a game, however long you manage to keep it up, eventually you lose.

◎

LYLE TOLD HIS parents he'd do his homework in the library and then take a subway to the CWA Detention Center in Brooklyn. There were visiting hours until 7 p.m. Getting home from there would take ninety minutes, so they wouldn't worry until 8:30 came and went. At first they'd figure he'd missed a train, had to wait for the next one. After that, well— After that they'd worry. They'd have to deal with it. He'd have to deal with it.

At 8:07 he was watching Manny lock the metal shutter he'd rolled down over the entrance to Nino's. Nino himself had left fifteen minutes earlier. Manny hefted a paper grocery sack, tucked it under one arm. The sleeve of his T-shirt rode up, exposing part of the tattoo underneath, dark ink showing a pair of skeletal hands gripping the shaft of a scythe. He'd joke about it sometimes as he spun a circle of dough in the air: *Everybody loves pizza. Whatcha think he carries that big slicer for?*

Lexington down to Grand Central, the shuttle to Times Square, underground through stinking tunnels to Port Authority. It wasn't anyone's idea of a pleasant commute, but Manny bore it patiently, and Lyle, walking twenty yards behind, bore it too. Manny had a Walkman to pass the time, headphone band lost in his shaggy cap of hair. Lyle had gotten one himself for his last birthday (not an actual Walkman, of course, some off-brand tapedeck his parents had found at Radio Shack), but right now it was safely zipped in his jacket pocket and the headphones stowed in his bookbag. This wasn't a time for distracting himself with music.

For the last leg of the trip, sitting in the front row on the bus to Jersey City, Manny let his eyes slide shut and his head tip back against the seat. Lyle hustled on by, relieved; that had been the riskiest moment, since there wasn't much chance Manny wouldn't have noticed him walking past him down the aisle, baseball cap or no baseball cap.

Following Manny the rest of the way from the bus stop wasn't hard. The man didn't stand out in a crowd, but this time of night there wasn't much of a crowd for him to get lost in. Lyle hung back, skulked in doorways, bent once to tie his sneakers, but the truth was he didn't need to do any of that. Manny hadn't looked behind him even once.

The building he stopped at had three gray concrete steps leading up to a front door tagged with graffiti, but Manny didn't climb them. Off to one side, a set of steep metal stairs led down to a basement apartment. Manny took the stairs. A moment later, Lyle saw a light go on.

Now what? He had nothing to confront him with, no evidence, no proof. Just the knowledge that the coins were the one thing tying Kyle to the break-in, the quarters with his fingerprints on them (which, come to think of it, could just as easily have had Lyle's prints on them, from when he'd stuffed them in the payphone; just luck of the draw, which of them had put his fingers on which coins, and many years later, when he was an old man and no one had seen a coin-operated video game in ages, he'd sometimes think about this late at night, and it would make his wife turn to him in bed and ask if he was okay); and if someone had left those coins by the machines for the police to find, it had to be someone who'd been there when Kyle threw them...and who could seriously think it had been the old man?

Lyle hesitated at the top of the stairs. He had nothing to defend himself with either. Manny may not have been huge, but he was solid, stocky, with the broad back and strong arms the job had given him, plus he had ten years on Lyle, easy. He was a grown-up. A grown-up with the Grim Reaper tattooed on his arm. What the hell was Lyle doing going to the man's basement apartment, at night, in a city where he knew no one, where no one on earth would miss him or probably even hear it if he screamed?

But Kyle was spending the night in a detention center in Brooklyn. So Lyle went down the stairs and knocked.

Manny swung the door open and stood there staring. *Ah, Jesus.*

Past him, Lyle saw an off-white couch with a low coffee table in front of it. The paper bag lay on its side, a six-pack of Budweiser beside it. A joint lay on a ceramic dish, the smell of it in the air.

Nino give you my address?

No.

Then what, you followed me?

Lyle put one hand up against the door, maybe to keep it from slamming shut, though Manny didn't show any sign of trying to close it. The other was in his jacket pocket, trembling. *You did it,* Lyle said, *didn't you? The robbery? And pinned it on Kyle?*

Manny stood in the doorway and said nothing.

Why would you do that? To a kid who did nothing to you, ever?

Manny scratched his jaw with a thick finger. Lyle could hear the stubble scrape against the nail.

You put my friend in jail—

Pff. It's not jail. You're what, fourteen? Fifteen? They don't put you in jail at your age, not unless you kill someone.

He's locked up.

They'll let him out. Long as he doesn't throw a fit again like the other day.

That's not the point! He's locked up for something he didn't do!

Manny turned back into the apartment, walked over to the coffee table, picked out one of the beers and pulled the tab. Just like in Tapper, and it didn't spray when he cracked it open either. 3,000 bonus points right there.

Want a beer, kid?

What? No. No. Why would you think...?

Just offering. Manny took a long swallow from the can. *So what exactly* do *you want?*

You to tell the truth.

I'm not fourteen. They don't go easy on you at my age.

You should've thought of that before you did it.

I should've thought of lots of things, kid. Couple thousand dollars sounded pretty good, but you try paying your rent in quarters. Manny came back to the door, where Lyle was still standing, more or less frozen in place. *But I'm not giving it back, if that's what you were hoping. And I'm not getting your friend out of trouble by putting my neck in the noose. So you kinda made this trip for nothing.*

You have *to—*

Before he could get another sound out, Manny took hold of the collar of Lyle's jacket and pulled him close.

Now, listen. I don't have to do nothing. Your friend's gonna have to deal with his own problems. His fist bunched tighter in the fabric and Lyle felt the man's knuckles against his throat. *I'm not gonna do anything to you this time, cause you're just a kid. But if you ever come back here again I'll break your fucking legs. Do you understand me?*

Lyle nodded desperately.

Good. Now get the fuck out of here.

He shoved Lyle backwards. Lyle hit the stone wall across from the front door and sat down hard. Manny started swinging the door shut.

Hey! Lyle hated the breathless squeak his voice had become. But he needed to ask one more question. *Why'd you only rip off some of the games? Why not all?*

Manny smiled. *Took as much as I could carry. That shit weighs a ton.*

The door closed. Lyle heard the locks turn.

He picked himself up, took a few seconds to start breathing properly again. He waited until he was at the top of the metal stairs before pressing the STOP button on the tapedeck in his pocket.

◎

IT WAS 9:20 before they let him into the bullpen where Officer Ramirez had his desk. Lyle was missing Ms. Cohen's English class right now. He'd already missed homeroom. He'd miss Music too. He didn't care. Kyle had missed more than that.

Lyle was clutching the cassette tape in his hand.

You've got to listen to this, he said, waving it. *You're going to be sorry you ever took Kyle in.*

Sitting behind a stack of file folders and a cardboard cup of coffee, looking tired, looking beat, Ramirez leaned forward. *You want to hear me say I'm sorry? I am sorry. Very sorry. We've called Mrs. Johnson, she should be here momentarily.*

That's— Lyle stopped. *That's great. But how'd you know to call her already?*

We called her immediately, as soon we knew what happened.

It felt like he was riding a bicycle whose chain had come loose. The gears weren't catching. *How'd you find out?*

The detention center called us. It's got to be on the news by now, radio at least. Isn't that why you're here?

Isn't what why I'm here?

Your friend. Mr. Johnson.

Right, Kyle, Kyle Johnson. You're going to let him out, right? What's going on?

Ramirez pinched the bridge of his nose. *He was found unrespon-sive shortly before three a.m. this morning. They cut him down, tried CPR, but—* His hands dropped to the desk, lay there. *He took his own life. I'm sorry.*

◎

HE FOUND HIMSELF stacking and restacking the handful of quarters he'd dug out of his pocket, the ones that had tumbled onto the sidewalk before he'd taped his handmade sign on the phone and gone to get Kyle. Two stacks of three, three stacks of two, one stack of six. A four and a two. He sat and worked the quarters like a rosary. Not even thinking about Kyle, not really. Not thinking about much of anything really. The phone on his grandmother's nightstand hadn't rung in days, not between 7:30 and 9. His parents had kept him home from school, with the school's blessing. There would be depo-sitions, probably a court appearance at Manny's trial, but that was all in the future. Lots of things were in the future. Summer break. Eleventh grade. College.

For some. For Manny, for Nino, for Mr. Pourmontain, for Officer Ramirez, for Kyle's mom, for his vamoosed dad, wherever the hell he might be. For Lyle. Futures galore.

He opened his bedroom window, heard the sounds of traffic four stories below, delivery trucks taking Bowne Street as an alternative to Kissena Boulevard. He picked up the stack of coins, weighed them on his palm. Then he took each one, pressed it tightly between his thumb and index finger, and flung them into the street, as hard and as far as he could.

King's Row

By S. A. COSBY

"Mr. Parrish doesn't get many visitors. And you're his—?"

The nurse let the question hang between them. Maurice waited a moment before he answered.

"I'm his cousin," he said after a beat. "Two sisters' children." The nurse smiled at him. She had a pretty smile, a hint of a dimple in her left cheek. Maurice glanced at her hands. No ring. Just short fingers with short nails. The hands of a working woman. He liked that. He didn't go in for all that fancy stuff. The other night he saw a lady at the gas station with a ton of glitter and pictures on her fingernails. She looked like she had punched a Christmas tree.

"Well, I'm sure he will appreciate you coming by. It might not seem like it but he knows."

"He don't talk at all? My other cousin said he don't say nothing."

Actually, Maurice had talked to Parrish's nephew. He'd gone by Parrish's parents' house a few days after he'd been released. Parrish's sister had stared at him like she was measuring him for a casket but Maurice didn't hold against her. He'd told her he was an old friend of Parrish's.

"You ain't his friend. I remember you." she'd said. She was a broad woman with a face as wide as a Smithfield ham. Maurice had thought about trying to sweet talk her anyway. Fifteen years inside was a long time. But the daggers she was shooting at him put that idea out to pasture.

"I just want to talk to him," Maurice had said. "We used to hang out. I just want to see how he doing."

Parrish's sister scowled so hard Maurice thought she was having a stroke. "You and boys like you the reason he in that damn place now," she said. "Calvin was a good man. He was smart. Could've been an doctor or a lawyer. But then he got hooked up with boys like you. Now he gets to eat pudding all day."

Maurice had fought back the urge to roll his eyes. Yes, Calvin Parrish was smart. There wasn't any denying that fact. Her other assertion though, that he was a good man, well, that was bullshit. Cal would slit the throat of a baby if he thought it could put money in his pocket.

"We was all youngsters back then. We all made mistakes."

"Yeah, but you can still wipe your own ass. Now get out of my house."

Maurice could have gotten nasty. Grabbed her pinky and pulled it backwards until she told him where Parrish was being housed. Instead, he got up and nodded at her before walking out the door. He didn't like the rough stuff, especially when it came to women. He'd just have to find another way to locate Parrish.

When he got to his car, a loaner from his own sister and her husband who were also letting him crash with them, a kid was waiting for him. The kid was taller than Maurice but rangy. All knees and elbows. Maurice put him at fourteen or thereabouts.

"My mama does not like Uncle Cal's friends," the kid said.

"Friends? Other people been looking for Parr—for your uncle?"

The kid nodded. "Yeah. A bunch of people have come here looking for him. Mama usually cusses them out or say she gonna call the cops. They stomp out the house like you did. And I'll give you the same deal I gave them. Fifty dollars for the address."

"Alright." Maurice pulled out two twenties and a ten. He had a little bit left in his nest egg but it wasn't nearly enough. Especially when his share was still floating around. He held out the money and the kid made it disappear like a street magician.

"When the last time you seen your uncle?"

"About a month ago. Mama used to go up there every week back when everybody said he was faking. Now that she thinks he ain't faking she don't go as much."

"What you think? You think he faking?"

The kid snorted.

"Man, he is *gone*. You could shove a cactus up his butt and he wouldn't flinch. My pops used to tell my mom that all the time. Last time he said she started crying so he don't say it no more. But...I think its true. You go up there, he don't talk. He don't look at you. He just make some noises and tap his foot. It like he a zombie."

AND NOW MAURICE was about to sit and talk with the zombie. The nurse guided him through the halls of Whispering Oaks Sanitarium. He'd expected it to smell like a nursing home. Or the infirmary. Instead, it was bathed in some soft cinnamon scent that filled the halls and every crack and crevice. It was like falling in a bucket of potpourri.

"What's in the box?" the nurse asked.

Maurice shook the box and it rattled like it was full of bones.

"Checkers. When we were hanging out back in the day we used to play all the time. I never could beat him. I thought he might like to see the board. Maybe I'll set it up. We can play. I'll just move his pieces for him."

The nurse smiled again.

"That's so sweet," she said.

Maurice smiled back. Parrish used to whip his ass in checkers, chess, dominoes. Anything that required strategy and foresight. Checkers was his favorite though. Maurice figured he'd appreciate the effort.

The nurse stopped at a large glass door in a heavy aluminum frame. She held her badge up to a sensor that beeped. Maurice heard a click, and then she opened the door.

"He seems to like sitting outside," she said.

Maurice followed her through the door onto a wide concrete patio. A few patients in wheelchairs were gathered around a table covered with ashtrays. The patients were puffing away like their lives depended on it. Maurice figured it did. Being in a place like this would drive him crazy. He would smoke three packs a day if he had to stay here. The big fake fireplace in the lobby and the wood-land-inspired wall art couldn't hide the fact this was a prison too. And everyone here was serving a life sentence.

They walked over to the corner of the patio. The whole area was enclosed by an ornate wrought iron fence. Sitting in the corner where two panels of fencing met was Calvin Parrish.

He was thinner than Maurice remembered. His dark brown face seemed to be drawn down into a perpetual frown. His thin black flattop had been reduced to a balding smattering of hair in patches all over his head. He wore a dark blue bathrobe and plush red slippers. His hands were in his lap. Time hadn't changed them at all. They still looked capable of crushing an apple into applesauce.

"He ain't in a wheelchair." Maurice said.

"No. If you guide him by the arm he can kind of shuffle along. Here let's move this table over there so you can set up your game." Maurice helped her move a plastic circular table in front of Parrish. Then she grabbed him a plastic lawn chair.

"Enjoy your visit." The nurse said.

Maurice waited until she had re-entered the building before he took out the checkerboard and the pieces. He unfolded the board and sat it on the table. The edges of the board were a little worn and the red and black squares had a few scratches but you could still play on it. Maurice took out two small cloth bags. One red, one black.

"Hey P. You look like shit. I guess your hair never grew back when they had to cut your head open and get that bullet out."

Maurice shook out the checkers onto the table. Parrish kept looking straight ahead. Not into the sun though, Maurice noted.

He said, "I don't guess you heard Keith died. I was in Coldwater. He was in solitary in Pentonville. Chewed his own wrists open. I'd heard he'd gone crazy but I never figured he do something like that. I guess you never know how much somebody can or can't take."

Maurice placed the black pieces on his side of the board and the red ones on Parrish's side. He glanced over his shoulder, saw that the smokers had wheeled themselves over to an awning. They were sitting in the shade, a quiet rumble of conversation bubbling across the patio.

"Brenda's dead too. OD'd while I was inside. My boy is with a foster family. He ages out in a year. I knew she was going through it when she stopped coming to visit me. Last time I saw her she looked like a wolf with rabies. They wouldn't let me attend the funeral. Her mama sent me a copy of the program. They didn't even list me as her husband."

Maurice's mouth had gone dry. Talking about Brenda made him feel like he was standing on the edge of some kind of cliff. If he talked about her too much he felt he would fall over that cliff and never find his way out of that yawning valley.

"Tommy is missing. Don't know what happened to him. He got out, said he was gonna beat his money out you and that was the last time anybody seen him."

He moved one of his pieces up one space.

"I mean Tommy could get into an argument with a mime," he went on "He lived to piss people off. So, you know, anything could have happened to him. That just leaves you and me. And look at you. That cop put two in your head and now you're worse than a mime. You a mannequin. I bet you never thought he'd shoot with you holding on to that girl, did you? But he couldn't let you go. You had killed his partner and a citizen. You was always smart but you sure made a dumb move that day. You were gonna grab a little girl, should have picked a white one. He would never have took a chance hitting her."

He moved one of Parrish's red pieces.

"That was smart though. Having two cars painted red like brand new candy apples leaving the bank in opposite directions while the gold bars was in Helen's purse. Me and Tommy and Keith and Willis draw the cops away while you walk down the street and Helen disappears down the subway. She puts the bars in your safe and we all meet up later to split the money."

He moved his black piece up another space.

"Then you had to backhand her. Jesus, ain't you ever heard about a woman scorned? She dropped that dime an' it hit all of us like a brick. Too bad about what happened to her and her mama. Guess you can't testify if you trailer blows up, huh?"

He jumped the black piece with Parrish's red piece.

"You must have been nervous," he went on. "They was running all kinds of tests on you when you came out of surgery. That's what I heard anyway. How'd you do it? Did you send a message by your sister? Did you get Skunk to do it? or Azon? I know Skunk doesn't like killing women. I can't lie, I thought we was in the clear when I heard she was gone. Without her there was nothing to tie us to the bank robbery. But of course, dumb ass Keith had grabbed two handfuls of bills and stuffed them in his coat. Him testifying was all they needed."

Maurice moved a black piece, then double-jumped a red.

"You didn't have anything to do with that, did you? Call in a favor on old Keith? Nah. You're a vegetable, right? You don't know what time it is. Or what day it is or even the year, right? You got another what, five years before the statute of limitations runs out on that manslaughter? Why they dropped the charge to manslaughter I'll never know. You figure you'll have a miraculous recovery right about then?"

A thin spidery length of drool unspooled from Parrish's lower lip. Maurice watched as the light caught it and for a moment it was quicksilver flowing like liquid lightning.

Maurice used a red piece to jump one of his own black pieces.

"Because here's the thing. We both know you're faking, Parrish. You shot that cop when they came to get you. Ricocheted a bullet into that old dude's dome and then grabbed that girl who was running through the parking lot. I talked to a friend of a friend whose girl worked at the hospital when they brought you in. Them shots you took was bad but they didn't necessarily leave irreparable damage. You're just holding out until the state runs out of time, ain't you? If anybody could it would be you."

He drew a breath. "You know I used to look up to you? I have never met nobody who was so slick. I thought you was the man. Right up until I ended up doing three nickels."

He rubbed his face.

"And you got to sit here in your comfortable goddamn slippers while my wife was running horse down her arm and my boy in some stranger's house."

Maurice leaned closer to Parrish.

"I know you can hear me, you goddamn son of a bitch. Here's something'll get your attention. I found your damn safe."

Maurice sat back, his eyes on Parrish's face. He studied the folds and crinkles and sallow creases under his chin. He searched that weathered expanse for the slightest tremor or twitch or spasm. Anything to indicate he had heard and understood what Maurice had said.

He saw nothing.

"It took some doing, but I found it. Those gold bars are still inside there, ain't they? Just waiting for the day when you can drop this act, right? Well, here's some more news. The old house where you hid it, where you told Nannie Billups it would be safe? Nannie stopped paying the taxes on that place. The county is gonna auction it off. Someone is going to get that safe and blow it open and then all your plans are gone. And so is my cut."

Maurice pushed one of his men forward on the board.

"I've tried to drill into it. I've tried to pick it. I don't know enough about explosives to blow it up. You had to get the best safe in the business, didn't you?"

Was that a twitch on Parrish's face? Or just the random firing of a nerve ending?

"Okay. Here it is. I need the combination. And you need to give me the combination. Because if you don't then we both lose everything. Fifteen years for nothing." Maurice felt a red-hot poker of rage sliding between the space in his heart where the love for his wife used to live and his desire to grab Parrish by the throat and squeeze.

He willed his temper into submission.

"I'll make you a deal. I know you think they are watching you. And I can't lie. I think they are. You killed a cop. They don't let that shit go."

Parrish didn't blink. Maurice leaned in, lowered his voice.

"There's numbers painted on the checkers. Little white numbers. All you have to do is move the pieces with the combination. That's it. Anybody watching will just think you're having a moment. You give me the combination and I'll make sure your cut of the gold is kept safe until you get out."

Parrish's hands didn't move. Those big soup bones just stayed in his lap. Maurice's mouth felt dry, his tongue a briar patch against the roof of his mouth.

"I know you can hear me, you motherfucker. You might have these nurses and the cops fooled but I know you. I've seen the things you've done. What you're capable of. And I know you're faking this catatonic shit. I was in that hellhole for fifteen years. Fifteen years. I never got to kiss my wife goodbye. My boy is bouncing from house to house fighting off old men who want to put their hands on him. You owe me."

Maurice slapped the table with his left hand. The checkers jumped off the board. An aide who was helping a patient eat their pudding raised her head and looked in his direction.

Maurice took a deep breath. He picked up the checkers, rearranged them on the board.

"Listen. I promise you I won't screw you over. I just want what's mine. I want to get my boy back. You don't know what it's like out there. I don't know how to do anything except hold a gun and hurt people. That won't cut it nowadays. Nobody robs banks anymore. People stopped using cash. They got all their money tied up in something called Bitcoin. I don't even know how that shit works. I need this, Parrish."

Maurice snapped his fingers in front of Parrish's eyes.

The bear trap hand shot up and grabbed his wrist. Crushing pain ran up Maurice's arm like a fire racing through a drought-stricken plain.

The aide who was helping with the pudding came running over. She grabbed Parrish's hand and pried it from Maurice's wrist one finger at a time.

"They should have warned you about that. He has sudden reactions to certain stimuli."

"Ain't nothing fucking wrong with him." Maurice said. He stood up from the table. During the whole incident Parrish had never turned his head. His blank watery brown eyes kept staring at nothing.

"It's a reflex," the aide said. "It's like a parrot. He's doing it but he doesn't even know he's doing it."

"Bullshit. You hear me, Parrish? I know its bullshit!" Maurice was shouting. The aide ran toward the door and yelled for help.

Maurice leaned on the table. He screamed in Parrish's face. His spittle landed on Parrish's eyelashes like drops of morning dew.

"Fifteen years, you piece of shit! And you're just gonna sit there like it don't matter? I'll beat that combination out of you. Do you here me, you fuck? I'll take it out of you one tooth at a time! My boy found her! He found his mama dead!!"

He felt hands on his shoulders and arms around his waist. He was being pulled away by men at least half as strong as he was. They dragged him, wrestled him towards the door.

"You had Tommy killed, didn't you? Send somebody after me! I dare you!" Maurice twisted and bucked but the orderlies were old hands at this kind of embrace.

Maurice looked back at Parrish over the shoulder of one of the shorter orderlies.

For a man with such huge hands Parrish had nimble fingers. He took one of the red checkers and jumped six of Maurice's black ones. His piece landed on the back row. Parrish had told him once they called it king's row in England where the game was called draughts.

They locked eyes for a moment so brief it might have been in Maurice's imagination.

Then Parrish looked away, careful not to stare into the sun.

The Babysitter

By Jeffery Deaver

"Your move," Kelli said.

She and the two children sat on the sumptuous oriental carpet in the family's game room. On the walls were posters of Las Vegas and Atlantic City. Nearby was a six-sided table for card games. A bar too, presently locked tight.

Kelli Lambert, seventeen, was in jeans and pink Hollister sweatshirt. Her blond hair was pulled back tightly into the ponytail that made her look all the more like the cheerleader that she was.

"No, me!" said William. The five-year-old, also blond, was fidgety. He'd sat still in one place for nearly ten minutes, which was maybe a record. His father was sure he would grow up to be an ace soccer player.

"It's your sister's turn," Kelli said to the boy. She nodded to Mab, seven. The girl had given herself the nickname, no one knew from where. Her given name was Barbara. Her parents had no predictions or expectations about her future career, athletic or otherwise—beyond growing up to be a woman as beautiful as her mother.

"Me!" William said firmly and with a frown.

Kelli cocked her head. "You won the last game," she explained. "Another player goes first now. The player to your left. That's your sister." They were sitting in front of the colorful board game Candy Land.

He made a face and said to the babysitter, "That's not in the rules!"

"It's in *my* rules." She gave him a kind, but firm, look through her blue-framed glasses that made her pretty face appear studious. Her braces matched the shade.

The teen was sitting across from her charges, in the lotus position, and her knees rose and fell. After the children were asleep she sometimes did yoga until the parents returned.

Kelli nodded to Mab, who, concentrating hard, solemnly lifted a card from the shuffled stack, as if she were rolling the dice at a craps table in Vegas, after betting the house.

She drew blue, which let her take a huge shortcut through Peppermint Pass.

"Yay!" she shouted.

Her brother shot an I-hate-you look her way. "Me!"

"No," Kelli said patiently. "My turn."

William sat back, arms crossed, brows furrowed. "I want to use dice, not cards."

Kelli drew orange and moved her gingerbread man marker, telling the boy, "You can't use dice. Only cards. Some of them have instructions on them."

"I get two sixes all the time. It's called snake eyes."

"Snake eyes," Kelli explained, "are two ones."

Undeterred, he bragged, "I get those too. I've had them a thousand times."

"According to the laws of probability, you'd have to roll the dice 36 thousand times to get a thousand of any particular combination."

"Yes, I *have*. I've rolled dice a million times!"

"Good for you."

Cards were drawn, the plastic gingerbread men advanced. Mab won this game and then the next.

William sat back glumly. "She cheated!"

"Did not!"

"Yes, you did."

"William," Kelli said sternly. "No talk of cheating."

It wasn't even clear how anyone *could* cheat at Candy Land—especially given that the babysitter watched the board the way the eye in the sky at Vegas casinos scanned the tables. "You're going to apologize right now."

"No."

"I didn't cheat!" Mab was on the verge of tears.

"William." Kelli's voice was ominous.

He said nothing.

She added evenly, "Bed for you right now. No Disney, no cookies."

A debate. Then: "All right, sorry." He didn't mean it but no matter.

"Thank you. Mab, accept his apology."

"I accept."

"Good. You guys tired of Candy Land?"

"Yeah, kinda," Mab said.

"Your parents have any other games?"

"I guess," Mab said. She was looking around. "Something... pin... Pinocchio."

A smile. "No, not for us."

William frowned and thought for a moment. "Dad plays Poke Her."

Kelli blinked and stared.

"With his friends. They come over. They play it with cards and chips."

She laughed. "Poker. Not for us either. A few years, maybe."

The tall, lanky girl rose and looked in the closet, then the drawers in the game table and a buffet. "Nothing here."

Next door was the office. She walked inside, flipped on the overhead light then the one on the cluttered desk. She looked in that room's closets too. She returned to the game room. "No luck. Sorry, guys. I'll bring some other ones next time."

"Monopoly Junior!" Mab called.

"Okay, I will. Now, let's get cookies and—"

The screen went dark.

Rachel Winston stepped back from the computer keyboard and stood with arms crossed over her chest. She and her husband both continued to stare at the monitor that had been showing the security video of the babysitting session earlier that evening. Their luxurious home was seeded with cameras.

Erik fidgeted like his son might do.

She snapped, "I told you she saw."

"Shit," he muttered.

"Why on earth would you leave them out?"

He said nothing. His tongue slipped from his mouth and touched his lip. A nervous habit that she found repulsive. Snakeish.

Rachel tapped the long, red nails of her right hand on the opposite arm's bicep. Her shoulders were raised and rigid.

The Winstons might be described as beautiful people. Thirty-eight, nearly six feet tall and voluptuous, Rachel resembled an actress who sometimes won awards but whom few people could actually name. Erik was an inch or two over her height and still had the physique of the baseball player he'd been in college. Attractive too, with thick dark hair that could be unruly; he'd had to become an expert at taming it with comb and spray. At the event where they'd met it had been his hair that drew her to him, across the crowded room, at the same time that he gravitated toward her because of her abundant chest. Only later did they learn they had a few substantive interests in common.

Rachel muttered, "She looked at it. She looked right at it." She'd made her point but her fury pushed her to repeat herself.

"Looking isn't seeing."

She sighed and closed her eyes momentarily. "And that means what?"

"You know how you look at something and don't see it. Like ads in magazines. You look at them but you don't focus. It doesn't register."

"How could it not register? You want me to run the tape again?"

The "it" was a diagram of the Golden Luck casino, located on a Native American reservation about thirty miles from Gardenview, the suburb in which this palatial home was located. In exactly one week an "accidental" electrical fire would break out in the basement of the casino, resulting in its near-total destruction.

The absence of a casino would throw the residents in this part of the state into abject panic. But not to worry; the syndicate that Rachel and Erik headed would leap in and fill the gap—miraculously in a matter of weeks. Their casino, known as the Half Moon, would be located in a nearby resort and up and running before the ashes of the Golden Luck had cooled. The prep work had already been done on the sly and the right money had gone to the right officials on the Gaming and P&Z Commissions.

In a final coup, Rachel's idea, the Native American employees from the Golden Luck would find new employment at the Half Moon, making a much higher salary. This would not only supply staff for Rachel's and Erik's venture but would leave the Roberto organization, owner of the Golden Luck, with no employees trained in the art of separating gamblers from their life savings.

A brilliant plan…

Except for one glitch.

A goddamn seventeen-year-old cheerleader had now glimpsed the blueprints—with the big, bold printing on top: *Golden Luck*.

Which for some reason her goddamn husband had not thought to tuck away into a drawer.

When the story hit the news, the girl would think, "Hey, Mr. and Mrs. Winston had this map or something of that same casino. Holy cow!"

Or "Holy shit!"

Or whatever teenagers nowadays said.

Rachel shivered with rage.

Erik said delicately, "Really, honey, it's not so bad. First, we're not sure she actually saw it. And even if she did she'd have to watch the news to hear about the fire, and what kid nowadays does? They're on their phones and doing Tok-tik and Facebook and shit. And even if she *does* watch the news she'd have to watch it at exactly the same time as the story about the fire's on. And you know how short TV stories are. What're the odds?"

Rachel said nothing. Her mind was clicking, as it tended to do. This was a gift. She didn't like to get her hands dirty in their projects but she could come up with a dozen different smart ways to solve problems. She'd hand those solutions over to somebody else and get started on something new.

"So, it'll be fine," Erik concluded breezily, looking her way with fragile confidence. "Anyway, what is there to do about it now?"

His wife scoffed, as if he'd asked the stupidest question in the world. "What there is to do is we kill her." She pulled out her phone.

◎

TO HIM, THEY were not people.

They were Objects.

Some of those in the profession thought of those they were hired to kill as Targets. Or just Them. Some actually liked to think of them by their names—but they tended to be the emotional ones, the sadistic ones and, driven by the thrill of taking lives, didn't last very long in this business.

Michael himself had settled on Objects, and that worked for him.

They weren't male, female, black, white, any nationality or creed, whatever creed was. Objects.

Replaying in his mind Rachel Winston's phone call, the hulking man, with a sallow complexion and sunken eyes, stepped off the bus in the Mapleton section of town. While the city itself was for the most part gray and tough and gritty and industrial—which is where he handled most of his jobs—the outlying areas could be pretty. This 'hood didn't have the mini-mansions of Harper or the sleek and chic high-rises of Wilmington but the residents here kept up their unpretentious homes nicely and tended their trim lawns and gardens.

Michael appreciated their efforts regarding the gardens in particular. Those who knew his professional specialty might be surprised that he himself enjoyed pulling on work gloves and knee pads and puttering about in the small yard behind his colonial home. He raised mostly vegetables. Some of these he gave away but many ended up in the dishes he prepared. Minestrone soup, breaded eggplant, ratatouille. He wasn't a great cook but the food he prepared was hearty and flavorful. Rich with oil and butter and salt. He didn't care about cholesterol or blood pressure. He figured his lifespan was limited, due not to physiology but factors like the criminal justice system and the guns that the Objects occasionally possessed and were not reluctant to use. So his circulatory system worried him zip.

Michael began walking west from the bus stop through the cool, overcast autumn evening. He owned a nice car but he traveled almost exclusively by bus when he was on a job. No tag numbers to trace and city conveyances did not have very good security cams, if at all.

In this business it was important to blend in. He didn't wear a porkpie hat or camo gear or long coat that might conceal an automatic weapon. Today he was in a tan sportscoat, black slacks, blue dress shirt and burgundy tie: a middle manager at an insurance agency, a supervisor at Outback. No one paid him any mind. He might be heading home to any one of these houses from a busy day at work.

Home to hug the wife and children. To water his green beans and Italian parsley.

Michael was thinking of his most recent job. The Object was a labor organizer. Had Michael's client's business unionized, as the Object was attempting to accomplish, profits would have plummeted, and so the man had to go. Michael had spent some days working up a plan to make the death appear accidental.

He was successful. Everyone bought the drunk driving scenario (the Object had certainly done his part). The hit was clean, it was elegant and, most important, it didn't get much scrutiny by the law. Cops here were overworked, understaffed and more than happy to accept a mishap at face value, and move on to busting inner city kids for selling drugs and the brown-toothed cookers for supplying them.

This job didn't permit that kind of sophistication. For one thing, the death had to happen fast. Also, the murder of the Object would raise many an eyebrow, and even the best organized apparent accident wouldn't put suspicion to rest. So, the plan was a quick shooting, and let the chips fall where they might (quite the ironic metaphor, he thought, given that a casino was at the center of the job).

The police would go into gear and investigate. So what? Michael thought, let them. He would melt the clear plastic gloves he wore when shooting. The weapon had been stolen from a gun show and the suppressor he was going to use he'd made himself, all of which meant the ballistic profile of the bullet would lead investigators nowhere.

But fast didn't mean impulsive or careless. He'd plan out the time and the place with his typical care. There'd be considerable surveillance work to do.

He now paused beside a particularly nice garden—filled with autumn flowers in abundance and zucchini ready to harvest and tomatoes red as fresh blood—and looked across the street to an unassuming, white-sided bungalow.

It was Kelli Lambert's house.

He saw the girl walk into the front room, carrying a glass of milk or soda or something. A moment later the lights dimmed, replaced by flickering blue. In his household, growing up, children didn't watch TV on school nights. But Michael had come to learn that it was a very different world nowadays.

⊚

THE ROUND, HANDSOME woman of about fifty looked her over in a particular way.

It was the gaze mothers gave babysitters. Part friendly greeting, part probing analysis.

Kelli was used to it.

"Good evening, dear."

"Hello, Mrs. Bailey."

They were in the entryway of a cluttered but clean house in Harbor Grove, a neighborhood popular because of the school district and the view of Ambrose Lake.

"Come on in."

The woman led her into the family room and they sat on a couch that you sank down into.

This was a try-out. Some parents didn't want to commit to an entire evening with a new babysitter, even those who had references like Kelli's, but would schedule an initial session for an hour or two while they visited with neighbors up the street or had a fast bite at a neighborhood bar. Any emergencies could be resolved in minutes. There were, Kelli had learned, a whole bunch of rules and arrangements in the babysitting world. These were called "protocols" in the business world, her mother had explained—Clara Lambert was a senior planner in the shipping company her husband had founded.

Kelli liked it that she'd learned a new word.

Protocol...

She shifted on the squooshy sofa, feeling a twinge in her joints. In cheer the team was trying a new routine that launched a student high into the air. Kelli had volunteered to be the "volleyball," she'd joked. Fine with the others; no one was really up for trying it. The move had gone pretty well the first couple of times but on the third, she'd spun a bit too far and, when she landed in the arms of the girls on the floor, it was on her side, not back. A muscle somewhere got pulled. Then she'd insisted she try it once more, even though her coach said she didn't need to. The final move had gone perfectly.

Only a bit of ache remained.

"So, honey," Mrs. Bailey said, "your references are wonderful. Mrs. Arthur said you straightened up her kitchen when you didn't need to."

"Just cleaned a little."

"Well, you don't have to do that for us. Oh, and I liked the notes you included from the children you've sat for."

Kelli never asked, but sometimes the kids wrote her something. Mab Winston, for instance, had written a glowing review and drawn a picture of Kelli, which was not half bad. (The little demon William had offered neither praise nor a portrait.)

"You live nearby, right?"

"Mapleton."

"Pretty there."

"It's nice."

A pause. Mrs. Bailey's face grew still. "You live with your mother, right?"

She nodded. "My father passed away."

Which was the question that Mrs. Bailey was really asking.

The topic had come up because it suggested that Kelli would take her job seriously; without the main breadwinner in the family, the girl would need money to help her mother and to save up for important things like college tuition. She wouldn't risk her babysitting reputation by sneaking boys into the house or drinking the parents' vodka and refilling the bottles with water.

"I'm so sorry."

"Thank you."

Then Mrs. Bailey sat back, nodding. "Well, I think the girls are going to like you just fine. I'll go get them."

The woman rose and stepped out of the room. Kelli looked around. It was hard to avoid the wall decorations. Mr. Bailey was a hunter. There were a half-dozen deer heads mounted on plaques, the creatures' glassy eyes staring into the room. Directly at her, it seemed.

Creepy.

Something else caught her attention too: a large wooden cabinet with glass doors. Inside, four rifles sat with their ends pointed upward. She rose and walked to it. The guns—of dark brown wood and glistening blue-black metal—were impressive, like the works of art the Winstons had scattered throughout their mansion. Mr. Bailey must have spent a lot of time caring for and polishing them.

She tugged at the door. It was securely locked. But looking up, she saw a small piece of metal protruding from the top. Hearing that Mrs. Bailey was still upstairs, Kelli reached up and took the key. She tried it and the door opened. Inside, on the floor of the cabinet, was a large, dusty box. She lifted the lid carefully and found some pistols. She closed the lid. And relocked the door.

Her father had owned guns and they had always fascinated her. She'd wanted to go shooting with him but he'd said absolutely not.

"Can't I just go shooting once?"

He'd used that line that infuriated her. "When you're older."

Now, looking at the deer, she thought: could I ever really shoot anything? She tried to imagine it. Like anybody who had the internet or TV, she knew how guns worked.

Pulling that slide thing back...

Lifting the gun...

Pulling the trigger...

Seeing what happened when the bullets hit their target...

But actually taking a life?

Without seriously considering the question, she returned to the couch. She pulled from her backpack the board game, with its colorful images of the happy characters sprinting through the fantasy landscape.

Candy Land was the perfect game for young children. Kelli had looked into it. Totally G-rated, the game had been developed by a retired teacher in the 1940s, recovering from this really bad disease, polio. She found herself in a ward filled with school kids who were recovering like her. To distract herself—and the children—the teacher came up with the idea of a game that involved a journey through a land of candy, where the players tried to be the first to the Candy Castle. The worst danger was getting stopped on square of sticky candy until you drew that same color of the space you were on. Even Lord Licorice, who looked a little weird, didn't pose any real danger.

It was not, Kelli had thought, Grand Theft Auto with a sweet tooth.

She'd read that more households with young children had Candy Land than had chess sets (though she wondered if, after *The Queen's Gambit*, that was still true).

As she was laying out the board, two twin girls about six charged into the room. One shouted, "Candy Land!"

Kelli smiled and said hello to Monica and Marion as they sat down across from her.

Mr. and Mrs. Bailey appeared in the doorway and, after the typical recitation of departing parents—bedtimes, snacks, toothbrushing, and which were the preferred stuffed animals to accompany the girls to sleep—they departed.

Without even looking at the gun cabinet.

Much to Kelli's great relief. If they had, they might've noticed that the key was no longer on top of the piece of furniture and wondered where it might have gone.

Never guessing that it sat deep in their babysitter's back pocket.

◉

REMOVING AN OBJECT is mostly about research and preparation.

The fatal shot would take only a few seconds. The time leading up to it would require days or weeks.

Michael sat in a coffee shop—a nonchain establishment, one with a fake security cam over the counter (he knew all the brand names). An ear bud was plugged in. Never use wireless; hacking and eavesdropping via Bluesnarfing and Bluebugging are so easy that even a fifty-year-old can do it, Michael had once joked.

He liked music, classical mostly, light classical, not weird classical, and now, with a slowly vanishing cappuccino in front of him, he might have been listening to Bach inventions or Mozart's *Queen of the Night* aria as he was preparing for a presentation or studying an important spreadsheet.

However, he happened to be listening to surreptitious recordings of a half-dozen conversations and staring, somewhat blankly, at a map of the city. Later he would turn his attention to that. Now, his whole world was listening to the words.

Some recordings had been made via X-treme883 Shielded pick-ups, which were very sensitive, though they distorted the tone (it rendered Kelli's voice higher than it naturally was). In other recordings, conversations had been vacuumed up via a SoundStealer, a $2000 microphone that could pick up a human voice from hundreds of feet away. The early models were dangerous. Say you were listening to someone on the other side of the street and a motorcycle with a bad muffler shot past. The decibels in your earphone might shoot from 80 to 130 in a second. That could blow your eardrums out and Michael knew one man in this business who that had happened to. He never recovered fully.

The new models, though, contained software that muted the sound instantly when the dBs rose to a dangerous level—like the shooting earmuffs that activated only when you fired the gun; you could carry on a normal conversation until you pulled the trigger.

Michael was jotting notes. He preferred to plan jobs on paper. Paper could be burned; paper could be soaked and wadded up and pulped in a garbage disposal. In this day and age you couldn't escape bits and bytes but if he had to communicate electronically he used Department of Defense-level encryption and Pretty Good Privacy, which despite the modest name could have been called Really Damn Good Privacy.

Always aware of his surroundings as he worked, he had noted that a woman nearby, in a dark skirt and white blouse, kept looking his way. She was a little younger than him, maybe mid-forties. She was attractive, a bit heavy. The looks were mere glances—but not too quick. Once or twice she lingered. Michael got this some. He was a good-looking man with a full head of salt-and-pepper hair and he was, as he had to be in this job, in good physical shape. He did not acknowledge her look, of course. While he certainly felt that tug, low in his gut, he would never pick up anyone in a venue like this, or at a time like this. His attitude was not out of fidelity to Anita, of course (she was presently off-shift from the Good-Night Gentlemen's club and was probably making several thousand dollars in the nearby Day's Inn). No, it was purely for security. Never mix lust and work.

The woman was merely pretending to read her novel—she'd flipped pages once in the past five minutes. Maybe this was because she'd come to Joe's in hopes of meeting a man.

But she might also be part of an operation. Meet Michael, go home with him, look for evidence.

Or shoot him in the back of the head.

Such was Michael's life.

Always risk.

But reward too: the satisfaction of using his God-given skills and removing Objects from the earth. While making a great deal of money.

The conversations on the recordings ended and he studied his notes. He had enough. He wiped the SD card and, when no one was looking, dropped it into his napkin, where he broke it into several pieces with his powerful hands. They went into his pocket; he would later pitch them into the roadside grass on his drive home.

He sipped some of the cinnamony beverage and turned his attention to the map, moving his mouse to the venue that he'd heard mentioned on the tape.

Ameri-Mall was a large indoor shopping center/entertainment spot about five miles from downtown. It was quite the attraction. There were the typical stores you'd see at such a place: from cheap to glitzy. One of the big draws was the rides—a portion was actually a mini amusement park, with a small roller coaster and Ferris wheel and bumper cars and arcades. Especially popular with teens.

After ten minutes of studying the map—and examining some architectural drawings he'd scored—Michael sat back, eyes on the stained acoustic tile ceiling. It would be impossible to do the job in the mall itself, of course; the place would be far too crowded—and the killing had to be at peak hours, to escape safely afterward. But one advantage about the venue was the maze of underground parking. Much of it was patrolled and covered by security cameras but there were many blind spots.

He was satisfied. Barring a turn of bad luck, the hit would work.

After downing his drink, cold but just as tasty as when it was steaming, he rose. Michael was halfway to the door when he heard a voice.

"Excuse me."

He turned. He was looking at the woman in the white blouse. She was smiling.

His unresponsive, almost cold, eyes did nothing to deter her.

"I knew it! I saw you at Fitness Is Us. The spinning class Tuesday. Don't tell me I'm wrong."

He had no idea what a spinning class was. "No."

"No, I'm not wrong? Or no you weren't there?"

"I wasn't there." He noted that her blouse was one button less secure than it had been five minutes ago.

"Are you sure?"

How could that possibly be a question?

"Okay. Maybe you don't spin, but you sure work out." She scanned his body.

"I have to go."

"Sure I can't buy you another cappuccino?" she asked. So she was all-in, no coyness present.

Which he respected.

"No. I have to get home. Sorry." He added the last word not because he was, but because it was something that one said at a time like this. And he needed to appear normal.

"Maybe I'll see you in here again."

"Maybe."

Michael walked outside into the cool evening air, reflecting that, no, it hadn't been an LEA op. No undercover cop in the world would be that clumsy.

Nor was she one of those pushy people who might just stand up, walk out the door with him and, inundating him with one-sided conversation, accompany him in the direction of his home.

This was particularly good news. It would have been a considerable inconvenience to kill her.

A DILEMMA.

Erik Winston paced in his office.

The office where he'd left out in plain view the damn documents about the plan to torch the competitor casino.

Of *course* the babysitter hadn't appreciated anything incriminating in what she'd seen—if, like he'd told his wife, she'd seen anything at all.

He'd once watched a TV show in which an audience was shown a scene of a streetside scuffle between a couple of men. While it was going on someone in a gorilla suit walked by in the background, stopped and waved. Ninety percent of the audience never noticed the creature.

It was the same in Kelli's case. She was so focused on looking for a game for the kids, the diagrams didn't even register.

Besides, there was a practical risk in killing her. What if investigators found that the victim had babysat for the very couple opening the casino that replaced the Magic Luck? A sharp cop might start to make connections.

The *lesser* risk was to let her live and take the slim chance that she had seen the casino's name.

He now rubbed his eyes. He was no saint; he'd ordered hits before and had come close to carrying out a few himself. (The two jobs his father sent him out on didn't work out, but that wasn't his fault. It really wasn't.)

No, Erik Winston didn't care about taking lives...

But a kid?

That was harsh. And he couldn't believe that his wife had actually found a hitman willing to tap a teenager.

Rachel had always been more brutal than he was. They'd met at the funeral of her cousin, an enforcer of the organized crew that her uncle headed up. Erik ran a small numbers and gaming operation that paid a cut to the uncle's crew. Their marriage was traditional in one sense—the wedding night lasted three energetic hours—but was also a business arrangement. He merged his operation into hers, sort of a reverse dowry.

He was grifting and scam, not guns and blood, his wife's preferred approach. Slash and burn was what she was known for.

But this was too much.

No, it was wrong and dangerous to kill the girl.

What to do about it, though?

He poured another scotch and sat back, considering the quandary.

Well, maybe there *was* a solution.

Erik considered himself an expert at human nature. He knew his wife. She was good at coming up with schemes and plans—solid ones, profitable ones—but once she'd done so, her attention jumped to the next job and the next. The earlier schemes faded from her mind.

He knew the psyche of hitmen too. They were stone cold, and in the business for one thing only: money.

A plan formed. Their hitman was making 50K for the job. Erik would contact him and offer 100K, cash or Bitcoin, to get sick the day of the hit. Something gut-wrenchingly bad, puking, high fever. So bad he was laid up in bed.

Rachel would try to find another hitman but given that she was focused on other projects and that it was hard to find a suitable killer before they burned down the Magic Luck, the hit would end up in the back of her mind. The arson would happen, the story would run but Kelli would never hear about it. The whole problem would go away.

Erik walked to the front of the house and looked through the curtains. His wife's car was not in the circle.

He pulled his phone from his pocket and texted the killer, laying out his plan.

There was a delay of only ten seconds.

I keep the original 50?

Erik debated. This seemed unfair since the man was being paid a bonus to *not* finish the job, which meant he was avoiding any risk of jail time. But he saw no other option.

Okay.

And the reply.

Deal. Cash. McMurtry's one hour.

Erik told the man he'd meet him there. He drained his glass and hurried to his car. He had to be gone by the time Rachel returned.

◎

KELLI PUSHED THROUGH the thick doorway from the parking garage and stepped into the light. It was so bright she blinked.

She headed to the rendezvous spot, where Tiff and Joanne and Kisha and Sha'ana were clustered together. Two of the girls she knew from cheer, one from the cafeteria and one from Computer Club. They were sitting in mesh chairs, leaning forward, huddled and holding phones.

Tiff held hers up, to the "Awws" of the others.

It wasn't of a boy, Kelli knew. That would have been a different tone of *Aww*. This would be of a cute cat. Maybe a baby goat.

Kelli strode up.

"Yo!" Joanne said.

They nodded and smiled greetings.

"Drop some screen, girl," Kelli said to Tiff.

She'd been wrong about the vid, but close. It was a puppy doing a Tik Tok dance.

"Aww," Kelli echoed.

"I need jeans," Joanne announced, and this would be quite a project because she was so tall and thin. But her crew, Kelli included, was up for the challenge.

They rose from the chairs and started down walkways. Kelli had no doubt that they'd be successful. You could find anything you wanted at Ameri-Mall, the Emerald City of shopping centers.

◎

AT MCMURTRY'S, IN the business district, Erik ordered a smoky Lagavulin and watched some of the more attractive women in the place. It was a watering hole for businesses in the area and most of the female clientele had jobs in the tall office buildings that created dim canyons in this part of downtown. But stepping inside here was like slipping into a different dimension. Jackets came off, buns got undone, fresh makeup was applied. There was definitely Tinder action going on here, figuratively as well as literally, and Erik knew that hooking up at McMurtry's invariably meant good sex...and even, he'd heard, the occasional marriage. He took pleasure in the observing the turgid jousting around him, even if he was no longer allowed to play.

He looked at his watch.

The killer was five minutes late.

He had a fantasy that the man had had another job before he was to meet Erik, but something went wrong and he got shot dead. That would take care of the dilemma right there. Not only would Kelli the babysitter survive but he'd save his 100K.

Win win.

He had just lifted the sweet pungent liquor to his lips when a woman's voice said in a snarling whisper, "Are you out of your mind?"

Shit and a half.

He closed his eyes momentarily.

Rachel lifted his glass out of his hand. She set it loudly on the bar.

"He told you?" Erik whispered.

"Of *course* he told me. He's a murderer but he's honorable." She pointed a bright red nail at her husband's chest. "A deal..." A painful poke with the long nail into his breastbone. "Is."

Poke.

"A."

"All right, I got the message."

"Deal!"

Poke.

"Ouch."

"Shut up. And our money?" she asked snidely. The pronoun was a reminder that, in a way, he'd tried to rob *her*.

He handed over the envelope. She pocketed it.

She leaned close and he smelled some floral scent, a delicate one. It went perfectly with her petite, sensual physique. It did not, at all, match her icy, hateful eyes.

People around them had turned, surely registering her scary face and harsh words. She glared back and they resumed their drinking and flirting. She whispered to Erik, "Do you like what we do at night?"

Oh, hell, this again.

He nodded.

"Do you *really* like it, Erik?"

"Yes."

"Am I creative? Do I know what you enjoy?

"Yes. But it's just I kept thinking, she's a kid, she's a kid."

Rachel said, "Whips or kid. You choose."

"Honey, I love—"

"Whips or kid?"

"All right," he muttered.

"There's my boy." She picked up his whisky and downed it, then strode out the door, saying, "Pay up and let's go. I want this over with."

◎

KELLI LOOKED AT her phone to get the time.

No kids wore watches anymore. Older people gave them as birthday and graduation presents but they ended up in drawers. A phone was everything, a clock, a calculator, a newscaster, a game, a camera, a lifeline.

Having said goodbye to her friends (the jeans mission successful), she walked along the brightly lit hallway of Ameri-Mall in the direction of the parking garage. Here was Claire's, full of trinkets. Here was Justice, full of Chinese shirts and jeans covered with American logos.

Unlike some friends, Kelli was not addicted to shopping and had no need for retail therapy but sometimes it was just good to be in a place that was a bubble from the outside, the real world. A place that was undeniably cheerful, where you could find a new outfit, friendly people, a mochaccino with whipped cream—a place where you could forget, momentarily, that you'd be returning to a home without a father.

Something now caught her eye—in the window of a store just past Justice. A hairclip in the window. It was in the shape of a feather and would go well with her hair when she wore it up, which she did at cheer so she didn't get blinded during a spin or twist routine. It sparkled and shone—it seemed to call her name, an expression of her father's when he'd noted she saw something she liked.

Oh, go ahead, girl, splurge.

She did, and a moment later was walking to the exit, swinging the shopping bag in her hand.

She stepped through the double doors and into the dark stairway that led to what she called the "secret" portion of the garage, always deserted, so there were plenty of places to park. It was spooky, with the dimness, the dripping pipes, the groans, the rat droppings, the graffiti—why tag a wall here, when only a few people would see it?

Spooky...

Of course, it wouldn't be, she thought, if you had a gun in your pocket or purse.

Any threat she'd pull it out, aim it and—if he didn't back off—start firing.

But that wasn't going to happen.

She had no weapon on her.

Sure, when she'd found the guns in the cabinet at the Baileys', she'd thought about borrowing one, taking it into the woods and trying it out. He probably wouldn't even know, considering that he didn't seem to open the dusty box very often.

But she'd decided, no. A gun wasn't for her. You couldn't take it to school; the safety officer sometimes had the police come in with metal detectors and do spot checks. Besides, shooting was a skill, like anything else and, she sensed, it wasn't one of her talents.

She'd stick to what she was good at: coding, Latin and cheerleading. Oh, and babysitting, of course. She couldn't forget that.

◎

MICHAEL WAS IN the garage beneath the Ameri-Mall.

Hiding in one of the spots he'd identified in his research. This part of the facility wasn't near the main entrance, and the stalls were mostly empty.

He'd been following the Object in the mall—certain he hadn't been seen—and was now near where the hit would take place. When he got within about fifteen yards from the kill zone, he stopped.

He'd created the shooting solution in the coffee shop and rehearsed it in his head a dozen times.

Research and preparation…

He pulled on the clear latex gloves and took his gun from his back waistband (the best place to stow larger pistols; they invariably displayed a profile when in a holster on your hip or even under your arm). The SIG-Sauer was a fine weapon, more complicated than a Glock but, in his opinion, more accurate. The caliber was 9mm and, compensating for the medium-sized caliber, the slugs were hollow points that expanded upon hitting their target, devastating organs and muscles.

From his pocket Michael took a suppressor. He screwed the tube onto the muzzle. Pros like him objected to the word "silencer." For one thing, it was inaccurate; no gun would ever be silent. Also, hitmen didn't like filmmakers' and actors' portraying them referring to the accessory inaccurately. It made them seem amateurish.

Suppressors, over the years, evolved from crude devices, tubes filled with rubber baffles, which lasted only three or four uses and fired out bits of material that the police could trace. Today, they were far more sophisticated, containing rings in carefully designed shapes, scientifically mounted in the tube. They worked by catching the hot gas from a gunshot and dispersing it slowly, so that the huge sound becomes an audible but quiet *thunk*.

Michael took one more item from his jacket: a C-clamp, the sort you can buy at hardware stores around the country. This he affixed to a pipe running from floor to ceiling. He rested his gun on it and aimed toward the target area. When he was tagging an Object with a firearm, he always used a rest. No pro shot freehand.

He looked at his watch.

How long would he have to wait?

Only seconds, it seemed.

The Object stepped into view at that very moment.

Michael had earlier chambered a round in the SIG. Firearm safety dictated that you not mount a suppressor on a loaded gun, and under other circumstances he would have followed that rule. But here, he couldn't risk mounting the suppressor first and then pulling the slide to chamber a bullet. The noise would be too recognizable; even someone who'd never touched a gun knew the distinctive metallic snapping from TV.

He would shoot three times. To effectively kill, you needed to obliterate your target, not risk merely wounding. He rested the weapon on the C-clamp and controlled his breathing. In, out. In, out. He increased pressure on the trigger.

Aim, breathe, squeeze…

Now!

Thunk, thunk, thunk…

The gun kicked hard. Blood and tissue sprayed everywhere.

◎

RACHEL WINSTON BARKED a scream and threw her hands up when the bullets blew apart the head of the man she'd been talking to, spattering her with gore.

Her husband screamed too.

The man, whose name was Lester Markus, had been counting the money she'd just handed him when he collapsed. Bills fluttered everywhere.

"Jesus," Erik gasped. A pistol appeared in his hand and he swiveled around, crouching.

"No," came a whisper from the shadows.

Without a moment's hesitation Erik dropped the gun.

Sighing at her husband's cowardice, Rachel, not a bad shot, eyed the gun and debated scooping up the weapon.

"You too," the voice from the dark. "No." Whoever it was had seen her eyes—and therefore her intention.

She slumped.

A large man, pale, with thick salt-and-pepper hair, walked into the light. He was holding a suppressed gun, which was pointed toward them.

Rachel began, "Listen..."

"Shhh. Turn around."

"We didn't do anything," Erik whined. "We were just shopping. We—"

Rachel told her husband, "Shut up."

"Turn around," the man muttered, like a parent irritated at a difficult child. Just how they talked to William.

They turned around.

In the corner of her eye she was aware that the killer was bending down and collecting things. Probably Erik's and Markus's guns and the money.

He'd had them turn their backs so he could shoot them more easily if one of them made a move. She couldn't help but admire professionals, even at a time like this.

"All right," the killer said.

They faced him.

She said, "If you're from the Roberto organization—"

"Don't talk."

Erik began babbling. "We won't. We won't say a word, you let us go and—"

"Shut up." This time it was the shooter who'd snapped at him. The broad man now looked around carefully. He said, "It's good."

"What?" Rachel asked.

"I wasn't talking to you."

Another person stepped from the shadows and joined them.

Rachel gasped.

It was Kelli Lambert, the babysitter.

"Hi, Uncle Michael," she said to the gunman and kissed him on the cheek.

◎

KELLI LOOKED DOWN at the body.

"Who is he?" she asked.

Her uncle held up the man's wallet. "Lester Markus. I've heard of him. Trigger man out of Detroit. He'll tag anybody. Children, the elderly, the disabled." The tone of his voice made it clear how he felt about that.

She then looked over the married couple standing in front of the body, both of them spattered with blood and other icky stuff. Mr. Winston's face was totally comical. It was a smile in a way but kind of distorted. She guessed it meant he was way freaked out. Was he going to puke? Kelli stepped back. It was so gross when people did that.

His wife's expression was calmer but it was still: WTF?

Kelli said, "We don't have a lot of time. You know." She glanced at the blood running down the floor toward a drain. Soon it would be out of the shadows and visible. "So, like, let's get to business."

"Business?" Mrs. Winston muttered. Her face was growing red. Confusion had turned to anger.

Her uncle took over. "We know you're going to burn down the casino that Roberto and his crew owns and then start up one yourself."

Mrs. Winston grimaced and lifted her palms toward her husband, like she was saying "Told you so."

"We have it all on a tape. Do you want to hear it?"

"That's not necessary," Mrs. Winston muttered. She looked at Kelli with a cold smile. "I assume when you were *pretending* to look for your goddamn games, you left a bug."

"Pretty much."

Michael continued, "And we heard the call of you arranging to take my niece out. And meeting here to pay him." Generally pretty calm and cool, he was now mad. And having Uncle Michael mad at you was not a good thing.

Kelli squinted as she recalled listening to the tape. "You said there was a nosy little bitch you needed dead. I.e., me." She smiled brightly. "Hey, I just learned something in school. Want to hear? 'I.e.'? It's Latin for *id est*. It means, 'That is.'" Latin was her favorite class, after coding.

Her uncle said evenly, "You can go ahead and burn down whatever you want. We don't care. But if you don't transfer two million into this Bitcoin vault, a copy goes to the cops, FBI *and* the Roberto organization." He set a card on the concrete between them and stepped back. Mrs. Winston nodded for her husband to collect it.

Mr. Winston scurried forward. "But we're only clearing one mill. Where are we going to get—"

Uncle Michael said, "Not our problem."

"Shit." He collected the card.

Kelli said, "You know, I think we need another million. That 'little bitch' part. What do you think, Uncle Michael?"

He was nodding with approval. He added to the couple, "Midnight tonight."

Mrs. Winston whispered, "Three million? Impossible."

Kelli stared at her coolly and thought it was really neat when the woman looked away first.

A sigh. "All right. We'll get it."

Uncle Michael said, "Go on home. I'll finish up here." A nod toward the body and the hundred-dollar bills littering the garage floor. "And say hi to your mom for me. We'll be there Sunday for supper."

"Bye," Kelli said brightly and kissed his cheek once more. She started away but then turned back, looked toward the Winstons. "Oh, by the way: A five-dollar tip, for a whole *evening* babysitting? Seriously?"

◎

KELLI LAMBERT SAT at a metal table with rounded edges. It was bolted to the floor, as was the chair she was in. She was bored. She didn't have her phone with her and there was nothing to look at. No windows. Nothing on the walls, which were painted green and were scuffed. She would have painted them. She was pretty good with a roller and brush. She'd done her room when she and her mother moved into the new house.

There was a shadow outside, in the corridor.

Her heart beat a little faster and she smiled when the door opened.

The guard let the man inside. He was fifty-two and had broad shoulders and a thin waist. He wore a gray jumpsuit with short sleeves. His arms were thick and his left forearm bore a tat in the shape of a dagger.

"Daddy!"

"Honey!"

Contact was against the prison rules, but they didn't apply when you were Tomas Milandic, the most powerful mob boss in the state. Anyway, also against the rules, the guard had left them alone, so who was to notice any infractions?

"You're too thin," he said, frowning as he stepped back and studied his daughter.

"Dad. I eat like a horse. I'm at cheer practice five times a week, and we have a game every Friday night."

"Eat more."

"Then they can't catch me when I do an aerial. I'll be too big."

He glanced at her hair. "Hm. Nice. I like that."

She touched the feather clip she'd bought at the mall—at the store next to Justice: Tiffany's. It had cost $5,000. Sometimes you just needed to splurge—especially when she was going to make the family seven figures that night.

She asked, "How's it going with the doctor?"

"It's working out good."

The prison offered psychological counseling. Her father was in group therapy with some convicts diagnosed with antisocial personalities. They'd been convicted of all sorts of serious crimes, hijacking, robbery, assault and, some of the younger ones, hacking and cyber stalking and ransomware attacks. They were all recidivist offenders, and the prison officials were hoping to turn them around.

Her father, however, was not there to cure himself...or help cure anyone else. He wanted to make contacts he might use when he was released in four years and returned to the helm of the syndicate that his father—Kelli's granddad—had created thirty years ago.

"The Eagles?" he asked.

She grimaced. "Lost our second in a row." The John Adams High Eagles were not a stellar team.

"So, when I call my bookie?"

She thought for a minute. "They're playing Travis City. I say Travis. And the spread? Make it eight."

"I'll do it. How'd the babysitting gig go?"

She held up three fingers. "In the vault."

Her father beamed. "Three? One mill extra. You put together a good one. But then you always do."

Kelli had known from a young age what her father did—he'd had to tell her at ten or so that there were certain things about their life she couldn't talk about, to anybody. Money in the basement, certain visitors who arrived in limos with thick, tinted windows, the guns hidden behind books on the shelves.

He'd even told her there was a chance that "certain people"—i.e., the police—might catch him.

Which is just what happened last year. One of the lower-level runners in her father's company had turned them in. Her dad and some key friends in the crew were locked up for conspiracy.

Part of the sentence was forfeiting most of the family's money.

Young Kelli had liked the intrigue of his career outside the shipping business he ran...and liked the fact that her father had entrusted her with his secrets. She'd never participated, of course, but had quietly observed how he conducted business, whom he had over to the house, what they said and what plans they'd made.

After he was arrested Kelli, then sixteen, had done a lot of thinking about the situation. She'd come to visit him and said she had an idea. She was a popular babysitter. What if, on a job, she were to find something about the parents that was incriminating. They could blackmail them.

"Absolutely not," was his stern response.

At her next job, though, she'd left a plush bunny in the basket stuffed full of the children's toys in the family's living room. The cute thing had huge, floppy ears, a sweet smile, a round puffy tail... and, inside, a digital recorder. She'd collected the device a week later on another assignment at the house and listened to the ten hours of recorded conversations.

She told this to her father on their next visit.

"You did what?" he said angrily. "I said not to."

She lowered her head contritely. "I'm sorry, Daddy." But then she looked at him quizzically. "What's insider trading?"

His face softened. "Explain."

The bunny had caught the man using that phrase, along with the words that they had to be "really careful or we could get ten years."

Which told her that he was doing something that he wouldn't want anybody to know about.

And that he'd pay to keep quiet.

Her father thought for a moment, then said, "Have my brother get you a bug that's shielded from scanners."

"Oh, they make those? That's neat."

The next few recordings captured the men's plan to use information to buy stock illegally. Uncle Michael had visited them and played some of the recordings. The shocked man had immediately transferred a $250K to a Bitcoin vault that Kelli and her uncle had set up.

Kelli and her mother moved to their new house in Mapleton. Going by her mother's last name and claiming her father had passed, she'd amped up her babysitting business, trying to get jobs in the homes of men and women like the Winstons—from a list that her Uncle Mike had supplied, people he and her father knew were engaging in criminal activities.

On a job, Kelli would search the house for incriminating evidence, on the pretext of looking for games, and would plant the bugs. Her uncle followed up with the collection, making sure she stayed out of harm's way.

It would have been the same with the Winstons.

Except for hiring somebody to tag the "little bitch." Kelli wanted to visit them in person. Once her uncle learned that the hitman was going to be paid at Ameri-Mall, he'd told Kelli about it. She'd met with her friends beforehand and then headed down to the garage to wait until Uncle Michael had killed Markus. Then confront the pair.

Her dad now said with a frown, "Mike told me, the latest job? They were going to tag you?"

She shrugged. "They hired some asshole from Cleveland."

"Language," he said in that voice that parents sometimes used to correct their children when they don't really believe in the rule they were enforcing.

"Sorry. But it was cool. Uncle Mike was always there, right behind him."

"All right. But be careful. A father worries."

"I will. Promise." Then, "Oh, there's something else I want to do. I babysat for this family, the Baileys?"

"Are they on Mike's list?"

"No, this was a real job. They had this gun cabinet in the family room. Locked. But the kids could climb on a chair and get the key."

"Idiots," her father said, a dark expression on his face. He had very firm opinions about gun safety and youngsters.

Can't I just go shooting once?

When you're older...

"I opened the door and got a picture of the twins standing in front of it. I locked it up again and kept the key."

"What're you thinking? A hundred thousand to keep the pic off social media?"

"No, they're not bad people. They're just like, yeah, idiots. I thought I'd send them a copy of the picture and a note saying, 'Child Protective Services.' They'll get the message."

"That's my girl," he said, wearing a proud expression. "But they'll know it came from you. You'll never get a job from them again."

"No problem. Always a demand for babysitters with games and fresh-baked cookies."

The door opened. "Time," the guard said uneasily.

"Sure thing, Joey."

Father and daughter hugged again.

"See you next week, Daddy."

The man led her father into the hall and Kelli sat back down to wait for the escort to take her back to prison reception.

Paladin

By Tod Goldberg

Tuesday morning, before the worst of the storm hit, Bennie Toellner called me at the sheriff's office to see if I could go look in on his twelve-year-old son, Kurt. He was home sick and Bennie'd been called to help a disabled fishing boat. "I don't know the situation out on the water," he said. Bennie was with a Coast Guard rescue crew, operating out of the marina thirty miles west of Granite City, on the southern coast of Washington, at the tip of the Long Beach Peninsula. "If someone's hurt, could be I don't get back until evening. I tried calling the house, but Kurt didn't pick up or it didn't go through. Guess I'm a little worried."

I looked out the window. Rain was falling at a slant. "Wind's already pretty bad," I said. "Wouldn't be surprised if phone service out your way is spotty." This was 1985, but in my mind, it could be Tuesday. "Where's Jane at?" I'd known Bennie and Jane Toellner for my entire life. Bennie and I had gone to high school together and Jane, back when she was Jane Patterson, had lived down the street from Katherine, my late first wife. She was a stewardess now, working for Alaska Air.

"Brawton," he said.

"What's she doing up there?"

"We separated," Bennie said.

"Oh, shit, Bennie," I said. "When did that happen?"

"A couple nights ago," Bennie said. "It was a long time coming, to be honest."

"You should have called me."

"Me and Kurt have been trying to figure things out on our own," Bennie said. "I didn't want to bother you."

"It's no bother," I said, "we're friends."

"You got a lot of responsibility."

"Still."

Bennie was silent for a moment, then he said, "I don't even really know if Kurt's sick. He said his nose was stuffed up. I didn't want to fight about it. Shit, Morris, I'm a damn wreck and now this."

"I get it," I said.

"I tried to leave a message for Deena Vlach on the phone, see if she could come by after school to watch *General Hospital* and make dinner, but that's another couple hours. And who knows when she might get it."

"I'll head over," I said.

"Might be better if Deena brought Kurt to her place, now that I think about it."

"We'll figure it out," I said.

"Wind is already thirty knots at Point Komo," Bennie said. "It's gonna be an adventure."

"Be safe out there. I got your son handled."

"I appreciate it, Morris," Bennie said. "I get back, we'll get a beer or six."

That would never happen. By nightfall, Bennie Toellner would be lost to the sea, along with the entire crew of his rescue tug and the fishermen they went to save, plus fifteen miles of coastline. Half the hull of the Coast Guard tug washed up on a beach in Oregon a year later, but no bodies were ever recovered. But their ghosts, oh, they still walk the streets of Granite City.

BENNIE AND HIS family lived in a two-story ranch house on the south side of Yeach Mountain, about fifteen minutes from the center of town. Their property stretched for a dozen acres to the east—ending at Nel's Pond, which was fed by Yeach's annual snowmelt and which Bennie kept stocked with rainbow trout—and another few acres west, before it dropped into Patterson Gulch, which ran all the way to the Interstate and was named for Jane's pioneer ancestors. In the summer, Bennie and Jane let locals park on their property to hike out to the pond to fish or picnic. They even built a couple tables and put out some garbage cans, though most people were respectful and carried their own trash back out. Knock on the door and be polite, you could use their bathroom or get some ice for your cooler. It was just how it was.

On that day, however, the long gravel road leading up to the house was already under an inch of water, which made the drive perilous since half the road hugged the gulch and its forty-foot drop. Even in the best weather the gulch had claimed cars, ATVs, bikes, and at least one UPS truck over the years, their skeletons visible in fire season when the county would come to prune the thick brush. So, by the time I pulled up to the house, I'd already made the decision that Deena Vlach could stay home and I'd sit with Kurt.

I got out of my cruiser and ran up the front steps to the Toellners partially enclosed front porch. They had a wicker couch, two wicker chairs, a low wicker-and-glass coffee table, which was covered in books and painted miniature figurines—dragons, elves, wizards—and a stack of what looked to me to be maps. There were two cans of RC Cola on the table, too, and a plate that had a smudge of peanut butter and bits of crust. I picked up the plate and walked in through the screen door, which was propped open with an old tennis shoe.

The TV was on in the living room—someone was looking for a P on *Wheel of Fortune*—and there was another can of RC on the coffee table in front of the sofa and even more figures and maps, plus a bowl of half-eaten mac and cheese.

"Kurt?" I called out. "It's Morris Drew."

Nothing.

I went around the sofa and turned off the TV before Vanna could flip around a letter. Picked up the empty RC and the bowl of noodles, took them into the kitchen. There were bowls in the sink, a pan with dried mac and cheese on the stove, a note on the kitchen table for Kurt, along with a $20 bill:

Order a pizza or some Chinese. Be sure to take a couple Actifed. Love you, Dad.

There was a box of Actifed open on the counter, two pills missing. Kurt must have helped himself, gotten tired and headed to bed upstairs, so I washed the dried mac and cheese out of the pan, cleaned up the plate with the peanut butter, washed out the half-eaten bowl of noodles, went back out front and grabbed the empty RC cans, tossed everything in the trash outside, then finally headed upstairs to check on the kid.

All in, I was there maybe five minutes before I went upstairs. How many times in those early days did I play those minutes out? How many times did I wonder if it made any difference whatsoever, the order of things? What if I'd left my office ten minutes earlier? What if I'd had a deputy already out on the road head over? What if Jane hadn't walked out on both of them? My god. *What if* is the infinity that makes an old man wish to die in his sleep, if only sleep was so easy to come by.

When I came up the stairs, I saw that Kurt's bedroom door was open and I could hear that the radio was on. I never did know the name of the song that was playing, only that for the next several decades I'd hear it in the background while I bought groceries, or while I stood in an elevator, or on the soundtrack of some movie, and I'd be brought right back to Kurt Toellner's empty bedroom, to his unmade bed, to the spatter of his blood and tissue on the wall, the ceiling, soaking into his *Star Wars* sheets, and a scream would rise up in the back of my throat and I'd have to fight to keep it down, just as I had on that terrible day, so long ago.

◎

"I FOUND BRAIN matter on the pillow and walls," Dr. Louis Digiangreco, our medical examiner, said. He lived a mile away and had a truck, so when I radioed in, he was the first to arrive. It took one of my deputies, Porter, another thirty minutes to show up. Half of Granite City was already underwater. Porter was inside now, processing everything, so I waited out on the front patio. I'd already walked through the house without paying any mind, which might have corrupted the scene, so Porter needed to account for every room I'd been in. It gave me a chance to go through the books and maps and the tiny figurines, trying to figure out what the hell I was looking at.

"How much?"

"Too much to survive without."

"Shit."

"My guess? You're looking for a sledgehammer. Ten pound or more. The velocity to make those spatters must have been something. And then a body without much of a head."

"He was twelve years old," I said. "Who would do that to a twelve-year-old?"

"You get Bennie on the radio yet?"

"No luck," I said. "He was on a rescue."

"Jane?"

"We're sending local Brawton boys to get her. Phones are down up there already. This storm is no joke. We think she's probably at her mother's, but fact is, we don't know."

Louis shook his head. "Look, that blood was dry. Boy's been dead a bit."

"How long, you think?"

"Hard to say. Drop of blood dries in a couple minutes, but those pools? That's an hour, at least. Maybe two. Depends on the surface. There was still some stickiness, so I'd say anywhere between two hours and a day. With the weather like this? Lotta moisture in the air? You'd need a real forensic investigator to figure that out. I'm just hypothesizing. It could be yesterday."

"But Bennie called this morning," I said. A moment that lasted forty years passed between us. Louis knew the life I'd lived in Korea and Vietnam and the life I lived here, in Granite City, knew that I'd witnessed multitudes of mistakes and bad choices, most hallmarked by profound violence.

"Like I said," Louis said. "Could be a pretty big goddamn open window."

I picked up an intricately painted dragon figure. "What do you make of these?"

Louis put on his glasses. "Lizzie has a bunch," he said. Lizzie was his daughter. She was about Kurt's age. "Gets them down at the comic book shop over by the JC. Part of some game she's into." He picked up one of the books. "Yeah, yeah, this. All the kids are playing it." It was the Dungeons & Dragons Beginner's Guide.

I thumbed through it. It didn't make much sense to me. A lot of talk of spells and quests and magical beings.

"You play it alone?" I asked.

"No, no," Louis said. "You need friends."

"How many?"

"Lizzie, it's always three or four of them."

"Shit," I said and got up from the patio, ran out back to the garbage cans, where I'd dumped the RC Cola cans, fished them out, brought them inside and put them in evidence bags. They were soaking wet. Maybe we'd be able to get a fingerprint, other than my own.

"Sheriff?" Shanna from dispatch came through my radio.

"Go ahead," I said.

"Brawton police found Jane Toellner."

"Okay," I said. "They bringing her down?"

"Highway 37 is flooded out at the Meriss grade. They want permission to tell her the news."

"I can only confirm that Kurt is missing," I said. Which was true. But we wouldn't be able to start searching for him, or his body, for at least a day. I wasn't entirely certain how Louis, Porter, and I were even going to get off the Toellners' property. I looked out the window, tried to find the contours of Yeach in the distance, but storm clouds and rain obscured it from my vision completely.

"Okay," Shanna said. "We'll go with that."

"Tell her I'm on it, though, okay? Soon as the rain lets up, we're going to run a grid search through the land out back, but I can't have anyone trying to mess around in this weather. We've got lightning splitting trees out this way."

"Will do, Sheriff."

Porter came down the stairs then with bags of evidence. I showed him the cans, told him about the dishes I'd cleaned, took him out front, showed him the game materials. "Heard that game was Satanic," Porter said.

"How can a game be Satanic?" I asked.

"I'm just telling you what I heard," he said. "My mother saw it on *60 Minutes*. Makes kids kill themselves."

"Are you of the opinion that Kurt Toellner bludgeoned himself to death, Deputy?" Louis asked.

"Well, Doctor, no, I'm not," he said. "But if you believe in the inspired word of God as I do, you would know that Satan can enter a man and cause him to act in terrible ways. That's just a fact."

"Is it now?" Louis said.

"Okay," I said. "Let's not bring God into this. He can't take the stand."

"No, indeed not," Porter said. "And anyway, this was some Godless shit here, Sheriff."

IT WOULD BE another ten hours before the storm let up enough that we were even able to leave the Toellners' house. By then, the news about Bennie's Coast Guard rescue team being lost at sea was everywhere—Tom Brokaw led off the national evening news with it, along with shots of the devastation along the coast—so when I finally got home, my wife Margaret was sitting at the kitchen table, sobbing.

"I can't stop," she said. "First I think about Kurt being missing, then I think about Bennie, and then I think about poor Jane, up there in Brawton, powerless."

"I know," I said.

"When will you start the search? First light? Do you think he just ran off? I mean. Boys do stupid things. Could he have hopped a bus to Brawton?"

"Margaret," I said, "he's missing, but I don't think he's alive." I told her what we found at the scene.

"That just can't be," she said. She got up from the table, went to the cabinet above the refrigerator, pulled down a bottle of Jameson. Neither of us were drinkers, really, but she poured us both a couple fingers.

"I think there were other kids there yesterday," I said after a time. "We found evidence, anyway. We'll have search and rescue out at dawn, but I need to see who maybe he was playing with, hopefully someone just comes forward. We'll get a deputy out to the John Glenn Middle School in the morning, find out what we can."

"I hope so."

I crawled into bed thirty minutes later and already heard the drone of helicopters in the night sky, news and military, I figured, documenting and searching, though the end result was inevitable. Hope was for the living. A charade to appease the unknowable fear of reality. Bennie Toellner was dead. His son Kurt was missing and presumed dead. And Jane Toellner was an hour north in Brawton, sobbing on her mother's shoulder.

Just as I was drifting off to sleep, Margaret grabbed my wrist. "I need to tell you something," she said. She turned on the light on her bedside table. "I saw Bennie with another woman."

"When?"

"A few weeks ago," she said. "When I was in Spokane seeing my sister. We went to Riverfront Park and I saw him holding hands with someone who wasn't Jane."

I sat up on my elbows. "Why didn't you tell me?"

"It's not against the law to cheat on your wife," Margaret said. "I saw something I wasn't supposed to see. I didn't want to compound the situation."

It was hard to argue the point. "Did he see you?"

"Oh," she said, "I'm sure he did. I screamed at him. I made a fool of myself right there in the middle of the park."

"What did he do?"

"He listened, politely," she said, "and then told me I wasn't half the woman Katherine was, to keep my own house in order, and to stop worrying about his."

"I see why you didn't tell me," I said. I'd have hurt him. That's the truth. Katherine had been his friend, but her name did not belong in his mouth. Twenty years she'd been dead and I still was ready to put someone's teeth in their throat for talking out of turn about her.

"I have no idea who that woman was," she said.

"She might be from over the hill. Could be they work together."

"I guess, I guess," Margaret said. "God. Morris. If not, how will she ever find out?"

"It made the national news," I said. "She'll figure it out." I reached across Margaret and turned off the light. "I need to close my eyes for just a few minutes. If you think of anything else, I'm right here."

"It's not true, though, is it? About Katherine?"

"Bennie said it to be cruel," I said. "He was cornered. It was a shitty thing to say to you. But it's not true. Katherine would love anyone who managed to love me. And that includes you."

I kissed Margaret goodnight, and for a long time I just sat there in the darkness. In the shadows of my mind, I imagined my late wife overhearing this conversation from wherever her soul now lived and heard her rueful laugh so clearly it gave me a start. *This place is infected with evil,* I told her. *Well, you knew that, Morris. That's why you have the badge and gun,* she said. *Get some sleep.* And so I did, all through the night, something I would not do again for weeks.

◎

WEDNESDAY MORNING, THE skies over Granite City were ice blue; the storm that had devastated the coastline, flooded most of the western portion of the state, and killed Bennie Toellner, swirled southeast, manifesting in northern California and central Idaho as little more than drops on a windshield. But here, it was everywhere, still: The broken window at Shake's Bar. The accordioned roof of the Texaco station on Route 9. A dozen split trees dangling onto Manzanita Drive...and one through the front window of Mel's Cosmic Comics.

"I almost spent the night in the shop," Melanie Cummings said. She was sweeping water out of the store when I arrived, just after nine, a bag filled with Kurt Toellner's D&D materials under my arm. Racks of comics had been destroyed. "But then the power cut out and the idea of sitting in the dark waiting for trouble seemed absurd."

"You made the right choice," I said.

"Well, I just hate to see these things get destroyed," she said. She motioned to a rack of soaked books. "Me, I've got insurance, so I'll be fine. It's just, those comics, that's someone's work, you know? Gone." She brushed her bangs from her forehead then and I saw that she was teary eyed. "It's stupid. But see those couches over there?" There were three old couches in the far right corner of the store, a coffee table between them, all of it covered with chunks of water-logged acoustic ceiling panels that had fallen during the night. "After school, I've got kids sitting there all day. This is their spot. And now I don't know how long it will be before I can get some more couches, even."

"What do they do here all day?"

"Game, read, bullshit," she said. "Sometimes I'll order them a pizza."

"Out of your own pocket?"

"These kids," she said, "they just need someone who thinks they're cool." She sighed. "Anyway. What is it I can do for you on this shitty day, Sheriff?"

"I was hoping you could look at something for me." I unpacked the books and miniatures on her front counter. "You sell these?"

"Yeah," Melanie said. "I did." She picked up one of the books— *Wizards & Spells*—flipped it open, found a metallic sticker shoved between page 44 and 45, popped it out. "This is one of our security stickers." She looked over the miniatures. "All these are from here, too. Every single one. Whose are these?"

"Kurt Toellner," I said.

"Yeah, yeah," she said. She picked up the Paladin. It was painted orange and gold and silver, though the Paladin's hair was a shock of blood red. He held a long sword. "Man, he does a nice job on the painting and detail work. What's the problem? He paid for all of them, if that's what you're wondering. Nice kid. Bennie's been bringing him here forever."

"He came up missing yesterday," I said. "Was hoping maybe if he came in here, you might know who else he played with?"

"Kurt? Oh no. He's like the mascot to a bunch of kids. Guy who runs their game," she said, "he's a little older. He must be a junior. Jason something. Wait a sec." She went into the back, came out with a Granite City yearbook. "I buy an ad every year in this, mostly so if one of the kids shoplifts or something, I can identify them later." She flipped through the pages, turned the book around. "Here you go. Jason Gerard." I wrote his name down. Didn't sound familiar. About 35,000 people lived in Granite City then, so I didn't know everyone, but I knew most of them.

"New to town?"

"Been coming in for a year or so," she said. "He put up a note on the bulletin board maybe six months ago saying he was looking to DM."

"What does DM mean?"

"Dungeon Master," she said. "I saw him in here with Kurt a couple times last few months. Nothing weird."

I pulled out the maps. "What are these?"

"The aforementioned dungeons," Melanie said. She held one up. "This is beautiful work. Kurt's a real artist."

"Where is this place?"

"It's in Kurt's head," she said. When I didn't respond, she said, "You ever been to a movie before, Sheriff?" I told her I was familiar with the concept. "These maps are like the map of an entire movie set. They play in it. It's a visual tool for the kids to act out in. And Jason, he's the director. Again, nothing weird."

"Nothing weird about a seventeen-year-old hanging with a twelve-year-old? And he's the dungeon master? All of that sounds weird, Melanie."

"You need the context," Melanie said. "Neither of these kids are exactly popular. It's good they found each other." A thought came to Melanie. "When you say he came up missing," she said. "What does that mean?"

"He's not been seen in a couple days."

"Is there a reason to be concerned?"

"Yes," I said.

"Jesus," she said. "I've known Bennie forever. I'll give him a call."

"You haven't heard," I said.

"Heard what?"

I told her what I knew about Bennie, which at that point was scant beyond what had been reported, that his Coast Guard tug had been lost at sea, that all were presumed dead.

Melanie slumped against her counter. "My god," she said. "Who saves the Coast Guard? It doesn't make sense. None of this makes any sense."

I took out my wallet, counted out all the cash I had in it, put it on the counter. It was about sixty bucks. "Toward the pizza fund," I said.

JASON GERARD WAS in calculus when I got to Granite City High School, so the principal, Davy Hewiston, sent a kid to get him. Davy Hewiston had been principal going on five years already. He'd come down from Seattle after Loretta King died at her desk after thirty-five years of waking up at 5 a.m., going to every frozen football game, standing watch in the halls, and then spending a good two to four hours at Shake's, bullshitting, chain-smoking, and drinking a single Maker's and 7UP from a tall red glass she brought from home. We ended up spending a lot of time together, because in a town like Granite City, the sheriff and the high school principal end up eating a lot of pancake breakfasts together courtesy of the Lion's Club.

Davy and I did not have the same relationship.

"What's this about, Morris?" Davy asked. "Your cruiser out front already has half the city calling in to see if there's been a drug bust."

"I just have some questions for Jason about a kid he knows," I said.

Davy shifted around in his seat. "Jason's not yet eighteen," he said. "Don't you think you should get his parents' consent?"

"He's not a suspect in something," I said. "And I don't need anyone's consent."

"I know you don't *need* it," Davy said. "I'm talking about the polite thing. You know. Kid comes home and tells mom and dad Sheriff Drew came and talked to him, that ends up being my problem, not yours."

"Take it up with the United States Constitution," I said.

"You wanna give me a hint, then? So I don't go into battle with a squirt gun?"

I looked out the window. There was a crew cleaning up debris from the quad, another was putting a plywood sheet in the library's window. I'd gone to this very high school, over thirty years before. I'd gone straight from here to Korea, where I'd been a rifleman, and then eventually returned to Granite City, thinking it would be a life that made sense. It never was, it never would be. "A twelve-year-old was bludgeoned to death in his bed," I said. "I think Jason might have been the last person to see him alive. Or maybe not. Maybe he's the one who put the twelve-year-old's brain matter on the ceiling. I guess I'm about to find out."

"Brain matter?" He sounded stricken.

"Yeah," I said. "You hit someone hard enough with a hammer and you do it enough times, well, you're eventually gonna spatter their brains in a pretty defined pattern."

"Jesus fucking Christ," Davy Hewiston said. He grabbed a Kleenex, coughed into it, and then vomited right there on his desk. Mostly coffee. "Oh my god," he said. "I don't know what just happened."

I got up, checked my shoes. All clear. "That's your body's way of saying: Don't ask questions that you don't want answers to, Davy. I'll be outside. Get yourself together."

I went out and waited for Jason Gerard in the breezeway between the administration building and the main hall. He came walking up a few minutes later and I understood immediately what Melanie had meant about the context. Jason Gerard's entire face was a series of caramel brown freckles. The freckles were so densely packed that his untouched skin looked like tiny shards of daylight up against the tableau of his long, thick black hair. That said, he wasn't a bad looking kid, but he carried himself with the countenance of a person who was waiting for bad news, so though he was almost six feet tall, he seemed somehow smaller, like he'd been cooked down. He had on jeans and a black T-shirt and a fleece-lined denim jacket. He'd have to be dipped in wet cement to weigh 140 pounds.

We sat down at the same long metal picnic table I used to take all my meals at in 1950. There'd been a couple coats of paint put on in the intervening years, but if I looked closely, I'm sure I could find my own fingerprints on here somewhere.

I set Kurt's books and miniatures between us.

"You know why I'm here?" I said.

He picked up an elf with a long sword. Rolled it between his thumb and index finger. "I guess about Kurt and his dad."

"That's right," I said.

"I heard there were cops at John Glenn today," he said. "I figured someone would be coming by."

"When was the last time you saw Kurt?"

"Monday night," he said. "We did a pretty bad ass quest, honestly. Mr. Toellner played, too. It was hella fun."

"You like pretending to kill things?"

Jason laughed, but not in an altogether funny way. "Did you watch the *60 Minutes?*"

"Heard about it."

"You worried me and Kurt were conjuring Satan?"

"Not personally," I said. "But others will eventually. I'm just being honest with you."

"That's not what D&D is about. It's more about, like, hanging out and using your imagination. It's cool, seeing where your mind can take you. So for me, as a DM? I get to make up stories, get to imagine how people will react in certain situations. But in the end, I'm in control, you know, but only to the extent of my own ability to come up with stuff? But then, like, in the game itself? You're with people. Doing things. Helping each other. Casting spells and killing things, that's like part of it, but it's not why you play. It's not why I play, anyway."

"Mr. Toellner often play with you two?"

Jason shrugged. "He was into whatever Kurt was into. He was cool as shit."

"He was," I said.

"You know him?"

"Since I was your age."

"He was pretty fucked up about his wife boning out."

"Yeah," I said. "That makes sense." I examined Jason's hands for scratches, marks, anything that might tell me he'd been in a fight. Other than a hangnail on his right thumb, Jason Gerard had the softest looking hands I'd ever seen. If he was to swing a sledge-hammer, it would rip his palm apart. "What time did you leave Monday night?"

"Mr. Toellner drove me home Tuesday morning, actually," Jason said.

"You spent the night?"

"Yeah, he drove me home on his way to work. Basically I babysat Kurt on Monday after school and then just stayed over. I did that sometimes."

"Your parents don't mind?"

"I live with my mom's brother Frankie. You probably know him. He owns the bowling alley."

"Frankie Loomis?"

"That's right."

Frankie Loomis did in fact own the bowling alley out near the county line. It wasn't a bad place to knock down some pins, provided you also drove a Harley and dealt a little trucker speed.

"You okay out there?" I asked.

He shrugged. "It's temporary. My dad's doing a stint in Walla Walla. My mom thought it would be better if I came and stayed here while she tried to make some money up in Alaska." Walla Walla was where the state penitentiary was located. "Finding the Toellners made things easier. And Frankie's all right. To me, anyway. Makes sure I have what I need."

"When do you turn eighteen?"

"Three weeks."

"Then what?"

"I guess college, then law school, then wife, then gold dog, then I'll retire and die on my bed of money."

"You got it figured out," I said.

Principal Hewiston walked out then. I gave him a wave. The kind that says this isn't his problem and he should go back to his shitty little office.

"I'll be out of this place fast," Jason said eventually. "You can bet on that."

"So," I said, "clear something up. Were you friends with Bennie or Kurt?"

"I guess sort of both. Kurt was way into D&D and I guess I was too, but then I just sort of liked hanging out over there. Mrs. Toellner was hella nice, too." He took out a Kleenex and blew his nose. "They knew I could use the money, so they were real pleasant to me, often asked me to watch Kurt if they were going out, which was never a trouble, because Kurt, he's a cool kid." He shook his head. "You think they'll find Mr. Toellner?"

"No," I said.

"I heard they found blood in the house."

"Where'd you hear that?"

"Mr. Foder? The shop teacher? He has a police scanner," Jason said.

"What time did Bennie drive you home?"

"Early," he said. "Woke me at 6."

"You see Kurt in the morning?"

"No, I fell asleep on the sofa watching TV. Kurt was pretty sick. Kept throwing up all day. So Bennie said he was going to stay home with him. Guess he changed his mind."

"He probably got called in," I said. I'd need to check that. But I was beginning to get a sick feeling in my stomach. "Kurt ever say anything about his father? Was he...touching him or anything?"

"No, man. No." He thought for a moment. "I mean, not around me. They seemed to really care about each other. Better than my dad treated me. Mrs. Toellner was like the third wheel, if anything." A bell rang and kids started coming out of classrooms. Jason picked up another miniature. A fire breathing dragon. "Can I take this one? This one was my favorite."

"Sure," I said.

Jason brushed the hair from his eyes. "So Kurt's dead?"

"I think so," I said. "We've got people looking for his body. You can help after school. We've got people meeting out by Casper's Burgers."

"And his dad?"

I pointed up at a helicopter overhead. "They'll keep looking for a bit," I said. "But he's dead, Jason. I'm real sorry."

Tears filled Jason's eyes. "I don't know what I'm supposed to do," he said.

"Try and be happy that you're alive."

"If I cut," he said, "you're not gonna arrest me for truancy, are you?"

"Not today."

Jason nodded. He picked up another figure. "This was Mrs. Toellner's favorite. Some kind of high priestess. Kurt used to leave this in like the fridge and shit. Bury it in the mayo or the butter or whatever. It was kind of a joke between them." He handed it to me. "Maybe make sure she gets it."

I told him I would.

Kids walking by stopped to stare at us. They didn't even bother to pretend they were looking at something else.

"You're not making my life easier," Jason said.

"Three weeks," I said. "You'll be out of here. Take the GED, though, don't just walk out."

"You think Mr. Toellner hurt Kurt?"

"I'm trying not to think that way," I said. "But if not, it was you or a stranger who showed up out of the woods."

"It wasn't me," Jason said.

"I know," I said.

"When I walked up," he said, "you looked like you thought it might be me."

I picked up the miniature Melanie had pointed out earlier—the Paladin with blood red hair and the long sword—and touched my thumb to the tip of the sword. It was sharp. If I pressed, it would draw blood. "When I was a kid, younger than you," I said, "I didn't play with Army men. We didn't have anything like this stuff. Nothing even close. By the time I was your age, I already knew that I wanted to kill someone." I set the Paladin down, picked up a female miniature that was absurdly proportioned and nearly nude. "What's this character called?"

"She's a ranger," Jason said. He watched me closely.

"She'll freeze to death before she gets anywhere." I set her back down. "So when I turned eighteen, I enlisted in the Army. I was so angry by then. If you looked at me wrong, I would hurt you. That's the kinda guy I was. Two beers and I'd put your eyes out. And then I got my chance in Korea. And I got good at it. I got what you would call proficient at my job."

"That's not me," he said. "Beer makes me sick."

"I know it isn't," I said. "It's not me much anymore, either, unless I need it. I tell you this because if I thought you'd killed Kurt, you'd already be dead. Because I loved that boy, understand? Maybe Bennie wanted me to find what I found. Maybe he wanted me to find you, eventually."

"You think that?"

"I don't know. I'm working through some things." I examined the Paladin again. You could see the minute brush strokes Kurt had made. He'd even painted the eyes so they had an ethereal glow to them. The hours he must have spent. "The people in this town," I said, "they may look at you like you did something wrong. But I know, okay? I know. And I'll do what I can to protect you. But you're gonna get called in on this. Your fingerprints and hair will be everywhere in that house. State guys may take a run at you, too. We'll get you a lawyer, all that. Just be honest and communicative and this will pass, eventually."

"My uncle is going to trip," he said.

"Yeah," I said. "Listen. He has anything…problematic in the house? Tell him to get rid of it. Guns, drugs, whatever. No need to bring some heat on himself in this." I reached into my pocket and found one of my cards, gave it to him. "Frankie has a problem, tell him to call me, alright? You, too."

Another bell rang. "I better get going," he said and stood up. "What are you going to do with all this stuff?"

"Keep it as evidence for a bit, then turn it over to Jane."

"If she doesn't want anything, tell her to let me know. Me and Kurt, we painted most of these together."

I told him I would. He'd started to walk away when a thought came to me. "You happen to know if Deena Vlach is here today?"

"I haven't seen her in a week," he said.

"Really?"

"Yeah, I heard she broke her leg skiing down in Tahoe or something," he said. "It's why I ended up babysitting Kurt. Monday nights, I usually do inventory with my uncle, but Bennie called in a panic. She might even still be gone."

Shit. I'd left a message for her yesterday, too. If he'd known she was out of town Monday, wouldn't he have known she was out of town Tuesday?

"Why?" Jason asked.

"It's nothing," I said. "Just running down people who'd interacted with the family." I put my hand out and Jason Gerard shook it. "Keep your head down. Okay?" He said he would. A few seconds later he was gone, enveloped in the mass of kids heading to class. Over the years, I'd see Jason now and again, usually out by the bowling alley where he ended up working for his uncle until Frankie got a nickel for dealing speed, and once, many years later, in the front seat of a Mustang that had smashed headlong into a semi, plunging him, ironically, and tragically, into Patterson Gulch.

THE SEARCH FOR Kurt Toellner's body lasted, in earnest, for three weeks, and then petered into nothing but posters on light poles as winter turned to spring. Jane Toellner moved back into her house for a few months and then, as May became June, put it on the market in hopes of getting some tourist to fall in love with it. Because one thing was certain, no local was stepping foot in that house or on that land. Not any time soon, anyway.

Though what we knew for certain by then was little more than we knew the day after it all happened, the unknown was quantifiably worse, amplified as it was over those next months and years by rumor and innuendo and, eventually, an episode of one of those late-night forensics shows found down low on the cable listings. Because while the blood and brain matter in Kurt's bed were indeed Kurt's, a search of the house found more disturbing things than we could account for: luminol tests revealed significant blood stains in the master bedroom, the garage, and underneath where the couch was in the living room. We found traces of hair and blood in the bathtub that didn't belong to anyone we could discern. Jane let us dig up the backyard, the front yard, the side yard, and wherever a dog seemed to find something worthwhile on the property.

But there was nothing.

We even drained Nel's Pond and discovered nothing but trout, broken fishing poles, a thousand condoms, and three guitars.

There weren't even any missing persons in Granite City at the time, other than Bennie and Kurt Toellner.

So it was that I drove over to the house on a blistering June day with a bag of Kurt's Dungeons & Dragons books, maps, and miniatures. I found Jane out back, planting roses, surrounded by bags of potting soil and fertilizer.

"Those look pretty," I said.

Jane jumped with a start. "You scared the shit out of me, Morris," she said.

"Sorry," I said, "thought you heard me pull up."

Jane pulled off her gardening gloves, dropped them on the grass. "I've been getting a lot of kids driving up, mostly at night, presumably to view the haunted house," she said. "I've taken to ignoring the sounds of cars."

"You want," I said, "I can put one of my guys on the road for a few weeks."

"It's fine," she said. "I won't be here much longer." She took the bag from me, looked in. "This all of it?"

"Yeah," I said. "I gave one of the miniatures to Jason Gerard a couple months ago."

"That was nice of you."

"He's going through it," I said.

"Do you want to go inside?" she asked. "I can see if we have any coffee. I don't drink it anymore. I have a hard enough time falling asleep."

"No," I said.

"No," she said. "I suppose not." I followed Jane over to the small patio off the back door, where she had a little table, mostly to hold an overflowing ashtray, surrounded by two white plastic chairs.

"When did you start smoking?" I asked.

"You don't remember?" she said. "Katherine and I used to steal my mother's cigarettes all the time."

"Marlboros?"

"See, you have a good memory after all," she said. "I see her sometimes, you know."

"Katherine?" She'd been dead over twenty years by then.

"Sure," she said. "More lately. I swore she was beside me in Fleenor's the other day. I was talking to her in my head about everything and just pushing my cart down the aisle and for a moment, I was positive I saw her, just out of the corner of my eye. Does that ever happen to you?"

"Yes."

"I guess it's just our brains trying to make sense of things that make no sense. Chaos looking for order. I've been waiting for Bennie or Kurt to show up, but no luck. It makes me wonder if they're really dead."

"They are," I said.

Jane nodded. "You're a practical man," she said. "I guess I could learn something from you. Less magical thinking would probably be good for me, in the long run." She took the ashtray and dumped the contents into a bush, then opened up the bag of Kurt's belongings and spread out the contents on the little table. "They spent more time playing this dumb game and painting these toys together than they ever spent with me. I hate this stupid shit, I really do." She flipped through one of the books. "Warlocks and wood nymphs and maidens and faeries. Neither of them content to live in the real world." She slapped the book against the table.

"I need to ask you a question," I said. I reached out and took the book from her hands. "For me. Just for me. Off the record."

"Nothing is off the record," Jane said. "I've answered every question a thousand times, from cops, from attorneys, from the fucking news. It's my infinity."

"Why did you leave? Really?"

"I didn't love him. It's as simple as that. I told him I had a flight and instead just moved to my mother's. Simple as that."

"Why didn't you take Kurt?"

"He wouldn't have come, that much I knew," she said. "And now I wonder what he and Bennie were doing in this house when I wasn't here. I can't imagine. I can't even begin to imagine." She paused. "Do you think Bennie crashed his boat?"

"I do."

She nodded again. "He was never violent to me. I never saw anything strange. I just didn't love him. I had the sense he was probably cheating on me, probably with someone in the Guard, no one local, and so I honestly thought I was doing him a favor by being the one to leave. Because he would have just stayed here, mired in his passivity, until we both got old. I just knew that. And I didn't want that life."

"Margaret saw him with someone in Spokane," I said.

Jane looked mildly surprised. "When?"

"About a month before this all happened," I said. "We haven't identified who she was. No one came forward."

"It doesn't matter," Jane said.

"I suppose not," I said.

We sat there in silence for a few moments before Jane finally said, "Just say it, Morris. I can see it devouring you."

"Was it you?" I said. "Did you do it?"

"No," she said. "Is that better? Do you believe me?"

"No," I said, "it's not better."

"There's not always a why," Jane said. "That's what my mother used to tell me about things I didn't understand. Why is the sky blue? Why is water wet? Why is God invisible?"

"Two out of three of those have answers," I said.

"You know what I mean," she said. She got up then, brushed herself off. "Help me get some bags of soil out of my trunk and then go home to your wife and have a good life, Morris. Don't think about me or this horribleness anymore. It's done. There's no why anymore that any of us can possibly figure out."

She was probably right.

I followed her to the garage, where her Honda Accord was parked. She popped the trunk and I grabbed up two big twenty-five-pound bags, put them over my shoulder, and then, as Jane began to close the trunk, I saw—along with a hand shovel, shears, and a small rake, plus the normal detritus of bags, old sweaters, and receipts—a sledgehammer.

Psychiatrist

By Jane Hamilton

When we talked about the house, long after it was gone, we often ended up mentioning Psychiatrist. A horrible game, some of us said. Under other circumstances it would be fun, cousin Liz insisted. Back and forth we went on that score. We never played it again, not after the night Nora tore up the stairs and out the south bedroom window and onto the roof, scaling the peak. As if the end of the house began with that game, or our understanding that we were going to lose the place started right then. As if it should have been obvious that Nora screaming on the pitched roof, threatening to throw herself from the highest point could lead one thing to the next: first that girl and her breakdown, next the huge old Victorian house, the summer kitchen, the ice house, the boat house, every building razed with a few swipes of a big cat dozer. As if the future could be that clear, a dramatic moment naturally leading to the single inevitable conclusion. The fall of the sparrow, and all that.

This was how long ago? We have to do the math each time it comes up. Nora was fifteen, so, well over a decade has passed. We cousins in the family corporation were extraordinarily lucky to have such a house, an ancestral dwelling that packed to the gills slept thirty persons, built by the great great grandfather in the late 1800s, the first house on the Wisconsin lake. We claimed that, anyway. Our Captain of Industry, one of the first white children born in the swamplands that was Chicago. Oh, that house, on a hill overlooking the water, the mildew in the walls, the ash in the fireplaces, the warped books, the dusty photographs of the forebears up the staircase wall, the moth-eaten carpets, the grandmother's lavender scent forever lingering, the pent-up winter air coupled with the summer breezes, the windows, the French doors at last thrown open in June, the heat of the sun. We breathed in all of that when we arrived as if the fragrance was far past plain old air in its sustaining powers. Beyond food, beyond love, even, that smell, or it was love itself, we later privately thought.

The property was of us, it was in us, around us, it had made us, it would be a part of our children's children, it was out of time, it was eternal. We didn't say so out loud, too hokey, plus the reek of privilege. But however much you couldn't talk about that kind of ineffable poetic hoo-ha, the sacred aspect of those acres, we felt it. Everyone did.

We were truly a family that was always very close in spirit. Because of our shared heritage visible in the house, all the photographs and artifacts, the Civil War saber of the great uncle, for instance, and because we'd spent our summers together there. We were the fifth generation; Nora and her cousins, our children, the sixth.

She had been sent to us that July when she was fifteen as she'd been sent every July for many years, her single mother putting her on a plane in Seattle. This practice began when Nora was seven, one of us waiting to collect the waif at the airport. We had charge of her for three weeks at the lake not because cousin Gail asked us but because she informed us of the plan. *Nora will be with you on such and such a date, Nora so enjoys her cousins and the family history.*

Whoops, we always fantasized about saying to Gail on the phone, a day after Nora's arrival. *We forgot to pick up your daughter.* Not that we didn't dote on Nora. Still, we had the joke—punishing Gail who was great in theory but out to lunch on the basics.

Nora was scary smart, preternaturally mature, the neglect of her mother cultivating in her an aptitude for self-reliance. So it seemed. She'd lie on one of the iron beds in the south bedroom in the afternoons when the others were swimming or fishing or sailing, reading Great Literature, *Jane Eyre*, *Ethan Frome*, *Emma*, *Moby Dick*, even, all those books with proper names for titles. But also, my God, when she was eleven years old she discovered *In Cold Blood*. We said, "Where'd you get that! Give it here." She said serenely, as if the book wasn't about random, brutal murders, "I just finished it. It's amazing."

That year she was fifteen we as usual gathered after dinner for parlor games. That's what we did at the lake at night, as had taken place time out of mind. There was no Home Entertainment Center, no Wi-Fi, the outlets for charging a phone were wickety. As the years passed we had a NO PHONE POLICY, no devices at table, no devices where anyone could see or hear them. We wanted some semblance of the Victorianism we had suffered from when we were children, no girls in the upper boathouse, no boys allowed in the upstairs of the main house. Our grandmother's rules that required ingenuity to subvert, our transgressions solidifying our bonds.

In the evenings we most often played the reliable old standard, charades, but as we weren't super catholic in our tastes we'd added the hat game, the sofa game, the name game, the cat game to our repertoire.

A week into Nora's visit, cousin Liz, the therapist among us, said she'd learned a new game at Family Folk Dance Camp. Liz was always going off to do an uncommon activity to decompress from the common unhappiness she had to listen to in her professional life. She'd ridden horses across Iceland and her bicycle the length of Great Britain. Once she tried to teach us Hora Mamtera, we WASPS on the lawn trying to master the complicated turns of the Israeli dance, some of us so clumsy we fell down. Cousin Patty laughed herself to tears.

So, we're in the living room, at the ready for the evening, and Liz says, "I learned this hilarious game called Psychiatrist at Folk Dance Camp."

Her brother, our cousin Daniel, the Presbyterian minister said, "No."

"It's very, very, very fun, Dan," she explained.

We wanted to be good sports even if we didn't need three *verys* worth of amusement. Not after pot roast and mashed potatoes and however many bottles of wine. Liz explained that it was the kind of game where the person who is IT, has to figure out the pattern, has to learn what's going on between all the players. One of us said, "Nora would be good at that. She should be IT, she's so smart."

"I'm not, I'm really not," Nora said, already knowing to be alarmed.

"You'll be great," many of us chimed in. "You're brilliant and observant."

"It's a unique game," Liz said, "because we can only play it in this particular company once. A one shot game. You can only be IT once."

"Special," Cousin Jill said.

There were a few teenagers that night but on the whole it was a room of adults. Nora was easy to talk to and interested in our preoccupations, so that it didn't seem strange, pitting one girl against the ranks of her elders.

She was sent away while Liz went through the rules. There were eighteen of us who'd already moved chairs from the other rooms and arranged them in a circle.

The game worked like this: The person who is IT, who has to stand in the middle of the circle, asks questions of the players. The advice for the IT person: Avoid yes/no questions. Aim for questions that require explanation, that elicit personal revelation. What was the secret of the game? Each person, when asked a question, answers for the person on his left. If he answers in a way that is truthful to the person on his left, all is calm. If, however, his answer is not truthful according to the person on the left, then that player shouts, *Psychiatrist!* And everyone jumps up and rushes to another chair. The questioning proceeds, now with new people on each person's left.

Hilarious!

Nora's task was to discover the system. What do the answers indicate about the pattern of the game? And, why are people periodically shouting *Psychiatrist?*

◎

SHE WAS SUMMONED from the summer kitchen. We were sitting around as if, No big deal, this is merely another of our usual silly games, the games which, nevertheless, are our religion.

Nora was a thin girl with long dark hair that she didn't take care of, the ends ragged, she'd pull the whole mess into a bun on top of her head. The off-center tilting top-knot only made her teenage beauty more arresting. Her eyes were startlingly blue, her lashes dark, her puffy lips with a tiny space at the center when they were closed, like the circle on a baby doll for the nipple of the toy bottle. That feature in and of itself was beguiling. She had almost no bosom and her legs were wonderfully long.

She giggled nervously, she came to stand in the center as she was told, and bowed her head. *Help.* Everyone was happy to be looking at her.

She first asked things like, *What's your favorite food? What's the last book you read? What's the first car you owned?* There was some leaping up, some *Psychiatrist*-ing. If she'd gone around and asked each person, *What's your name?* the game would be over. No one ever figures out that's the question for instantly solving the mystery. We laughed at the wrong answers, the earnest attempts at answers, the person trying to channel her neighbor. That's what can be pretty funny, especially if the clowns in the crowd start impersonating the cousin on his left.

We remember the point at which the game began to turn. In retrospect, there was a delineation, before, after—that's how we tell the story. Nora's turning-point-question went to cousin Jill, the family beauty, lovely Jill aging along with the rest of us, her skin damaged by the sun we'd soaked up as teenagers on the pier. Also, smoking had done her complexion no favors. She'd been caught having an affair, the husband arriving home early, a total adultery cliché. Her marriage busting up. Everyone knew the details. To Jill's left was Marcia, an in-law, a woman who considered housewife her Godly profession. Pony tail, leggings, in terrific shape. She'd had her twins via in vitro fertilization. The girl and the boy were not her eggs; eggs from a bank. But the children were of her husband's sperm, not a thing wrong with cousin Bruce's swimmers. These facts were also known to us although we didn't know if Marcia knew we were in on the secret.

Nora says to Jill, aging beauty, "How many natural-born children do you have?"

That was Nora, going for poetry rather than prose.

Okay, so, Jill had two adopted bi-racial boys. She therefore had to think a minute. *Natural born?* It seemed a rude question. Jill was grateful her kids weren't around to hear that term. But, wait, she was supposed to answer for Marcia, the Stay-at-Home Mother of the World. Jill considered—*Natural-born, natural-born.* Those in vitro children, not Marcia's eggs—would you call that natural? Jill wanted always to be generous, to be understanding, they had suffered so much, Marcia and Bruce, trying for ten years to get pregnant—her heart truly went out to them. She said, "It is always a journey, to have children. Such a miraculous trip." She spoke in a wounded, but educational way. "All children, just so you know, are natural born." She added, "I have two."

"Right! Of course," Nora said. "I just meant, how many kids do you have? A simple question. Sorry."

"No need to apologize," Jill said. "I've got two incredible children. I don't care how they arrived, they are in my life. They are my life."

Because the not-eggs of Marcia's was private information no one laughed, no one looked at her to see if she was unsettled by the suggestion of mystery concerning the conception of her babies, or the whole journey thing, the whiff of hardship. Because of Jill's affair and the divorce and the ugly on-going custody battle, no one was going to laugh about her children, either.

Nora, moving on, said to Marcia, "Did you vote for our current president?"

Marcia was sitting next to cousin Bruce, her husband. She said, voicing her opinion as well as his, "The opponent was far more qualified. Also, the opponent, unlike the President, is an American citizen."

Some of us clearly read Nora's thought bubble, Nora staring down Marcia with those steely blue eyes of hers. *You couldn't vote for a black man. Why don't you just admit it.*

In those days we thought our cousins who'd voted as we had not, we thought them blinkered and small-minded, but we did not yet think their brains had been sucked from their skulls, the cavity then injected with a foam that bonded stupidity to evil. In those simpler times we figured, What could you do but laugh at them?

Next Nora asked Bruce, "What do you dream about?" Ah, a fun question, much room for error. He was sitting next to Julia, who worked for the EPA, and while she was not extreme, while we considered her reasonable, she was a dedicated environmentalist.

Bruce, married to Marcia, great sperm, fairly high up in a telecommunications company, chiseled & handsome, said, all groovy, laidback-like, "Hey, man, wow. You wouldn't believe my dreams, they are ka-razy psychedelic. The black rhino is huge in my night life, the giant panda, not to mention the tortoise, each of them has starring roles in my—"

EPA Julie starting shouting, "Psychiatrist! Psychiatrist!" We were laughing, changing our chairs as per the rules. Julie was not, and had never been into the hippie experience. She was crisp in her speech and would not say, *Hey man, wow*, not ever. Neither did she dream of the black rhino or the giant panda. Bruce, despite his terrific IQ, had gone too far.

"Oh, God," Nora cried. "Oh, my God, why does this keep happening?"

We did have to give credit to Bruce for knowing at least some of the animals on the endangered species list.

"You're doing great, Nora," we said. "You're asking the right kind of questions." We assured her we weren't laughing at her, we were laughing at ourselves. We took pains to say that.

Very likely because at dinner we'd been talking about the period, twenty years earlier, when a few of our aunts and uncles wanted to sell the property, that acrimonious time which ended with some of the cousins buying out the old folks, Nora said to Patty, "Would you ever sell this place?" Patty, who was now sitting next to Bruce.

Patty laughed at the question. She lived nearby, the only person who had moved to Wisconsin to be close to the property, who was the self-appointed caretaker. No one ever paid her, no one knew how much time she spent smelling the perfume of the house, enjoying the spring flowers, and engaging workmen to fix this and that. She was unmarried, she was a nurse, she considered the house her child. It seemed she'd never had a love interest, Patty of the round face and small eyes, a lifelong member of Weight Watchers. She lowered her head to glance to her left. Bruce, okay, she had to answer for the man she considered an asshole. She loved the guy, of course and forever, her littermate back in the day. "You want to sell this place?" she said to Nora. "Name your price, sweetheart."

It was a total Bruce answer. Everyone guffawed.

"Wait," Nora said. "You think that, Patty?"

Patty shrugged. "If there was enough money to be made, yeah, I'd consider it."

We were nodding, that's exactly what Bruce would say, Bruce who was removing gristle from between his wisdom teeth.

"You think this place runs for free, missy?" Patty went on. Perfect. Bruce was big into lecturing. "Do you? Think again. The taxes alone were thirty grand this year. In case you aren't aware, that's what it costs to have twenty acres of woodland and a two-hundred-foot shoreline. Think about the house, while you're at it. It's falling to pieces. I won't bring my friends here. The mildew, the cracked walls. The shower? How often do you get hot water—"

"Find new friends," someone yelled from across the room. "My friends find this place magical."

"When we were kids we had to wash in the lake." Another outburst. "No one took showers."

"That cruddy bar of Ivory is still on the ledge under the pier."

"Covered in moss!"

Laugher all around.

But Nora, a few of us realized, looked like she was about to cry.

"Ask another question," Jill called. "Really, you are on the right track."

"Would you ever sell this place?" Nora's voice was trembly. That time she asked the question of Don.

Don was in the Bruce camp when it came to money, to real estate, that whole *Let's Be Real* approach, no point in being overly sentimental when the stakes were high. No doubt that every family member loved the trees, the history, the memories, but again you had to be realistic. The expense of the place was crushing. And the taxes weren't ever going to go down, people. But so what, he was required to speak for Patty, to his left. "Over my dead body," he said evenly. "You sell this place over my carcass."

Nora bowed her head to her prayer hands, phew, if Don felt this way, then no worries.

Patty blinked once and again, she nodded, yes, the dead body, she would never let the place go, not if she could help it. What was it that Mrs. Wilcox said in the novel *Howard's End*. "To lose your house, it's worse than dying."

"Okay, okay," Nora said, as if she were getting it. That's when she started pulling out the stops. Like, holy major wow. She said to Patty, "Do you love everyone here?"

We all laughed and laughed. *Go, Nora!* This was not a yes/no question. The answer was naturally yes, but, again as we all knew, the feelings ran deep and wide: this guy is a lunatic, love him to pieces, that cousin is a whacko, bless her heart.

Patty was sitting next to Don's wife, Cheryl. Cheryl was a horsewoman and hospital administrator. The second wife. We'd all adored the first one and understood when she divorced Don. He was short with a broad chest and the Nora-type piercing blue eyes. A bull dog, you might say. He'd been the life of the party when we were younger, a very entertaining teenager doing accents of the globe before every kid was capable of that stunt. In middle age he'd become overly serious, we thought. A little sanctimonious. Cheryl was an interesting looking person of power, a woman with a lazy eye, mousy hair, veiny legs. How was Patty going to answer for Cheryl? We were psyched! *Do you love everyone here?*

"Um," Patty said, stalling. "I try to love everyone? But, quite frankly, it's a club you can't break into, this family. This family is fortified. A bank vault. And to be honest, I'm not sure I want to break into it."

Nora, supremely confused, said, "But...you *are* a part of the family, Patty."

"Think," Liz said to Nora.

"I AM THINKING." Nora surprised us with her scream. She covered her face, she said, "Sorry guys."

"You're doing great," we quickly called out, "so great."

What about Cheryl? Patty had just accused her of not wanting to be a family member. Which was in fact Cheryl's true feeling. Cheryl, it was clear, did not much enjoy the property or our company. Nonetheless, in normal tones she said, "Psychiatrist," causing the flurry. Even though we all knew that Patty was SPOT ON about Cheryl.

Despite the lying of some of the players the basic set-up seemed evident. Wasn't Nora going to crack the code in a second? She was smoothing her cheeks, collecting herself. No one thought she was in distress, first because she was so smart, and second, she would feel the affection in the room.

Nora next asked Liz if she loved everyone present, Liz having to answer for her brother Daniel, the minister. She said, "I know I'm supposed to. That's my training, you know. Love." (Big hint, Nora, Liz is speaking for a man of the cloth. But, it could be argued, a therapist was also required to be generous of heart. So, maybe her tip-off wasn't much of a clue.) Liz said, "I do, no, I really do. Love everyone. Equally and fairly. As the good book tells us to."

Yuk, yuk, the dour, pain in the butt minister who was probably the most bitter of us. Still, we all agreed that it was good to have an ecclesiastical figure in the family, such a deal, free memorial services and weddings.

Nora down the line had the good sense to ask Cheryl (the one disciplined eye, horsewoman, second wife of cousin Don), "You love everyone in the room?" Cheryl at that point was sitting next to Jill (aging beauty, adultery expert.) Also, of note, Cheryl was Jill's sister-in-law. Some people laughed to themselves because Jill was touchy feely, Jill was all about charity and forgiveness. Cheryl said in an effusive way not at all her own, in a way we'd never heard her speak before, she said, "I just love to hug people. I love to squeeze them until they can't breathe. Love to feel their bodies." Going full throttle as Jill. "Men, women, men, hug, hug, hug. I know certain people don't like it but I want them to know how much I love them—"

"Psychiatrist?" poor Jill said.

"Is it," Nora asked, when we'd settled, Nora choking, her hand to her throat—"is it when someone says something where you need a medical doctor, where you might need one, that's when you say Psychiatrist?"

"Think of the pattern," Liz again instructed.

"I AM," Nora again screeching.

"There's a pattern, Nora. You're going to get it."

"EVERY TIME THERE'S SOMETHING REALLY INSANE YOU PEOPLE—"

"Keep going," we cheered, "you're going to see it."

"IF YOU COULD KILL ONE PERSON HERE, WHO WOULD IT BE?" Nora shrieked this at Patty (nurse, caretaker of the house) Patty who was to answer for Jill (hug hug hug.)

So, okay. Jill, to review, sister-in-law to Cheryl, had just suffered a wound from Cheryl, being made fun of for having a big heart. Patty, speaking for Jill, says, "Who would I murder? Easy. I'd shoot Cheryl." To be fair to all parties, probably most people want at some point to murder their in-laws, in-law-fratricide not an unusual crime.

Jill did not challenge Patty's choice of victim.

"Jesus," someone said.

Cheryl rose from her chair and left the room.

"Bad question," someone else said. "I mean, bad juju you're putting out there, Nora. Maybe take it down a notch."

Don was hauling himself off the sofa, going after his wife.

But Nora, Nora was now cooking with oil. Even if she couldn't figure out the fucking pattern she'd stumbled into power. She might at least get each player, one by one, to leave the room. She stood erect, she yanked her tilting bun to the top of her head.

"If you could kill one person here...," she continued.

The Reverend, too, had had enough. He stood and departed.

Nora went on with the same question, Nora on a roll, moving around the circle. "Who would you kill, Julie?"

EPA Julie was sitting next to Patty. The women were of similar minds on most matters. "I want to say," Julie began, "that if Bruce or Don, if they ever sold this place? If they thought it was time to cash in? And, let's say they sold the property before those of us who want to put it in a conservation easement were able to do that. Let's say, because of their opposition to conservation, their resistance at every meeting to talk about it, they snow their siblings into voting with them. We all know they don't value the watershed that runs through the property, the watershed that's critical to the health of the lake." Julie suddenly felt so happy, letting it rip in her calm fashion. "Consider their ethos of money, the ethos that makes Don and Bruce hostile to preserving the environmental corridor we happen to own, the corridor which includes rare flowers, the skunk cabbage, for one, and the habitats of any number of animals. Let's say, worst case scenario, they sell it to some Illinois creep who develops it." (Most of us were from Illinois, but we understood the type.) "We all know Bruce and Don mean well, in their own terms—but, we know they also think they are above the law. So, if they subvert this group? If they prevent us from protecting the property for the generations to come? If we can't save one small patch of the planet?" She looked around to each of us. "You think I wouldn't kill both of them?"

One or two people tittered.

Julie lowered her voice. She spoke slowly. "I'd bash their enormous brains out of their skulls while they were sleeping."

Patty nodded solemnly.

For a second the gathering went still. Everyone was staring at the floor, as if there were a magic mirror there, as if the future had been revealed by word and now vision. As if all of us saw that big cat dozer. All of us with our future broken hearts.

Bruce left the room.

Nora burst into tears. "This is the worst game," she keened before she knocked over a chair and tore up the narrow, dark staircase.

"Oh dear," someone said.

Liz, instantly in therapist mode, steamed past us. By the time she got upstairs Nora was out the south bedroom window to the roof, scaling the pitched shingles to the peak, that sharp point. She was sobbing and screaming, both, alternating between despair and outrage. Some of us went out on the lawn as if we thought we might be able to catch her if she leapt. The women, in particular, were shouting up to her. "We love you, Nora." "It was just a game." "We're sorry." "You did great." Someone muttered, "She's read all the wrong books, all those hysterical females."

"And whales," someone else said.

Liz was on the flat section of the roof, trying to affect calm as she called to Nora, no way could she climb that pitch to reach the girl.

We thought, We're going to have to call cousin Gail in Seattle and explain that Nora broke her neck when she jumped from the top of the house. Death by parlor game. Gail's final punishment for being an inattentive mother.

Somehow or other Nora finally did come down. We were able to coax her to the summer kitchen, where she cried for an impressive length of time over her cup of hot milk. Not, as it turned out, so much about the game, but about the talk of the house, the taxes, the upkeep, the skunk cabbage. *There, there*, we said. *Everything will be all right. All will be well.*

When we at last did have to sell the property, Don and Bruce and Cheryl managing the sale, that trio wresting the process from us, we all remembered that night when our esprit de corps came into focus. And later, when we drove by the land, and saw all the trees cut down, and when we noted the eighteen thousand square foot house going up right on the shore line, the hill razed, too, and the thirty-seven units under construction in the upper pasture, we again thought of Nora. She who'd been in a psych ward two or three times through her twenties and into her thirties. How could she not be troubled? She no longer had us, she no longer had the web—the net made of time itself to hold her. Nora in a free fall, always falling from the roof. We imagined she screamed *Psychiatrist!* whenever anyone said even a single word that was not the truth.

Knock

By James D. F. Hannah

A rt shuffled the deck. The cards moved slowly between his stiff, meaty fingers. Goddamn, but getting old was a sucker's bet.

Jimmy reached across the table. "Here, let me—"

Art swatted the younger man's hand away like a child going for a cookie, continued the shuffle. Art guessed him to be early twenties—young enough to be his grandson had he ever had kids to begin with—but inclined to hurt feelings.

"Nothing personal," Art said. "I just don't trust you."

Jimmy shook his head, took a long chug from his bottle of orange Faygo. "We should do some trust-building exercises. I could fall backwards and let you catch me."

"I wouldn't recommend it. Floor'll hurt like a motherfucker when I let you fall."

Art dealt the cards. They'd been playing like this for a year now. The same time, every Saturday night, here in the bait shop beside the lake.

The shop was Art's, and he opened it every day of the season. He had a guy who worked Mondays and Tuesdays—the slower days— but Art liked the weekends for himself. The season was drawing to a close, but there were still customers for bait, sandwiches, and soda. Art had cheap poles he loaned to the kids and small boats to rent.

Even had a station set up across from the card table—a butcher block with fillet knives where he'd help less experienced anglers clean their catch. Enough years had passed, he'd gotten good at it.

Art finished the deal, ten to each, and laid the deck down, flipping over the top card. Six of diamonds.

"Gin rummy?" Jimmy said.

"As always," Art said.

Jimmy moved the cards around in his hand. "This was what you played in your old neighborhood, right?"

"Yeah," Art said, trying to sound nonchalant. "We played."

Nonchalant because Jimmy couldn't understand what the game meant, how it'd changed Art's life. Art turning twelve, and he'd already stopped going to school, realizing there wasn't much the nuns could teach him he wanted to know. No, Art's true education began at Martelli's Barbershop down on 29th Street, and the card games in back.

Martelli's had been a de facto business center for men of the neighborhood. They came for straight razor shaves, to play cards and read Playboy, to take phone calls and do business. The air was always thick with hair tonic, bay rum, and cigar smoke, and it was intoxicating to Art.

In the alley behind the shop, Art and a group of boys about his age hung out, shooting dice, playing dominos, smoking and lying about experiences with girls they didn't understand yet.

They modeled their actions after the men in the shop. Adult haircuts on children's faces. Hardened expressions they hadn't earned. None of that mattered. They were biding their time. Practicing for the future.

Whenever the phone rang and the noise echoed into the street, the boys shot to attention. Phone calls meant business and an errand to run, like delivering messages or betting slips or an envelope thick with winnings, and the runner earned five bucks. Five bucks may as well have been a million to Art back then.

But it was watching these men play gin rummy all day long where things truly changed.

"I thought if that's what they did, I needed to also," Art said. "Once I taught myself, I got the other guys going, and I made extra cash playing for points. John Agosti—"

"Johnny Two-Hat," Jimmy said.

Art thinned his lips. The kid was an encyclopedia of Art's life, and sometimes it made Art feel unnecessary for his own story.

"Yeah, John," Art said. "He liked my hustle. He took me into the back room at the shop where they had poker and blackjack. Making book on baseball games or horses." He sipped his beer. "It was better than standing in the stock exchange. You felt the electricity. I chased that feeling for years."

Jimmy said, "That why you pulled the Air National heist?"

And there it was: the inevitable nudge. Never subtle. That was how Jimmy was, jumping in feet first, right on top of your head.

Art inspected his cards. He had two melds: an ace-two-three of clubs run and a trio of queens. He'd watched Jimmy's discards, and he could guess the hand the younger man was trying to build.

He knew Jimmy didn't listen; he waited to talk. Jimmy wasn't observant, studying the quiet spaces between words and actions. Not the way Art did, and he thought of that as he tapped a thick finger across the top of his cards.

"There are court transcripts," Art said. "You want details? Read those."

"No one cares what you told the jury, Art. They want the truth." Jimmy set his cards on the table. "No one's coming after you, old man. This long, everyone's dead or rotting in prison, wishing they were dead."

"People got long memories," Art said. "You have men pissed about things that happened to their grandfathers. What you're talking about was only thirty years ago. That's nothing. It's yesterday's lunch."

The trial had been all over the news. Not only Chicago. Newspapers and magazines and TV stations around the world. Art had been walking into court one day when someone shoved a mic into his face and spat questions at him in Japanese.

The biggest Mob case in the city's history, and he'd been the star. The entire world had watched. It's why he hadn't believed the Feds when they claimed they could hide him somewhere no one would find him.

Damned if they hadn't been right. Thirty boring years and no one had looked at him twice.

Until Jimmy.

Art finished his beer and got up to grab another. Fishing through the cardboard case, thinking about the cops and men from the neighborhood both who'd still put him in the ground given half a chance. How if you lived long enough, your friends and your enemies all become the same.

"Mind fetching me another big orange?" Jimmy said.

Art grumbled as he brought the bottle of soda to the table, his beer in his other hand. He locked eyes with Jimmy and gave the bottle several vigorous shakes. The contents foamed wildly, bubbles the color of sunshine pushing for release. Art slammed the bottle hard onto the table.

"There," he said as he took his seat. "Gets tiring you never paying for shit. You run around like things don't come with a cost."

Jimmy set his cards down. "You're this way every week."

Art twisted his face into a scowl. "Because I know what's coming, and the answer never changes."

"Then change the answer. Tell the whole truth of your life. You know where the bodies are buried because you had the shovel in your trunk. Tell it all. No bullshit. No hedging. No changing names to protect the innocent. We do it, and you can check out with a clean conscience and your sins confessed."

"You talk like those old priests from the neighborhood, but I don't see you wearing a collar. You offering absolution on the side?"

"This is America, old man. You don't need absolution; you just need an audience."

It had been the previous summer when Jimmy came into the shop. Hadn't taken him more than thirty seconds before he approached the counter where Art was ringing up bait and spare line and said, "Aren't you Silvio Gualdoni?"

Art hadn't heard that name spoken aloud in decades. Now that person was a stranger to him. But it hadn't been that way in the beginning, when the Feds gave him a new name and a new home, running this shop. He'd struggled to adjust after an entire life as one person to wake up as someone else who had never existed before.

Art had rushed his customers out the door and closed up the shop and asked this kid who the hell he was and what the hell he wanted.

The kid's name was Jimmy. Visiting family nearby, he said. He was a true crime podcaster, and Art made him explain what that meant; Jimmy called it radio programs you listened to on your phone. Most true crime podcasts dealt with weird murders and unusual deaths—people enjoyed hearing about young blonde girls getting killed, he said—but that wasn't Jimmy's thing. No, he focused on Syndicate action. Drugs. Bank robberies. Smuggling. Crimes run by guys with "the" as a middle name. Old-school stories he recited with the enthusiasm of baseball play-by-play.

One he wanted to tell was the Air National job out of O'Hare—and who wouldn't? It was the stuff of legends. Seven million dollars stolen. The biggest airport heist in history. Nine dead in the aftermath. Money never recovered. And after months of chasing leads and watching security video and listening to wiretaps, the Feds busting through Silvio Gualdoni's front door, six in the morning, and the click of steel around his wrists. The beginning of the end for Chicago's 29th Street Crew.

But there wasn't anyone to talk to, Jimmy said. Dead or in prison, the whole lot. All except Silvio Gualdoni, who was standing in front of him now saying his name was Art.

Art remembered that windowless room that reeked of sweat and vending machine coffee and the Feds playing back the tapes. His voice, admitting his role in the plan. They had him on a dozen other charges—the extortion racket, the bookmaking, some casual black-mail on a few politicians—but Air National was the unmistakable elephant in the room.

The guard killed at the airport raised the stakes to a Federal murder beef, they told him. Electric chair or lethal injection, take your pick.

He was so utterly fucked that the only people in his corner were a couple of Federal agents and a prosecutor willing to deal. Which was a fucked feeling indeed.

Art took the witness stand. Sold out the rest of the 29th Street Crew. Men he'd known since they'd waited outside Martelli's bar-bershop, desperate for attention from the mean inside. He watched the faces of those men as honor and loyalty were cast aside to save his own ass.

Because the rule was, when you got caught—not if, but when—shut your mouth, you did your time.

Until Art decided fuck the rule. What good was honor if you died with a needle in your arm?

Occasionally, Art thought about Elaine, how without her, the Feds wouldn't have had a case. She'd been the one who got him on tape.

Elaine had a coke problem and a kid in foster care. Promises were made to place her in rehab and help her get the kid back if she did this one thing. Art had trusted her, confided in her, and when those Feds played his voice back to him...

He understood why Elaine did what she did. He'd grown up without his own mother. But it didn't change what had to be done, and the cops never found Elaine's body. Art knew he was okay, and Elaine's kid would be as well.

Art considered his cards. "A thing I learned a long time ago was this game, it's like life."

Jimmy rolled his eyes. "You having a stroke?"

"Think about every hand of cards. I can't see yours, and you can't see mine. Those are our secrets, and we want them hidden. You're pulling groups together. Melds. Those are your friends. You keep your friends, and you keep them close. The cards you can't use are deadwood. You get rid of that. Have as little deadwood as possible before you—" He tapped his knuckles on the tabletop, placed a four of diamonds into the discard, and laid out the rest in a spread. "Go out. That's when we show everyone what we've been hiding all along."

Jimmy shook his head. "Your metaphor doesn't work." He waved a finger toward Art's cards. "What I see is your friends and your secrets blurred together, and no one'll say that's healthy. Besides, my mother always told me to never trust someone with too much to hide."

Art smiled. "I was a crook, Jimmy. She probably would have told you not to trust me, anyway."

"You saying I shouldn't trust you?"

"It'd be your second mistake."

"What's my first?"

Before Art could answer, he heard the boards along the front entrance of the shop creak. A silhouette flashed across the dirt-crusted window and then disappeared.

Jimmy glanced back, trying to find what had the old man's attention. He couldn't, though, so he gathered the cards together and started a shuffle. "Nothing out there. Relax, and let's play this damn game."

Art ran a thumb slowly through the condensation across the beer can. "Someone's out there."

That stiffened Jimmy's spine. The nearby town had possessed a homeless problem until the chamber of commerce and the tourism board convinced the powers that be that panhandlers and encampments were dragging down the economy. The homeless were pushed out to the lake and the surrounding hills—public lands—where they roamed campsite to campsite, looking for food, begging for spare change. They came into the shop and bought cheap beer and nearly expired sandwiches, paying with singles and handfuls of quarters.

Art knew Jimmy thought of him as a harmless old man now, nothing but a declawed cat on a windowsill. The potential of a homeless person outside, an unknown threat, was different. That felt visceral and terrifying. Art saw Jimmy's fear in the tremble of his hands and how he tried to steady them by setting them flat across the table.

Jimmy might not have noticed things, but Art did. Senses sharpened by a life spent studying the small actions of others. Hand gestures and eye movements. Glances toward doorways and checking for witnesses. The fit of a jacket and the size of a purse.

Those had been the things that kept you alive in the world of Silvio Gualdoni. And unlike a name that seemed to mean nothing now, it wasn't something Art had forgotten.

Art still had his eyes on Jimmy's hands as a man burst through the door and raised a pistol into the air.

"Where's your fucking money?" Spittle flung from the man's lips. Stringy hair slicked back with sweat. Tattoos like children's scrawls crept up the length of arms exposed by a faded black tank top.

Jimmy turned and watched the man. Saw the gun. Heard his words but couldn't process what was happening. Like a faulty car ignition.

Click. Click. Click.

Nothing.

Then.

"Oh fuck."

He whispered the words like a secret. Sucked in one long breath and held it in his lungs as if it could protect him.

The man looked familiar to Art. He'd seen him earlier that day. Checking the shop out. Noticing the lack of security cameras, the "Cash Only" sign prominent on the door, no doubt.

Art watched how the pistol shook in the junkie's hand. It was a cheap six-shot revolver. A junkie gun. Passed hand to hand like an offering plate at church, serving a purpose and shuffled along to someone else.

The junkie swung the gun inches from Art's face to Jimmy's, back and forth like a pendulum. Finger on the trigger.

"I said, where's your fucking money?" he said.

Art jerked his chin toward the front of the shop. "Register's right there, but there's not much."

The junkie wiped his free hand across his forehead and then along the leg of his blue jeans, leaving wet streaks on the denim. "You're nothin' but cash, right?"

"That's what the sign says."

The junkie inched closer with the gun. "You being a smart ass?"

Jimmy made a small gulping sound like a floating toy being pulled underwater.

"Don't, Art," he said. "Please."

Art wondered if Jimmy had ever seen a gun up close. He'd sure as hell never had one pointed at him. What he talked about on his show—violence and murders—was nothing but anecdotes. When death isn't your experience, it can be your entertainment.

Art remembered Sister Beatrice telling him how God grants free will and yet knows every choice you'll ever make. Years later Art decided your life isn't really your own if everything's eventual, and maybe a loving God shouldn't have let someone like him loose in the world.

"You stand up," the junkie said to Jimmy. Then, to Art, "Open the fucking register."

Art heard the words like an echo in the distance. Mostly there was the steady thrum of blood in his ears. Hardened breaths and the soft scuff of his shoes across the floor as he walked. Noises understood when there's a gun pointed at your head. It made his heart rush in a way he didn't find uncomfortable.

The register was ancient—no credit cards, no need for anything fancy—and he only had to push a few buttons and the drawer popped with a loud ring. The junkie elbowed past him and started stuffing cash into his pockets.

"Where's the rest?" the junkie said when he was done. "There's gotta be more. You got people coming out of here all goddamn day."

Art pivoted on the heels of his boots and rested his shoulder blades against the shelves where he kept cigarettes. A whiff of the junkie floated by. The guy was sour, like something rotting in the sun so foul even the flies won't bother.

"That's what there is," he said.

The junkie ran his tongue over pale, cracked lips. Eyes fluttered, doing mental calculations, raging internal debates.

"What about an office?" he said. "You got cash, you got a safe, right? Show me."

Art pursed his lips and blew short huffs of air. Rolled back onto the flats of his feet.

"Come on," he said. They headed toward the rear of the shop.

Jimmy's eyes locked onto the junkie as he took blind steps backward and watched the gun in the man's hand. His feet swiped one behind the other, and the toe of his right caught the heel of his left, and he stumbled into the card table. The orange soda bottle rattled across the surface. The sound made Jimmy gasp, and a humorless smile flickered on the junkie's face. Pulled the corners of his mouth up into taut cheekbones, dusty with stubble, stamped with pus-filled sores. He jerked toward Jimmy and screamed, "BOO!"

Jimmy screamed and his feet jumbled harder against one another. His balance gone, he fell onto the table. The soda bottle jumped and fell to the floor. There was a loud pop as the cap flew off like a cannon shot, and an orange-colored geyser spewed.

The junkie looked down to watch the soda spray across his ankles. He didn't notice Art spin around and snap the gun from him until the weight of the weapon was gone from his hand. When he did, a slow-dawning defeat splayed across his face like spilled paint.

Art turned the pistol toward the junkie. The air seemed to shift in the room when Jimmy saw Art holding the gun. He released the breath he'd been clutching to like a life preserver and stepped toward the old man, placed a hand on his shoulder, had words in his throat when Art jerked away, grabbed the fillet knife from the butcher block, and slipped the blade between the junkie's ribs.

The junkie gasped as the knife pierced his skin, and the tip punctured his lungs. Art leveraged his weight to push it further, angling it upward, cracking a rib and slicing the man open. He twisted the blade and moved it around.

Like the name he knew but didn't recognize, the sensation felt both foreign and familiar. A knife offered intimacy. He was there for the junkie's last gulps for air, his eyes swimming to meet Art's. The junkie struggled to make one last human connection with the old man, but turned his head away when he realized there was nothing there.

The knife slipped out cleanly. Art stepped back to dodge a spurt of blood from the wound. The junkie grabbed at where the blade had been, tugged at his shirt and at folds of skin, trying to hold back a flow so red it was almost black.

Jimmy choked out soft sobs as the man's form folded against the butcher block and slipped downward inch by inch, blood running down his jeans and pooling on the floor. Art turned off the front light, flipped the door sign to "Closed," and pulled the blinds.

Pink foam frothed from the corners of the junkie's mouth. Art brought a handkerchief from his pocket, crouched and pinched the man's nostrils shut with one hand, then held the cloth over his mouth. The junkie heaved a few hard breaths and gave a last shake before his head went slack and lazed against his shoulder. Jimmy muttered curses and called out to Jesus Christ a few times. When no one responded, he dropped into his chair and stared at the dead man.

"You fucking killed him." He said it over and over, as though Art was somehow unaware of what had happened.

Art used the butcher block to raise himself to his feet. He had tarps and cleaning products in the back. Cinder blocks left from renovation work at the shop a few summers back. Those would get the job done.

"We gotta call the police," Jimmy said in a voice wet with potential tears. "We gotta—"

"No, we don't."

"But—"

"He's deadwood, Jimmy. Something you get rid of. But you and me, we're melds. We're in this together." Art looked at the knife still in his hand. He ran the blade along the leg of his pants, blood staining the fabric, and dropped it onto the butcher block.

Jimmy's breaths came fast and heavy, a struggle to control them. "You had the gun. You didn't have to do this."

"He had a fucking gun, Jimmy. Someone comes at you with a gun and they don't shoot you, you don't give 'em a chance to try again. That's how the world works."

"What world are you talking about?" Jimmy gestured around the bait shop. "Look at where you are. This is your world."

Art knew goddamn good and well what his world was. He'd spent the past year talking about it to Jimmy, remembering a life like another man's memories.

The idea had struck him a few months ago as he'd watched the way campers looked at the homeless when they were in the shop at the same time. The hesitation on the faces of people in designer cargo shorts and unscarred hiking books around someone in thrift store clothing. The contrast of those looking for escape versus those with nowhere else to go. Art could see the eagerness to be locked safely away in their Range Rovers and Escalades, and the anger they felt for the real world intruding on them.

This had been Art's world for so long he had forgotten how regular people—civilians—perceived danger versus its reality. Men like Art and the rest of the 29th Street Crew had spoken violence as a language. When he'd been Silvio Gualdoni, he had understood what it communicated. Those who weren't really aware of its meaning handled it like a blunt object—a cheap pistol perhaps, conveniently loaded and left somewhere easy to find—instead of how Art welded it. Like a honed blade.

The "Cash Only" signs. The pistol. Easily overheard conversations about late-night card games in the shop. Art had counted on someone desperate and hungry putting those pieces together, trying to score. He wasn't sure who it'd be, though. But everything's eventual, right?

He'd loaded the gun with blanks, though. He was an old man, after all, and if time had taught him nothing else, he knew to always measure your risks.

Art jerked a finger at Jimmy.

"You wanted a murder story; here's one of your own," he said. "You don't understand it until you've been there, and you'll never feel more alive than you do at this moment. Not until you have to do this again." He rested his weight against the butcher block. "The question now is what you wanna do with that feeling. Because you can choose if you're telling someone else's stories, and do you want to be the one they tell stories about?"

An owl called out a long hoot that shook Jimmy from the moment, and he looked toward the sound. When he turned back, he seemed almost surprised that Art was still there. The two men stared at one another as the owl continued to cry out into the darkness.

"I'm an old man," Art said. "But I will not go out dying like an old man, so fuck your little podcast. You and me are going to do some real business. I still got action in my bones, and you've got the youth to make it work. Between the two of us, we should be able to make money the right way." He looked over to the dead junkie. "But first things first; we gotta get rid of this chunk of garbage. We put him in the lake, and then we start making plans."

Jimmy tried to swallow, but he couldn't. He stared at the junkie, this dead man's own gaze directed into a blank void, as acid churned in his stomach and bile burned at his throat. His mouth moved, but no sounds came out. Eventually, he stood and walked into the back of the bait shop with Art, and they started to work.

They finished cleaning, and Jimmy dragged the tarp-wrapped body toward the dock to load into a boat. Art stood in the pale moonlight and watched, because he was an old man who didn't move dead bodies anymore. That was for the Jimmies of the world.

"By the way—" he said.

Jimmy paused, sweat beading across his brow.

Art turned to face the lake.

"Don't call me 'Art' no more," he said. "It's Silvio from now on."

Jimmy didn't say anything and kept on working.

The kid was scared, but scared was okay. He'd be good for the long drive back to Chicago, Art thought. But then what?

This whole year, Jimmy had pushed Art to relive his past. Tell him where the bodies were buried. But he could do better than that. Now he could show him.

With the Right Bait

By Gar Anthony Haywood

Reggie never gave a damn about games. Life was not a fucking game. Life was about winning and losing, yes, but the stakes were a lot higher than a $46 pissant pot in poker or bragging rights to a silver trophy. When Reggie Lymon went up against somebody, it was only with the goal of busting them in the teeth and leaving them gasping for breath, not gleefully shouting "Bingo!" when his numbers were called before some other guy's. Games were for losers.

But Reggie was in Huntington Memorial Hospital, had been for two days now waiting for part of his colon to be removed, and what the hell else was there to do for a seventy-two-year-old man imprisoned in a hospital but starve, play games and watch television?

Of course, playing a game had been Brenda's idea—"I know what we can do! Let's play a game!"—because showing childlike enthusiasm for the dumbest shit imaginable was his wife's greatest talent. He tried to decline in the most polite way possible, which was to say so many times he nearly slapped her across the face with his dinner tray just to get her to shut up, but she was relentless. No matter how many options he declined, she found another to offer him.

Cards? *No thank you.*

Chess? *Get serious.*

Trivia? *Not a chance.*

By the time she got around to naming board games, his will to deny her was all but exhausted. *Monopoly, Life, Clue, Scrabble…*

"Mouse Trap," he said, surprising even himself. "Do they have Mouse Trap?"

The kids' game had been his favorite growing up, something he and his older sister Emily had played non-stop. He hadn't thought about it in decades. But what he remembered now was how stupidly simple it was, a metaphor for life itself: build a trap, catch a rat.

And oh yes, Reggie knew all about rats. Dirty, filthy vermin skulking around in the dark, making plans to slip into a man's home and rob him blind. Reggie had a big rat needing extermination right now, and he was going to see the job done before he got rolled into an operating room in this godforsaken dump and came out with a sheet over his face.

His wife was the rat in question.

Besides being a lightweight intellectually, Brenda was also a gold digger. Reggie had known this for years. Maybe she was kinder and more selfless than most, and maybe whatever sleeping around she was doing behind his back was being done so discreetly, he'd yet to see any concrete evidence of it, but she was a gold digger just the same. What kind of idiot would Reggie have been had he married this woman eight years ago, seventeen years his junior and magazine cover beautiful, and not understood that his money was all she was really after?

Not that Reggie himself hadn't benefitted from the marriage. Up until his body started giving out on him three years ago, the devil's bargain he had made with Brenda had been paying off nicely. Service, companionship, and all the sex an old man could handle. He had little reason to complain. But underneath it all, for all the good stuff on the surface, he knew what motives were being hidden from him, the betrayal of trust that was coming. It was inevitable.

So as his doctor visits and medical bills piled up, as his physical ability to be a vibrant and active partner to his wife dwindled away, he began to pay closer attention to her, to watch and listen for the telltale signs of a woman looking past her current husband to her next one. And yeah, it wasn't his imagination, those signs were there now. The uptick in spending, in preparation for the free rein she'd have with his money once it was all hers; the lunches and dinners with "girlfriends" that had become more frequent and of longer duration; the weight she was losing to fit into clothes she never felt the need to fit into before.

If she wasn't already banging somebody on the side, it was just a matter of time.

His analyst would say this was all in his mind, a byproduct of his lifelong inclinations toward paranoia combined with the stress that went along with his declining health. But Reggie's analyst was full of shit. This was real. Brenda was counting the days until his death.

While she was waiting for him to die, however, secretly laying the groundwork for her next and better life without him, she was continuing to play the loving and devoted wife to the hilt. Sitting in on every meeting with his doctors, monitoring his diet and medications, encouraging him to stay positive and think only good thoughts. She prepared his meals personally, careful to avoid his numerous food allergies (shellfish, nuts, eggs—the list seemed endless), as if his life was as important to her as her own. Anyone other than Reggie would have thought Brenda was an angel.

But she wasn't an angel. She was a rat.

And soon she would be a rat in a trap. All Reggie had to do was live long enough to build the trap, bait it, and spring it on her.

◎

THEY HAD MOUSE Trap down in the hospital rec room, but much to Reggie's chagrin, it wasn't quite the game he remembered as a kid. At some point in the last sixty years, some genius had decided to change it, add "cheese pieces" for players to collect and dumb-down the Rube Goldberg-like machine that dropped a net over the losing player's plastic mouse at the end. The changes weren't fundamental, but just significant enough to make playing the game more of a challenge for Reggie than he'd been prepared for.

That first night, they set up the board and played for about twenty minutes. Brenda wanted to go a whole round but Reggie begged off, claiming to be tired but actually just acting on an inspired thought. He would stretch this thing out. Make the game last for three days, right up until his scheduled operation, so that it only ended when he was ready for it to end. Reggie had a soft spot for symbolism and springing the game's plastic trap on Brenda's green plastic mouse only hours before he sprang the trap on her for real, and for good, struck him as the height of poetic justice.

So they went slow. Took turns flipping the spinner, moving their little mice (Reggie's was red) down the meandering path on the game board, one or two squares at a time, building the convoluted mouse trap, piece by piece, as they went. The lamppost, the stop sign, the boot, and so on and so forth. Reggie might have actually been having fun if he weren't so fucking hungry all the time. The diet his doctors had him on since he'd been admitted held him in a constant state of what had to be malnutrition, the food he was served as distasteful as it was insubstantial. Plus, Reggie was too intent on winning to enjoy the damn game. He had to win, or what the hell was the point of this nonsense? And winning was going to be tricky, because this was a game of chance; no amount of genius or skill could guarantee the outcome. Unless he could figure out a way to cheat, which he would be more than happy to do if such a tack proved necessary.

Brenda, on the other hand, *was* having fun. Making jokes, laughing at all the game's twists and turns. Two steps forward, three steps back, it was all the same difference to his wife; she giggled and clapped her hands with glee either way.

Reggie just let her enjoy herself. She was on the clock even more than he was, and she didn't even know it.

"WHY DON'T YOU just write her out of your will or something?" Melvin had asked.

Reggie had known the question was coming. His nephew was a dim bulb, but he wasn't a total idiot.

This was a couple days before Reggie went into the hospital, in his bedroom at home while Brenda was out "at the spa," she said.

"Because I don't have time for all that. Phil would ask a million questions about my reasons and none of them would satisfy him. He'd insist I wait until after the operation to make sure I was in my right mind, and I want this shit settled before that."

"Phil" was Phillip Landsbury, Reggie's longtime attorney.

"*Are* you in your right mind?" Melvin asked, grinning.

"Look, do you want the job or not?" Reggie asked. He'd offered his nephew sixty grand in cash to arrange for Brenda's murder, and now he was starting to regret he'd ever brought the kid into his confidence.

"Sure, sure, Uncle," Melvin said. "I've got this, no problem."

Which had been spoken like the sociopathic little mobster Melvin was. A twenty-two-year-old health nut with muscles on top of muscles, he'd driven his mother, Reggie's sister Emily, to an early grave, dabbling in crimes both petty and felonious for most of his life, yet he and Reggie had always shared an odd affinity for one another. Maybe because they both recognized a fellow, conscienceless predator when they saw one. It was hard not to admire one's own mirror image, after all.

That Melvin was capable of murder, Reggie had no doubt. And Reggie knew he wouldn't much give a damn that Brenda was the one Reggie needed killed, either. Sentimentality stuck to the kid like wood to a magnet. But could his nephew be bought for a reasonable price, and counted on to do the job right? That was the great unknown.

"How will you do it?" Reggie asked.

"Don't worry about that," Melvin said, biting the end off one of his ubiquitous vegan energy bars. The crap he ate and drank in the interests of fitness and health sometimes made Reggie want to puke. Meatless breakfast sausage? As the kids today liked to ask, *WTF?* "Unless you want it done a certain way, in which case—"

"It'll cost extra. Yeah, never mind, then. Do it however you want. I'll let you know when."

REGGIE DECIDED "WHEN" should be Friday afternoon, the day Reggie was scheduled to be operated on. Hungry and tired and in constant pain, he was feeling more and more like he wasn't going to make it out of surgery and he wanted to know with some certainty, before the anesthesia kicked in, that Brenda had been paid her due.

He remained committed to killing her but, by Wednesday morning, he was fighting off second thoughts. In Reggie's experience, doctors were wrong almost as often as they were right, but maybe this time what Daniel Greene, his analyst, would have told him—were Reggie crazy enough to consult him—would have been on the money. Maybe Brenda's bad intentions really were all in Reggie's head. Maybe Reggie was just a paranoid lunatic hopped up on pain killers and food deprivation who was seeing a "rat" where none existed. Maybe his wife really did love him and wanted nothing but the best for him.

In playing the game with her for an hour and a half over the last two nights, he kept finding himself wondering why he hadn't tried harder to enjoy the simple things with this woman. Going out to a concert or a ballgame, driving out along the coast with the top down on the convertible, sitting by the pool eating grilled burgers and dogs. What would have been the harm? Was her laughter really that annoying, her childlike innocence that great an offense? But rather than take her for the uncomplicated soul she was and relish her company, he'd all but avoided it instead, only drawing near for a few minutes at a time to issue an instruction or lay his hands on her body as a means of foreplay. Like everyone else in Reggie's life, Brenda was only good for the bare necessities, a scratch or two where he had an itch and nothing more.

Watching her at the hospital as their rounds of Mouse Trap progressed, her brow furrowed with concentration as she struggled to put one new piece or another on the gameboard trap, he had a hard time maintaining the outrage he would need to go through with his plans to kill her. But he managed. His anger and suspicion were the only things keeping him alive now, and he either held on tight to both or perished.

Neither his surgery nor his cancer was supposed to kill him, if his doctors could be trusted to tell him the truth, but Reggie had already made up his mind that his life was over. There was so little current left running through the veins of his ancient body, so little desire to care what the next day would bring, he was practically dead as it was. So he was either going to die on the operating table in two days or at home in his bed six months from now, no matter what statistical arguments his physicians and wife offered him to the contrary, and he wasn't going to go without putting everything and everybody in their proper place. He'd been nobody's sucker in life and he wasn't going to be anybody's in death.

Maybe if Reggie had had someone other than Brenda to focus on, he would have directed his scorn elsewhere. But his wife was all the family he had, other than his nephew Melvin. He'd scared everyone else off: friends, partners, distant relatives. When you spent your entire life building an empire with a scythe in one hand and a bullwhip in the other, this was destined to be your reward: a cheering section of one.

And Brenda was the one. She was the one waiting to cash in on his demise, to take the fruits of his labor and squander them on God only knew what, perhaps starting as soon as the last of his ashes were poured into the urn. Even if she meant no harm, if there was no malice intended in such self-gratification at her late husband's expense, the injustice of it would have been crime enough to satisfy Reggie. Had she earned the wealth she was in line to inherit? By blowing and banging him a few times a month, keeping him fed and his home well maintained? By giving him someone to talk to when he needed to rant, helping him in and out of the bath when he was too weak to be trusted doing so alone? No. No!

And if she'd been doing all that while fucking some guy at the tennis club, or the bank, or the gym where she seemed to be spending more and more of her time lately? Even if she was just *thinking* about it?

Death was too good for her.

So Reggie's resolve held. The game went on and his plans for murder remained in effect—until an unexpected complication threatened to render them useless:

"There's no diving board," Brenda said.

◎

"WHAT DO YOU mean, there's no diving board?"

"I mean, it's not here," Brenda said. "It's not in the box."

And hell if she wasn't right. The damn diving board was not in the game box. Reggie shuffled through the remaining pieces of the trap himself and couldn't find it.

"Shit!"

What the hell was he supposed to do now? The game had to end tomorrow night, only hours before Melvin was scheduled to earn his sixty grand by murdering Brenda in whatever fashion he had devised, and there was no way to end the game without a goddamn diving board. A diving board from which the diver could jump, into the wading pool, triggering the net that would drop like a feather onto Brenda's little green mouse, foreshadowing with perfect precision her own fatal downfall the next day.

"It's okay, baby," Brenda said, trying to head off one of Reggie's signature tantrums before she had to call a nurse. "We can play something else."

"Bullshit! We're damn near finished, we can't stop now!"

"But what can we do? If we don't have all the pieces—"

"Go buy another copy of the game. And don't come back here without one."

"Are you serious? You really want me to buy another copy of Mouse Trap just to get the diving board?"

"Tell me: Do I look serious? Or do I look like I'm joking?"

It was a question his wife might have once been dumb enough to actually answer, but tonight, she just let out a big sigh, kissed him on the forehead, and left, nearly colliding with her step-nephew Melvin as they passed each other at the door.

"Did I miss something?" Melvin asked, taking a seat at his uncle's bedside.

"The fucking game's incomplete," Reggie said, nodding at the game board and the partial Rube Goldberg machine spread out across his lap.

"What the hell is this?" Melvin couldn't help but grin, tickled by all the colored plastic. "Is that—"

"Yeah. So what?"

"Mouse Trap, right? You guys have been playin' Mouse Trap? For real?"

"I've got my reasons. Did you come here just to piss me off, or was there something else?"

Melvin started peeling a banana he'd taken from his jacket pocket. The sonofabitch was always eating something. Reggie hated bananas but his mouth watered, all the same. "We've got a business deal to close, Uncle. Remember?"

"You'll get your money, Melvin. Don't worry."

"Uh-huh. And when would that be, exactly? Before your surgery or after you die in the middle of it? Come on, Uncle." Melvin took a bite out of the banana. Reggie watched his jaws work with an envy that almost had him sobbing. "I don't mean to be a downer or anything, but we both know you may not be around after Friday."

"And I'll tell you something else we both know, asshole: That I'd be a complete idiot to pay you sixty grand now for a job you may never actually do if, as you say, I'm not around after Friday."

"Okay. Point taken. So how about this." He bit off another two inches of banana. "You can get your hands on fifteen thou by tomorrow, can't you? As a retainer?"

Of course Reggie could. It would be complicated, but it was doable, and there wasn't much point in Reggie denying it. Still...

"No," Reggie said.

"No? Seriously?"

"You heard me."

Melvin nodded and finished off the banana, tossing the peel into a nearby trash can. "Okay. No problem. To be honest, I thought this might happen, so it's all good."

"What? You thought *what* might happen?"

"That you'd lose your nerve and back out. I mean, it's understandable." He stood up to leave. "This was a very big adventure we were about to embark on, you and me, and not everybody's got the stomach for it."

"You think I've lost my nerve? Fuck you!" Reggie said, gasping for air. "Nothing scares me, you little punk! Nothing!"

"Then we're still on for Friday?"

"You're damn right we are."

"And you'll have fifteen grand here, waiting for me to pick up, by tomorrow afternoon at three?"

Reggie realized immediately what had just happened: his nephew had played him. Used Reggie's pride as a lure and drawn him into a mouse trap of his own, *snap!*

"Yeah, sure. Fifteen grand, by three tomorrow. Now get the hell out of here before I call for security."

◎

BRENDA ARRIVED AT the hospital Thursday morning with fifteen thousand dollars in cash and a new copy of the Mouse Trap game. Reggie told her the money was to pay off an old gambling debt and a man would be coming by later to collect it. Her husband liked to bet on sports from time to time, always seeming to lose more than he won, so Brenda didn't question his explanation. She gave him a big kiss and promised to come back in several hours for their last evening round of Mouse Trap before his operation the next day.

And how would she be spending her time in the interim, Reggie asked?

At the tanning salon, she said.

It was another mark against her, this feeble addition to all her other sorry alibis (the gym, the spa, the tennis club, etc., etc.), and Reggie had spent the last eleven hours doing a final tally: Should he kill the woman or not? He wasn't losing his nerve, as his nephew suggested the night before, he was simply making sure. Testing his suspicions against his perceived evidence. Lying flat on a gurney tomorrow at 4 p.m., watching a parade of fluorescent ceiling lights march past his fading vision as they wheeled him into surgery, he wanted all his doubts erased. If he was going to have a change of heart where his wife was concerned, now was the time.

But no—there would be no reprieve for Mrs. Brenda Lymon. Given the choice between having an innocent woman murdered in error and letting a guilty one go free, Reggie would take the former every time.

So it was with almost no regrets whatsoever that he gave Melvin his retainer when his nephew came looking for it that afternoon. He was doing the right thing. A man had to trust his instincts, right up to his last breath.

"I tell you what, Uncle," Melvin said, biting into the sandwich he'd brought with him today. A goddamn *sandwich*, the sonofabitch! Reggie's last meal had been a limp green salad and a bowl of chicken-less chicken soup. "I'm gonna give you a few more hours to think about this. Just to make absolutely certain this is what you want."

"I don't need any more time to think about it. I just paid you, didn't I?"

"All the same. If you want me to go through with it, you're gonna have to give me a call. Say, around eight. Leave a message if I don't answer."

"A message? What kind of message?"

"Make it simple." He took another bite of his sandwich, which from where Reggie was sitting and salivating, looked like ham and cheese, no doubt on some kind of gluten-free excuse for sourdough. "Something like, 'The eagle has landed.'"

"Are you *shitting me?*"

"Of course I'm shitting you," Melvin guffawed, crumbs flying out his mouth in all directions. "Just say, 'We're on for Friday.' As if you're talking about your surgery tomorrow. Okay?"

"Okay."

"Nothing happens if I don't get that call. Are we clear?"

"We're clear. But—"

"Yeah?"

"Do me one last favor before you go, will you, kid? Please."

◎

WHEN REGGIE GOT a good look at Brenda's left hand that night, as they were setting up the board for their final round of Mouse

Trap, he knew he could make the call his nephew was waiting for with a totally clear conscience. Because what married woman who wasn't cheating on her husband went around without wearing her $38,000 wedding ring?

"Are you okay, baby? You aren't worried about tomorrow, are you?"

Brenda had picked up on his sense of distraction. Of course he was worried about tomorrow; for all he knew, Friday was going to be his last day on earth. There was no avoiding the fact. But that wasn't what was most on his mind at this moment. The game was. For three nights now, he'd engaged in this idiotic throwback to his childhood for one reason and one reason only—to put a fitting exclamation mark on his wife's impending murder, to exit the world (if that was to be his fate) on one last, fiendishly clever act of sticking it to anyone who had the audacity to cross him—and it was all for nothing if he didn't end the exercise by winning. When all was said and done, he had to drop a red plastic net over a green plastic mouse to symbolize the justice he was about to mete out against his wife. This liar, this adulterer, this *rat* sitting before him now.

He had to win. He had to.

And finally, relying on the strength of his intellect and the power of his luck, he did it. He got Brenda's fucking mouse on the space of death, right where he wanted it, and he pulled the trigger. Down went the little silver ball along the winding blue staircase, around the red chute and into the yellow bucket; up the ball went from there, propelled on the arm of a blue, broomstick catapult, to take another red chute ride into a similarly-colored bathtub, where it fell down the tub's oversized drain onto the previously missing diving board below. At the other end of the board, a green diver was kicked into a yellow washtub, which upset the delicate balance of a red net perching at the top of a connected yellow pole. The net fell, inching down the pole's serrated surface, and landed as soft as a feather, Brenda's mouse trapped hopelessly in its clutches.

Game over.

Reggie laughed like a kid at the circus. He couldn't remember the last time anything had felt this good to him.

And Brenda, God bless her clueless ass, laughed right along with him, until she realized laughing wasn't all her husband was doing.

"Reggie, what's that you're eating?"

He took another celebratory bite, a big grin on his face. "It's a sandwich. What's it look like?"

His first guess had been right: ham and cheese, though the bread wasn't sourdough, or gluten-free. It was just a stale, garden variety white. His nephew's palate was beginning to show signs of normalizing.

"You can't be eating a sandwich! Are you crazy? Where did you get that?"

Brenda stood and reached for what remained of the half-sandwich in his hand, but he pulled away, laughing again, and stuffed the last of it in his mouth. After eight days of hospital slop, ham and cheese tasted like a Porterhouse steak on his tongue.

"Oh, my God," Brenda said, near tears. "What have you done? Nurse!" She snatched up the call button on Reggie's bed. "*Nurse!*"

Reggie just went on laughing, enjoying the show. His wife's final performance of "The Loving Partner" before he made the call to Melvin that would end her acting career forever. In the several minutes that followed, chaos reigned. The nurse rushed in and together with Brenda, began peppering Reggie with questions. They found the plastic wrap he had peeled off Melvin's sandwich and took turns sniffing it for clues.

It was hysterical, and Reggie would have laughed through it all had he not been preoccupied with the suddenly arduous task of breathing. Out of nowhere, he was having a lot of trouble getting air into his lungs. And swallowing. Two things he had never had trouble doing before. Something was happening to him and it wasn't good.

Recognizing his distress, Brenda began to scream, sending the hospital staff into overdrive. A doctor appeared and two other nurses. It could have been an army of medical personnel and it wouldn't have made any difference. They couldn't clear his airway in time to save him.

With the last few minutes of life he had left, Reggie did the math and came to a few conclusions. The first was that he very possibly owed his wife an apology, because they always made you take your jewelry off at tanning salons and Brenda might have simply forgotten to put her wedding ring back on after today's session in the booth. Maybe it was fortunate that Reggie would never be able to make that phone call his nephew was waiting for.

His second conclusion was that a man with as many food allergies as Reggie should have known better than to eat anything Melvin considered edible, no matter how ordinary it appeared. Meat was never just meat with Melvin and dairy was never just dairy. If a nut could be used as the basis for something instead of the milk from a cow—almonds, for instance—you could bet Melvin had it in his refrigerator.

And finally, just as his lights were about to go out for good, Reggie's last cogent thought was that, of all the things you could bait a mouse trap with, one old standby was still the most reliable. Got the little bastard almost every time.

Cheese.

Two Norths, Two Souths, Two East, Two West, Two Reds, Two Whites, and Two Greens

By Elaine Kagan

"Well, I don't know," Madge said, shaking her head. "Dolores, who did you pray to when Frank was dying?"

"The devil!" Dolores said, smiling.

"Ha ha," Madge said. "I'm serious." She took a small handful of peanuts and delicately placed one in her mouth.

Geraldine pushed her mahjong tiles to the side of her rack, turning them over, moving them so they were in pairs or threes or whatever she saw as possibilities in her hand. "Come on, Dolores," she said, taking a swig of cold Chardonnay. "Don't be glib."

"I'm never glib, kiddo," Dolores said. "I was praying to whoever would take Frank out, the bastard."

The click of ivory tiles, the dry wind pushing at the curtains. Babe's front door was open and someone across the street was talking to someone else and although you couldn't make out the words, you could hear the murmur of voices, the hum of an occasional car shifting gears up Benedict Canyon, the comforting sound of Tommy Schraeder bouncing a basketball in the Schraeder driveway. It was a hazy hot September afternoon in Los Angeles with just a hint of the Santa Ana that was promising to blow havoc later in the week.

Four women around a card table, four perfumes struggling to be the top note. Four old dames, Frank would have said. Although the word *old* may be relative, sixty-something-year-old upper arms could give it away.

Madge lifted her chin. "I always liked Frank."

Dolores gave her a look. "That's because you always went for the bad guys."

"I did not. What about Irwin?"

"Irwin was a dork."

"But he wasn't a bad guy," Madge said firmly.

"Who's Irwin?" Babe said, walking in from the kitchen. She had a bottle of Chardonnay in one hand and a bottle of Tito's vodka in the other. Babe was still perky, Dolores would say—she still had that accomplished strut. Dolores was probably the only human alive who would use the word perky, but if you squinted you could imagine the cheerleader Babe once was. A compact little blonde who probably still had her pom-poms.

"Dolores?" Babe asked, extending the vodka bottle towards her glass.

"Yeah…" Dolores said, "…what the hell…what time is it?"

"Nearly three."

"Okay." She took a tile off her rack and placed it in the center of the table. "One bam."

Madge took a tile from the wall and put it on her rack. She discarded a flower. "Irwin was a very nice guy I went out with after Paul and I got a divorce," she said to Babe.

"Before I met you."

"Before anything," Madge said.

"He was one of those guys who had a plastic holder in his shirt pocket to keep pens," Dolores said.

"A pocket protector," Madge said.

Babe grinned. "You're kidding."

Dolores lifted her hands like she'd just scored a touchdown. "I rest my case."

Madge sighed. "Okay, he did. But he was a very nice guy and that's not what we were talking about anyway." She took a tile off the end of the tile wall, put it on her rack and discarded another. "Two cracks," she said.

"I should have put a pocket protector on Frank's cock," Dolores said.

"Oh, Dolores," Madge said, but they all laughed.

Babe filled Geraldine's glass with Chardonnay, poured a slug of vodka into her own glass, put both bottles on a stunning pine sideboard in her living room and sat down at her place at the card table. The living room was very chic and very French. At least Babe said it was. Many chintz pillows precisely placed on perfect beige sofas, expensive porcelain vases made into lamps, thick Persian rugs. Or maybe they were Chinese. Everything in place in case photographers from *Architectural Digest* showed up unannounced. Babe said she wanted the living room to feel like the lobby of the Plaza Athenee Hotel in Paris where Joe took her on one of their lavish trips before they lost a shitload of money in a ponzi scheme. The other girls had never been in the lobby of the Plaza Athenee Hotel in Paris, except Dolores who said she only remembered Charlotte Rampling sitting in the lobby drinking champagne, cozying up to some guy who was extremely unattractive. Who was it? Well, she had no idea but he must have been *somebody*, but she certainly didn't remember anything about the lobby decor. So they took Babe's word for it. Babe Norton always seemed to know what she was talking about. After all, she was the most popular, most likely to succeed, most everything.

The card table was the only thing out of place—a typical card table with four typical pull-open bridge chairs—the setup that occurred every fourth Tuesday afternoon when the maj game rotated to Babe's house. Babe's tiles weren't really ivory—they were a beautiful rich yellow like little frozen rectangles of Velveeta and were made of Bakelite. Some people will tell you their inherited tiles are made of ivory but that's rare—they're probably bone. The flowers or knobby pieces of bamboo or red dots or tiny feisty green dragons painted on each tile were still vibrant colors despite years of hands. The four racks were see-thru plastic—red, green, blue, and yellow—and the dice were still a crisp white. The long card, which listed the acceptable mahjong hands, unfolded between the player and the rack of tiles in front of her and changed every year. Babe's set belonged to Babe's grandmother, Ida Mae Magill, and the story was that although Ida Mae was high Episcopalian she was a whizbang at mahjong and all her girlfriends were Jews. Of course, Ida Mae would have never said *Jews*. She would have referred to her girlfriends as 'of the Jewish Faith' the same way she never called Jesus Jesus, but 'Our Lord Jesus Christ'. The Magills were old money, Los Angeles money, very Hancock Park.

Babe was fifteen when Ida Mae decided it was time for Babe to learn mahjong. "This game has been a part of American Jewish culture since the 1920s," Ida Mae said, lovingly taking the tiles out of the black leather case and putting them on the card table. She cleared her throat and went on, as if she was teaching World History. "But it originated in China in the 1800s," she said with authority. Babe's grandmother could sometimes take on the air of Eleanor Roosevelt— or at least how Babe pictured Eleanor Roosevelt—very grand. Of course, Eleanor Roosevelt probably didn't wear pink lipstick that was seeping into the tiny lines around her mouth.

"Uh huh," Babe said, picking up a tile, tucking her shoes on the rung under the chair. "What's this one?"

"That's a wind, darling. There are four winds: north, south, east and west. There are cracks and bamboos and dots and flowers," she said, her eyes smiling.

"Okay," Babe said, putting down the north and picking up another tile.

"And that's a joker," her grandmother said. "You can never use a joker to make a pair."

"Okay."

"Mahjong is a game of skill, strategy, *and* luck, dear. Always remember that. Luck," she repeated.

"I know, Grammie."

"No, you don't," Ida Mae said, adjusting the strand of pearls around her neck. "Mahjong is played all over the world," she went on in her wobbly voice. "From Southeast Asia to Brooklyn," Ida Mae said triumphantly, mixing the tiles in a big circle in the middle of the table. Babe was pretty sure her grandmother had never set foot in Brooklyn but if she asked it could be another three hours of story so she just smiled.

"Your mother never understood mahjong," Ida Mae said.

"Mommy doesn't like playing games."

"Well, that's a matter of opinion," her grandmother said. "Go ahead. Mix them up. That's right."

Babe's young freckled hands, her grandmother's papery old ones, Ida Mae's diamond rings catching the light from the windows in her living room making rainbows around the thick white walls. It was the music of clicking tiles combined with talk, Babe would say later, that's what hooked her.

"In Jamaica the men play. For *money*," Ida Mae said, shaking her head in disapproval. "Now you build a wall," she said, stacking the tiles into a double row and backing them up against the rack in front of her. "That's right," she said, watching Babe copy her moves. "If you're lucky you'll find the perfect foursome." She put her hand on Babe's. "Now you take three tiles and pass them to the left, then three across and then three to the right...that's called the Charleston. Which I understand is only played in American mahjong and came into being around the same time as the Charleston dance. Isn't that funny?" she said but didn't stop talking, and it was at that moment it occurred to Babe that her grandmother was practically giddy explaining this game. "We'll pretend we have two other girls here," Ida Mae went on quickly moving tiles. "And, if you're lucky, your foursome could go on for years…" she said, smiling, "through births and deaths…when Anne died we had to replace her…oh, what a time that was," Ida Mae said, patting the strand of pearls. "But we played. Oh, we played through everything. Wars. Even divorce," Ida Mae said, frowning. There was nothing worse in Grammie's book than divorce. "Uh huh, so let's see what you have here," Ida Mae said, bending her powdered face close to Babe's, her pale blue eyes taking stock of the possibilities, catching Babe in a cloud of Chanel No. 5.

"The romance of mahjong," Babe said to Dolores years later. "Well, I call it romance."

"I get that," Dolores said. "But part of that was the essence of your grandmother, cookie. My grandmother smelled more like chopped liver than Chanel."

BABE SCOOCHED HER chair in closer. "It's hot, huh? Should I turn on the air conditioning?"

"I think it's nice," Madge said.

Dolores exhaled. "We're fine." She pushed her hair back behind her ears. It was still brown except for some wiry gray streaks—she pulled it up in the back and clamped it with a couple of shiny gold clips she'd slid from her jeans pocket. Dolores' jeans were not chic. If there was a way to buy jeans that still looked like you were spending the summer at your Uncle Pete's cabin at the Lake of the Ozarks, Dolores found them. Probably at K-Mart, Babe said. One would never know Dolores was the famous Dolores James, a federal judge who had spent a good chunk of her life sending bad guys to the slammer. Dolores' jeans weren't chic and neither was her vocabulary. She loved the old words, she said. Gay as in gay at a cocktail party, slammer or clinker for jail—or *the big house*, which Geri thought was hilarious—calling people kiddo or cookie or jack. Dolores was a skinny brunette with sharp eyes and sharp bones, a big brain and a lot of...moxie. Which was probably still the right word.

Babe repositioned herself on the chair, adjusting her skirt so that it wouldn't wrinkle. "I love fresh air. Joe always keeps it so cold in the house. He has a fit when I open the doors, says it's not safe nowadays but I know it's his fixation on regulating the air conditioning. He's obsessed. Do you guys want more of the little sandwiches?"

"Honey, I can't eat any more cucumbers," Geraldine said. "They give me gas."

Dolores gave Geri's arm a little smack. "You're a riot," she said.

"I am indeed."

"So, where are we?" Babe asked, taking a sip of vodka and studying the tiles in front of her.

"Well, we were talking about who you pray to," Madge said.

"When?"

"You know. When you pray."

Babe looked up. "What do you mean? Like Jesus?"

"Well, sure. I mean, if that's who you pray to."

"Well, sure. Uhhh..." She took a tile from the wall, slipped it between tiles on her rack and discarded a green dragon. She looked at Madge. "How do you picture him?"

"How do I picture *Jesus*?" Madge asked, taking the green dragon and discarding a west wind.

"Sean Connery," Geri said. "Only thinner."

Dolores let out a whoop of laughter. "You're kidding."

"Sean Connery?" Madge said. "With a beard?"

"Well, not when I was a kid," Gerri said. "When I was a kid in Queens I pictured him more like that actor who died young...

with the ice blue eyes and muscles... I can't remember his name... Jeffrey something?" She shifted some tiles on her rack. "Of course we weren't supposed to. If Sister Mary Annunciata had known we were picturing Jesus looking like a movie star she would have taken out her ruler."

"Child abuse," Dolores said.

"Well, I guess," Geri said. "But then when I was older, I kind of pictured him like Sean Connery, but not when he was Bond. Not in a suit and tie with Miss Haypenny or the Goldfinger gal or holding a gun..."

"Miss Moneypenny," Babe said. "Not Haypenny."

"She was M's secretary," Madge said. She pulled a tile from the wall, put it in her hand, and discarded a red dot.

"Right," Geri said.

"I never pictured him like that," Babe said.

"No? How did you picture him?"

"Probably more Episcopalian," Dolores said, laughing, "thinning beige hair, black vestments, a collar..."

"No...not like that... I don't know...more like an old guy..." Babe said. "You know...in the clouds. Not his whole body...more like his face..."

"Oh, wow," Dolores said, looking at Babe. "I pictured him kind of like that. But smelly. With crumbs in his beard. Kind of like my Uncle Nachman who pulled quarters out of your ears and reeked of pickles."

Babe laughed. "We pictured God the same? Oh, boy. What if we find out I'm Jewish?"

"No way, kiddo," Dolores said. "Jews do not make cucumber sandwiches."

"How did this come up anyway?" Babe asked, touching the clasp of Ida Mae's pearls that were around her neck. "This praying thing?"

"I asked," Madge said.

"Why?" Babe's head whipped around to Madge. "Are you worried?"

Madge sighed. "Well, it's not like I have any more breasts to give. You know. I only got here with two."

The three of them looked at her. It wasn't like they hadn't all prayed plenty when she was diagnosed four years ago. Trying to rationalize the doctors' snappy dialogue about how the removal of two breasts would be cheaper than the removal of one. "He *said* that?" Babe had been beyond furious. She even frowned, which was practically impossible with all the Botox that had been shot into her forehead. "He actually *said* that to you? Like a bargain?"

Dolores piped up, "Like a special. Attention K-Mart shoppers, two breasts for the price of one! Step right up, ladies!" Her eyes slid to Madge. "That son-of-a-bitch."

"Well, I think he was trying to be funny," Madge said. "You know, make it lighter?"

"Right," Dolores said. "Lighter! It's like a goddamn mammogram. If a man had to put his cock in between two icy sheets of plastic while a nurse squeezed the plastic tighter and tighter and then waltzed out of the room saying *hold your breath, honey, don't move!* there would be a cure for breast cancer!"

There had been talk that their husbands were going to go over to the doc's office in Beverly Hills and confront him. Babe's husband, Joe, was all set to punch the fucker. Joe was in construction, had about forty guys who worked for him and was known to have punched in the past, but Geri's husband, Dave, who was a cardiologist, felt it would be more appropriate if he called the surgeon and they had a doctor-to-doctor talk. Which he did. No one was apprised of that particular dialogue but knowing Dave it was probably well thought out. Dr. Dave was a mild man. Knowledgeable. Proper. Even when he was barbecuing hamburgers in their yard wearing bermuda shorts with one of those impossible jungle print short-sleeved shirts, you still pictured him in a white starched lab coat with a stethoscope looped around his neck.

Dolores' husband, Frank, was already a *dead duck* at the time. Dolores' expression. After years of fighting a heart condition, Frank had finally succumbed to a heart attack in their driveway with one foot still inside his Porsche. Dolores was going out with a couple of guys but neither of them were serious enough to take on the oncologist.

Madge didn't have a husband at the time, which meant that her ex-husband, Jerry, who was some big-shot at Warner Bros. and was remarried to some spray-tanned self-proclaimed life-coach in Brentwood, walked a tricky line—showing up to see Madge and schlep their two kids back and forth, while smiling his fishy smile. Jerry, who had an ego that was probably bigger than the entire population of California, thought the world revolved around him and Madge's breast cancer had definitely catapulted her to the lead. Jerry had a hard time being second. "Maybe he'll work himself up into a cardiac arrest to get back on top," Dolores had said.

It wasn't like the girls hadn't been involved from the very beginning. Individually and together. Because all women find themselves vulnerable when the news strikes home or even down the block. *BREAST CANCER.* There you go, ladies. All caps. Italicized. With a drum roll. Rechecking your breasts, lifting your arms up in the shower or sprawled across the bed, feeling yourself up until you're bruised. *"Honey, do you feel anything here?"* And then there was the practical side of being involved when it was your girlfriend. Taking turns standing by her bed, lifting the straw of lukewarm water between her chapped lips, reassuring her kids, helping her take a shower, changing bandages with sticky dressings. Checking angry stitches that Geri said actually reminded her of the thread her mother used to tie up the Thanksgiving turkey. *Oh my heart.* The news of Madge's double mastectomy rippled out across L.A. from Santa Monica to the Hollywood Hills, over Laurel Canyon into Studio City and west, past Sherman Oaks. It was discussed at Dolores' yoga class at Temple Emanuel where the rabbi's wife taught Hot Yoga, and at Geri's women's choir practice at the Church of the Good Shepherd where she sang second soprano, and across eighteen holes of perfectly clipped emerald green grass at the Riviera Country Club where Babe teed off at eight a.m. every Wednesday with three other women wearing tiny skirts. It was discussed in every Ladies Bathroom from the la-di-dah Grill on the Alley to the everyday Nate N Al's. Opinions wavered according to individual female history. Paula Stefano's Aunt Connie had both breasts removed, weeks of chemo and then radiation— sick as a dog—topping it off with reconstructive surgery and a year later the fucking cancer came back in her lungs. "So, there you go," Paula said, when she and Geri were taking their morning walk. Amy Ransahoff's mother had a lumpectomy with no chemo or radiation and was totally fine for more than thirty years until she died from a cerebral hemorrhage in her kitchen while she was whipping up an angel food cake. "The whole thing sucks," Amy said, eating around the potato salad on her plate because she was off carbs.

You had to know the type of cancer. You had to know the stage. You had to read reams, but most of all you had to ask. Women in their surrounding circles compared viewpoints and stories. Everybody had a story. The bottom line being: "Well, would you do both breasts or take your chances and just do one?" It was discussed over a tuna-melt and under the din of their grandchildren playing. It was hashed and rehashed by each of their grown children, especially the daughters. "I wouldn't do it," Dolores' daughter Juliana said, chasing her four-year-old around Dolores' kitchen.

"You'd just say no thank you?"

"Well, I'd certainly get a second opinion," Juliana said with a tone.

Dolores exhaled. "Darling, so far we've got about thirty-four opinions. Take one breast, take two, don't take any...you could lose your mind along with your boobs."

"Oh," Juliana said.

It wasn't like they hadn't taken turns crying. And praying.

◎

THE THREE OF them looked at Madge. They waited. Babe scooched her chair in closer. Geri put her hand on Madge's arm. Dolores frowned. Madge kind of pursed her lips together. She used to do it for her kids—purse her lips together like Kermit the Frog's scrunch face—but sometimes she didn't even know she was doing it. "I mean...what's next?" she asked, trembling. "Two lungs?"

"Did you feel something?" Babe asked, eyes wide.

"Okay, wait a minute here," Dolores said, in her *judge* voice. "Madge, did you have a doctor's appointment? Did they say something to you?"

"No... I just..."

"You're just scared," Geri said, patting Madge's arm. "It's totally understandable."

"And I thought..." Madge's eyes filled. "I don't know..." She moved her hand through the thin amount of hair that was still on her head. Little faded tufts. No longer deep red. More like the color of weak tea. As if she'd accidentally run her head through the rinse cycle in her Whirlpool with Clorox. She looked at the three of them. "They don't want me to color my hair anymore," she said. "The oncologist said he didn't think it was a good idea." The tears slid down her cheeks. "I'm going to have white hair. White hair and no breasts!" she said, suddenly sobbing.

"Oh, for chrissakes," Dolores said, glancing at the tile she had taken from the wall and still had in her hand. She slid it into the other tiles on her rack and flipped them over. "Mahjong," she said.

◎

THE TILES SWIRLED. Like two colors of paint merging. The backs of eight freckled hands moved the little yellow rectangles in a fast clicking circle, shuffling them for the next game. Well, they weren't really freckles anymore, were they? Age marks? Madge had called Dolores one June afternoon and asked, "What are you doing?" And with her usual deadpan, Dolores mouthed off, "I'm connecting the dots on the tops of my hands."

These eight hands had been shuffling tiles for nearly thirty years, give or take an occasion, a Tuesday with a problem: When Madge's mother died—when all their mothers died actually, except Babe's, who at ninety-three still lived in her own house and had only just recently given up driving her Lincoln, "I'm not going to drive any-more, dear." "Why, Mommy?" And in her still-perfect ritzy girl accent, Mrs. Bushfield smiled and said, "I no longer like to merge."

A funeral, a vacation, taking one of your kids to college, coming down with the flu or getting *BREAST CANCER*. There were cer-tain priorities in life that could stop a mahjong game. But not many.

"I think you're overreacting," Geri said to Madge. "Let's put the color of your hair in perspective." She took a breath. "I mean, given the alternative..."

"I know," Madge said, "but..."

"Remember when they did Babe's cataracts? And she couldn't wear mascara?" Geri said, making a disbelieving face. "You would have thought she'd been shot. Such carrying-on."

"Well, it was very upsetting to me," Babe said.

"It was on the front page of the *Los Angeles Times*," Dolores said. "Woman up Benedict Canyon deprived of Maybelline Long Lash!"

Babe gave Dolores' shoulder a little push.

They moved the tiles into stacks, some backed against the racks and some in a perfect diagonal wall across the bridge table. "Resembling the great wall of China," Dolores had once said. "But really the great wall of mahjong."

"I'm just trying to put this in perspective," Geri said, looking at Madge. "Would you feel better if we all stopped coloring our hair?"

"What?" Babe said. "Are you *kidding?* I can't stop coloring my hair!"

Madge laughed.

"I don't even know what color my hair is!" Babe said.

"So, let's be serious," Geri said, gazing at Madge. "Why were you praying? Or asking about praying?"

"Right," Babe seconded.

Geri was the sound one, the most reliable, the most calm in all matters of emergency. When Babe's youngest, Ryder, fell face down on a sprinkler head at the playground, it was Geri who whipped off her T-shirt and wound it around his little blond head, scooping him up in her big arms and running with him to Babe's car. It was Geri who was covered with blood in the ER, pacing in a bra and size 14 chinos until a nurse gave her a paper hospital gown to put over her beige Bali double D cup with wire. It was Geri who held Babe's hand until the others arrived.

One has their place in a foursome. The steady one, the beautiful one, the smart one, and Madge. It wasn't always easy to pinpoint Madge.

"Well," Madge said, wiping the remaining tears off her face with one of Babe's pink linen luncheon napkins. "I was thinking...maybe I've been praying to the wrong person."

"What?" Dolores asked, looking up, "What person?"

"Well, Jesus."

"Jesus Christ, you mean?"

A little half sob came out of Madge. "Yes. I mean, I was thinking...what does Jesus know about breasts?"

Babe blinked. "What?"

"Holy shit," Dolores said.

"Well..." Geri said. "It's not really whether He understands about breasts, is it? I mean...it's about faith and believing..."

"Oh, I believed alright," Madge said, eyebrows up. "Didn't I believe? My whole life. Please Jesus this and please Jesus that…and, where did it get me?" She spread her fingers wide in front of both sides of her chest. "So long little breasts, bye bye sweet titties," she said, stifling a new sob. "All this time. I should have been praying to Mary."

"Mary…?" Babe repeated, her bottom lip lowering into a perfect Revlon coral scallop.

"Mary?" Dolores repeated.

"Sweetheart," Geri said, leaning in, ready to protest but Dolores interrupted. "Oh, don't be so Catholic," she said to Geri.

"Dolores…" Geri said, her face going pink.

"Just give her a minute. Go on, Madge," Dolores said. "I'm fascinated."

"You see?" Madge said, nodding at Dolores. "Mary had breasts. Mary would have understood. Here I am praying all this time, oh please Jesus don't take my breasts and look what happened. What does he know about breasts? What does he know about being a woman?"

"Well, of course," Geri said. "But, wait a minute…"

"Wait a minute yourself," Dolores said, sitting back in her chair. "Just because you still go to Mass every Sunday doesn't mean you know everything about beliefs. I think Madge has a point."

"You see?" Madge said. "We've been praying to the wrong guy." She frowned. "I mean, you know…the wrong God…"

"Well, not me," Dolores said, "I haven't prayed in years. But I hear your argument."

"You don't pray?" Madge said, looking at Dolores.

"Well, I don't know. I mean, *please don't let that car hit me,* or *please let me make it to the bank before that bozo closes the window.* Stuff like that, but it's not specific to a particular god. Jesus, God, whoever…it's more random."

Babe blinked. "Well, Mary would definitely be more appropriate."

"Right. Instead of Jesus," Madge said. "Jesus is a guy. You see?"

Geri exhaled. "Madge, I know you're frightened, but…"

Babe held out her hand. You couldn't tell what tile she was clutching but it was probably a dragon—you could see a little bit of green sticking out from under her thumb. "Mary would definitely understand. And not just breasts," she said, emphasizing. "What about ovaries? And a vagina!"

"What?" Geri said.

"Mary had to have had a vagina. I mean, we know she had a baby. She probably had everything we have," Babe said, taking a gulp of vodka. "She probably had periods. How old was she anyway?"

"Young, I think," Madge said.

Dolores pushed at her hair. "Well, that rules out menopause. You couldn't pray to her about that joy—hot flashes, night sweats—she didn't make it that far."

"You can't be serious," Geri said.

"Geri, why can't you be more open? I think Madge has an intriguing idea here."

"It's blasphemous."

"Well that's taking it a little far, don't you think?"

"I do not."

Madge shifted in her chair. "I wasn't trying to be irreverent. I was just thinking…"

"You're always poo-pooing everything," Dolores said, giving Geri a look. "You're so closed."

"I am not," she said, turning to Babe. "Am I closed?"

"Well, sometimes…a little."

"Madge's got a point," Dolores said. "Men don't get it. It's like trying to explain to your gynecologist what a yeast infection feels like."

"I think it feels the way my Kermit the Frog scrunch face looks," Madge said, pursing her lips together like Kermit.

"HA! That's it! Exactly."

Madge nodded. "You see, Geri? We could pray to Mary about female things."

"Well, she certainly knew about being married," Babe said. "Living with a man…"

"Right," Dolores said. "What do you think good old Joseph said when she told him it wasn't his kid. That there was some star in the East or whatever she cooked up. *Don't give me that crap, baby. I'll bet he was livid.*"

"Being married…" Babe went on. "Living with a man…doing everything you do with a man. Touching and sucking…all of that…"

Geri took a breath. "Now, Babe…I don't think…"

"What? Think about it. Mary was married. She certainly knew about everything we know about. Being with a man…washing his stinky socks, freezing because of all the goddamn air-conditioning…"

"What?" Madge said.

"Oh, you know. Everything we put up with. Their power and their taking us for granted."

Madge nodded. "Oh, that."

"And how they're dismissive…" Dolores said. "It didn't matter what I did, as far as Frank was concerned. It was never enough. My career, my mothering, my piece of the marriage. I could have made it to the Supreme Court and it wouldn't have been enough. The only thing I did right as far as Frank was concerned was making a *pretty good* grilled cheese."

"We could start a new church," Babe said, eyes wide.

Dolores finished off the vodka in her glass. "Ha. Well, I don't know if you'd get that far," Dolores said.

"We could pray to all the Marys. There were three Marys, you know," Babe said.

"You've lost your minds," Geri said. "We're not praying to three Marys. Mary Magdalene was a whore!"

"They didn't prove that," Madge said.

Dolores shook her head. "See? There you go. Don't be such a hardass, Geraldine. You think everyone is a whore."

"I do not."

"Oh, yes you do. Miss Goody Two Shoes. You've been like that since the kids were in middle school and I told you Frank and I had watched porn. So judgmental. So holier than thou. Like we were having the neighbors over to eat pot roast and fuck."

"I never..." Geri said.

"Hold on..." Babe said.

"Dolores, wait a minute..." Madge said.

But she was on a roll. Back in court hammering in the 'closing' argument. "Are *you closed?* For chrissakes, Geraldine, let's be honest here. Sex is a dirty word to you," Dolores said. "You wouldn't even go with us when Anita and Stephanie Zweifel were selling that crazy line of lingerie—silk panties with slits and tiny heart cut-outs in the bras for nipples—which turned out to be pretty spectacular— but you said oh, no, you wouldn't go, you didn't even want to see it! That it was dirty. Filthy, you said, like we were whores! And I thought, well, what do you think goes on in their house? Poor old Dave, that's why he goes around all..." She stopped. She moved her hands through her hair, readjusting one of the gold clips. She took a big breath.

"Goes around all what?"

"Wait a minute here," Madge said, her hand on her throat.

"What about Dave?" Geri asked again, face flushed. "He goes around all *what?*"

"Oh, never mind."

"All what?" she asked again, her voice raised.

"Girls, stop," Babe said. "We don't have to talk about this now. Really. We should wrap it up. Whose turn is it?"

"What? He goes around all *what?*" Geri asked again.

"Oh my goodness. What time is it?" Madge asked.

"All what?" Geri shouted.

"All dying for affection," Dolores said, "that's *what*. That's how he goes around! You probably wear gloves when you touch him."

Babe's mouth opened. "Dolores...hold on..."

"Oh, dear," Madge said.

"And you probably don't ever suck his cock."

Now everyone's mouth dropped.

Geri's face went from pink to white and with a sound like a tree falling, she collapsed. Head bent forward over the table, sturdy shoulders shaking, trembling fingers covering her face. Her elbows hit her mahjong rack dislodging a few tiles. A red crack and two green bamboos slid across the table and dropped to the rug.

"Oh my God," Dolores said, reaching out for Geri. "I'm so sorry. I'm such a jerk."

"Geri," Babe said, touching Geri's back.

"Oh my goodness," Madge said.

"I'm out of my mind," Dolores said. "I'm probably shitfaced."

"We should get her some water," Madge said. But the three of them didn't move, eyes fixed to the top of Geri's frosty curls, definitely transfixed. In all the years of Tuesdays this was the first time they had seen her fall apart, much less cry. This was more than unpredictable behavior. Geraldine was their rock.

They kind of took turns patting her until she lifted her head and wiped at her face.

"I'm so sorry, Geraldine," Dolores said.

"Oh my goodness," Madge said again. "Are you alright?"

Geri looked at them. "I don't," she said, her big shoulders heaving, "I don't do any of that."

"Don't do what?" Madge said.

"Oh my God," Dolores said, eyes wide.

"I never liked it," she said, wiping her cheeks on the sleeve of her pale blue linen shirt. "Well, that's not true..."

"What?" Madge asked, looking at Dolores. "What didn't she like?"

Babe blinked and took a swig of her vodka.

"Sex," Geri said. She pulled a folded kleenex out of her pants pocket, opened it and blew her nose. "Sex with Dave," she said, exhaling. "I can't believe I'm telling you this."

"It's because you're upset," Madge said. "You don't mean it."

"I do mean it," Geri said, sniffling, wiping her nose. "I don't touch him. I mean, I love him, we had two children, but I don't... you know."

"What do you mean *never?*" Babe asked softly. "You never liked it?"

"No."

The room went quiet. There was only the sound of someone's gardener blowing leaves. A car turned off Benedict Canyon; you could hear the radio blasting something with a thudding drum beat. No one spoke until the noise faded.

"Did you ever like sex with anyone else?" Dolores asked. "Oh, man, I can't believe I asked you that."

"Well, that's the thing..." Geri said and then she stopped.

"What thing?" Madge asked.

"Well..." Geri said, sighing, "Oh, dear. I wish I still smoked."

"I have some cigarettes," Babe said.

The three turned to her. "You have *what?*" Dolores said.

"Wait a minute," she said, getting up from the chair, straightening her shirt and moving to the kitchen. "They're for emergencies," she said over her shoulder.

"Well, this would certainly apply," Dolores said.

"This is so crazy," Geri said, wiping at her nose. She gave Dolores a long look. "I'm sixty-four years old."

"I know, honey."

"I never told anybody."

"Well, I think it's okay," Dolores said, "I mean, it's us, you know. Whatever it is."

Babe came running back to the table, a flip box of Marlboros in one hand and a kitchen box of matches in the other. "Here," she said, holding both out to Geri. "I never knew you smoked."

"Well," Geri said, shaking a cigarette out of the box and lighting it. "I haven't since the day I found out I was pregnant with John. What is that? Forty-two years ago?" She inhaled and blew the smoke out over their heads. She held the kitchen match in her other hand.

The three of them didn't move.

Geri took another drag and tilted her head, looking at them. "I guess I'm a lesbian," she said and exhaled.

Babe's lower lip dropped.

Madge gave a little giggle. "Don't be silly," she said.

"Well, I don't know..."

"Give me one of those," Dolores said, holding out her hand for the cigarettes. She took one and lit it.

"Maybe you should start at the beginning," Babe said.

"Maybe I should start at the end," Geri said. "Babe, do you have an ashtray?"

"Oh, what the hell, just use the plate," Babe said.

"But it's your mother's Wedgwood."

"Geri, please, she won't know."

Dolores exhaled. She gave Geri a long look. "Why do you think you're a lesbian?"

"Because I never liked it with Dave. I hated it."

"Well, maybe Dave is no good at it."

"Dolores!" Madge said.

Geri looked at them. "It was different with Marilyn."

"Marilyn?" Babe said. "Your friend when you were little?"

"Right."

"Geri, just tell us," Dolores said. "I'm too old for this. I could have a goddamn heart attack before you finish the goddamn story."

Geri stubbed the cigarette out on the little blue plate. She carefully set the kitchen match next to it. "Well..."

"Go ahead, honey," Babe said.

"Well," she said, frowning, remembering, "I was nineteen... I can't believe I'm telling you this..."

"Geraldine," Dolores said.

"Okay, alright..." She sighed. "I was nineteen..."

Babe gave her a reassuring nod.

"I was still living with my folks in Elmhurst and taking the subway and Marilyn was still living with her folks, taking the subway. We had jobs in the city. Silly jobs, I guess, but we thought they were a big deal. You know, you're going to go into the city and...I don't know..."

"Knock their socks off," Dolores said.

Geri smiled. "Exactly." She inhaled, looked at the three of them. "You remember how I've talked about Marilyn, how we were best friends, we sang together in the choir at St. Bart's and we lived three blocks from each other, you know, we were together practically every second since kindergarten. She was engaged to Saul that summer, we were nineteen—did I say that?"

"Yes, nineteen," Madge said.

"Right...it was June. And she was going to get married right after the first of the year..." She took a few seconds. Eyes focused somewhere in the distance. "It was a hot muggy Saturday. That's all it was. Raining off and on. Humid. Sticky. You know how New York can be in the summer. Awful. My parents didn't have air conditioning." She ran her hand across her cheek and through her curls. "My mother was making chicken with garlic, that's all you could smell in the house was garlic frying, you know, and my father was doing something in the garage..." Geri smiled, ran the kleenex across her nose. "He was always doing something in the garage...and Marilyn and I were supposed to go out with the girls to a supper club in the city called D.J.'s and I was figuring out what to wear, pulling hangers out of the closet and somehow I got my finger caught in the closet door, you know, the door smashed it, I don't know how, and Marilyn was holding my hand looking at it, it was all bloody, and...she kissed my palm...and then... she kissed me."

The three of them didn't move.

"And I kissed her...and...everything." Geri took a big breath and cleared her throat. She looked at Dolores. "She died last Thursday."

Dolores blinked, leaned forward. "Marilyn died," Dolores said. She stubbed her cigarette out on the little blue plate.

"Yes."

"And, the two of you were lovers."

"Yes."

"All these years?" Babe asked.

"Oh, no," Geri said. "No, no, only until her wedding. Six months. She got married in January. Her wedding to Saul. I was the maid of honor," Geri said, frowning. "Honor..." she mumbled. "Well, that's terrible. Here we had been having this...affair? Is it an affair when it's two girls who aren't married?"

Babe shook her head. "Well, you were free."

"Well, not exactly."

Dolores nodded. "Oh, sure, two Irish Catholic girls steeped in the church. Ha! Free as birds."

"Free as birds," Geri said softly.

"And what happened? After Marilyn married Sam?" Madge asked.

"Saul," Geri said.

"Saul. Sorry."

"She lived happily ever after," Dolores said, lighting another Marlboro.

"Well, maybe," Geri said. "I don't know."

"Now I'm being glib," Dolores said.

"Did you see each other?" Babe asked.

"When I left New York. You know, when I said goodbye to everyone. But not like that, you know. She was married to Saul and I started going out with Dave and then he applied to med school and, you know, he got into USC and we got married and we moved here."

"And then what happened?"

"Nothing. I mean, you know, everything. We each had two kids and we kept in touch, you know, an occasional postcard like when we went to the zoo in San Diego or they went to Disney World in Florida and always a Christmas card and one on her birthday."

Babe took the vodka bottle and poured some in her glass. "But you never saw her?"

"Twice," Geri said, smiling. "Once when we took the kids to New York to see the Statue of Liberty and everything. I met her for a cup of coffee while Dave took the kids on the boat that goes around the island. But she only had a half an hour in the city. She still lived in Queens, you know."

"Oh, right, we did that," Madge said. "The boat that goes around New York City."

"And then years later when Dave and I went in—he had some medical conference and I met her at a little park on 55th Street. It had a little waterfall and some chairs, you know, little wrought iron chairs. I don't remember the name of it. It was so cold. Too cold to be sitting there. All bundled up in our coats and gloves. Marilyn had this big beautiful green wooly scarf she had all wrapped around her neck and her head." Geri laughed. "It was the color of her eyes," she said. "We sat and talked for maybe an hour. We were frozen." She looked at the three of them. "I loved her."

They were quiet. Dolores put her hand over Geri's. "Okay," she said. "It will be okay, kid."

"All these years," Madge said.

"What are you going to do, honey?" Babe asked, looking at Geri.

"Do? Well... I don't know..." Her eyes filled and then she laughed. "Go home and make Dave supper?"

If you were driving past Babe Norton's house you might have heard the four of them laughing. It actually took a few minutes before they could stop.

Geri wiped her face with the crumpled kleenex. "I'll have them say Marilyn's name at mass on Sunday."

"That will be good," Dolores said. "We'll go with you."

Babe nodded. "Absolutely. We'll all go together."

"Of course," Madge said.

The four of them began to scoop up the mahjong tiles, placing them carefully in the box in rows. They folded the cards, lifted the empty racks. Babe began stacking plates, Madge was picking up napkins and Dolores kind of took Geri's arm when they stood up.

"Madge," Geri said, "I think you were right. I think I may have made a big mistake."

"What?" Madge said, turning.

"Here I am all these years praying to Jesus. Maybe I should have been praying to Mary."

A Crokinole Tale

By Avri Klemer

The board rests between us, large and smooth and round, as visual as it is tactile. The hole in the center precisely the right size to receive my shiny new disks. The circle of eight pegs guarding the hole. The larger circles marked under the varnish separating the sections of the board, separating a good shot from a great shot.

My hand rests gently relaxed on the golden-brown Canadian Maple surface, pointer finger sitting just behind a beautiful wooden disk, ready to start a Crokinole game in our monthly meet-up.

The hall is quiet tonight, not too many players, not a whole lot of action yet, as my long-time opponent settles into his seat, unpacks his disks. I see him note that I'm not playing with my usual set, but he says nothing.

A subtle, almost nonchalant flick, and my disk slides across the mirrored, waxed surface past the ten- and fifteen-point lines, settling with a satisfying click into the center hole. Twenty points.

It is a full body experience, that tiny twitch of my right-hand pointer finger. "The pleasure of small motions" as I once heard it described. That it was in reference to pool makes it no less accurate.

My opponent, my friend, reaches across the table and half fills my glass with rye. I prefer scotch or bourbon—ideally a bourbon that tastes like a scotch, or vice versa—but tonight it is his turn to provide the drinks and, after my first taste, I have to admit that the bottle of small batch rye he has cracked is quite excellent.

It's not a case of trying to gain an edge against me. It is just part of the ritual. We are both aware that we flick better as the booze goes down, letting our bodies understand that, despite what we might have been taught in high school, when it comes to Crokinole the angle of incidence does not in fact equal the angle of reflection.

Shoot what you see.

My body knows the shot, the feel, the strength necessary far better than my head, and if my head is otherwise occupied—say perhaps with good whiskey or better conversation—the more likely it is my disks will dance and slide around and off the board the way I see them do it in my head.

"They finally let us visit the campsite over the weekend."

I like to talk while we play.

"It's been almost two years since I was up there, about as long as I've ever been away. First summer I wasn't there in a quarter century. I went to see my tree—have I ever told you about my tree?"

While I talk, we play, feeling for the rhythm that we both enjoy so much. His disk follows mine to the hole, and we trade twenty-point shots back and forth until I finally leave a disk short by a fraction. My opponent fires my disk off the playing surface, into the ditch that surrounds the board, and in doing so leaves me a target for my own next shot. We are as evenly matched as ever.

It is going to be a close game, a long night.

"I was just a baby, in my twenties, in love with life, in love with a beautiful girl, in love with possibility. All the possibilities. I was responsible for a dozen twelve-year-old boys, living in a group of cabins at the top of a hill in the middle of the woods in upstate New York. And just outside the door to my cabin were two saplings, less than five feet high, as young and as flexible as I was myself. And every time the boys would come out of their cabin, they would tear up the hill and grab a hold of the young trees to swing themselves off in the direction of the washhouse.

"I was so sure of myself. So certain and so angry. Arrogant by my own admission, and I thought the word a compliment. I told the kids every time. I told them to quit swinging on the trees, that they would damage them, break them.

"About the only person more arrogant and oblivious than a twenty-something in love is a twelve-year-old away from his parents for the first time."

More rye. It is smooth now, all bite taken away by the previous sips, by the beautiful numbing that comes over a person when they are a few drinks deep. And my game is all the way in the zone now, the disks seemingly controlled by my mind—the hand, the finger incidental to the process.

Of course, wherever it is that I am, my opponent is in the same place. The reason we love these meetings so much—more than the booze, more than the tales, more than the human companionship—it's the competition, and the fact that we are perfectly matched.

I find that I finish ten points up in one round, then the next two rounds are tied, before he claims five points on another. As we flick, again and again. I miss the hole by a whisker. He slides my disk off the board as if it is on rails while his own nestles comfortably, inevitably into the hole. We flick, and the cat and mouse continues.

Explosive power in the inch and a half my finger moves in an instant to send his disk flying from the board, trying to will mine to career off a peg and into the hole. But the angle is not quite right, the weight behind my fingernail not exact enough this time (let's blame not enough rye at this point of the evening) and instead my disk is snuggled safely, a peg between itself and my opponent, my friend.

"Weeks went on like this with the trees slowly growing, and the boys slowly growing, and not-so-slowly swinging on the trees as they ran up or down the hill.

"I remember the wild turkeys that used to wake us every morning, squawking and gobbling just out of sight in the valley, calling us to the day. Calling us to the lake and the fields, to the theater and the hiking trails.

"Remember when our pastimes were so much more physical? When we would compete across a soccer pitch, or over fifty meters in the lake. Even the ping-pong table got our heart rate up. Not like this. Not like the gentle exertion of flicking, of breaking in a new set of wooden disks.

"What's that? My shot?"

I stop staring at the past, place my disk touching the outer line, and see that he has left his own vulnerable, leaving me to picture the sequence that will take my new disk into my old to fire his off the board and into the ditch.

As it is thought, all the disks respond on the board exactly as they do in my head, and I continue my tale.

"I remember waking at 7 a.m. to get the boys up and cleaned and dressed for breakfast and the day. Ready for fourteen hours in the sun, running and swimming, creating and laughing and singing.

"And somehow at the end of the day, instead of falling into bed once our charges were down, we—my fellow counselors and I—would walk down the hill to the bar off the highway. It would take us forty minutes to walk down that hill. The walk back up would feel like forty seconds at the end of the night, and the next morning we were ready and eager to do the whole thing again."

Another exchange of turns, and with the final disk of the round my friend knocks out one of my two, leaving him up five points for the round. If tonight is like every other, we'll go back and forth like this all night, edging up slowly, slowly toward the 100-point goal until one of us blinks.

For some reason, the last round is never close.

"It was always going to happen.

"It was why I was so insistent about it, made such a big deal when they swung on the baby trees. Did you know I had a temper back then? I wasn't famous for it yet. I wasn't important enough for people to really notice it, but it was there. We've all got our buttons, and my biggest one is when I see an unwanted outcome, when I show people to how to avoid it, and it happens anyway.

"You had the last shot of this round. You to shoot first in the next."

A top-up from the rapidly emptying fifth, a slight raising of our glasses, a slow sip, a long moment to savor. My opponent, my friend puts down a disk on the back line. I blink and the disk is in the center hole.

"I think I could be heard all over the 260 acres of the campground when it finally happened.

"One of them was running too fast, held on too tight, too long. His legs went out from under him, and he never let go as he kept sliding on the loose dirt. I turned in time to see the sapling break, splinter near the ground, and I heard the cracks as the tree, all that it could have been, died.

"It wasn't the one boy I got mad at. I vented on all of them equally. Any one of them could have been the one to end it. Which one finally did the deed was unimportant. It was done, and I was furious. I don't remember what I said. I don't remember the words, but I remember the shape and feel of the rage.

"I remember I was hard on them.

"I remember the faces. And I remember that they did not touch the other tree for the rest of the summer. Not with the sad stump of the sibling less than two feet away, less than eight inches high, a constant reminder of what they had done. Of how angry and disappointed I could be.

"I wonder if both trees could have survived so close together. I wonder if in killing one tree my boys helped the other to survive and thrive. There's probably a metaphor in there but after this much whiskey I'll be damned if I can articulate it."

We're now at the peak of our powers, riding the whiskey high. It's Canadian rye, I now notice, like the wood of the board, like the game of Crokinole itself.

A clean game, untainted by the devilish connotations of billiards or playing cards. The Montgomery Ward catalogue marketed the game as having 'no objectionable features'. Does that make our insistence on making it a game played over drinks ironic?

Like the origins of the game then, our play now is clean and uncomplicated—we're hitting the center hole more often than not, and our scores are never more than a few points apart. We are riding the crest of a wave, and that's a metaphor that I can recognize even in my current state.

I know the inevitable crash that follows—the question is, for which one of us?

"Ten months later I'm back for another summer of caring for other people's children, and I'm back living in the same cabin. My tree has grown a little, but now there is no sign that there was ever another.

"And every succeeding year now—two, three, four of them—I still work in the group of cabins at the top of the valley, and my tree keeps growing. Initially some of the same kids are around, and when I tell the story of the sibling tree, they nod knowingly, share glances with their new bunkmates, and I see the fear I've put in their eye.

"I used to have a temper.

"And as time passes and I'm still nurturing the eleven- and twelve-year-olds up there in the woods, I tell the story and the fear is replaced with wonder, as these boys from streets of Brooklyn and Queens, from the swamps of Florida and Manhattan, see this tree now taller than them, too thick to put one hand around, solid enough to hold when hit with a shoulder while running at full speed. I can see the unspoken question—*this* tree was small enough that someone their size could break it by accident?

"Want the last drop from the bottle? No? It seems we've drunk all the rye. Good choice by the way."

I'm feeling good—relaxed and cocky and invincible, and all the other adjectives that come with drinking just a little too much just a little too quickly. With telling a story you're really feeling, to a friend that you trust, over a game you love.

I used to get this way playing pool, too—hitting a sweet spot of loose and confident where I knew at the precise moment that the tip of the cue connected with the cue ball whether or not the balls would do on the table what I saw them doing in my head.

The distances on the Crokinole board are shorter, and the speeds higher, so often the shot is over before you are exactly sure what has happened. But with the right amount of whiskey, with just the right company, the line between what you anticipate happening and what happens in reality simply disappears.

My opponent, my adversary, my friend has left a disk vulnerable, outside the ten ring, out to my left, towards my side of the board. It sets up my favorite shot, a seemingly simple flick, just hard enough, with all the English my body can provide. Not just the fingernail hitting the disk, like a cue tip on a cue ball. My whole being moves, my top half to the left, my bottom half to the right. All so that when my disk hits my enemy's, and fires that sucker right into the ditch with a satisfying "thunk", my own disk seems to take an unnaturally hard right, slips between two pegs, and settles into the twenty hole.

"Thanks. It was a pretty shot, wasn't it?

"More years pass. My summer hobby has become a year-round career, an escape from the disappointments of teaching, an opportunity to make a difference shaping and molding young minds, like sawing and sanding one of these pucks into the perfect shape.

"I'm finally persuaded to follow my young charges into teenagerhood. I leave the beauty and perfection of the cabins on top of the valley and move half a mile away, to the other side of the lake. To what feels like a new frontier—the wild west—and a set of bunks clinging to the side of a different hill.

"I'm still happy, even if I don't have any stories about the trees on this side of the camp. And every year, before all the kids arrive, I take a pilgrimage across the lake and up the hill to visit my tree, three times my height now, seemingly having been here forever.

"I know better.

"While my tree endures, the cabin I used to call home is worse for wear. The slope leading down to the porch has turned muddy, and rain sends that mud sliding down into the room where I got so little sleep for so many summers. When it rains, a puddle appears in one corner of the room. I'm not sure anyone but me really notices—there are fewer kids of this age coming to the camp, and my cabin, watched over closely by my tree, is no longer needed.

"My past, forgotten, by all but me."

More disks flicking back and forth across the board, we are in a groove, in a zone, and we now have an audience.

Ours is the last game still going on tonight, everyone else already vanquished or victorious, and the closeness of our abilities means every third round is still a tie. When someone does edge ahead it is only by five or ten or occasionally fifteen points. We have sixty-five points apiece, while the 100-point threshold has long since been passed by everyone else and, winners and losers, they now watch us play.

Whether it is the melancholy of my recent return to the site of past glory, or some property of this particular rye, I am unable to just play. The words continue to flow from my mouth, and never mind that the people who hear them don't know me the way that my opponent does. I have to tell my story.

And it seems they have to listen.

"Soon after being promoted to the teens, I met the woman who would be my wife. She would hang out with me over the weekend while I refereed a soccer match, or led a hike, or hosted a live reading of a comic book. Of course I told her the story of my tree, although I never took her to see it.

"I regret that now.

"By now I'm no longer just a camp counselor. I'm a supervisor responsible for dozens of teenagers, and also for all of the twenty-somethings watching those teens. My portfolio had grown like my tree, until the summer when I took the day off to go to my best friend's wedding.

"In England.

"There are still campers of mine from that day—men in their thirties now with wives and kids of their own—who don't believe I went to England on my day off. But there was no way I was going to miss the first wedding of my group of friends, the wedding of the boy who would eventually be my own best man.

"Kennedy to Heathrow, we were on the ground in England for less than twenty-seven hours. A quick nap on arrival and a change. A perfect English wedding with Pimms and rain and country dancing. Another nap and then a train back to the airport.

"The beginning of the end? It certainly started the end of something.

"Oh, rough bounce there. You've left me an opening. Booze wearing off?"

His disk is hanging half on and half off the hole. It's a trivial thing to flick my disk straight and true to knock his flying off the back of the board and leave mine scoring twenty. But my touch is off—skewed and far too light—and the disk doesn't come anywhere close to where it is supposed to be.

It would be ditched even if my opponent had no disks on the board, since it never reaches the fifteen-line. As it is, before my disk has finished settling in place off the board where I have swiped it, the next disk is slipping over the waxed wooden surface, clacking so satisfyingly against the hanging disk and depositing it in the hole, while the new disk settles perfectly behind a peg nearer to my side of the board.

I need a drink.

"Nice shot. Serves me right for gloating.

"Coming home on the red-eye, going straight from JFK to the Hudson Valley, my soon-to-be fiancée headed back to the Upper East Side alone for now. I arrived at camp that morning just ahead of a thousand parents and grandparents, aunts and uncles, siblings and friends. It is Visiting Day, and I haven't slept more than a handful of hours in seventy-two. It always had the probability of getting ugly.

"I don't remember much about that morning and afternoon. After many years of interacting with campers and their parents—both at camp during the summer and in the city office over the winter—and with the thousand-yard stare of my sleep deprivation, the day was one of functional autopilot, a triumph of muscle memory. But there are two moments which are still clear, all these years later.

"I remember my rounds that day took me up to old haunts. One of my campers had a younger brother living up by my old tree, and it was there that I went to touch base with his parents. I remember reassuring them that their son was doing well, that he was making friends, was joining in, was happy to be here. I remember someone asking how long I'd been working for the camp, and on hearing my answer, asking how long I thought I'd stay.

"I told them the story of my tree.

"I told them that's how long I'd been there—long enough for a sapling to grow three and four times my height. I also thought, but I didn't say it out loud, that I'd be around for as long as that tree stood. That my tree would outlast me.

"That perhaps I would like the tree to be my legacy."

I'm behind in this round, in danger of getting blown out, but now it's my opponent's turn to start miscuing.

After I manage to clip the small piece of disk that's visible behind a peg—knocking it into the ten-ring and leaving mine hidden in front of me with all the pegs between it and the new disk—the next shot cannons back off the front pegs and is ditched. I remove the stray disk with a clean connection, his disk buried in the ditch, mine seeming to reverse itself like a cue ball with backspin, leaving it near my first disk.

Another dud shot from my opponent. I think about trash talking, but my middle feels hollow, the start of the hangover or the gnawing of what's coming next in the story. I sink a twenty, he knocks out one of my live disks. I finish the round by clearing out his final disk, and he takes five points for the round. I've avoided disaster for now.

"The other thing I remember from that day was in the evening, after we had seen all the parents off, after we had served a dinner none of the campers would eat, still stuffed with the favorite foods their families had brought them, still intent on all of the treats and sweets left behind and awaiting them in their bunks.

"After a concert in the outdoor theater, as I lead the thirteen-, fourteen-, fifteen-year-olds back to our side of the lake, my fatigue and my temper combine to help set the course of the rest of my life.

"After I stop at the entrance to the far side of camp, as I watch the campers stream by, on their way to be counted, to make sure they are all here, I notice I'm only seeing campers, no staff. A hundred teens flow by me before I see the first counselor, and I realize that my blood is beginning to boil.

"I'm also aware that I'm barely seeing straight. Once I find enough counselors and send them to the places where they need to be, I stalk into the little cabin that serves as an office, and I fire my walkie-talkie into the wooden wall, smashing one and denting the other.

"Much like all those years before, when the tree was broken, I'm pretty sure everyone in camp hears my bellow of frustration.

"I yell at every supervisor I see. My temper, unfortunately now legendary to the point of parody, on this one occasion is untempered by what shred of self-control I can usually muster in the worst of moments, and I do not hold back. I shred my voice and my coworkers.

"The next day I'm not sure I'm still going to be employed beyond the last few days of the summer."

I shot last, I shoot first, and my disk is short again. Not so short as to be ditched, but only barely touching the fifteen line, and a simple shot for an experienced player like my opponent to remove it while leaving his disk safe behind a peg again. This is exactly what he does, and my response is a shot which flicks his disk, and leaves both in the fifteen ring, one on either side of the hole.

It's the best I can do, to keep complicating the position, and hope that eventually I am more capable of extricating myself than my opponent.

This could get messy.

"After this summer, which ends with all eyes on me, and not many of them friendly, I take a vacation to the lazy pace of Mystic, Connecticut. I exhale, and when I come back to Manhattan I find that the bookkeeper is gone. 'We think you can do it,' I am told, and just like that I am out of the field and into the office.

"But it turns out not only can I do it, I am good at it. And while I still have a temper, it is revealed far less often when I am dealing with numbers rather than people. I still get to spend my summers at camp, albeit more in an office than on the lake. And every year I go to see my tree, and every year it gets bigger and stronger, a physical manifestation of my connection to this place, this job, this life."

The next shot leaves all three disks hovering around the center hole, the bounds and rebounds of the pieces against the pegs and each other a tiny example of Brownian motion in action, and I see my opponent drop his hands.

That wasn't what he saw in his head.

Is it that single sip more I had compared to him? Did I get both first and last shot from the rye bottle, and so I'm holding onto the sweet spot that moment longer? The crowd is watching closely, listening to my every word, but they don't know that I've already won.

I flick my next disk without really thinking about it—my body, my finger knows better than my eyes now—and all three disks in the center fly off the board while the new one settles in the hole.

There is something like a sigh from the crowd.

"I was back up at camp this weekend and I went to see my tree.

"Somebody told me last week that it was gone. I didn't want to believe it, I had to see it for myself. They said it was unstable on the hill above those cabins. Said it was going to fall and do real damage one day."

His focus is all on the board, but I'm not talking for him. His shot is too hard and slides over the hole, almost reaching the fifteen line on my side of the board.

I flick, and again his disk slides out with a "clack" as mine settles in the hole.

"It was gone, just like they said. A little dent in the ground where they had dug out the roots, and then filled it in. Two decades, thirty-five feet, gone. And even knowing it had been there, I could barely tell."

He shoots again, going through the motions as he slips from buzzed to drunk. He's not interested anymore. In the story. In the game. But I'm relentless. I have something to play for.

Another disk knocked out. Another twenty.

"It took a little asking around, but I found where they had taken the logs once they had cut it up and hauled it off. They let me take one."

His own muscle memory kicks in, but it's too late. I match his twenty with one of my own. Only a few shots left. His disk sits in the fifteen ring, and I leave mine touching it, clogging up the middle. Complicating. His last shot sits in the fifteen while knocking the two already there into the tens. Seventy points to me, and the match.

"What did I do with the log?"

With a deep breath and a long exhale, I smile as I open up the pocket on my bag and carefully start putting away my newly blooded, undefeated Canadian Maple disks.

Red Billie

By Joe R. Lansdale

(This one is for Lewis Shiner. Thanks for the tips.)

This happened back when I was a kid, during a scorching summer so hot it was rumored birds fell dead and smoking from the sky, and the clouds looked like unpleasant faces. I don't doubt it.

Those were the good old days, actually.

I'll come to that.

◎

THE GIRL WE came to know as Red Billie moved into our town one night with who we assumed were her gray-faced parents, both of them stooped and homely as moldy sacks of old sin.

They arrived during a terrible hot spell in a coughing, clattering pickup that was made of rust and a bad promise. It was so worn out, neither model or year of its production could be identified. It had one headlight, and that one looked tired, like a sick, one-eyed monster looking forward to retirement or a quick death from an auto crusher.

Billie and the withered adults showed up along with three slinking hound dogs in the bed of the truck. The dogs were dust-colored and bony. The dogs stayed close together, as if they had just recently been unglued from one another and were unaccustomed to independence.

Folks and hounds ended up stuffed into a sagging gray house with a leaky tar paper roof with only candle light at night and an outside shitter that leaked out of the side of the hill like radioactive honey, steamed in the heat, and carried its aroma, which was strong enough to part your hair and call you Bobby, down from the hill and into the edge of the Dirt Yard.

The Dirt Yard was the remains of an old quarry where the ground had given up stone and earth, and then, had been shit on from above.

There was a light on a pole at the top of the hill, almost in the yard where Billie lived. From down in the pit, it looked like a second moon.

All us boys gathered in the Dirt Yard beneath where the light dropped its gold spot. It was cooler at night and more bearable against what was then record heat.

We played marbles, drank stolen beers, and talked about the girls we claimed to have screwed. Class was not our middle name, not even the name of a distant ancestor. We were fifteen, just a few years above booger eating and knock-knock jokes.

From the Dirt Yard, when the moon was bright, you could see greasy smoke rising from the nearby factories. Further along the hill were other houses, most of them built on the fly and constructed as if sacrifices to the wind.

Most of the boys in our group lived in those houses, which were only a couple of steps in quality above the one where Billie lived. That one was abandoned and no one wanted it. Billie and her folks, and those hounds, were squatters. No one rushed to throw them out, as my guess was the person who owned that house and property was either dead or had moved off, or had no more interest in that place than one might have in trying to give a rattlesnake a tonsillectomy with a pair of tweezers.

East side of town was known as Hell's Five Acres. No one was thinking a lot of brain surgeons were coming out of that section. I lucked out in a lot of ways. My parents weren't as poor as the others, and they had other interests besides beating a kid's ass and drinking a twelve-pack nightly. At least my hopes and dreams didn't wear chains and concrete boots.

One night, with the bugs swarming around the pole light thicker than the Milky Way, we saw Billie out on the sagging porch up there, sitting with her hounds, looking down on us like a hawk picking which mouse she was going to swoop down on.

We kind of knew who she was, as we'd all observed her and her strange family for a couple weeks or so, but at that moment in time, of course, we didn't know her name, and none of us had spoken to her. She watched us play marbles for a while, then came down, using a path to the Dirt Yard that would be precarious even for a mountain goat. She was carrying a bulging brown cloth bag.

Billie was peculiar looking, about our age at first glance. Because of her peculiarities, one of the meaner kids, Charlie, immediately thought of her as an object of fun, way she looked and acted.

Her short, fire-red hair made tufts on the sides of her head that stuck up high like horns, and she was ruddy-faced, and her skin appeared to have been pulled back tight to her ears by invisible wires and a serious winch. She had on jeans and a dirty, brown sweatshirt that her breasts poked against like a couple of door knobs. She had little feet in little black shoes.

She shook the cloth bag. It rattled like lug bolts and broken glass.

She said, "My name is Billie. Some call me Red Billie. Some call me Little Red Billie, some call me Bill, and some don't call me at all. I'd like to play marbles."

Charlie, who lived with his grandmother because his parents were in prison and his older brother had been shot dead in a washateria robbery, said, "Looks to me, girl, like you collected an ugly bill, and got paid in full."

Billie hit him in the mouth with a sharp left jab that made Charlie sit down so quick you'd have thought he wanted to.

Billie said, "Don't write a check your ass can't cash."

Charlie realized he didn't even have a checkbook, and stayed seated.

Billie broke open her bag of marbles then, and just to show she had style, unfastened the string that closed the bag, and dumped all the marbles into the circle we had drawn in the dirt.

Those marbles were wonders of color, and some of those colors I had never seen before. There was one marble that looked clear. I noticed it when it fell out of the bag and rolled onto the packed earth. As it rolled it turned blue and green, then it sparked with orange and red lights, like tiny fires set by mischievous fairies.

We all studied those wondrous orbs for a bit, then Red Billie dropped her empty marble sack into the circle, said to Charlie, "You. Pick those up and bag them, then let's get down to business."

Charlie moved into the circle, still on his knees. He picked the marbles up, examining them as he put them in the bag with all the caution of a collector handling miniature Faberge eggs.

There was only one shooter marble in her collection, bigger than the rest and black as a dead man's night. Just looking at that marble made my heart beat faster.

"Now," Red Billie said, "which game do you pussies play? Straight marbles, or for keeps?"

We did a bit of both from time to time, but it was difficult to afford a bag of marbles on a regular basis, so normally we didn't play for keeps.

Charlie, now fully indoctrinated with left-jab diplomacy, said, "How do you like to play?"

"I play for keeps or I don't play. I was only pretending to ask. And we're going to play, aren't we, boys?"

We all agreed to play. It seemed better than a jab in the snout, possibly some lost teeth.

"Now," she said, "we'll play with your marbles, not mine. Not until I say so. Except the shooter. I'll use my shooter."

"That sounds good," Charlie said. In that moment he would have spit polished Billie's little shoes with his tongue and wiped her ass with a silk handkerchief. He might have even reversed that order.

The wind was kicking up the usual stink of sewage and foundry, but I could smell Billie too. She smelled like charred wood smoke and burnt pork ribs coated in a mist of sulphur fumes and the residue from a sticky bean fart. She added strong tobacco stench to her scent by pulling a black cheroot out of her pocket, poking it between her thin lips, and lighting it with a match she popped to fire with her long black thumbnail. Her thumb knuckle was as big as a willow tree knot and dark with grime.

Charlie poured his bag of marbles into the center. Letting them roll every which way.

Red Billie was so short she could have walked under a kitchen table with a hat on, but she threw a bigger shadow than her height deserved. That shadow lay over the circle of marbles like a rain cloud.

We all squatted around the circle to watch Billie attempt to hit her first marble. She crouched low, and the smoke from her cheroot veiled her head in a Vesuvius cloud. She eyed her target. Then with a slow release of tobacco breath, she flexed her thumb against that big black shooter marble and let it fly.

Her shooter was a tumbling shadow. It hit a green and blue cat's eye so hard it shattered it. Fragments flew about like shrapnel.

You could hear all of us let out our breath. You might run over a marble with a truck tire and crush it like that, but a thumb shot? It could happen, but not the way that happened.

Billie's shooter didn't go out of the ring. It spun about for a moment in the center of it like a happy drunk in a four-wheeler.

Since she had destroyed the cat's eye, she was up for another shot.

"I'll go light," she said.

And so it went. Each shot banging a marble, knocking it out of the ring, but not shattering it like the first. She had been showing off, but I didn't doubt she could explode other marbles as easily as the first. Her shooter never once went out of the ring, so she kept on shooting. She shot fast, and by the end of it, all of Charlie's marbles, by standard rule, belonged to her.

When Billie completed her run, her face was popped with sweat and one got the strong impression that the only thing that might satisfy her as well as shooting marbles was stomping kittens.

Billie wanted us to shoot, so more marbles were dumped, and without her participating, normal games were played with marbles being bumped out of the ring. It seemed lethargic after her performance.

No doubt, I played the best. I could shoot hard and had a good eye, though my results were far less dramatic.

Even as the time for me to be home ticked by on my genuine used Timex watch, I didn't inch my way away from there. I was hoping to see Billie shoot again.

But that was it for the night. Her family dogs had begun to howl, and this seemed to be like a siren call for her. She smiled and told Charlie he could keep his marbles she had won. She took her bag of marbles, said, goodnight motherfuckers, and made her way back up the hill, never faltering as she went.

We couldn't have been more in awe than if Santa Claus had turned out to be real and was living as our next-door neighbor and spent his spare time fucking a stray dog in public.

When I got home, I eased into the house, passed the living room where Mom and Dad were watching some sort of variety show. They nodded at me, and my dad tapped his watch to signify I was late. I nodded back. I wasn't that late, and they weren't so strict as to lose a lung over it, but they hadn't lost sight of the time. A reminder they cared about me.

On TV, cloggers, men and women dressed in cowboy shirts, jeans and boots, were dancing what is sometimes referred to as the

Ignorant White Folk Dance, or Irish dancing without the good parts. Someone was playing a fiddle. I like a good fiddle. This wasn't one.

I eased into my room, which I shared with my eight-year-old brother, Lenny. He was in the process of dismantling his transistor radio with a hammer.

"Can't get the batteries out," he said.

"That's okay. You aren't going to need them."

I lay on my back on the bottom bunk, and listened to Lenny hammering away. He was destroying everything but the hammer. I could hear the TV going, and the variety show was over by then, and the news was on, and the main topic was the weather. Unseasonably hot. Tar and roofing shingles melting like chocolate, dripping off and onto the ground. That was one reason my parents weren't too hard on me about being late. During the day it was almost too hot to breathe. The air conditioner panted in the house like a dying dog, sucked that Freon as if with a straw.

I thought about what I had seen out at the Dirt Yard. I could still smell Red Billie's aroma on my clothes. It had soaked into them like dye. I finally undressed and showered and put on my pajamas and went to bed.

I dreamed that night of Billie and her odd hair tufts, her enormous thumb and jet-black nail, the big black shooter, and that exploding marble. Its fragments blowing out in slow motion, tinkling to the sun-dried earth like hail stones.

◎

I CONSIDERED NOT going back the next night, as the whole thing had both amazed and spooked me, but, then again, I had never seen such a thing, met such a person, and I had once seen a drunk guy who could dance barefoot on broken glass.

Next summer night, the moon and stars were bagged up in wet-cloud darkness, and what should have been a cool, late-night breeze had turned humid. At the Dirt Yard, something swift and flickering moved inside the light on the pole at the top of the hill. Beat at it like a moth captured in a jar.

Now and again, Billie would pause, look up at the light, sigh, bend down again, and thump her shooter and knock another marble out of the ring. She even busted one or two to show she could.

◎

ONE LATE AFTERNOON, the sun bleeding between houses, I was walking on the little oozing blacktop road set slightly above Red Billie's house.

I was going to buy some milk and cereal, maybe a comic book. I was thinking that night I would definitely skip the marble show. I had begun to feel odd about it, as if I were waiting for something not so pleasant to happen, and I need to abandon ship.

As I was passing Billie's house, I saw she had gone out to sit on a bench near the edge of the hill so she could look down on the Dirt Yard. She was surrounded by her dogs. Little dust-colored shadows that slinked close to her feet.

She turned her head in time to catch me walking by, called out to me.

"Hey, come sit with me a while."

There was a plaintive tone in her voice, like a child that had thrown a birthday party only to have no one show up. I thought about an excuse, decided against it, and went over.

The dogs gathered around me as I walked into the yard. They were a bedraggled bunch. With hot spot patches where fur had been. Maybe a touch of mange. One had a phlegmy eye, and that was the good one. The larger dog had two peckers.

"They won't bite you," Billie said. "Unless I tell them to. Come. Sit."

I sat on the bench beside her. One of the hounds licked my ear, like a chef testing the specialty of the house right before it was served;

a chef with hot breath that smelled like a rotting carcass, and with a tongue like sandpaper.

"Are you happy?" she asked me.

Not a question I would have expected.

"I think so. Nothing hurts and I'm okay."

"I've never been happy. Not where I come from."

"Where's that?"

"South."

"What was it like to make you so unhappy there?"

"Where I'm from, time crawls like a slug. Sometimes, though, it wobbles and comes loose. There are cracks through which you can escape. My life is like a dream in a trash can."

I was as confused as a Martian tourist, but I said nothing. The air crackled and snapped slightly. In the distance I could see dry lightning dancing and the air began to taste of ozone and turn even warmer than it had been. Sweat dripped off of me.

"I slipped through the cracks. But they'll be looking."

"Who will be looking?"

"Her. It won't be long. She comes cold and snowy."

Looking at Billie and her surroundings, those horrid dogs, I couldn't figure what she was talking about. Someone looking for her? Cold and snowy? What the hell?

I said, "You have your parents to look after you?"

"The dogs do a better job. And those two are not my parents. Guardians."

I certainly had questions, but I was afraid to ask them.

As we sat there and the summer night ticked onward with the stars swarming above like the bugs at the pole light, I was possessed with a sudden thought.

Looking at Red Billie, I found I was looking past her peculiar hairdo, her strange clothes, her little feet, and I saw a girl there, scared and almost pretty if you squinted just right. Admittedly, at the age I was then, the old gear shift had a tendency to switch out of Park and into Drive at the vaguest hint of sexual attractiveness.

I said, "Would you like to go get an ice cream cone?"

It wasn't a pick-up line on the equal to how about a trip to Paris, but it's all I had. My cousin used to ask girls to wrestle. That worked pretty well, he said.

Red Billie turned her head and looked at me. In her eyes there was movement. I could almost see thoughts drive by like cars on the interstate. Then her eyes went soft, and her face turned soft as well.

"You don't have ideas, do you?"

"About what?" I said, and I felt my gear shift back into Park. "It's not marble time yet. We got a couple hours or so before we play?"

She smiled at me.

"Just thought you might want an ice cream cone," I said. "I'm getting one."

I stood up.

"Okay," she said.

WE WALKED DOWN the street to the ice cream shop. When we went in, the older teenagers turned to look at us. Of course, it was Billie's curious looks that drew their attention.

At the counter we ordered. Billie went for a hot fudge sundae and I ordered a banana split. I paid for it all, just like I had money to spare. I wouldn't be buying cereal and milk this night.

We sat in the back at a lone table separated from the others. As Billie ate her ice cream, it steamed little pale clouds out of her mouth and nose.

"Are you embarrassed?" she asked.

"About what?"

"Being with me."

"No. I'm not embarrassed."

"My mom always says I was the peach that fell off the tree and lay too long on the ground."

"Your mom said that?"

"Not good for the confidence you know," Billie said. "I run off whenever I can. But she always comes for me, and I always have to go back. I really hate it there. I keep trying to stay away."

"Your father?"

"No one mentions his name. It's not to be said. He pretty much ignores me. I don't know if that's better or worse."

We ate our ice cream, and by the time we had stepped back out into the street, the air had been touched with a chill, which made no sense.

Red Billie trembled, looked up at the sky. I couldn't see much up there because of the street and store lights. Billie seemed to see well enough, though.

She said, "The universe has shifted."

"Yeah?"

"Yeah."

"All manner of this and that from then and now are coming loose of their regions."

"No shit?

"No shit."

We walked slowly back to her house. She took my hand. It felt like a hot water bottle freshly filled. Other than that, we were just two teenagers on a cool, soft night with the universe having shifted and something coming loose of their regions.

When we arrived at her house, the dogs came out to see us. Billie slowly let go of my hand, turned to look at me, said, "Go home. Don't come back. Go home."

"Oh," I said.

"It's best. You being there are not won't change a thing. Thanks for being kind."

◉

MY PARENTS WERE on the couch in front of the TV. I went over to acknowledge I was home.

I left them there, had a sandwich, and went to the bedroom. My little brother had worn himself out early beating an old record player to pieces with his hammer. At least I wouldn't have to hear the god-damn singing chipmunks anymore.

He lay on the floor, hunched over his damage, asleep from physical exhaustion. The hammer was next to his hand. I was going to recommend to Mom and Dad that for Christmas they buy him an anvil, or some angle iron to beat on. His toys were just about extinct.

I picked up the hammer, went outside and flung it into the shrub-bery. The air was warmer again, and the stars had lost their sense of wonder. Pollution from the foundry floated in front of the moon.

"Don't come back," Billie had said, but I started walking back to the Dirt Yard.

◉

A NUMBER OF the kids had shown up, as Billie was still the number one attraction in our section of town. They stood, hands in pockets, heads bent, waiting for Billie and a display of her phenomenal marble shooting. Charlie seemed more anxious than any of us.

Down from the hill she came. Tonight, she wore a dark, leather jacket. Her hair had been brushed and the red tufts on the sides of her head had been combed back. A bit of hair dangled on her fore-head in a spit curl. She looked quite fetching, if overdressed for a summer night. That coat would have smothered me.

Following her, came the hound dogs, as well as her Guardians, walking like sticks in shoes. Billie came to stand by the circle. She looked at me and smiled.

"I told you not to come back."

"I know."

She gave me a thin smile that hit me in my back pocket.

Some of the kids were looking away from Billie, in the other direction.

I turned. Coming down the back trail was a tall, wisp of a woman in white shirt and pants, white tennis shoes, no socks.

She had night-black hair, skin like porcelain, eyes like fire. She had a white purse; the long strap that supported it was slung over her shoulder.

Four white cats, their fur touched with frost, strolled after her. The air was not only bite-ass cold all of a sudden, there was flecks of snow blowing about. What the hell?

Up close, the woman smelled of jasmine, damp earth, and gentle decay.

"It's time to come home," she said to Red Billie, facing her across the circle.

"I don't have to," Billie said.

"I believe you do. Things are out of whack. I see you took our dog."

Dog, I thought, there were three of them. But when I looked, the hounds were pushed up tight to one another and I couldn't see where they separated. The Guardians had bent their long bodies so that their hands touched the earth. They had the appearance of insects. Enormous white crickets ready to hop. Out of their backs grew transparent wings.

I hadn't seen that coming.

When I turned to look at the Wisp, the cats were no longer there. In their place were long, cool women, silver-haired, bare and pale with expressionless faces. There was nothing sexy about them. No gears shifted from Park to Drive. They might as well have been marble statues in a cemetery.

One of the women licked out with her tongue and touched her nose, giving it a wipe.

"You're over your time," said the Wisp. "It's time to catch the boat, honey. I have your fare."

The insects around the light buzzed like harpies, cast shadow dots on the poorly lit ground.

"I'd rather not," Billie said. "I'll take my chances with the game."

"You know how that turns out before you start."

"Not always. Remember that time in Death Valley?"

"I've always suspected you cheated."

"And Krakatoa."

"Don't talk to me about Krakatoa. Definitely a cheat, Billie."

"And Chernobyl."

"I give you that one. I wasn't feeling myself that day."

"I think I have to be home," Charlie said. His attachment to Red Billie having faded during the transformation of the dogs and Guardians. I was about to suggest I go with him.

"Everyone will stay," said the Wisp. "The night is sealed."

"Sealed?" Charlie said.

"That means you can't go," the Wisp said, "and if you try to, they'll find you inside a block of ice. Go that way, you'll be ash. So, I suggest you stay."

"Okay," Charlie said, and looked at me.

I shrugged. I was kind of hoping he'd make a run for it. I was curious which direction he might go, and how he'd turn out. Ash or ice.

"Shall we play?" the Wisp said.

"We always do," Billie said.

"I have brought the coins for your eyes," said the Wisp. She flipped two large silver coins onto the ground. They rattled and wobbled before becoming still. "Flip it."

Billie eyed the two coins. It was obvious there was a ritual here we didn't understand, and it had been happening for quite some time.

"What's going on?" Charlie said. "What is this?"

"Shush," said the Wisp. "I don't like my concentration bothered. Understand, you little worthless shit?"

"Yes, ma'am," Charlie said.

Billie picked up one of the coins, and flipped it, said, "Heads."

In those moments the Dirt Yard was all there was of the world. Hot wind blew, and cold wind followed. Snow flicked, and insects caught fire. The air swirled with Billie's smell, the sewer, the pollution, and the sick sweetness from the Wisp. The three-headed dog growled. The women mewed and swayed. Between heat and ice, I shivered and swooned.

The flipped coin sailed up high, catching the light, the edge of it sparkling like a diamond, spinning, seeming to hang for a moment, then it dropped fast.

Billie stuck out her palm and caught it. She stepped into the circle, extended her hand, showed it so all could see. Tails.

The Wisp smiled, removed her purse and dumped her marbles on the ground outside the circle. The marbles steamed like dry ice. Her shooter was a ball of blue ice. She picked it up and rolled it across her fingers, turned her hand and let it fall into her palm. She curled her fingers, straightened them, and now she held the marble between thumb and index finger.

Billie emptied her sack of marbles into the circle. The Wisp, having won the right to first shot, bent forward with her ice-blue shooter, and with her thumb, delicate and long, her nail like a chip of ice, she thumped her shot at a bright red marble.

The shooter-marble tumbled in the air, dipped within the circle, made a little mushroom cloud of dirt as it struck the ground. It smacked the red marble. There was a scratchy streak of tiny lightning and Billie's marble blew apart. Fragments rattled about like scarlet hail.

"One," the Wisp said.

I looked at Billie. Her face was a wad of wrinkled flesh. In that moment she looked ancient and less confident or attractive than before; had the look of an unwrapped mummy.

Wisp moved around the circle, and her women followed. She found a spot where she could lean down and shoot again, the player having to shoot where the marble landed.

She thumped her shooter. Like a heat missile, it found a marble the color of a harvest moon. Another explosion and a rip of lightning, and the golden marble blew apart.

"Two," Wisp said.

Charlie said, "Aww."

When I looked at him, he was touching his face. A piece of the marble had cut his cheek. Blood ran out from under his fingers.

"Damn," he said.

"Shut up, little boy," said the Wisp.

The walls of the pit were no longer visible. Looking up, there was only the light on the pole. No stars. No moon. For a brief instant I saw something move up there, a crack of light, as if night's curtain was being parted by a nervous thespian taking a peek at the audience.

On the third shot, the Wisp broke another marble. It had been all the colors in a crayon box.

"Three," she said.

The Wisp's success finally turned sour. Her shooter rested in a really bad spot, and she had to reach pretty far to thump it. Her arm stretched slightly, or seemed to in that overhead pole light, but as she reached, the circle grew wider, and the marbles were farther away from her. She missed her shot.

Red Billie stepped forward, having kicked off her shoes to show hooves, like those of a goat. By this time, I would have expected no less.

"Dump yours," Billie said.

One of the women had collected all of the Wisp's marbles and put them back into her purse.

The Wisp nodded. The woman dumped the purse again. The marbles rolled into the ring and wobbled about. These two played their own way. Perhaps somewhere they had a kind of rule book tucked away.

Billie pushed her fingers together, cracked her knuckles. Her face looked like a drama mask, the one where the lips drooped. She eyed an icy-white marble, and thumped.

I can't describe the impact, because the sound of it brought me to my knees. I felt dazed and confused. My thoughts felt as if they returned to me by rickshaw. When they did, I saw that Billie had been shooting for a while. She had destroyed half a dozen of Wisp's marbles.

Billie was examining her possibilities for a shot. Billie took a deep breath. The corners of her lips turned up. She saw a shot, and it was easy to see that she felt she would make it.

And then I knew. I can't say how. But I knew. My mind was so wide open you could have driven a train to it. The world had shifted again.

It was as if the answers, or at least some of them, were in the air. Truthfully, I merely felt something. It's only now, much later, that I understand it more. A truth is first felt before realized.

If Billie won, the earth would grow warmer, and even the air would burn. But if Wisp won, Billie would return to where she had escaped from, and the weather would balance, or at least hold on. I still can't explain how I knew these things, but in that moment, I felt a cosmic truth move through me like a dose of laxative.

And the way it looked now, Billie was going to run the circle, destroy all the marbles.

Billie looked at me.

"You'll be all right. I can take you with me," she said.

Take me? Where?

I don't know what made me do it, but just as Billie was about to shoot, I looked down at the blue and green marble she was aiming for, and stepped into the circle.

I knew then I wasn't in East Texas anymore. I was floating in the black of space and there were marbles and fragments of marbles whirling in the void, some were like stars, others appeared to be worlds. They were bigger than marbles, but I was bigger than they were. I was a cosmic parade float hung in space and time.

And then I saw one of the marbles swirling closer. Or was I coming closer to it?

It was blue and green, and when it was about to pass me by, I saw it for what it really was.

Earth.

I grabbed it. I clung to it. Hugged it like a life preserver. I felt the heat slipping from my body like water running down a drain. The only thing that mattered to me then was clinging to that marble—clinging to Earth.

A moment later. A century later. I couldn't tell you for sure, my body felt as if it were being grated with sandpaper. Still, I clung. A piece of light cracked open the darkness.

It was the pole light. I was on my back. I had the marble—the Earth—clutched in my fist. My shoulders burned. My clothes were flecked with fragments of ice. There were hands on my shoulders.

Wisp's hands.

Wisp leaned down and looked at me. That sweet smell of hers wrapped me up like mummy bandages. She smiled. It was a shiny smile of straight white teeth, reminiscent of the sheen on a glass marble.

I knew then why my shoulders burned.

Frost bite. Wisp had yanked me out of the circle.

In the next moment, her minions were lifting me to my feet, holding me steady until I could stand on my own. The Wisp took the marble out of my hand, dropped it into her purse, which a minion was holding for her, wide open.

And there was Billie. A crooked smile on her face. She was crouched, the ebony shooter marble resting against her thumb and forefinger. The three-headed dog growled at me and the stick Guardians stood up and were old folks again.

Billie had refused to take her shot.

She had refused to shoot with me in that circle. She had refused to destroy me and our planet. Was it respect for what I did, though I had no real idea what I was doing at the time? Or was she suddenly thinking about our ice-cream date, that moment when we had connected?

Slowly Billie stood up straight. The marble rolled from her hand and plopped onto the dirt outside the circle.

One of the Guardians snapped it up, bagged it in Billie's sack. When I looked into the circle, there were no longer marbles there, just perfectly round gray rocks.

The walls of the pit became apparent. The stars and the moon were bright in the heavens. The air had cooled. I could smell shit from the sewage radiating out of the wall of the pit.

The Wisp stared across the circle. Her minion women were gone. White cats had once again replaced them. They leaned against her legs and purred.

"You have defaulted, Billie," Wisp said. "You didn't shoot. You refused your shot."

Billie nodded.

She looked at me. The expression on her face was hard to identify. Disappointment? Desire? A bit of anger. A bit of admiration. It all seemed to be there in that look.

"It would have been less lonely for me," Billie said, looking at me.

"It really is time," the Wisp said.

Billie found the coins the Wisp had tossed at her, placed them over her eyes, and then, as if those coins were bifocals, she turned and trudged up the hill, followed now by three hounds and the Guardians. When she was at the peak of the hill, she threw up her hand and extended her middle finger.

Not long after, we heard that old truck starting up. One cyclopean light blazed momentarily over the hill, then swung around. There was a rumble and an engine cough, and then the truck, Billie, and her companions were gone.

I turned to look at the Wisp. Her cats were gone. Her purse was gone. There was only her. She smiled at me. Her hair lifted on the cool wind and came apart like ripped away shadows. Her clothes jumped away. She stood naked and beautiful and translucent in the glow of the pole light before she faded into thin air.

"Now that was the shit," Charlie said.

I went over and picked up Billie's shoes. They fell apart in my hands.

◎

WE LEFT THE pit then. As you might guess, we were all done with marbles. I threw all of mine away the next day.

My brother grew up and went into the business of demolition. Knocking down old buildings, blowing holes in the earth for mining. He never lost that gleam in his eyes when something came apart and fell down.

Me. Environmentalist. I might as well have gone into trying to catch cicada farts in a jar, for all the good I've done.

You only get to dance so much, and then the music stops and the lights go out. My music had stopped and my lights were flickering.

But maybe, I had done something. Something big. I had to ask myself that now and again.

Had I saved the world? Part of the universe with an ice-cream date?

Well, not completely. Billie hadn't totally lost. She'd knocked some things out of whack. Outside my window on the land where great pines had been, there is only a stretch of sandy earth. No birds flew. No bees buzzed. Outside the air is heavy and thick, like breathing wool socks. Inside, the central air only manages to skim the edge off the heat, but not remove it.

Somewhere, between the cracks, Billie waits. Thinking how she missed her shot, building her strength, wanting all the marbles, looking for a way to escape.

If she does, this time there'll be no stopping her. It occurs to me, the way we humans treat our Mother Ship, we may be responsible for the widening of those cracks. Giving her enough room to slip through.

Yet, I wonder if now and again, in moments of nostalgic reflection, Billie thinks pleasantly of me, and our one beautiful ice-cream date.

Lightning Round

By Warren Moore

Wednesday night at The Little End was trivia night, which meant that Noah Pearsall was heading for his usual seat. He sat in the corner opposite the door, across from the bar, and under one of the televisions that ran sports every night—usually baseball or basketball in season, or whatever else was on ESPN. There were four TVs, which seemed like a lot for a bar that size, but the owner kept the sound down, so Noah didn't have to pay attention to them if he didn't want to. Instead, the soundtrack was generally supplied by what the sign said was "Kentucky's Third-Best Jukebox."

Noah figured that was like being the tallest skyscraper in Morristown, Tennessee, but he had to admit that for Greensburg, Kentucky, the jukebox wasn't bad, with everything from Wes Montgomery to Buck Owens, from the Jive Five to Django Reinhardt, and most importantly, no Bob Seger or Linkin Park. While Noah had never figured out whether Greensburg was a small college town or a town with a small college in it, he figured The Little End was a more-than-adequate local bar. And since he had a three-year contract teaching history at Greensburg College, more-than-adequate wasn't a bad deal.

He had discovered The Little End a few months into his stay at Greensburg—someone from Student Services told him that there had been a Greensburg prof who didn't get tenure, so he opened a bar instead. The guy had been an English prof; everyone called him Doc, and apparently the bar's name came from *Gulliver's Travels*, but Noah hadn't bothered to look it up. It made sense to him, though—running a bar in a college town might not be a bad gig, if you did it right, and the students went somewhere else to drink (maybe because of the jukebox), so it wasn't a bad place to be.

Of course, Pearsall thought, Joey Wolfson made it better. Joey was the mistress of ceremonies every Wednesday, and even if trivia night wasn't enough in itself, Pearsall thought Joey looked a hell of a lot better than the games on TV. She was medium height, with enough silver in her dark brown hair to put her on the right side of forty. The hair made a nice contrast to her fair skin and blue eyes, and she looked like someone comfortable being who she was.

After he had been coming to trivia night for a while, Pearsall struck up a conversation with Joey before the game started, while she was arranging her notes and making sure the P.A. was working. She turned the notes face-down when he approached. "I'm not a cheater," he said.

"I know," she said, "but it's kind of a habit." After a second, she added, "It's amazing how many people *will* cheat, just to get a twenty-five-dollar gift card here and to get their name on the wall for a week. After a while, you get to know which tables to check, which parties are going to have their phones out. Not you."

They picked up the conversation now and then, from Wednesday to Wednesday. He found out that there was a guy in Louisville who apparently ran a lot of these games, putting lists of questions together and sending them out each week. He'd find folks to emcee the games at bars all over the state, or maybe even the region. Apparently, the bars subscribed to the guy's service, and the host or hostess got paid a cut from the home base—Joey said it was forty bucks a week. Noah thought it was more complicated than he would have expected, but a lot of things were. "Tell him to include more music questions," he said. She laughed.

After a few weeks, Pearsall asked Joey if she might be free on some night other than Wednesday. She shook her head, even though she smiled.

"That's sweet, Noah. But I'll tell you the truth; I was in a really bad relationship before I came here. I mean," she paused, "*really* bad, like restraining order bad. So I guess I'm just not at a place where I'm ready to be with anyone right now. But you're nice, and I like seeing you here."

She smiled. "Besides, if we went out, it wouldn't be fair to the other players if my boyfriend was in the game, right?" He had dealt with harsher turndowns, and he figured right now wasn't necessarily forever, so he told her to let him know if she might be interested some time, and let it drop, and kept coming back on Wednesday nights. He even won every so often, which felt pretty good—a lot of other folks from the college played, and of course, the townies were there too (since the students weren't), and anyone could get hot on the right night. At some point, it's luck of the draw, depending on what the guy from Louisville came up with.

And really, it was a pretty good group of regulars each week. At the night's end, players might talk about the questions they got or didn't get, how they had seen that movie but couldn't remember the actor, or how Joey (or the guy in Louisville) could have thought *anybody* would know a given answer. Some weeks were solo nights, and others were team nights, so you got to meet people that way, too. And even if it was a bad night, at least you had the Third-Best juke playing between questions and rounds, and as Noah knew, Joey was pleasant, and nice to look at. She was smart, too—she had told him that she usually knew the answers to the questions without having to check the sheets. She did check the sheets, though; she said she had made mistakes before. She said that with a tone that made

Noah think she wasn't just talking about the game, but that wasn't his business, so he let it pass at face value.

◎

TRIVIA NIGHT BECAME a regular part of Noah's week. He'd get there early to get his seat under the TV, with a clear view of the DJ booth that Joey used as an "office" and scorer's table during the games. It was October of his third contract year, but the dean had told him that his evaluations had been good, that the kids liked him, and while he wasn't guaranteeing anything, if a tenure line became available, would Noah be interested in being considered?

So he was in a good mood as he walked from the parking lot into The Little End. He walked toward his corner table, but as he was sitting down, he heard a playoff game on the TV, and the bartender said, "No trivia tonight."

"How come?"

"Joey called—she said she slipped in the shower and would have to take the night off. Should be back next week," he said.

It happens, Noah thought, and forty dollars didn't seem worth the trouble of coming in. So he ordered an overpriced Mexican Coke at the bar, chatted with a couple of the other regulars, and after the baseball game was over, he listened to Gordon Lightfoot on the Third-Best. He was still in a good mood—the lure of tenure is a strong one, but he had hoped to share the good news with Joey between rounds.

Greensburg is a small enough town that eventually everyone sees each other at Walmart. Noah frequently said he could probably hold office hours there, so he wasn't really surprised when that Friday evening, as he was buying some soy sauce in what the store called the "international aisle," he saw Joey Wolfson pushing her cart toward the far end of the aisle. He called her name; she flinched as she turned, like a small bird being chased from a backyard feeder. But she stopped, and Noah closed the distance. "Feeling better?"

A frown flickered across her face, as if she were trying to recall a test question, but she said, "Oh, yeah. A little sore, but I'll be fine." Noah noticed a bottle of extra-strength ibuprofen in her cart, next to the pasta sauce and some bottled water.

"Yeah—you've gotta watch out for those attack showers," he said. "They'll jump you with no warning at all. Do you know how you fell?"

"I just misstepped as I was getting in. I tripped on the edge of the tub, went face-first into the wall, and half-slid down on my left knee." Looking closer, Noah saw some swelling on Joey's lower lip, and something not quite dramatic enough to be a shiner, beneath some concealer under her left eye.

Noah winced. "That had to hurt. Did you go get checked out?"

She gave her head a quick, small shake. "No—it wasn't that bad. It just uglied me up a little, and like I said, I'm kind of sore." *It would take more than that to ugly you up*, Noah thought, but he kept it to himself.

Instead, he asked if she was going to be at The Little End next Wednesday. She said she would, "because ten bucks is ten bucks."

He laughed. "Geddy Lee, right?" Bob and Doug McKenzie jokes—like she wasn't terrific enough.

"Five points," she said. She glanced toward the checkout lanes. "Um, I've got a ride waiting for me. I'd better get moving."

Dammit, he thought, and it must have shown, because she said, "Not like that, but I need to go." She looked at the bottle of Kikkoman in his hand. "Try not to drink all that in one place, okay?" And he laughed and said goodbye as she moved toward the front. He picked up a bottle of Sriracha to go with the soy sauce, and headed out himself.

Joey beat him out the door, but he saw her getting into the passenger side of a Ford truck that was held together by Bondo and holes. The truck had Indiana plates, and a Colts sticker decorated what was left of the tailgate. The driver—a guy ("*Not like that,*" Noah) reached across as if he were helping Joey up into the cab, but he seemed to have her wrist more than her hand as she stepped up. Noah put his bottles into the passenger's seat of his Nissan Versa, and made his way to the Chinese place to get some take-out.

Noah spent the weekend grading papers, and made it through the first half of the week's classes smoothly enough. In the cafeteria on Monday, he heard some students at the next table talking about a creepy old guy ("He was at least *forty*") who had been coming on to some of the Beta Xis at The Liar's Den. They had turned him down ("Because, *Ewww*"), and he had turned nasty before a couple of guys from the lacrosse team had braced him. "So he got into this shitty old truck in the parking lot and left rubber, but later we saw Mindy's car was keyed."

"You think it was him?"

"Well, Mindy *does* have her letters on the back window. But it's not like you can prove anything, you know?"

"God—what a creeper."

"I know, right?" And the girls stood and took their trays to the conveyor belt, and after a couple more minutes, Noah left as well.

◎

WEDNESDAY NIGHT CAME around as it tends to do, and Noah got there early enough to get his seat. He saw the clapped-out truck parked across the street from The Little End, but he didn't see anyone sitting in it, and he parked behind the building, in the lot by the back door.

He went in, got a Three Philosophers from Doc, and took his usual seat. He saw Joey in the booth, and went over to get a pencil and some answer sheets from her. As he made his way over, he saw an unfamiliar face across the way. The guy looked big—maybe not muscular, but hard fat. The goatee didn't quite make up for the double chin, and he scratched at some stick-and-pokes that had blurred on a tanned, hairy forearm. He didn't look biker mean, but had something of a bully vibe. He wore a ball cap, but whatever had been printed on it had long since flaked away. His black T-shirt had some sort of spiky logo—it could have been a heavy metal band's or it could have belonged to one of those companies that sells to MMA fans, like TapOut, Affliction, Eye Gouge, something like that. Noah didn't feel the need to go ask.

By then, he was at the booth, and as he picked up his pad and pencil, he glanced at Joey. Her frown could have been from getting the microphone cable untangled, but she looked even a little paler than usual, so he said, "Hey—you okay?"

"Fine," she said. Did she glance over across the room at the new guy? "Um, I'm really kind of busy now."

Really? The other players hadn't shown up yet, but Noah didn't want to be a jerk, so...

"Oh, okay. Catch you later," and back to his table. He sipped his beer and kept an eye on the TV over the bar, which had a replay of one of the previous weekend's college football games. A couple of punts and an interception later, it was time to start.

Each week's game was broken into three rounds of three questions each, with breaks after the rounds, and then a final round called the "two-minute drill": ten questions, separated by twelve seconds each, with a double score. During the first two rounds, contestants had the length of whatever song Joey chose from the Third-Best to jot down and turn in their answers.

Joey faded the jukebox down as the night's contestants settled in, and clicked her microphone on. After welcoming everyone and explaining the rules, she said the game would start in a few minutes, and reminded everyone that this was supposed to be fun, and that cheating took the fun out of it for everyone, so please refrain from using cell phones or other electronics while the game was in progress.

The regular players knew the spiel; a couple of newcomers nodded and put their phones in their pockets and purses. The stranger across the bar stared at Joey while he peeled the label off his bottle of PBR.

The early round had easy questions, with the degree of difficulty rising as the night went on. The process was simple, Noah thought: Hear the question, write the answer and your name on a slip, and hand it in to Joey. He aced the first round, handing the answers in within the first minute of the music each time, which gave him time to glance at the ball game—he figured *something* interesting must have happened in it, or why would they be replaying Sacramento State versus Eastern Washington, for God's sake? And of course, he also saw Joey. She still seemed tense, he thought. She had fluffed a couple of the questions on her script, but we all have bad nights sometimes.

True to form, the second round was tougher, but Noah made it through unscathed again, thanks to the knowledge that Burkina Faso had previously been known as Upper Volta. He glanced across the room, and saw that the stranger had five empties in front of him, and a couple of empty shot glasses as well. Apparently he had gone into the boilermaking business.

The third round was a little disappointing—Noah thought he should have known that Jim Bunning was the only Baseball Hall of Famer to serve in the U.S. Senate—but he also noticed that during the break before the two-minute drill, the stranger switched from his table in the corner to one between Joey's booth and Noah's table. Noah couldn't hear over the jukebox, but it looked like the man said something to Joey. She mouthed something that looked like "Not now," and the stranger jabbed her in the upper arm with his forefinger, like someone emphasizing a point. Joey started to shrink back as the man leaned forward, but the last song of the break was winding down, so she turned away and went to the microphone.

Noah thought her voice held a note of false cheer as she began to speak. "Okay, it's time for the Two-Minute Drill. Remember—points are doubled in this round, and a new question comes up every twelve seconds. After I'm done, you'll have two minutes to get it all written down, and, um, check your answers. Tonight's category...is music! Are we ready? Let's go!

"Question 1: This Beatles album contains the songs 'Another Girl,' 'You've Got to Hide Your Love Away,' and 'The Night Before.' Name the album.

"Question 2: The girl group the Angels took this song all the way to Number 1 on the charts. What was it?

"Question 3: This West Coast band's song "Let the Day Begin" was a theme song for Al Gore's 2000 presidential campaign. Who were they?

"Question 4: Henry Padovani was the original guitarist for what 80s superstars?

"Question 5: If the British punk band 999 had been American, what would they have been called?"

"Question 6: Finish the title of this Thin Lizzy album—*Live and* _____.

"Question 7: In the Talking Heads' concert movie *Stop Making Sense*, what opener features frontman David Byrne accompanied by a boom box?

"Question 8: Jacksonville's Ronnie and Johnny Van Zant have both served as singers for Lynyrd Skynyrd—" Someone at one of the other tables hollered "FREE BIRD!", and everyone chuckled. Joey continued. "What band was led by the third Van Zant Brother, Donnie?

"Question 9: What cheesy 1970 single was a hit for R. Dean Taylor?

"Question 10: What golden oldie featured a solo played on an early synthesizer called the Musitron?

"Okay, make sure you get those answers written down, check them over, and turn them in. You have two minutes." Noah had been writing all along. He reached his left hand into his pants pocket, where his phone was, as he glanced at his pad. As he walked up to Joey, past the man in the baseball hat, the phone fell from his pocket. He picked it up, dragging his thumb across the screen, and walking back to his position. Joey looked at his answers and nodded, and then the other players brough their answers forward. The man in the baseball cap sat there, apparently none the worse for his evening's drinks. *If I'd had that many,* Noah thought, *you could iron shirts on me.*

He recopied his answers when he took his seat again—he was sure they were right. Once more, Joey cut the sound on the jukebox.

"Well, it was a close game tonight, with only eight points separating first and third place." She named the runners up, and then said, "But tonight's winner, with forty-eight out of a possible fifty points, is Noah Pearsall. Come up and claim your gift card, Noah!" He walked forward, and heard the sirens before the blue lights started flashing through the front window.

Heads turned toward the front door, and then swiveled back as the man in the baseball cap yelled, "You set me up, you bitch!" He was reaching into his waistband when Noah hit him with his beer bottle. The stranger jerked his hands up, the pistol he had reached for tumbling to the floor to lie next to the freshly fallen baseball cap. Noah collapsed on top of it as if it were a fumbled football, which earned him a kick from the stranger, but he stayed on top of it as the police came through the door.

After the police had separated everyone, and after Joey told them about her restraining order and the outstanding assault warrants on the stranger, The Little End emptied out pretty quickly. Noah twisted to the left, trying to stretch where he had taken a boot to the ribs. Now it was Joey's turn to ask if he was all right.

"Yeah, I think so. But could you do me a favor?"

"I think I owe you one," Joey said. "What is it?"

"Well, I'd just like your autograph." She raised an eyebrow. He continued: "On my answer sheet." He handed her his copy.

Help
My Boyfriend's Back
(The) Call
(The) Police
911
Dangerous
Psycho Killer
.38 Special
Indiana Wants Me
Runaway

She laughed and signed the paper. "I was hoping you were as much of a music buff as I thought. Anything else?"

"Um, this may not be the best time, but—"

"Yes, Noah, we can get together sometime soon. Maybe this weekend?"

"Sure! But what about next week's game?"

She laughed, and he loved how it sounded. "Tell you what—why don't you help me keep score?"

"I can do that," Noah said.

He felt like a winner already.

The Puzzle Master

By David Morrell

"**M**ary left this on our front bench," Beth said.

"This" was a cardboard box about two inches thick and twelve inches square. It had an illustration on the front. Its contents rattled when Beth held it up.

"What is it?" Quentin asked.

"A jigsaw puzzle."

"Ah," Quentin said without interest.

Mary was their next-door neighbor. She'd left a note on the box: *We finished this yesterday. Had a lot of fun. Thought you might enjoy it.*

"A jigsaw puzzle," Quentin repeated.

"When I was a kid, my parents often had one spread out on a coffee table," Beth said. "Finding a piece that fit, I always laughed. Why do you look like that? Didn't you ever put a jigsaw puzzle together?"

Beth went to the dining-room table, picked up a cactus bowl, set it on a counter, and opened the box. The illustration on it showed what looked like a square in a New England village, with rustic shops, Victorian houses behind them, and a tree-covered hill in the distance. A farmer's market was in progress. Smiling families paused at tables that displayed tomatoes, peppers, apples, and jars of what a sign said was strawberry jam. Another sign advertised honeycombs. The title on the box said, *Summer Harvest.*

Beth opened the box and dumped the pieces on the table. They clattered softly.

"So many," Quentin said.

"The box says one thousand."

"That'll take forever."

"You finished your new book yesterday," Beth said. He wrote detective novels. "You're always nervous, waiting for your editor's reaction. You can clean your office and fix things around the house, or else you can help me sort these pieces."

Quentin sighed. "What's the principle?"

"Group them in colors. Anything that has a straight edge goes in its own pile."

"What if a piece is part green and part yellow, like the one you just picked up?"

"Decide which color there's more of."

"Looking for the straight pieces sounds easier." When Quentin finished, he asked, "Now what?"

"Sort the straight pieces into colors, also. Those eight white pieces look like they go together."

"Two of them have black spots." Quentin placed one straight piece to the right of the other. When they didn't fit, he tried them the opposite way and imagined hearing a click as he joined them. He looked at the illustration on the box. "A guy buying tomatoes has a Dalmatian on a leash." The dog was at the bottom of the puzzle, so Quentin moved the two white pieces with black spots in that direction. "The other white pieces have tiny gray lines."

"Part of the church steeple. High on the left." Beth pointed toward the illustration on the box.

He tried those white pieces in various combinations until they all clicked into place. He felt oddly good.

"You can do it faster if you pay attention to the shapes along with the colors," Beth said. "Some tabs point down. Others go straight to the side or up. Some pieces have as many as four tabs. Others have none. Some have as many as four slots for the tabs. Others don't have any."

Quentin noticed pieces that were green with little black lines in them. "I bet these are the grass on the bottom left."

"You're getting the idea."

He pointed toward the illustration. "There's a cat sitting in a window in this shop on the left."

"The closer you look, the more details you notice," Beth said.

"There's a squirrel in this tree. There's a line of crows on this wire," he said.

Three hours passed.

In the kitchen, a television news announcer described the day's accumulation of violence, greed, and hate, along with the increasing death count from disease, floods, earthquakes, forest fires, tornadoes, hurricanes, and various wars.

"When everything's falling apart—" Quentin pushed another puzzle piece exactly into place. "—it feels good to put something together. It's sort of like writing a novel, except a novel's never perfect. There's always another way to do it. With this puzzle, there's only *one* way."

Doing his customary research, he scanned the Internet and learned that jigsaw puzzles had reviewers the same as novels did. The reviewers assessed not only the art but also how sturdy the pieces were. Some puzzles were wooden. Some had round edges instead of straight ones. Some were three-dimensional and formed objects such as intricate clocks. There were jigsaw-puzzle tournaments and a movie, *Puzzle*, about a woman and a man who competed in them. Quentin learned that puzzle artists even had agents, copyrights, and royalty agreements, as authors did.

They finished *Summer Harvest* in two days.

"Ask Mary if we can borrow another," he said.

Its title was *Lakeside Idyll*. Like the first puzzle, the painting was by their neighbor's favorite puzzle artist, Morgan Case. The box showed part of a log cabin on the right. An elderly man sat on its porch, smiling at adults and kids on a lake that occupied the rest of the painting. Some of the people were swimming, others getting in a canoe at a dock, others waving to someone fishing in a rowboat. A hill rose from the far side of the lake. The sun gleamed above distant trees. Ripples glistened. A man stood on the left, facing an easel and canvas, painting the scene.

After Quentin and Beth emptied the box and started sorting, he noticed another group of pieces that were white with black spots. He glanced toward the image on the box and saw a Dalmatian jumping into the lake.

"There's a Dalmatian in *Summer Harvest*, too. You'd think the artist... What's his name?"

"Morgan Case."

"You'd think he'd bother to vary the details. Maybe use an Irish setter in this one. Red instead of white."

Beth pointed toward the image on the box, saying, "There's a blond-haired woman getting in a canoe."

"So...?"

"The other puzzle had a woman with blond hair buying a jar of something at the farmer's market. I remember finding the piece with the color of her hair," she said.

Because they'd returned *Summer Harvest* to Mary, Quentin brought the iPad from the kitchen and went to the website for the company that made both puzzles. He found the page for *Summer Harvest* and compared its artwork to the image on the box for *Lakeside Idyll*.

"Hard to see details in this website image, but the Dalmatian seems to have the same brown collar in each," Quentin said.

"The blond woman seems to have the same gold-colored bracelet," Beth said. "The elderly man smiling at the people on the lake—he's wearing bib overalls—looks like the same elderly man in bib overalls who's selling tomatoes at the farmers' market."

"The man holding the Dalmatian's leash in *Summer Harvest* looks like the man who's painting the scene in *Lakeside Idyll*," Quentin said.

That man wore spectacles. In his mid-forties, he was thin, of medium height, with dark hair that was tied in a ponytail.

Quentin noticed the white tip of something on the crest of the hill in the background. The detail was so tiny it was visible only on a puzzle piece and not in the illustration on the box.

"Is that sunlight glinting off a house?" he asked.

"No, it looks like the tip of a steeple," Beth said.

"A church steeple?" Quentin wondered. "Could that be the tip of the church in *Summer Harvest?* Are we supposed to get the feeling that the town's on the other side of the hill?"

He went to the ARTISTS section on the puzzle-company's website. Morgan Case, he learned, was a movie-poster artist, who also created jigsaw puzzles about an imaginary New England community called Granite Falls.

"Do all Case's puzzles fit together the way the pieces of each puzzle fit together?" Quentin wondered.

He ordered the rest of Case's puzzles—seven—from the website. Rather than borrow *Summer Harvest* again, he bought that puzzle, too.

After he and Beth completed *Lakeside Idyll* in two days, rather than take it apart as they had with *Summer Harvest*, Quentin slid it onto a section of cardboard and put it under the dining-room table.

By then, Fed Ex had delivered the box of puzzles Quentin had ordered. The first one he and Beth assembled was *Antique Paradise*. A smiling crowd perused old tables, chairs, cabinets, crockery, framed paintings, and a spinning wheel outside a red barn with an eight-pointed blue star above its open double doors.

"People in Granite Falls sure smile a lot," Beth said.

"There's that Dalmatian again," he noted.

"The man with the ponytail is looking at an old rocking chair," she added. "The blond woman's looking at a painting."

"Behind everything, above the trees—" Quentin pointed at a small detail in the finished puzzle. "—there's the white tip of the church steeple."

The next puzzle, *Halloween Happiness*, showed costumed children approaching a Victorian house that had a scarecrow in the front yard. A jack o' lantern glowed on a table next to the front door.

"The blond woman's at the open door, holding a bowl of what looks like candy," Beth said.

"The man with the ponytail is in the hallway behind her," Quentin said. "Their hands are showing. They each wear a wedding ring."

The next puzzle, *Festive Barbecue*, depicted a smiling crowd at a backyard party. The man with a ponytail cooked hamburgers on a grill. The blond woman carried a tray of glasses to a group at a table.

In *Autumn Frolic*, happy townspeople raked leaves on a rustic street. The blond woman laughed at someone leaping onto a pile of leaves. The man with the ponytail watched from a porch.

"He isn't smiling anymore," Beth noticed.

Quentin studied the piece that showed the ponytailed man's face. "You're right." He scanned the other completed puzzles arranged on cardboard on the floor. "In fact, when I look closely, he isn't smiling in several other puzzles."

Each of Case's puzzles had a year next to his signature. Quentin arranged them chronologically and learned that, starting five years earlier, Case had created two puzzles each year, except for the current year, in which only one puzzle had been released: a total of nine.

"In the first three puzzles, the ponytailed man smiles. But after that..." Quentin shook his head. "Why did he stop? What made him unhappy?"

"You're talking about him as if he's a real person."

"More like a character in a... Do you suppose these puzzles tell a story?"

"If they do, it isn't obvious."

"Maybe that's the point," Quentin said. "Maybe Case is playing a game. Everyone smiles in the first three puzzles. In the remaining six, one person alone looks unhappy. Case's paintings are so precise, he must have realized what he was doing."

"A hidden plot. That sounds like one of your detective novels," Beth said. "Makes me think of the clues hidden in photographs in—what's that movie by Antonioni?—*Blow-up*."

"Or the clues in audio recordings in Coppola's *The Conversation* and De Palma's *Blow Out*," Quentin said. "But here..."

"The clues are in jigsaw puzzles. So, why is the man with the ponytail suddenly unhappy?" Beth asked.

They studied the puzzles on the floor.

"Well...," Beth said.

"Yes?"

"Still thinking."

"How about...?" Quentin began.

"Yes?" Beth asked.

Quentin pointed. "In *Festive Barbecue*, the man with the ponytail is grilling hamburgers, but now I realize he isn't paying attention to them. He's frowning past the grill toward his wife, who's carrying a tray of drinks to a group at a table."

"But why is he looking at her like that?" Beth wondered. "Did they have an argument?"

They continued to study the puzzles.

"The handsome man at the table," Beth said. "The rest of the group is talking among themselves. He's the only one looking at the blond woman as she brings the drinks."

"Could be he's thirsty," Quentin said.

"For what?" Beth wondered. "Here in *Lakeside Idyll*, the blond woman is getting into a canoe with the handsome man. The pony-tailed man painting the scene is frowning past the easel toward them."

"And in *Antique Paradise*, the ponytailed man isn't paying attention to the rocking chair for sale in front of him," Quentin noticed. "He's frowning toward his wife in front of a painting. I used to think she was interested in the painting, but now it seems she's half turned toward the handsome man next to her."

"The painting," Quentin said. "It's tiny. Hard to tell. But does it look like the image for *Lakeside Idyll?*"

"Now that you mention it."

"Why would Case include a painting from another o f his puzzles?"

"Maybe he's reminding us," Beth decided.

"Of what?"

"That the ponytailed man is a painter. Could it be a self-portrait? Could the ponytailed man be Morgan Case?"

Neither of them said anything for a while.

"We still have one last puzzle to do," Quentin said.

It was titled *Christmas Splendor*. The box showed the always-smiling townspeople hanging Christmas lights and decorations in the town square. The man with the ponytail stood at the edge of the crowd. In the box's reduced image, his facial expression was hard to read.

With now-practiced speed, as if at a tournament, Quentin and Beth hurriedly set out the pieces. Instead of starting with the edges, they began the hard way by concentrating on the section of the crowd that featured the ponytailed man.

"He's not just frowning," Beth said as they assembled his face. "He's scowling."

"At what?" Quentin asked.

The image on the box showed the part of the Christmas crowd that the ponytailed man glared at.

"There's the handsome man. He's propping up a Christmas tree," Beth said.

"Where's the blond woman?" Quentin wondered.

They scanned the image on the box but didn't see her. They assembled more of the puzzle, searching for her.

"She isn't here," Quentin said.

"She *has* to be," Beth said. "She's in all the other puzzles."

But at midnight, after they inspected every piece and pushed the final one into place, the blond woman was nowhere to be seen.

"What happened to her?" Beth asked. She sounded like she wondered what had happened not just to a character in a story but to a real person.

Quentin walked along the row of puzzles. "Does Case want us to think that the wife was having an affair, that she and the man with the ponytail argued, that the marriage broke up and she left town?"

"*But the handsome man's here*," Beth emphasized. "The two of them didn't leave town together."

"Maybe the handsome man wasn't serious about the affair," Quentin said. "Maybe she left town alone."

"There aren't enough clues," Beth complained.

"Or else we need to look even closer. What's this on a hill past where everybody's putting up Christmas lights and decorations?"

"Tiny rectangular objects. A half dozen of them. Close together in a neat row. Don't you think it's strange that a Christmas jigsaw puzzle doesn't have snow?" Beth asked.

"Maybe *that's* a clue. Snow would have covered those distant objects. What's that narrow brown strip in front of one of the tiny rectangles? Maybe...?"

"What?"

"Are we looking at a cemetery? Are those gravestones? Is the brown strip..."

"A fresh grave? Do you think the reason the blond woman isn't in the puzzles anymore is she's dead?"

"Look at this row of shops," Quentin said.

"What about them?"

"All their names are blurred, except for one."

"The sign says it's a drug store. Does Case want us to conclude the wife died from an illness?"

"But that wouldn't explain why the husband keeps glaring at the other man," Quentin said.

"Unless she killed herself with an overdose of sleeping pills. The husband blames the other man for his wife's suicide."

"The final clue will be in Case's next puzzle," Quentin said. "Or rather, something *won't* be in the next puzzle: the handsome man. If I'm right, the man with the ponytail will have done something to him. The handsome man will be gone."

Quentin phoned the puzzle company, made his way through an answering system, and managed to reach a human being.

"My wife and I love Morgan Case's puzzles. We wonder when your company will release his next one?"

The young woman's voice—enthusiastic at the start—became solemn. "We won't."

"Do you mean he went to another puzzle company? Can you tell me its name?"

"No. He didn't go to another company. He..."

"Yes?"

"...died."

"Died?"

"In a fire." The woman's voice sounded so low and dejected that Quentin had to press his cell phone close to hear it. "Three months ago. His house burned down with him in it. We're still in shock. Mr. Case's puzzles had a special quality."

"As if the people and the town were real," Quentin said.

"Exactly," the woman said.

"I'm sorry," Quentin murmured.

He pushed the END button.

He and Beth searched the Internet. They found Morgan Case's obituary from three months earlier. It indicated that Case's wife of fifteen years had died suddenly a year earlier.

"Is 'suddenly' a euphemism for 'suicide'?" Beth wondered.

The obituary indicated that someone else had died in the fire: a man who was described as Case's closest friend.

"Maybe we don't need the next puzzle for us to know that the handsome man wouldn't have been in it."

"The man with the ponytail wouldn't have been in it, either."

"No," Quentin said. "A dead man can't paint a puzzle."

"We could have imagined everything," Beth said.

Quentin nodded.

"I feel as if I know these people," Beth said.

Quentin nodded again.

"I don't want to put jigsaw puzzles together anymore," Beth said.

Challenge Cube

By Kevin Quigley

My father hadn't moved much by the time I got back. I set my latte down on his bedside table and settled into the chair that had become so familiar over the last few days. The inventory was a little shocking: his thin arms, his pale legs, his withered chest. Back when I was small, he had been a giant to me. Towering. Imposing.

"Hey Dad," I sighed, placing the paper bag I'd been carrying on the floor between my feet. "I brought you something."

He rolled his eyes toward me, not speaking. He couldn't speak. His forehead was slick with sweat and I dabbed at it with the small towel I kept on the nightstand.

"It's a present, sort of. I couldn't believe it when I saw it. It—"

Now he made a loud groaning sound and squirmed a little on the bed, as much as his body would allow. He was hard to watch like this. I could remember him bursting in the front door every night, hale and hearty, his face ruddy, his sweaty hair plastered to his skull. To look at the man, you wouldn't have guessed him a thinking sort of fellow, let alone an intellectual. You could mistake him for any other public works guy; dungarees, orange reflectorized vest, hard hat plastered with stickers from the unions to which he belonged. He was the sort of man you imagined ate sloppy Italian sandwiches in his underwear in front of the television at night. A brooding man. A dull man.

Far from it. The only time we saw the version of my father that patched potholes and climbed into sewers is that brief span of minutes it took for him to get from the front door to the shower, where he would sing Billy Joel songs and scrub the grime of the day off. For the rest of the night, we got Smart Dad.

I was terrified of Smart Dad.

But that came later.

My first memory, the only one I cherished for so many years, starts with watching my dad throw back his head and bellow laughter. I had to have been five or six, and all of us were at the dining room table: Dad, Mom, my big sister Pepper, and Jessie and Jack, the twins. Family Game Night was every Tuesday and Thursday, and it was always a word game. He didn't see the point in something like Hungry Hungry Hippos or Candyland or Chutes and Ladders, which he said were all about greed and acquisition and chance. Once in a while, we could get him to budge on Clue, but wordplay was his coffee and cake. "Your mother and I aren't in the business of raising stupid children," he'd tell us, setting up the Scrabble board. Only it wasn't Scrabble that night, even though it was Dad's favorite. That night was the twins' turn to pick, and they always made it Boggle Night.

"Do you remember that night?" I asked my father. "It's always so clear in my mind. Everyone happy and laughing. I can smell Mom's perfume and the soap you used in the shower. Each of us kids got three cookies. And the box. The Boggle box. I was fascinated with it. The idea that you guys could have the game out and playing on one side of the table and that there was a picture of that *very same game* on the box...well, I know it probably sounds silly now, but the concept of that blew my little mind."

The Boggle cube was so simple and so elegant. There was a tray with sixteen square indentations set into a grid; sixteen oversized white dice fit into those squares, letters on every side. A square dome made of smoky-dark plastic fitted over the tray, and you were supposed to shake the whole thing so that the letters would face up all mixed up when you removed the dome. Pepper always shook too vigorously, earning disapproving glances from Mom, but never from Dad. Dad loved it when everyone else got into the game as much as he did.

From that jumble of letters, you were supposed to find words, joining letters up and across and diagonal, all while an (included!) plastic hourglass ran out white sand. Depicted on the box against a backdrop of appealing sky blue, two sets of hands were scratching out words on notepads that had emerged from the chaos: *eat* and *ate* and *tar* and *hats*. I didn't understand those words then, not me, not at six; now, they are seared into my memory.

The challenge was to get *unique* words, words that none of your opponents could find. And to make things just a little bit harder, the box advertised a red cube, darkly brilliant against a yellow banner emblazoned across the box's lower corner. This was the Challenge Cube, and on each of its sides it contained more difficult letters: M. K. And that weirdest and most exciting of all, Qu. If you played Qu, you got to count it as two letters. That was a concept I understood early, even when most of the other rules still seemed foggy. You could swap the Challenge Cube out for any of the regular letter cubes. When it was in play, the red leapt out in that sea of white, like a judgmental eye, staring and mocking and borderline furious.

Despite all the laughing and fun on the other side of the table, everyone took the game seriously. Even at six, I understood the value my father placed on word games, and what fierce competition it was to win the day and his continued approval. On the night of my first memory...

"The game was winding down. You were ahead, but not by much. Jack was closing in. Was that why you asked me to play? To shake him up?" My father stared at me. I knew he remembered, even if he couldn't say anything. "Your voice comes back, Dad. Booming, like it might shake the world down. 'Hey Petey! Wanna see if you can find a few words?'"

Everyone had stopped, like players in a game of Stop Stop Go. Had Mom favored him with a disapproving look then? Maybe, although that could be my memory playing tricks on me. She wouldn't have said anything, that's for sure. In the course of time, I would discover that my brothers and sister had been reading at a junior high level since they were four. And I? I couldn't read the words on the Boggle box.

But I don't really remember any of that. Like a movie you stumble on in the middle and start watching, my memories emerge from nothing with my turning away from the Boggle box and toward the Boggle game, and Dad grinning widely and asking me to join in the fun. How happy I had been! How thrilled to be included in his reckoning!

The room got silent as I looked into the grid. Looked *through* the grid. All at once, the letters seemed to be moving, shifting. Was it magic? Anxiety flooded me, although I didn't really know what anxiety was then. My therapist has been instrumental in helping me get to the core of my responses to my father's capricious love. When I finally found a word that made sense to me, I tapped the letters, one by one. D-O-U-L-A. The U faced up from the face of the red Challenge Cube.

"You were all in shock. None of the rest of you had managed to find that one, even though you and Mom had used a doula with the twins and me. Poor Pepper. What none of you knew was that it had been pure accident. The letters I thought I was picking were R-O-F-I-D. I couldn't sound them out and I had no idea what they meant next to one another. I may not have entirely understood the point of the game."

That didn't matter. Dad had clapped a hand on my back and smiled broadly and proclaimed his son a genius. Was there a measure of relief in that declaration? Memory is hard like that, but I think there was. I think, now with the virtue of knowing what life was like before that Boggle night, Dad decided that there wasn't a runt of the litter, like he'd feared. *All* of his children were smart.

"What a joy that must have been to you!" I declared, standing up and grabbing my coffee and pacing around the little room, trying to get a sense of how to proceed. It was stuffy in here, like sickrooms often are, but I didn't think opening a window was a good idea. Dad's eyes tracked me as I wandered around the room. What was he thinking? Did he remember as clearly as I did? Did he regret?

In any event, the celebration was short-lived. Dad took me book shopping a few days later and I picked out books whose covers appealed: books with dogs and horses and kids on bikes on the cover. The woman at the counter revealed the title to me, *Bike Buddies: Dan's Disappeared*. "It's a little scarier than the other ones, but my little guy says it's his favorite." I offered her a confused smile. How old was her little guy? How long had he been reading?

At dinner, we rarely spoke as a family; we were all supposed to read as we ate, and afterward, before Game Night, we sometimes talked about the books we were reading. I've mentioned this setup to friends later on in life, and all of them seem to think this was some idea of paradise on earth. I don't tell them that I couldn't read. I don't tell them that when I stared at the letters, sometimes they seemed to move on the page, to rearrange themselves in new and confusing ways.

"I couldn't really explain that then," I told my father now, settling back down at his bedside. "I didn't have the vocabulary for it. I don't even know if I knew I was faking it. I'd sit at the table and shovel beans and casserole and stuff into my mouth and turn pages just like everyone else. Maybe I thought it was a game. Maybe I didn't really understand the purpose of books. All I knew is that you wanted us to look at them, and so that's what I was going to do."

How long did it take him to find out I was full of shit? How long before I understood more clearly that something was wrong with me? There are websites and seminars now that proclaim that dyslexia is a gift, and maybe it is for some people. Not for me. Not in his house.

Dinner was over and everyone still sat around the kitchen table, books in hand. I was six, still six, so it must not have been long after Boggle Night. On some level, I had to know that I was supposed to be doing something beyond just looking at the pages. Hadn't the woman at the counter said this was scary? What was scary about looking at pages? But of course I knew: holding *Dan's Disappeared* in my hands, some of the anxiety I'd felt right before I accidentally spelled *doula* simmered in me again. Scary was the not knowing. Scary was the growing understanding that there might be repercussions for not knowing. Despite my memories cycling up where they had, there must have been echoes of what had come before. I was right to be scared.

As I stared down at the pages some of the words seemed to coalesce into something almost understandable. Everything else was like the Boggle cube on that box: a jumble of letters that people smarter than me could make sense of. "And you asked me what it was about. Do you remember that? You asked me what it was about."

Dad closes his eyes now, slowly and intentionally. Maybe it's to say he's sorry. It would be easy to forgive him now. My therapist says that the long journey of recovering from my past starts with forgiveness. I just don't know if I can.

"Bikes," I'd spat out at once. And then everything inside had me locked up. Silence spun out like yarn from a loom. One by one, everyone closed their books and looked at me. Even Pepper, who hadn't taken her nose out of the new Stephen King book since she'd come home from the library with it. That was when my father, like a levitating monolith, rose from his seat and stalked over to my spot near the end of the table. He grabbed the book from me, jabbing a finger at the page. "Read this sentence." It wasn't a voice but a growl.

Any second, I expected his jaw would open wide, wide, wide and swallow me whole.

I didn't speak. Didn't move. My mother, her tight mop of curly red hair and thin face offering no assurance, hesitantly suggested he was scaring me. Dad, his face now more brick-red than ruddy, pounded his fist onto the table surface. All the dishes rattled. "You shut your mouth if you don't want me to shut it for you," he snarled.

Real terror cycloned into me then, maybe the first of my whole life. *Maybe* is a tricky word, though. Smart Dad had scared me since before I could remember. A trickle of pee escaped me. I couldn't read the sentence. He knew I couldn't read the sentence. And before too long, he tore the book from my hands and hurled it with all his might. It fluttered briefly before connecting with the grandfather clock in the living room, then lay at its base like a bird who has murdered itself flying full force into a clean window. Without warning, he grabbed me by the back of the neck, and his callused hand scratched my skin so hard it felt as if was filled with little knives. For a moment, I thought he was going to lift me and fling me across the room, too. He could have. Maybe he wanted to. Instead, he marched me into the parlor, opened the closet door, and threw me inside. I collided with the back wall, and before the light from the parlor slimmed down to a thin line, then disappeared, my head swam. I felt like I was drowning in air. The door closed, and a lock turned. I collapsed to the hard wood floor, the pungent smells of winter shoes and wool jackets surrounding me out of context, making my darkness feel even more alien.

Deep in those shadows, I curled into a little ball, my knees and forehead against the floor, and cried as quietly as possible. I cried until I finally fell asleep.

Now I got up from the chair, turning my back on my father and going to the high window. The sun was going down now, and my coffee was getting cold. "It's the first time I could remember crying in that closet, but that doesn't mean I hadn't done it time and again before that. *All* of it felt familiar. Was it familiar to you? Comforting to you? Did it make you feel strong, Daddy? Or could you just not help it? My therapist has tried to help me understand your anger. Where it came from. Why it was directed the way it was. Sometimes I want to know. Mostly, I don't care."

It was Pepper who pulled me out of the closet hours later. Later on, she told me she found me sucking my thumb and still crying in my sleep. I woke up while she was cleaning off my legs. She was so sweet to me. She was always my favorite. She said, "I knew you got a slow start. Mom told me she was teaching you. She said you could read all of the Dr. Seuss books." But I couldn't. Every time I opened them, I could hear Mom's voice in my head, and every turn of the page. The words as written meant nothing to me. I just memorized what she said.

"You have to learn," she whispered, slipping me into bed. I shared a room with the twins and she didn't want to wake them up. "This is going to keep happening."

For the first time since dinner, I spoke. "Did he ever put you in the closet?"

"God, yes," she said. "I got it bad because I was the first. I *had* to read at four. I'm surprised he gave you this long. Maybe it's because you're the baby."

"I'm not a baby," I said to her, but without conviction. I'd peed myself and sucked my thumb that night.

"The first time I came home with a B, he broke my arm. Mom was screaming but he still put me in the closet. I was there for an hour. He wouldn't let Mom come with us to the hospital and he told me on the way that if I ever embarrassed him like that again, he was going to call up his old Army buddies and have them cut me up. Cut up my face." I thought of her shaking the Boggle cube so hard that the strain showed in her face. Was she remembering that night in the hospital, and what my father promised her? Of course she was. It wasn't vigor. It was terror.

Now I watched my father, lying helpless and immobile on this bed in this terrible room. It was impossible to drum up compassion for him, even in this state. "You said you'd cut up her face, Dad. Her *face*. Because she wasn't smart enough for you. Did Mom know that? I don't think she did. You know Mom killed herself, right? Jessie told me. Her and Jack both."

Eventually Dad didn't even let me try at Game Night, even though I had the growing suspicion that he liked watching me fail. He just put me in the closet before bringing out the Scrabble or Boggle or Bananagrams sets. Every night, Mom would read to me, desperately trying to get me to understand the words, sounding them out one by one. It helped some, but it was difficult to learn anything when she broke down crying so often.

"I suppressed a lot of this," I told my father, standing by the window and watching him. He blinked once, twice. Was that a yes or no? "I had to. For a little while, I kept remembering Game Night as a time when everyone laughed and got along. That first memory was everyone laughing hysterically. I was the fly in the ointment. I was the odd man out. Everyone was laughing in spite of me. Only that wasn't it, Dad, was it?"

Jessie had been shaking as he recalled it, the hellish cheer and the hideous laughter. I almost stopped him, not wanting to curdle my only good memory. "We were all on the verge of screaming," he told me years later. "Jack especially. Sometimes he started laughing so hard he couldn't stop, and I would bring him up to bed early. I wasn't surprised when I found out what he did. Even before you came along, Petey, Dad was cruel. After...his cruelty took on the tenor of invention." One of the unspoken rules was that you were supposed to be reading a new book every night. If you hadn't devoted enough time to reading in the day, enough to finish the book you were on, you were slow and stupid and unworthy of Dad's favor. More than once, he dumped Jack's dinner into a dog bowl and made him eat it on all fours, because dogs were dumb creatures and Jack was nothing but a dog.

"Sometimes he kicked him over. Sometimes he hit him with his belt. Made him eat faster."

"What about you?" I asked.

A tear escaped him. "Nothing so banal. You see, I knew that I had to have a new book at dinner. Often, then, I wouldn't finish the stuff I was reading. I'd just grab something new from the library pile. I don't know how he found out. But one night, after we'd returned our library books and gotten new ones, Dad asked me how the ending of one of my old books had gone. I think it was *Great Gatsby*. We usually got to pick our own books but Dad made sure we were versed in the classics. He asked me the ending and I made something up. I thought I was going into the closet, but you were already there. He got up from the table and came back with two things: his own beat-up paperback copy of the novel…and his gun. It was shiny and silver with a snub nose and he held it to my head and told me to finish the book."

Mom had screamed and he'd hit her. Jack and Pepper had simply watched in horror as Jessie struggled to read as cogently as possible, knowing that there was going to be a quiz, and knowing that if he failed the quiz, Dad was going to splatter his brains everywhere.

"I've wondered a lot if you were crazy," I told Dad now, coming back to him. "My therapist says we're not supposed to use that word. She tells me that, from your point of view, you were just trying to help us. Make us smarter so we'd have the tools to succeed in the world. You didn't want us working grunt jobs like you'd been forced to take out of high school because you barely graduated. Your whole journey of learning and betterment might have been inspiring if it weren't so fanatical. My therapist says there's no one so intense as the newly converted. Intense. That's so mild a word for what you did."

It was on the tip of my tongue to ask him why he didn't have me tested. Dyslexia and learning difficulties weren't as well-understood then as they are now, but it's not like they were unheard of. He could have made a project out of me with some patience and the right tools and training. But Dad couldn't answer now and besides, I knew the reason. If he could pick himself up and make himself smarter, his children should be able to do the same. In my father's imagination, all that made sense. A learning specialist, developmental training, textbooks that helped me tackle my issue...none of that would have fit his idea of learning by brute force.

He didn't want to understand me. What he understood was pain, intimidation, and humiliation. By the time I was seven and in second grade, that had grown abundantly clear. But I believed, despite all evidence to the contrary, that making my father proud of me would take all that away. If I could do the things he'd asked of me, I wouldn't have to be afraid anymore, ever. That euphoric feeling of that first Boggle night could follow me everywhere, always. It would live in my heart and I could build new memories from it, good ones. So when Dad enrolled me in the school spelling bee, determination to make him love me like he had the night he thought I spelled *doula* nearly overwhelmed my terror. Nearly.

"You know what I did?" I asked him, finding myself laughing a little. "One day after school, I pulled the Boggle set down from the shelf and slipped the challenge cube in my pocket. It was going to be my good luck charm. All those difficult letters, white against the red die; if I could only absorb those letters, I knew that I could win the bee. If I did that, I would stop going into the closet. Every night before bed, I would pull that cube out and stare at it in the glow from my nightlight, trying to make sense of the letters, trying to understand what was so wrong with me that I couldn't."

For a long while after, I couldn't understand why the whole family didn't come to the spelling bee that night. Mom had offered some token protest about the very concept of me doing it, but he shut her up. He was good at shutting up dissenting opinions, and when you live with a maniac long enough, you learn not to have dissenting opinions too often. I spent the drive over to the school envious of them, getting to spend a night without my father. I didn't know that they were busy packing. I didn't know that they were trying to escape.

I didn't know that they were abandoning me.

"In the scheme of things, it wasn't long," I told him now, dabbing at his sweaty forehead. "Court was terrifying, but I was used to terrifying. Still, she had to have known how you would take it when you came home with me and she and the others were gone. There had to be a thought in her head that you would hurt me so badly I would never recover. I hated her for a long time for that. But that forgiveness thing works for almost everybody. Eventually, I understood where she'd been coming from. How could I not?"

Did he think, in his own twisted wisdom, that his private humiliations simply weren't enough to turn me into the genius he needed me to be? Was he convinced that my reluctance to learn would fade away if the whole school saw just how stupid I was? I'd managed to hide so much of my problems from my teachers, who knew I wasn't a fast learner but also knew I wasn't stupid. If they read stories aloud to the class and asked us questions after, I was the first to raise my hand. I'd gotten good at memorizing things. Pepper and Jamie and Jack helped me with the little homework I had. It might have all been enough for me to squeak through.

But there was nowhere to hide when you were standing on the stage in the school auditorium, looking out at the sea of parents' faces. Some of them were smiling, proud of their children even before the bee began. I couldn't understand that, not then. Love, in my experience, was a conditional thing. You either earned it or you got the closet. Or worse. Dad sat right in the front row, watching me with crossed arms and a stern expression. A statue that hands down judgment.

"I watched your face. The whole time I watched you. I think that even if I had been able to spell or read right, the presence of you would have unnerved me too much to go on. When they called my name, I slipped my hand in my pocket and there was the Challenge Cube, red and heavy and comforting. The proctor told me my word was *harpsichord*. When he said that, your face changed. Do you remember that, Dad? Do you remember your face changing?"

Not stoic, as he had been; not furious, as I'd feared. No, the expression I'd seen on my father's face in that auditorium was glee. Over the years, I've tried hard to puzzle out whether this was a false memory, or something like confirmation bias. All these years later, I don't think so. Neither does my therapist. Maybe he thought that this was going to be the moment that changed me or shocked me into being smart. That a massive failure like this was going to change me fundamentally, bring me in line with the rest of his family. But I think he was just excited to watch his stupid child get humiliated in public. If I wasn't going to be smart, I was going to be shamed.

"I don't know if seven-year-olds have heart attacks," I told him now. "But I thought I might have one on that stage. I stared down at you. *Harpsichord*. The word was *harpsichord*." My pulse slamming in my throat, constricting my brain. I could picture the instrument in my head. I knew what it *was*. *Harpsichord*. Dad in the front row, and was that when he started laughing? I had to pee. The silence spun out. *Harpsichord*. Even now I can't see that word without panicking, without wanting to cry, without wanting to scream my throat bloody.

My father's eyes locked on mine, full of that awful joy. I said the letter "A," and that's when my stomach lurched and I started puking all over the stage. The smell hit me. Chaos erupted. I started sobbing and then his arms were around me, my father's arms, and I thought for a moment he was going to finally comfort me, hold me, tell me I was good and that he was still proud of me. Then we were out of the auditorium and outside and the night air bit my sweaty forehead and cheeks and ravaged my eyes and he said, "If you puke on me or in my car, I will kill you. Do you understand that, you retard? I will murder you and no one will cry for you. You don't want to learn the words, then choke on them. *Choke* on them."

The ride home was silent. His good cheer had dissipated and when we got home, he bellowed for the rest of the family to come down and witness his idiot child in the depths of his humiliation. But they weren't there. Maybe they were already checked into the motel I wouldn't see for two more days. Maybe they were still driving.

The irony was that I figured it out before he did. I went into my bedroom and the folder with Jack's baseball cards was gone, and Jessie's small pile of notebooks where he wrote his stories. They had vanished, along with Pepper and Mom. Dad spent over an hour searching the house, calling their names from the back porch. He even phoned the local Dairy Queen where he took us sometimes if he was in an especially generous mood. Only slowly did he figure out that his family had left him. Only gradually did he realize that only I was left.

But I knew. And for a very long time, I hated my mother and my brothers and sister for leaving me with the monster. I hid in the parlor closet, maybe reasoning that if he knew I was punishing myself, he wouldn't feel a need to hurt me any more than he already had. I could taste vomit on my tongue and my throat was on fire. The Challenge Cube was in my pocket still and I grabbed at it, wishing in the futile darkness that maybe now its magic would protect me.

"Of course it didn't. Were you drunk when you finally pulled me out of there? I don't think you were. It would be convenient to blame that. You twisted my foot so hard you sprained my ankle. The doctor found that later. I thought about Pepper telling me how you broke her arm and didn't take her to the hospital for an hour."

He had a hardcover book in his hand. I can't entirely trust my memory here, but I'm pretty sure it was James Herriot's *All Things*

Bright and Beautiful. I was screaming. Dad was screaming. And my only thought was, *He's going to try to make me read that whole thing and kill me when I can't.* That's all I had time to think before the book came whistling down on my face, and the pain swallowed everything rational. The book didn't stop coming down, and soon the darkness took even the pain away.

I would swim out of that darkness only a few times over the next few days. Did my mother's conscience finally overwhelm her enough to come rescue me in the middle of the night, stealing me from my bed like a kidnapper, hand clamped over my mouth as she moved silently back down the stairs and out into the night? Or had that been the plan all along? I didn't resist her when she came, even though I didn't know what was happening until I was back in the car. Either I was too weak, or I was ready for anything to take me away from my father's anger. Kidnapping sometimes meant that the kids got killed. I was ready for that, too.

Now, Dad watched me as I reached under the chair and produced the bag I'd brought in with me. "I've been looking for one of these all week," I told him. I'd found it in one of the dusty antique shops lining the streets of this tourist town where nobody knows me other than a face in the crowd. After all that looking, there it had been, serendipitously at eye level, as if it wanted me to find it. The same pale blue box. Those two sets of hands on the front, and the lists of words I can now read easily. Time and patience, that's all it took eventually. But they, unlike anger and fanaticism, were things my father had in short supply.

"Vintage. I paid twenty bucks for it. I wanted it to be the exact one," I said. "I checked to make sure all the cubes were in there. The Challenge Cube, too."

I opened the Boggle box and presented it to my father, whose eyes were wide and staring. They blinked up at my face and then back down to the box. Did he look scared? I couldn't tell. The only time I remember him really looking scared was when the judge passed down the sentence, much of which had to do with how many times he had hurt me in the few days I was alone with him. They'd brought me into court with my head bandaged and showed the jury my back, which was still purple with welts. The jury didn't need much convincing.

He'd been sentenced to twelve years. He got out in less than half that. I worried for a while that he would come after us. That he would want revenge. But he never did. He'd come out a changed man. I guess that was good for him. By all accounts, he lived a life of quiet solitude now, reading and working in a garden and bothering nobody. His intimidating size diminished. His rage dwindled. I found out all this from Pepper, who had been in occasional, fraught contact with him. I want to be happy for him. I want to forgive him. But I don't.

I removed the ball gag from his mouth and he gasped in a breath. His voice was raw and cracked with panic. Sudden tears dribbled down his cheeks. "Jesus Christ, Peter, what the fuck do you think you're doing?"

His wrists and ankles had chafed significantly from pulling against the ropes with which I'd secured him to the bed. The red weals screamed like fire in the dim room. I bet he had a whopper of a headache from the chloroform, but that's probably dissipated by now. I pulled the Challenge Cube from my pocket, the one I started carrying with me when I was only seven years old. The letters have mostly worn off, but I can recite them by heart. I. Qu. M. K. L. U. That Qu, the only one you can count it as two letters. Whenever I play with my friends, I pray for that Qu. I'm very good at Boggle these days.

"You see, Dad, I don't think it was about us being smart at all. I think it was about you not being dumb. Anything that threatened that idea of yourself had to be punished. Am I close?"

"You have to believe me," he pleaded. "All I wanted was the best for you and your brothers and sister. And your mom. The mistakes I've made, I've paid for them. I've rehabilitated, Peter."

"After all these years," I told him. "I never realized how often you sound so stupid."

I reached out and pinched his nose. His mouth gaped open and I dropped my Challenge Cube into it. It rattled against his back teeth, and that's when I tipped his head back so that it would travel a little further down. His hot breath stopped tickling my wrist. I let his nose go and watched his eyes bulge out. If he managed to swallow that one, there were sixteen more cubes to go. Plus my new Challenge Cube, although I wanted to leave this room with that in my pocket.

"They're your words, Dad," I murmured to him, wiping flop sweat from his brow as he bucked and convulsed on the bed. "So choke on them. *Choke* on them."

That's when I started to laugh.

A Tip on a Turtle

By Robert Silverberg

The sun was going down in the usual spectacular Caribbean way, disappearing in a welter of purple and red and yellow streaks that lay across the wide sky beyond the hotel's manicured golf course like a magnificent bruise. It was time to head for the turtle pool for the pre-dinner races. They held the races three times a day now, once after lunch, once before dinner, once after dinner. Originally the races had been nothing more than a casual diversion, but by now they had become a major item of entertainment for the guests and a significant profit center for the hotel.

As Denise took her place along the blazing bougainvillea hedge that flanked the racing pool a quiet deep voice just back of her left ear said, "You might try Number Four in the first race."

It was the man she had noticed at the beach that afternoon, the tall tanned one with the powerful shoulders and the tiny bald spot. She had been watching him snorkeling along the reef, nothing visible above the surface of the water but his bald spot and the blue strap of his goggles and the black stalk of the snorkel. When he came to shore he walked right past her, seemingly lost in some deep reverie; but for a moment, just for a moment, their eyes had met in a startling way. Then he had gone on, without a word or even a smile. Denise was left with the feeling that there was something tragic about him, something desperate, something haunted. That had caught her attention.

Was he down here by himself? So it appeared. She too was vacationing alone. Her marriage had broken up during Christmas, as marriages so often did, and everyone had said she ought to get away for some midwinter sunshine. And, they hadn't needed to add, for some postmarital diversion. She had been here three days so far and there had been plenty of sunshine but none of the other thing, not for lack of interest but simply because after five years of marriage she was out of practice at being seduced, or shy, or simply uneasy. She had been noticed, though. And had done some noticing.

She looked over her shoulder at him and said, "Are you telling me that the race is fixed?"

"Oh, no. Not at all."

"I thought you might have gotten some special word from one of the hotel's boys."

"No," he said. He was very tall, perhaps too tall for her, with thick, glossy black hair and dark, hooded eyes. Despite the little bald spot he was probably forty at most. He was certainly attractive enough, almost movie-star handsome, and yet she found herself thinking unexpectedly that there was something oddly asexual about him. "I just have a good feeling about Number Four, that's all. When I have a feeling of that sort it often works out very well." A musical voice. Was that a faint accent? Or just an affectation?

He was looking at her in a curiously expectant way.

She knew the scenario. He had made the approach; now she should hand him ten Jamaican dollars and ask him to go over to the tote counter and bet them on Number Four for her; when he returned with her ticket they would introduce themselves; after the race, win or lose, they'd have a daiquiri or two together on the patio overlooking the pool, maybe come back to try their luck on the final race, then dinner on the romantic outdoor terrace and a starlight stroll under the palisade of towering palms that lined the beachfront promenade, and eventually they'd get around to settling the big question:

his cottage or hers? But even as she ran through it all in her mind she knew she didn't want any of it to happen. That lost, haunted look of his, which had seemed so wonderfully appealing for that one instant on the beach, now struck her as simply silly, melodramatic, overdone. Most likely it was nothing more than his modus operandi: women had been falling for that look of masterfully contained agony at least since Lord Byron's time, probably longer. But not me, Denise told herself.

She gave him a this-leads-nowhere smile and said, "I dropped a fortune on these damned turtles last night, I'm afraid. I decided I was going to be just a spectator this evening."

"Yes," he said. "Of course."

It wasn't true. She had won twenty Jamaican dollars the night before and had been looking forward to more good luck now. Gambling of any sort had never interested her until this trip, but there had been a peculiar sort of pleasure last night in watching the big turtles gliding toward the finish line, especially when her choices finished first in three of the seven races. Well, she had committed herself to the sidelines for this evening by her little lie, and so be it. Tomorrow was another day.

The tall man smiled and shrugged and bowed and went away. A few moments later Denise saw him talking to the leggy, freckled woman from Connecticut whose husband had died in some kind of boating accident the summer before. Then they were on their way over to the tote counter and he was buying tickets for them. Denise felt sudden sharp annoyance, a stabbing sense of opportunity lost.

"Place your bets, ladies gemmun, place your bets!" the master of ceremonies called.

Mr. Eubanks, the night manager—shining black face, gleaming white teeth, straw hat, red-and-white-striped shirt—sat behind the counter, busily ringing up the changing odds on a little laptop computer. A boy with a chalkboard posted them. Number Three was the favorite, three to two; Number Four was a definite long shot at nine to one. But then there was a little flurry of activity at the counter, and the odds on Four dropped abruptly to five to one. Denise heard people murmuring about that. And then the tote was closed and the turtles were brought forth.

Between races the turtles slept in a shallow, circular concrete-walled holding tank that was supplied with sea water by a conduit running up from the beach. They were big green ones, each with a conspicuous number painted on its upper shell in glowing crimson, and they were so hefty that the brawny hotel boys found it hard going to carry them the distance of twenty feet or so that separated the holding tank from the long, narrow pool where the races were held.

Now the boys stood in a row at the starting line, as though they themselves were going to race, while the glossy-eyed turtles that they were clutching to their chests made sleepy graceless swimming motions in the air with their rough leathery flippers and rolled their spotted green heads slowly from side to side in a sluggish show of annoyance. The master of ceremonies fired a starter's pistol and the boys tossed the turtles into the pool. Graceless no longer, the big turtles were swimming the moment they hit the water, making their way into the blue depths of the pool with serene, powerful strokes.

There were six lanes, separated by bright yellow ribbons, but of course the turtles had no special reason for remaining in them. They roamed about randomly, perhaps imagining that they had been returned to the open sea, while the guests of the hotel roared encouragement: "Come on, Five! Go for it, One! Move your green ass, Six!"

The first turtle to touch any part of the pool's far wall was the winner. Ordinarily it took four or five minutes for that to happen; as the turtles wandered, they sometimes approached the finish line but didn't necessarily choose to make contact with it, and wild screams would rise from the backers of this one or that as their turtle neared the wall, sniffed it, perhaps, and turned maddeningly away without making contact.

But this time one of the turtles was swimming steadily, almost purposefully, in a straight line from start to finish. Denise saw it moving along the floor of the pool like an Olympic competitor going for the gold. The brilliant crimson number on its back, though blurred and mottled by the water, was unmistakable.

"Four! Four! Four! Look at that bastard go!"

It was all over in moments. Four completed its traversal of the pool, lightly bumped its hooked snout against the far wall with almost contemptuous satisfaction, and swung around again on a return journey to the starting point, as if it had been ordered to swim laps. The other turtles were still moving about amiably in vague circles at mid-pool.

"Numbah Four," called the master of ceremonies. "Pays off at five to one for de lucky winnahs, yessah yessah!"

The hotel boys had their nets out, scooping up the heavy turtles for the next race. Denise looked across the way. The leggy young widow from Connecticut was jubilantly waving a handful of gaudy Jamaican ten-dollar bills in the face of the tall man with the tiny bald spot. She was flushed and radiant; but he looked down at her solemnly from his great height without much sign of excitement, as though the dramatic victory of Number Four had afforded him neither profit nor joy nor any surprise at all.

The short, stocky, balding Chevrolet dealer from Long Island, whose features and coloration looked to be pure Naples but whose name was like something out of *Brideshead Revisited*—Lionel Gregson? Anthony Jenkins?—something like that—materialized at Denise's side and said, "It don't matter which turtle you bet, really. The trick is to bet the boys who throw them."

His voice, too, had a hoarse Mediterranean fullness. Denise loved the idea that he had given himself such a fancy name.

"Do you really think so?"

"I know so. I been watching them three days, now. You see the boy in the middle? Hegbert, he's called. Smart as a whip, and damn strong. He reacts faster when the gun goes off. And he don't just throw his turtle quicker, he throws it harder. Look, can I get you a daiquiri? I don't like being the only one drinking." He grinned. Two gold teeth showed. "Jeffrey Thompkins, Oyster Bay. I had the privilege of talking with you a couple minutes two days ago on the beach."

"Of course. I remember. Denise Carpenter. I'm from Clifton, New Jersey, and yes, I'd love a daiquiri."

He snagged one from a passing tray. Denise thought his Hegbert theory was nonsense—the turtles usually swam in aimless circles for a while after they were thrown in, so why would the thrower's reaction time or strength of toss make any difference?—but Jeffrey Thompkins himself was so agreeably real, so cheerfully blatant, that she found herself liking him tremendously after her brush with the Byronic desperation of the tall man with the little bald spot. The phonied-up name was a nice capping touch, the one grotesque bit of fraudulence that made everything else about him seem more valid. Maybe he needed a name like that where he lived, or where he worked.

Now that she had accepted a drink from him, he moved a half step closer to her, taking on an almost proprietary air. He was about two inches shorter than she was.

"I see that Hegbert's got Number Three in the second race. You want I should buy you a ticket?"

The tall man was covertly watching her, frowning a little. Maybe he was bothered that she had let herself be captured by the burly little car dealer. She hoped so.

But she couldn't let Thompkins get a ticket for her after she had told the tall man she wasn't betting tonight. Not if the other one was watching. She'd have to stick with her original fib.

"Somehow I don't feel like playing the turtles tonight," she said. "But you go ahead, if you want."

"Place your bets, ladies gemmun, place your bets!"

Hegbert did indeed throw Number Three quickly and well, but it was Five that won the race, after some minutes of the customary random noodling around in the pool. Five paid off at three to one. A quick sidewise glance told Denise that the tall man and the leggy Connecticut widow had been winners again.

"Watch what that tall guy does in the next race," she heard someone say nearby. "That's what I'm going to do. He's a pro. He's got a sixth sense about these turtles. He just wins and wins and wins."

But watching what the tall man did in the next race was an option that turned out not to be available. He had disappeared from the pool area somewhere between the second and third races. And so, Denise noted with unexpectedly sharp displeasure, had the woman from Connecticut.

Thompkins, still following his Hegbert system, bet fifty on Number Six in the third race, cashed in at two to one, then dropped his new winnings and fifty more besides backing Number Four in the fourth. Then he invited Denise to have dinner with him on the terrace. What the hell, she thought. Last night she had had dinner alone: very snooty, she must have seemed. It hadn't been fun.

In the uneasy first moments at the table they talked about the tall man. Thompkins had noticed his success with the turtles also. "Strange guy," he said. "Gives me the creeps—something about the look in his eye. But you see how he makes out at the races?"

"He does very well."

"Well? He cleans up! Can't lose for winning."

"Some people have unusual luck, I suppose."

"This ain't luck. My guess is maybe he's got a fix in with the boys—like they tell him what turtle's got the mojo in the upcoming race. Some kind of high sign they give him when they're lining up for the throw-in."

"How? Turtles are turtles. They just swim around in circles until one of them happens to hit the far wall with his nose."

"No," said Thompkins. "I think he knows something. Or maybe not. But the guy's hot for sure. Tomorrow I'm going to bet the way he does, right down the line, race by race. There are other people here doing it already. That's why the odds go down on the turtle he bets, once they see which one he's backing. If the guy's hot, why not get in on his streak?"

He ordered a white Italian wine with the first course, which was grilled flying fish with brittle orange caviar globules on the side. "I got to confess," he said, grinning again, "Jeffrey Thompkins not really my name. It's Taormina, Joey Taormina. But that's hard to pronounce out where I live, so I changed it."

"I did wonder. You look—is it Neapolitan?"

"Worse. Sicilian. Anybody you meet named Taormina, his family's originally Sicilian. Taormina's a city on the east coast of Sicily. Gorgeous place. I'd love to show you around it some day."

He was moving a little too fast, she thought. A lot too fast.

"I have a confession too," she said. "I'm not from Clifton anymore. I moved back into the city a month ago after my marriage broke up."

"That's a damn shame." He might almost have meant it. "I'm divorced too. It practically killed my mother when I broke the news. Well, you get married too young, you get surprised later on." A quick grin: he wasn't all that saddened by what he had learned about her. "How about some red wine with the main course? They got a good Brunello here."

A little later he invited her, with surprising subtlety, to spend the night with him. As gently as she could she declined. "Well, tomorrow's another day," he said cheerfully. Denise found herself wishing he had looked a little wounded, just a little.

◎

THE DAYTIME ROUTINE was simple. Sleep late, breakfast on the cottage porch looking out at the sea, then a long ambling walk down the beach, poking in tide pools and watching ghostly gray crabs scutter over the pink sand. Mid-morning, swim out to the reef with snorkel and fins, drift around for half an hour or so staring at the strangely contorted coral heads and the incredibly beautiful reef creatures. It was like another planet, out there on the reef. Gnarled coral rose from the sparkling white sandy ocean floor to form fantastic facades and spires through which a billion brilliant fishes, scarlet and green and turquoise and gold in every imaginable color combination, chased each other around. Every surface was plastered with pastel-hued sponges and algae. Platoons of tiny squids swam in solemn formation. Toothy, malevolent-looking eels peered out of dark caverns. An occasional chasm led through the coral wall to the deep sea beyond, where the water was turbulent instead of calm, a dark blue instead of translucent green, and the ocean floor fell away to invisible depths. But Denise never went to the far side. There was something ominous and threatening about the somber outer face of the reef, whereas here, within, everything was safe, quiet, lovely.

After the snorkeling came a shower, a little time spent reading on the porch, then the outdoor buffet lunch. Afterwards a nap, a stroll in the hotel's flamboyant garden, and by mid-afternoon down to the beach again, not for a swim this time, but just to bake in the blessed tropical sun. She'd worry about the possibility of skin damage some other time: right now what she needed was that warm caress, that torrid all-enfolding embrace. Two hours dozing in the sun, then back to the room, shower again, read, dress for dinner. And off to the turtle races. Denise never bothered with the ones after lunch—they were strictly for the real addicts—but she had gone every evening to the pre-dinner ones.

A calm, mindless schedule. Exactly the ticket, after the grim, exhausting domestic storms of October and November and the sudden final cataclysm of December. Even though in the end she had been the one who had forced the breakup, it had still come as a shock and a jolt: she too getting divorced, just another pathetic casualty of the marital wars, despite all the high hopes of the beginning, the grand plans she and Michael had liked to make, the glowing dreams. Everything dissolving now into property squabbles, bitter recriminations, horrifying legal fees. How sad: how boring, really. And how destructive to her peace of mind, her self-esteem, her sense of order, her this, her that, her everything. For which there was no cure, she knew, other than to lie here on this placid Caribbean beach under this perfect winter sky and let the healing slowly happen.

Jeffrey Thompkins had the tact—or the good strategic sense—to leave her alone during the day. She saw him in the water, not snorkeling around peering at the reef but simply chugging back and forth like a blocky little machine, head down, arms windmilling, swimming parallel to the hotel's enormous ocean frontage until he had reached the cape just to the north, then coming back the other way. He was a formidable swimmer with enough energy for six men.

Quite probably he was like that in bed, too, but Denise had decided somewhere between the white wine and the red at dinner last night that she didn't intend to find out. She liked him, yes. And she intended to have an adventure of some sort with *someone* while she was down here. But a Chevrolet dealer from Long Island? Shorter than she was, with thick hairy shoulders? Somehow she couldn't. She just couldn't, not her first fling after the separation. He seemed to sense it too, and didn't bother her at the beach, even had his lunch at the indoor dining room instead of the buffet terrace. But she suspected she'd encounter him again at evening turtle-race time.

Yes: there he was. Grinning hopefully at her from the far side of the turtle pool, but plainly waiting to pick up some sort of affirmative signal from her before coming toward her.

There was the tall dark-haired man with the tiny bald spot, too. Without the lady from Connecticut. Denise had seen him snorkeling on the reef that afternoon, alone, and here he was alone again, which meant, most likely, that last night had been Mme. Connecticut's final night at the hotel. Denise was startled to realize how much relief that conclusion afforded her.

Carefully not looking in Jeffrey Thompkins' direction, she went unhesitatingly toward the tall man.

He was wearing a dark cotton suit and, despite the warmth, a narrow black tie flecked with gold, and he looked very, very attractive. She couldn't understand how she had come to think of him as sexless the night before: some inexplicable flickering of her own troubled moods, no doubt. Certainly he didn't seem that way now. He smiled down at her. He seemed actually pleased to see her, though she sensed behind the smile a puzzling mixture of other emotions— aloofness, sadness, regret? That curious tragic air of his: not a pose, she began to think, but the external manifestation of some deep and genuine wound.

"I wish I had listened to you last night," she said. "You knew what you were talking about when you told me to bet Number Four."

He shrugged almost imperceptibly. "I didn't really think that you'd take my advice. But I thought I'd make the gesture all the same."

"That was very kind of you," she said, leaning inward and upward toward him. "I'm sorry I was so skeptical." She flashed her warmest smile. "I'm going to be very shameless. I want a second chance. If you've got any tips to offer on tonight's races, please tell me. I promise not to be such a skeptic this time."

"Number Five in this one," he replied at once. "Nicholas Holt, by the way."

"Denise Carpenter. From Clifton, New Jer—" She cut herself off, reddening. He hadn't told her where he was from. She wasn't from Clifton any longer anyway; and what difference did it make where she might live up north? This island resort was intended as a refuge from all that, a place outside time, outside familiar realities. "Shall we place our bets?" she said briskly.

Women didn't usually buy tickets themselves here. Men seemed to expect to do that for them. She handed him a fifty, making sure as she did so that her fingers were extended to let him see that she wore no wedding band. But Holt didn't make any attempt to look. His own fingers were just as bare.

She caught sight of Jeffrey Thompkins at a distance, frowning at her but not in any very troubled way; and she realized after a moment that he evidently was undisturbed by her defection to the tall man's side and simply wanted to know which turtle Holt was backing. She held up her hand, five fingers outspread. He nodded and went scurrying to the tote counter.

Number Five won easily. The payoff was at seven to three. Denise looked at Holt with amazement.

"How do you do it?" she asked.

"Concentration," he said. "Some people have the knack."

He seemed very distant, suddenly. "Are you concentrating on the next race, now?"

"It'll be Number One," he told her, as though telling her that the weather tomorrow would be warm and fair. Thompkins stared at her out of the crowd. Denise flashed one finger at him. She felt suddenly ill at ease. Nicholas Holt's knack, or whatever it was, bothered her. He was too confident, too coolly certain of what was going to happen. There was something annoying and almost intimidating about such confidence. Although she had bet fifty Jamaican dollars on Number One, she found herself wishing perversely that the turtle would lose.

Number One it was, though, all the same. The payoff was trifling; it seemed as if almost everyone in the place had followed Holt's lead, and as a result the odds had been short ones. Since the races, as Denise was coming to see, were truly random—the turtles didn't give a damn and were about equal in speed—the only thing governing the patterns of oddsmaking was the way the guests happened to bet, and that depended entirely on whatever irrational set of theories the bettors had fastened on. But the theory Nicholas Holt was working from didn't appear to be irrational.

"And in the third race?" she said.

"I never bet more than the first two. It gets very dull for me after that. Shall we have dinner?"

He said it as if her acceptance were a foregone conclusion, which would have offended her, except that he was right.

The main course that night was island venison. "What would you say to a bottle of Merlot?" he asked.

"It's my favorite wine."

How did he do it? Was everything simply an open book to him? He let her do most of the talking at dinner. She told him about the gallery where she worked, about her new little apartment in the city, about her marriage, about what had happened to her marriage. A couple of times she felt herself beginning to babble—the wine, she thought, it was the wine—and she reined herself in. But he showed no sign of disapproval, even when she realized she had been going on about Michael much too long. He listened gravely and quietly to everything she said, interjecting a bland comment now and then, essentially just a little prompt to urge her to continue: "Yes, I see," or "Of course," or "I quite understand."

He told her practically nothing about himself, only that he lived in New York—where?—and that he did something on Wall Street—unspecified—and that he spent two weeks in the West Indies every February but had never been to Jamaica before. He volunteered no more than that: she had no idea where he had grown up— surely not in New York, from the way he spoke—or whether he had ever been married, or what his interests might be. But she thought it would be gauche to be too inquisitive, and probably unproductive. He was very well defended, polite and calm and remote, the most opaque man she had ever known. He played his part in the dinner conversation with the tranquil, self-possessed air of someone who was following a very familiar script.

After dinner they danced, and it was the same thing there: he anticipated her every move, smoothly sweeping her around the open-air dance floor in a way that soon had everyone watching them. Denise was a good dancer, skilled at the tricky art of leading a man who thought he was leading her; but with Nicholas Holt the feed-back was so complex that she had no idea who was leading whom. They danced as though they were one entity, moving with a single accord: the way people dance who have been dancing together for years. She had never known a man who danced like that.

On one swing around the floor she had a quick glimpse of Jeffrey Thompkins, dancing with a robust redhaired woman half a head taller than he was. Thompkins was pushing her about with skill and determination but no grace at all, somewhat in the style of a rhinoceros who has had a thousand hours of instruction at Arthur Murray. As he went thundering past he looked back at Denise and smiled an intricate smile that said a dozen different things. It acknowledged the fact that he was clumsy and his partner was coarse, that Holt was elegant and Denise was beautiful, that men like Holt always were able to take women like Denise away from men like Thompkins. But also the smile seemed to be telling her that Thompkins didn't mind at all, that he accepted what had happened as the natural order of things, had in fact expected it with much the same sort of assurance as Holt had expected Number Five to win tonight's first race. Denise realized that she had felt some guilt about sidestepping Thompkins and offering herself to Holt and that his smile just now had canceled it out; and then she wondered why she had felt the guilt in the first place. She owed nothing to Thompkins, after all. He was simply a stranger who had asked her to dinner last night. They were all strangers down here: nobody owed anything to anyone.

"My cottage is just beyond that little clump of bamboo," Holt said, after they had had the obligatory beachfront stroll on the palm promenade. He said it as if they had already agreed to spend the night there. She offered no objections. This was what she had come here for, wasn't it? Sunlight and warmth and tropical breezes and this.

As he had on the dance floor, so too in bed was he able to anticipate everything she wanted. She had barely thought of something but he was doing it; sometimes he did it even before she knew she wanted him to. It was so long since she had made love with anyone but Michael that Denise wasn't sure who the last one before him had been; but she knew she had never been to bed with anyone like this. She moved here, he was on his way there already. She did this, he did it too. That and that. Her hand, his hand. Her lips, his lips. It was all extremely weird: very thrilling and yet oddly hollow, like making love to your own reflection.

He must be able to read minds, she thought suddenly, as they lay side by side, resting for a while.

An eerie notion. It made her feel nakeder than naked: bare right down to her soul, utterly vulnerable, defenseless.

But the power to read minds, she realized after a moment, wouldn't allow him to do that trick with the turtle races. That was prediction, not mind-reading. It was second sight.

Can he see into the future? Five minutes, ten minutes, half a day ahead? She thought back. He always seemed so unsurprised at everything. When she had told him she didn't intend to do any betting, that first night, he had simply said, "Of course." When his turtle had won the race he had shown no flicker of excitement or pleasure.

When she had apologized tonight for not having acted on his tip, he had told her blandly that he hadn't expected her to. The choice of wine—the dinner conversation—the dancing—the lovemaking— Could he see everything that was about to happen? *Everything?*

On Wall Street, too? Then he must be worth a fortune.

But why did he always look so sad, then? His eyes so bleak and haunted, those little lines of grimness about his lips?

This is all crazy, Denise told herself. Nobody can see the future. The future isn't a place you can look into, the way you can open a door and look into a room. The future doesn't exist until it's become the present.

She turned to him. But he was already opening his arms to her, bringing his head down to graze his lips across her breasts.

She left his cottage long before dawn, not because she really wanted to but because she was unwilling to have the maids and gardeners see her go traipsing back to her place in the morning still wearing her evening clothes, and hung the DO NOT DISTURB sign on her door.

When she woke, the sun was blazing down through the bamboo slats of the cottage porch. She had slept through breakfast and lunch. Her throat felt raspy and there was the sensation of recent lovemaking between her legs, so that she automatically looked around for Michael and was surprised to find herself alone in the big bed; and then she remembered, first that she and Michael were all finished, then that she was here by herself, then that she had spent the night with Nicholas Holt.

Who can see the future. She laughed at her own silliness.

She didn't feel ready to face the outside world, and called room service to bring her tea and a tray of fruit. They sent her mango, jackfruit, three tiny reddish bananas, and a slab of papaya. Later she suited up and went down to the beach. She didn't see Holt anywhere around, neither out by the reef as he usually was in the afternoon, nor on the soft pink sand. A familiar stocky form was churning up the water with cannonball force, doing his laps, down to the cape and back, again, again, again. Thompkins. After a time he came stumping ashore. Not at all coy now, playing no strategic games, he went straight over to her.

"I see that your friend Mr. Holt's in trouble with the hotel," he said, sounding happy about it.

"He is? How so?"

"You weren't at the turtle races after lunch, were you?"

"I never go to the afternoon ones."

"That's right, you don't. Well, I was there. Holt won the first two races, the way he always does. Everybody bet the way he did. The odds were microscopic, naturally. But everybody won. And then two of the hotel managers—you know, Eubanks, the night man who has that enormous grin all the time, and the other one with the big yellow birthmark on his forehead?—came over to him and said, 'Mr. Holt, sah, we would prefer dat you forgo the pleasure of the turtle racing from this point onward.'" The Chevrolet dealer's imitation of the Jamaican accent was surprisingly accurate. "'We recognize dat you must be an authority on turtle habits, sah,' they said. 'Your insight we find to be exceedingly uncanny. And derefore it strikes us dat it is quite unsporting for you to compete. Quite, sah!'"

"And what did he say?"

"That he doesn't know a goddamned thing about turtles, that he's simply on a roll, that it's not his fault if the other guests are betting the same way he is. They asked him again not to play the turtles—'We implore you, sah, you are causing great losses for dis establishment'— and he kept saying he was a registered guest and entitled to all the privileges of a guest. So they canceled the races."

"Canceled them?"

"They must have been losing a fucking fortune this week on those races, if you'll excuse the French. You can't run parimutuels where everybody bets the same nag and that nag always wins, you know? Wipes you out after a while. So they didn't have races this afternoon and there won't be any tonight unless he agrees not to play." Thompkins smirked. "The guests are pretty pissed off, I got to tell you. The management is trying to talk him into changing hotels, that's what someone just said. But he won't do it. So no turtles. You ask me, I still think he's been fixing it somehow with the hotel boys, and the hotel must think so too, but they don't dare say it. Man with a winning streak like that, there's just no accounting for it any other way, is there?"

"No," Denise said. "No accounting for it at all."

It was cocktail time before she found him: the hour when the guests gathered on the garden patio where the turtle races were held to have a daiquiri or two before the tote counter opened for business. Denise drifted down there automatically, despite what Thompkins had told her about the cancelation of the races. Most of the other guests had done the same. She saw Holt's lanky figure looming up out of a group of them. They had surrounded him, they were gesturing and waving their daiquiris around as they talked.

It was easy enough to guess that they were trying to talk him into refraining from playing the turtles so that they could have their daily amusement back.

When she came closer she saw the message chalked across the tote board in an ornate Jamaican hand, all curlicues and flourishes:

TECHNICAL PROBLEM NO RACES TODAY YOUR KIND INDULGENCE IS ASKED

"Nicholas?" she called, as though they had a prearranged date. He smiled at her gratefully.

"Excuse me," he said in his genteel way to the cluster around him, and moved smoothly through them to her side. "How lovely you look tonight, Denise."

"I've heard that the hotel's putting pressure on you about the races."

"Yes. Yes." He seemed to be speaking to her from another galaxy. "So they are. They're quite upset, matter of fact. But if there's going to be racing, I have a right to play. If they choose to cancel, that's their business."

In a low voice she said, "You aren't involved in any sort of collusion with the hotel boys, are you?"

"You asked me that before. You know that that isn't possible."

"Then how are you always able to tell which turtle's going to win?"

"I know," he said sadly. "I simply do."

"You always know what's about to happen, don't you? Always."

"Would you like a daiquiri, Denise?"

"Answer me. Please."

"I have a knack, yes."

"It's more than a knack."

"A gift, then. A special—something."

"A something, yes."

They were walking as they talked; already they were past the bougainvillea hedge, heading down the steps toward the beachfront promenade, leaving the angry guests and the racing pool and the turtle tank behind.

"A very reliable something," she said.

"Yes. I suppose it is."

"You said that you knew, the first night when you offered me that tip, that I wasn't going to take you up on it. Why did you offer it to me, then?"

"I told you. It seemed like a friendly gesture."

"We weren't friends then. We'd hardly spoken. Why'd you bother?"

"Just because."

"Because you wanted to test your special something?" she asked him. "Because you wanted to see whether it was working right?"

He stared at her intently. He looked almost frightened, she thought. She had broken through.

"Perhaps I did," he said.

"Yes. You check up on it now and then, don't you? You try something that you know won't pan out, like tipping a strange woman to the outcome of the turtle race even though your gift tells you that she won't bet your tip. Just to see whether your guess was on the mark. But what would you have done if I *had* put a bet down that night, Nicholas?"

"You wouldn't have."

"You were certain of that."

"Virtually certain, yes. But you're right: I test it now and then, just to see."

"And it always turns out the way you expect?"

"Essentially, yes."

"You're scary, Nicholas. How long have you been able to do stuff like this?"

"Does that matter?" he asked. "Does it really?"

He asked her to have dinner with him again, but there was something perfunctory about the invitation, as though he were offering it only because the hour was getting toward dinnertime and they happened to be standing next to each other just then. She accepted quickly, perhaps too quickly. But the dining terrace was practically empty when they reached it—they were very early, on account of the cancelation of the races—and the meal was a stiff, uncomfortable affair. He was so obviously bothered by her persistent inquiries about his baffling skill, his special something, that she quickly backed off, but that left little to talk about except the unchanging perfect weather, the beauty of the hotel grounds, the rumors of racial tension elsewhere on the island. He toyed with his food and ate very little. They ordered no wine. It was like sitting across the table from a stranger who was dining with her purely by chance. And yet less than twenty-four hours before she had spent a night in this man's bed.

She didn't understand him at all. He was alien and mysterious and a little frightening. But somehow, strangely, that made him all the more desirable.

As they were sipping their coffee she looked straight at him and sent him a message with her mind:

Ask me to come dancing with you, next. And then let's go to your cottage again, you bastard.

But instead he said abruptly, "Would you excuse me, Denise?"

She was nonplussed. "Why—yes—if—"

He looked at his watch. "I've rented a glass-bottomed boat for eight o'clock. To have a look at the night life out on the reef."

The night was when the reef came alive. The little coral creatures awoke and unfolded their brilliant little tentacles; phosphorescent organisms began to glow; octopuses and eels came out of their dark crannies to forage for their meals; sharks and rays and other big predators set forth on the hunt. You could take a boat out there that was equipped with bottom-mounted arc lights and watch the show, but very few of the hotel guests actually did. The waters that were so crystalline and inviting by day looked ominous and menacing in the dark, with sinister coral humps rising like black ogres' heads above the lapping wavelets. She had never even thought of going.

But now she heard herself saying, in a desperate attempt at salvaging something out of the evening, "Can I go with you?"

"I'm sorry. No."

"I'm really eager to see what the reef looks like at—"

"No," he said, quietly but with real finality. "It's something I'd rather do by myself, if you don't mind. Or even if you do mind, I have to tell you. Is that all right, Denise?"

"Will I see you afterward?" she asked, wishing instantly that she hadn't. But he had already risen and given her a gentlemanly little smile of farewell and was striding down the terrace toward the steps that led to the beachfront promenade.

She stared after him, astounded by the swiftness of his disappearance, the unexpectedness of it.

She sat almost without moving, contemplating her bewildering abandonment. Five minutes went by, maybe ten. The waiter unobtrusively brought her another coffee. She held the cup in her hand without drinking from it.

Jeffrey Thompkins materialized from somewhere, hideously cheerful. "If you're free," he said, "how about an after-dinner liqueur?" He was wearing a white dinner jacket, very natty, and sharply pressed black trousers. But his round neckless head and the blaze of sunburn across his bare scalp spoiled the elegant effect. "A Strega, a Galliano, a nice cognac, maybe?" He pronounced it *coneyac*.

"Something weird's going on," she said.

"Oh?"

"He went out on the reef in one of those boats, by himself. Holt. Just got up and walked away from the table, said he'd rented a boat for eight o'clock. Poof. Gone."

"I'm heartbroken to hear it."

"No, be serious. He was acting really strange. I asked to go with him, and he said no, I absolutely couldn't. He sounded almost like some sort of a machine. You could hear the gears clicking."

Thompkins said, all flippancy gone from his voice now, "You think he's going to do something to himself out there?"

"No. Not him. That's one thing I'm sure of."

"Then what?"

"I don't know."

"A guy like that, all keyed up all the time and never letting on a thing to anybody—"

Thompkins looked at her closely. "You know him better than I do. You don't have any idea what he might be up to?"

"Maybe he just wants to see the reef. I don't know. But he seemed so peculiar when he left—so rigid, so *focused*—"

"Come on," Thompkins said. "Let's get one of those boats and go out there ourselves."

"But he said he wanted to go alone."

"Screw what he said. He don't own the reef. We can go for an expedition too, if we want to."

It took a few minutes to arrange things. "You want a guided tour, sah?" the boy down at the dock asked, but Thompkins said no, and helped Denise into the boat as easily as though she were made of feathers. The boy shook his head. "Nobody want a guide tonight. You be careful out there, stay dis side the reef, you hear me, sah?"

Thompkins switched on the lights and took the oars. With quick, powerful strokes he moved away from the dock. Denise looked down. There was nothing visible below but the bright white sand of the shallows, a few long-spined black sea urchins, some starfish. As they approached the reef, a hundred yards or so off shore, the density of marine life increased: schools of brilliant fishes whirled and dived, a somber armada of squids came squirting past.

There was no sign of Holt. "We ought to be able to see his lights," Denise said. "Where can he have gone?"

Thompkins had the boat butting up against the flat side of the reef now. He stood up carefully and stared into the night.

"The crazy son of a bitch," he muttered. "He's gone outside the reef! Look, there he is."

He pointed. Denise, half rising, saw nothing at first; and then there was the reflected glow of the other boat's lights, on the far side of the massive stony clutter and intricacy that was the reef. Holt had found one of the passageways through and was coasting along the reef's outer face, where the deep-water hunters came up at night, the marlins and swordfish and sharks.

"What the hell does he think he's doing?" Thompkins asked. "Don't he know it's dangerous out there?"

"I don't think that worries him," said Denise.

"So you do think he's going to do something to himself."

"Just the opposite. He knows that he'll be all right out there, or he wouldn't be there. He wouldn't have gone if he saw any real risk in it."

"Unless risk is what he's looking for."

"He doesn't live in a world of risk," she said. "He's got a kind of sixth sense. He always knows what's going to happen next."

"Huh?"

Words came pouring out of her. "He sees the future," she said fiercely, not caring how wild it sounded. "It's like an open book to him. How do you think he does that trick with the turtles?"

"Huh?" Thompkins said again. "The future?" He peered at her, shaking his head slowly.

Then he swung sharply around as if in response to some unexpected sound from the sea. He shaded his forehead with his hand, the way he might have done if he were peering into bright sunlight. After a moment he pointed into the darkness beyond the reef and said in a slow awed tone, "What the fuck! Excuse me. But Jesus, will you look at that?"

She stared past him, toward the suddenly foaming sea.

Something was happening on the reef's outer face. Denise saw it unfolding as if in slow motion. The ocean swelling angrily, rising, climbing high. The single great wave barreling in as though it had traveled all the way from Alaska for this one purpose. The boat tilting up on end, the man flying upward and outward, soaring gracefully into the air, traveling along a smooth curve like an expert diver and plummeting down into the black depths just beside the reef's outer face. And then the last curling upswing of the wave, the heavy crash as it struck the coral wall.

In here, sheltered by the reef, they felt only a mild swaying, and then everything was still again.

Thompkins clapped his hand over his mouth. His eyes were bulging. "Jesus," he said after a moment. "Jesus! How the fuck am I going to get out there?" He turned toward Denise. "Can you row this thing back to shore by yourself?"

"I suppose so."

"Good. Take it in and tell the boat boy what happened. I'm going after your friend."

He stripped with astonishing speed, the dinner jacket, the sharply creased pants, the shirt and tie, the black patent leather shoes. Denise saw him for a moment outlined against the stars, the fleshy burly body hidden only by absurd bikini pants in flamboyant scarlet silk. Then he was over the side, swimming with all his strength, heading for one of the openings in the reef that gave access to the outer face.

She was waiting among the crowd on the shore when Thompkins brought the body in, carrying it like a broken doll. He had been much too late, of course. One quick glance told her that Holt must have been tossed against the reef again and again, smashed, cut to ribbons by the sharp coral, partly devoured, even, by the creatures of the night. Thompkins laid him down on the beach. One of the hotel boys put a beach blanket over him; another gave Thompkins a robe. He was scratched and bloody himself, shivering, grim-faced, breathing in windy gusts. Denise went to him. The others backed away, stepping back fifteen or twenty feet, leaving them alone, strangely exposed, beside the blanketed body.

"Looks like you were wrong," Thompkins said. "About that sixth sense of his. Or else it wasn't working so good tonight."

"No," she said. For the past five minutes she had been struggling to put together the pattern of what had happened, and it seemed to her now that it was beginning to come clear. "It was working fine. He knew that this would happen."

"What?"

"He knew. Like I said before, he knew everything ahead of time. Everything. Even this. But he went along with it anyway."

"But if he knew everything, then why—why—" Thompkins shook his head. "I don't get it."

Denise shuddered in the warm night breeze. "No, you don't. You can't. Neither can I."

"Miss Carpentah?" a high, strained voice called. "Mistah Thompkins?"

It was the night manager, Mr. Eubanks of the dazzling grin, belatedly making his way down from the hotel. He wasn't grinning now. He looked stricken, panicky, strangely pasty-faced. He came to a halt next to them, knelt, picked up one corner of the beach blanket, stared at the body beneath it as though it were some bizarre monster that had washed ashore. A guest had died on his watch, and it was going to cost him, he was sure of that, and his fear showed in his eyes.

Thompkins, paying no attention to the Jamaican, said angrily to Denise, "If he knew what was going to happen, if he could see the fucking future, why in the name of Christ didn't he simply not take the boat out, then? Or if he did, why fool around outside the reef where it's so dangerous? For that matter why didn't he just stay the hell away from Jamaica in the first place?"

"That's what I mean when I tell you that we can't understand," she said. "He didn't think the way we do. He wasn't like us. Not at all. Not in the slightest."

"Mistah Tompkins—Miss Carpentah—if you would do me de courtesy of speaking with me for a time—of letting me have de details of dis awful tragedy—"

Thompkins brushed Eubanks away as if he were a gnat. "I don't know what the fuck you're saying," he told Denise.

Eubanks said, exasperated, "If de lady and gemmun will give me deir kind attention, *please*—"

He looked imploringly toward Denise. She shook him off. She was still groping, still reaching for the answer. Then, for an instant, just for an instant, everything that was going on seemed terribly familiar to her. As if it had all happened before. The warm, breezy night air. The blanket on the beach. The round, jowly, baffled face of Jeffrey Thompkins hovering in front of hers. Mr. Eubanks, pale with dismay. An odd little moment of déjà vu. It appeared to go on and on. Now Eubanks will lose his cool and try to take me by the arm, she thought; now I will pull back and slip on the sand; now Jeffrey will catch me and steady me. Yes. Yes. And here it comes. "Please, you may not ignore me dis way! You must tell me what has befallen dis unfortunate gemmun!" That was Eubanks, eyes popping, forehead shiny with sweat. Making a pouncing movement toward her, grabbing for her wrist. She backed hastily away from him. Her legs felt suddenly wobbly. She started to sway and slip, and looked toward Thompkins. But he was already coming forward, reaching out toward her to take hold of her before she fell. Weird, she thought. Weird.

Then the weirdness passed, and everything was normal again, and she knew the answer.

That was how it had been for him, she thought in wonder. Every hour, every day, his whole goddamned life.

"He came to this place and he did what he did," she said to Thompkins, "because he knew that there wasn't any choice for him. Once he had seen it in his mind it was certain to happen. So he just came down here and played things through to the end."

"Even though he'd *die?*" Thompkins asked. He looked at Denise stolidly, uncomprehendingly.

"If you lived your whole life as if it had already happened, without surprise, without excitement, without the slightest unpredictable event, not once, not ever, would you give a damn whether you lived or died? Would you? He knew he'd die here, yes. So he came here to die, and that's the whole story. And now he has."

"Jesus," Thompkins said. "The poor son of a bitch!"

"You understand now? What it must have been like for him?"

"Yeah," he said, his arm still tight around her as though he didn't ever mean to let go. "Yeah. The poor son of a bitch."

"I got to tell you," said Mr. Eubanks, "dis discourtesy is completely improper. A mahn have died here tragically tonight, and you be de only witnesses, and I ask you to tell me what befell, and you—"

Denise closed her eyes a moment. Then she looked at Eubanks.

"What's there to say, Mr. Eubanks? He took his boat into a dangerous place and it was struck by a sudden wave and overturned. An accident. A terrible accident. What else is there to say?" She began to shiver. Thompkins held her. In a low voice she said to him, "I want to go back to my cottage."

"Right," he said. "Sure. You wanted a statement, Mr. Eubanks? There's your statement. Okay? Okay?"

He held her close against him and slowly they started up the ramp toward the hotel together.

Chance

By Wallace Stroby

T he gun was a .38, as Rainey imagined it would be. Anything larger would make too much of a mess. Smaller, and there was no guarantee it would get the job done. So yes, a .38.

The man who'd called himself Darnay was holding the gun out butt first, both of them in a circle of overhead light, the rest of the room dim. Rainey sat on an armless wooden chair. The concrete floor under him was lined with clear plastic sheeting.

He took the gun. It was lighter than he expected. Short-barreled, blued steel with hard rubber grips. There was a fleck of something on the barrel, close to the muzzle. He scraped it off with a thumbnail. Blood.

The others in the room were lost in shadow and a haze of cigarette smoke. No chairs, everyone standing. Rainey had gotten a better look at them when he'd entered the loft. There were maybe twelve, mostly men. Only two women he could see. One of them, a tall, thin blonde in a black evening gown, now stood closer to him than the others, her face expressionless. She held a fluted champagne glass.

At the back of the room was the betting table. Behind it sat the big man with the steel-gray crew-cut who'd met Rainey in the basement parking garage, brought him up on the elevator. There was a briefcase open in front of him. Nearby was a bar cart.

"Our third—and last—pilgrim of the night," Darnay said. "Another gambler, in the truest sense of the word. We salute you." There was a smattering of applause.

Rainey turned the revolver over in his hand, thumbed the cylinder lock, let it fall open. Six empty chambers, the faint smell of gunpowder.

Darnay raised a hand, and the room grew quiet. This was the closest Rainey had been to him. He was hairless, his scalp shiny. A vein pulsed in his right temple, like a worm beneath the skin. He wore a leather vest over his bare chest, leather pants. He was painfully thin, and Rainey could see the outline of each rib. There was a piercing where his right eyebrow would have been. He smelled of sweat and something harsh and metallic.

Rainey gave the cylinder a quick spin to make sure it moved freely, then closed it again, handed back the gun.

"The weapon is inspected," Darnay said. "The player approves. Wagering is now open."

People crowded around the betting table. The blonde stayed where she was, watching him, sipped from her glass.

Rainey took a deep breath, let it out slow. He rubbed the pale spot on his finger where his wedding band had been. He wondered where Alisha was tonight, what she would think about what he was doing, if she would understand why.

He looked around the room, his eyes acclimating to the dimness. Canvas tarps covered the windows. They'd hide the light up here from anyone on the street below, muffle the sound. The rest of the building would be empty.

Past the edge of the plastic sheeting was a video camera on a tripod, the red Record light already glowing. Rainey wondered how many of these they'd filmed, how much they'd charge those who wanted to see one.

He had no watch or cellphone, had lost his sense of time. Maybe an hour since the Town Car had picked him up at 81st and Lexington, where he'd been told to wait. It was close to midnight then. The driver, a lean Hispanic man with gothic type tattooed around his neck, had been silent on the drive downtown. He'd pulled into the underground garage—trash on the floors, graffiti on the walls—and stopped in front of the elevator. There were a half dozen vehicles parked there. A limo, two luxury SUVs with tinted windows, a new Mercedes, a Jaguar, and something low-slung and Italian that he couldn't identify.

As soon as Rainey got out, the driver had turned around, driven back up the ramp to the street. The elevator rattled as if on cue, came to life, the sound of it echoing through the garage. When the doors opened, the crew-cut man was inside. He wore a thigh-length black leather jacket despite the heat, a black silk shirt. Rainey could see the butt of a dark automatic in his belt. He didn't speak when Rainey got on, just gestured for him to raise his arms. He'd stiffened when the man searched him, ran hands down the legs of his jeans, stopped short of his boots. The man straightened then, pushed the button for the eighth floor. The elevator had risen jerkily with the squeal of metal, the clatter of cables.

The last of the bettors were at the table now. A cork popped in the shadows.

"You risk only your money," Darnay said to them. "Our player risks his life. Be bold. Honor him with your wagers."

Rainey's left leg began to shake, the calf muscle twitching. He'd stayed calm on the ride here, had found that familiar flatline state that made him feel he was outside himself. But now that calmness was gone, the fear and uncertainty washing over him.

It had taken him a year to find these people, this game. Rumor had led him finally to the bartender in Red Hook. Two hundred in cash had gotten him a phone number. The deal was simple, the bartender had told him. A payout of ten thousand dollars for every round played, with an agreed minimum of three rounds. A ten-grand bonus if the player went four or more. A lucky man could do well in one night, the bartender said. Walk out the door with fifty grand and his life.

Rainey had left three messages at the number before his call was returned. The next game was a week away. He was told where to wait and when.

Now he felt his stomach tighten, tasted the bile rising, fought it back down. He'd come this far, would see it through, do what he had to.

"Final wagers," Darnay said.

Rainey met the blonde's eyes. She didn't look away.

How many of these has she watched? How many would be enough?

A man came forward, refilled her glass from a bottle, then kissed the back of her neck. She ignored him, lifted her glass to Rainey as if in a toast.

"Betting is closed," Darnay said.

The room went quiet again. Darnay held up the gun, opened the cylinder, exposing the empty chambers. "A Taurus Model 865, as before. Empty now. You've all seen what it can do. It's small, but mighty."

He reached into a vest pocket, took out a bullet. It had a shiny brass casing and a dull lead nose. He held it up between thumb and forefinger to show the bettors. "One live round. No substitutions, no sleight-of-hand, no blanks."

"Get on with it," someone said.

Darnay slipped the bullet into a chamber, locked the cylinder back in place. "Not so empty now."

Rainey closed his eyes, tuned out the people, the room around him. He had to find that calmness, that flatline, again, to do what he had to do. He wondered about the first two players. Had one of them left here with their winnings, or were they both wrapped in plastic sheeting in another room?

"Our moment of truth," Darnay said.

Rainey opened his eyes. Darnay was holding out the gun. After a moment, Rainey took it.

"And we begin," Darnay said.

A draft billowed a window tarp. Rainey heard a distant siren, fading as it went farther away. He looked at the blonde. She was touching her breasts through the dress.

The betting over, the crew-cut man had come out from behind the table to watch, a thumb hooked in his belt near the gun. Rainey knew if he aimed the Taurus at anyone other than himself, the man would shoot him dead.

Stop stalling. One chance out of six. The odds are in your favor.

He put his thumb on the hammer, drew it back until it locked. With the flat of his left hand, he spun the cylinder clockwise, the chambers clicking fast as they went by. He spun it a second time, then a third, the cylinder gathering speed, then slowing, stopping.

Do it.

He put the gun to his head, just above his right ear, the muzzle cold against his skin.

He imagined the path the bullet would take. A contact wound, so even if his hand shook at the last second, the muzzle wavering, the gun would do the trick. The bullet would plow through tissue and bone, shatter his skull, keep going. Lights out.

Silence in the room. The trigger was tight under his finger. He began to squeeze, felt it give, closed his eyes.

The hammer snapped down. Empty chamber. Someone yelled, "Yes!"

Rainey lowered the gun. His hand was shaking. The floor seemed to tilt under him.

"Bravo," Darnay said.

Rainey breathed slow. *Don't pass out.*

"You are now ten thousand dollars richer than you were only a few moments ago," Darnay said. "And maybe minutes away from another ten." Then to the room: "Wagering is open." The crew-cut man went back to the table, the others gathering around it.

Rainey set the gun in his lap, wiped his wet palm on a jeans leg. A draft moved the tarp again. A bottom corner fluttered free, exposing the window. He caught a glimpse of a red crescent moon beyond.

"It's easier the second time," Darnay said. "You'll see."

Rainey flexed his stiff right hand. "Before I go again, I have a question."

"There are no questions here. And no answers. Only the moment."

"One question. One answer. What do I have to do to earn it?"

Darnay frowned. "Are you worried about your money? We always pay winners in full. If we didn't, and word got around, no one would want to play the game, would they? And they always do. Some of them more than once."

"It's not about the money."

"Let him ask," the blonde said.

Darnay looked at her. "We're here to play, not talk."

"I say let him ask."

"Two bullets," Rainey said.

Darnay looked back at him. "What?"

"Two bullets this time. Increase the odds, make it more interesting. Will that earn me an answer?"

One of the men hooted. Another yelled, "Do it!"

Darnay smiled finally. "A true sportsman. 'Dead game,' as they say. Two bullets it is." Then to the bettors, "A change in the odds. Adjust your wagers accordingly."

He held out his hand for the gun. Rainey gave it to him. Darnay popped the cylinder, raised the gun as he'd done before. He took another bullet from his vest, slid it into a chamber, snapped the cylinder closed. "Final wagers, please."

He handed the gun back. "You won your question. What is it?"

Rainey cocked the hammer. "This time last year, there was a game here. Did you run that one too?"

Darnay looked uneasy. "What possible difference could that make?"

Rainey spun the cylinder once. "I'm asking. I want to know before I pull the trigger."

The bettors went back to their places. The crew-cut man came out from around the table again.

"I brought the game here," Darnay said. "There are others in other cities. People come to wager—either their lives or their money—because they know we run an honest game, with total discretion. Players come to us, just as you did. Word travels where it needs to."

"So it was you."

Darnay looked at the crew-cut man, then back at Rainey. "Play."

No hooting now. Rainey set the cylinder spinning again, waited for it to come to a stop.

"Last year," he said. "There was a man here, a boy really. Twenty-three. His name was Andrew. Do you remember him?"

"Players don't have names here," Darnay said.

"He left a journal behind at the place where he'd been living. He'd found out about the game. He was a good kid having a bad time, trying to stay sober. He needed money, but he wasn't the type could go out, rob someone, hurt anyone beside himself. He wrote about what he was going to do, said he wasn't sure if he could go through with it. And he couldn't, could he? Not after he got here."

"Anyone who plays the game does it by choice."

"Did he get scared at the last minute, try to leave? You wouldn't let him though, would you? Not after what he'd seen. Did you force him to play? Did one of you hold a gun on him while he did it? That the way it happened?"

"None of us can run from our fate," Darnay said. "Luck. God. Destiny. Call it what you want. We're all born to a path."

"They found his body where you left it, under that bridge in Brooklyn. I never showed the journal to the police. I wanted to find you myself."

"Who was he to you?" Darnay said.

"My son."

Darnay took a step back, looked at the crew-cut man and said, "Shoot him."

The man drew the gun from his belt. Rainey stood, aimed the .38 at him, pulled the trigger. The hammer clicked. The man smiled, took careful aim, his gun in a two-handed grip.

Rainey jerked the trigger twice more, fast. The gun went off, bucked in his hand. The bullet caught the man in the right shoulder, knocked him back and down. The sound of the shot echoed off the walls. A woman screamed.

Rainey dropped the gun, pulled up his jeans leg, reached into his boot and felt the cold metal of the small .25. He drew it out. Darnay had his hands up, was backing away. Rainey fired at him twice, heard him grunt. Then the crew-cut man was up on one knee, aiming the automatic again, one-handed this time. Rainey saw the muzzle flash, felt the punch to his stomach. He stumbled back, hit the chair and took it down with him, landed on his side on the sheeting.

The man was on his feet now, coming closer, trying for a clear shot. Rainey raised the .25, fired once, twice, kept firing as the man fell. Then the gun was empty, the slide locked. Gray gunsmoke drifted in the air.

Rainey couldn't breathe. He dropped the .25, touched his stomach. No pain there yet, but his fingers came away wet with blood.

Darnay was crawling across the floor toward the betting table. There was a slug-like smear of blood on the concrete behind him.

Rainey pushed the chair away, rolled onto his knees, gasping for air. The pain hit him then, deep and burning. He picked up the .38 again, forced himself to stand, breathe.

The blonde was alone. All the others were gone. She'd moved farther away to stay out of the line of fire, but there was no fear in her eyes.

"Get out of here," he said. When she didn't move, he raised the gun.

"You've only got one bullet left in there," she said. "Are you sure you want to waste it on me?"

He lowered the gun, weary now. "Just go."

"There's a lot of money in that briefcase."

He pointed the gun at her. "Go." His voice was hoarse.

She left the room. He heard the unhurried click of high heels on concrete. Then, after a few moments, the clatter of the elevator.

Darnay had stopped crawling. He rolled over onto his back, panting. There were two small black holes in the center of his chest, streaming blood.

Rainey stepped across to straddle him, cocked the .38, spun the cylinder. When it came to rest, he pointed the gun at Darnay's face. Darnay looked up at him, coughed. There was blood on his lips.

"He was just a kid," Rainey said, and squeezed the trigger. The hammer fell on an empty chamber.

"Lucky," Rainey said. He left him there, went over to the crew-cut man. He lay face up, eyes half-closed, shirt dark with blood. He wasn't breathing.

Rainey went back to the chair, righted it, sat.

I'm sorry, Andy, he thought. *Sorry for all the things I couldn't do.*

He looked at the lens of the camera, put the gun to his head, slowly squeezed the trigger. Felt the tension there, then the sudden release.

The hammer rose and fell, clicked. He pulled the trigger again. Another click. Three more pulls, one after the other, the cylinder rotating each time. Three clicks.

You fuck up everything, don't you?

Last chamber. The bullet for sure.

He closed his eyes. His hand began to shake.

Do it. You'll see him again.

He opened his eyes, looked at the camera, the red light.

"No," he said aloud.

He took the gun from his head, aimed at the lens, fired. The gun kicked back, and the camera exploded, pieces flying away across the room. The tripod fell over.

He let the empty gun drop from his hand, stood, ears still ringing from the shot. He kicked the gun across the floor. Pain spiked in his stomach again, bent him.

Don't die here. Not in this place.

He looked at the betting table, the briefcase there. Whoever found the bodies would find it too. A lucky day for them.

Left hand pressed against his stomach, he made his way out of the room and down the hall. He punched the elevator call button, left a bloody thumbprint on it.

The bell dinged, and the doors opened. He went in, hit the G button, left another bloody print. When the elevator started to descend, he had to grip the handrail to keep from falling. The car rattled and shook, brought a fresh wave of pain, finally jerked to a halt. The doors slid open.

The blonde was leaning against the fender of the Mercedes, smoking a cigarette. One of the SUVs was still there. The other vehicles were gone.

He stepped out of the elevator, hand tight over his stomach. He felt weak, the pain a live thing inside him.

The woman dropped the cigarette, ground it out with the toe of her shoe, then walked past him and got on the elevator. She pushed a button, watched him as the doors closed.

He went up the ramp and onto the empty street. The red moon lit the clouds. He walked past darkened storefronts and empty buildings, his legs like lead. He didn't know where he was.

Engine noise behind him. He turned, saw the roof lights of a cab, raised his right hand. It steered to the curb in front of him.

He got in back, shut the door, left bloody handprints on the vinyl. They pulled away.

"Where you going?" the driver said.

Rainey was cold all over now, sleepy. He watched the dark buildings pass by. The driver twisted to look at him through the Plexiglas divider. Rainey took his hand away from his stomach. The blood was everywhere.

"Man, you're in bad shape," the driver said. "You need to get to a hospital."

Rainey didn't answer. He saw Andy's face again, heard his voice. It made him smile. He let his head fall back, and closed his eyes.

Strangers on a Handball Court

By Lawrence Block

W̲e met for the first time on a handball court in Sheridan Park. It was a Saturday morning in early summer with the sky free of clouds and the sun warm but not yet unbearable. He was alone on the court when I got there and I stood for a few moments watching him warm up, slamming the little ball viciously against the imperturbable backstop.

He didn't look my way, although he must have known I was watching him. When he paused for a moment I said, "A game?"

He looked my way. "Why not?"

I suppose we played for two hours, perhaps a little longer. I've no idea how many games we played. I was several years younger, weighed considerably less, and topped him by four or five inches.

He won every game.

When we broke, the sun was high in the sky and considerably hotter than it had been when we started. We had both been sweating freely and we stood together, rubbing our faces and chests with our towels. "Good workout," he said. "There's nothing like it."

"I hope you at least got some decent exercise out of it," I said apologetically. "I certainly didn't make it much of a contest."

"Oh, don't bother yourself about that," he said, and flashed a shark's smile. "Tell you the truth, I like to win. On and off the court. And I certainly got a workout out of you."

I laughed. "As a matter of fact, I managed to work up a thirst. How about a couple of beers? On me, in exchange for the handball lesson."

He grinned. "Why not?"

◎

WE DIDN'T TALK much until we were settled in a booth at the Hofbrau House. Generations of collegians had carved combinations of Greek letters into the top of our sturdy oak table. I was in the middle of another apology for my athletic inadequacy when he set his stein down atop Zeta Beta Tau and shook a cigarette out of his pack. "Listen," he said, "forget it. What the hell, maybe you're lucky in love."

I let out a bark of mirthless laughter. "If this is luck," I said, "I'd hate to see misfortune."

"Problems?"

"You might say so."

"Well, if it's something you'd rather not talk about—"

I shook my head. "It's not that—it might even do me good to talk about it—but it would bore the daylights out of you. It's hardly an original problem. The world is overflowing these days with men in the very same leaky boat."

"Oh?"

"I've got a girl," I said. "I love her and she loves me. But I'm afraid I'm going to lose her."

He frowned, thinking about it. "You're married," he said.

"No."

"She's married."

I shook my head. "No, we're both single. She wants to get married."

"But you don't want to marry her."

"There's nothing I want more than to marry her and spend the rest of my life with her."

His frown deepened. "Wait a minute," he said. "Let me think. You're both single, you both want to get married, but there's a problem. All I can think of is she's your sister, but I can't believe that's it, especially since you said it's a common problem. I'll tell you, I think my brain's tired from too much time in the sun. What's the problem?"

"I'm divorced."

"So who isn't? I'm divorced and I'm remarried. Unless it's a religious thing. I bet that's what it is."

"No."

"Well, don't keep me guessing, fella. I already gave up once, remember?"

"The problem is my ex-wife," I said. "The judge gave her everything I had but the clothes I was wearing at the time of the trial. With the alimony I have to pay her, I'm living in a furnished room and cooking on a hotplate. I can't afford to get married, and my girl wants to get married—and sooner or later she's going to get tired of spending her time with a guy who can never afford to take her anyplace decent." I shrugged. "Well," I said, "you get the picture."

"Boy, do I get the picture."

"As I said, it's not a very original problem."

"You don't know the half of it." He signaled the waiter for two more beers, and when they arrived he lit another cigarette and took a long swallow of his beer. "It's really something," he said. "Meeting like this. I already told you I got an ex-wife of my own."

"These days almost everybody does."

"That's the truth. I must have had a better lawyer than you did, but I still got burned pretty bad. She got the house, she got the Cadillac and just about everything else she wanted. And now she gets fifty cents out of every dollar I make. She's got no kids, she's got no responsibilities, but she gets fifty cents out of every dollar I earn and the government gets another thirty or forty cents. What does that leave me?"

"Not a whole lot."

"You better believe it. As it happens I make a good living. Even with what she and the government take I manage to live pretty decently. But do you know what it does to me, paying her all that money every month? I hate that woman's guts and she lives like a queen at my expense."

I took a long drink of beer. "I guess our problems aren't all that different."

"And a lot of men can say the same thing. Millions of them. A word of advice, friend. What you should do if you marry your girlfriend—"

"I can't marry her."

"But if you go ahead and marry her anyway. Just make sure you do what I did before I married my second wife. It goes against the grain to do it because when you're about to marry someone you're completely in love and you're sure it's going to last forever. But make a prenuptial agreement. Have it all signed and witnessed before the marriage ceremony, and have it specify that if there's a divorce she does not get one dime, she gets zip. You follow me? Get yourself a decent lawyer so he'll draw up something that will stand up, and get her to sign it, which she most likely will because she'll be so starry-eyed about getting married. Then you'll have nothing to worry about. If the marriage is peaches and cream forever, which I hope it is, then you've wasted a couple of hundred dollars on a lawyer and that's no big deal. But if anything goes wrong with the marriage, you're in the catbird seat."

I looked at him for a long moment. "It makes sense," I said.

"That's what I did. Now my second wife and I, we get along pretty good. She's young, she's beautiful, she's good company, I figure I got a pretty good deal. We have our bad times, but they're nothing two people can't live with. And the thing is, she's not tempted by the idea of divorcing me, because she knows what she'll come out with if she does. Zeeee-ro."

"If I ever get married again," I said, "I'll take your advice."

"I hope so."

"But it'll never happen," I said. "Not with my ex-wife bleeding me to death. You know, I'm almost ashamed to say this, but what the hell, we're strangers, we don't really know each other, so I'll admit it. I have fantasies of killing her. Stabbing her, shooting her, tying her to a railroad track and letting a train solve my problem for me."

"Friend, you are not alone. The world is full of men who dream about killing their ex-wives."

"Of course I'd never do it. Because if anything ever happened to that woman, the police would come straight to me."

"Same here. If I ever put my ex in the ground, there'd be a cop knocking on my door before the body was cold. Of course that particular body was *born* cold, if you know what I mean."

"I know what you mean," I said. This time I signaled for more beer, and we fell silent until it was on the table in front of us. Then, in a confessional tone, I said, "I'll tell you something. I would do it. If I weren't afraid of getting caught, I would literally do it. I'd kill her."

"I'd kill mine."

"I mean it. There's no other way out for me. I'm in love and I want to get married and I can't. My back is to the proverbial wall. I'd do it."

He didn't even hesitate. "So would I."

"Really?"

"Sure. You could say it's just money, and that's most of it, but there's more to it than that. I hate that woman. I hate the fact that she's made a complete fool out of me. If I could get away with it, they'd be breaking ground in her cemetery plot any day now." He shook his head. "*Her* cemetery plot," he said bitterly. "It was originally our plot, but the judge gave her the whole thing. Not that I have any overwhelming urge to be buried next to her, but it's the principle of the thing."

"If only we could get away with it," I said. And, while the sentence hung in the air like an off-speed curveball, I reached for my beer.

◎

OF COURSE A lightbulb did not actually form above the man's head—that only happens in comic strips—but the expression on his jowly face was so eloquent that I must admit I looked up expecting to see the lightbulb. This, clearly, was a man who had just Had An Idea.

He didn't share it immediately. Instead he took a few minutes to work it out in his mind while I worked on my beer. When I saw that he was ready to speak I put my stein down.

"I don't know you," he said.

I allowed that this was true.

"And you don't know me. I don't know your name, even your first name."

"It's—"

He showed me a palm. "Don't tell me. I don't want to know. Don't you see what we are? We're strangers."

"I guess we are."

"We played handball for a couple of hours. But no one even knows we played handball together. We're having a couple of beers together, but only the waiter knows that and he won't remember it, and anyway no one would ever think to ask him. Don't you see the position we're in? We each have someone we want dead. Don't you understand?"

"I'm not sure."

"I saw a movie years ago. Two strangers meet on a train and—I wish I could remember the title."

"Strangers on a Train?"

"That sounds about right. Anyway, they get to talking, tell each other their problems, and decide to do each other's murder. Do you get my drift?"

"I'm beginning to."

"You've got an ex-wife, and I've got an ex-wife. You said you'd commit murder if you had a chance to get away with it, and *I'd* commit murder if I had a chance to get away with it. And all we have to do to get away with it is switch victims." He leaned forward and dropped his voice to an urgent whisper. There was no one near us, but the occasion seemed to demand low voices. "Nothing could be simpler, friend. *You* kill *my* ex-wife. *I* kill *your* ex-wife. And we're both home free."

My eyes widened. "That's brilliant," I whispered back. "It's absolutely brilliant."

"You'd have thought of it yourself in another minute," he said modestly. "The conversation was headed in that direction."

"Just brilliant," I said.

We sat that way for a moment, our elbows on the table, our heads separated by only a few inches, basking in the glow generated by his brilliant idea. Then he said, "One big hurdle. One of us has to go first."

"I'll go first," I offered. "After all, it was your idea. It's only fair that I go first."

"But suppose you went first and I tried to weasel out after you'd done your part?"

"Oh, you wouldn't do that."

"Damn right I wouldn't, friend. But you can't be sure of it, not sure enough to take the short straw voluntarily." He reached into his pocket and produced a shiny quarter. "Call it," he said, tossing it into the air.

"Heads," I said. I always call heads. Just about everyone always calls heads.

The coin landed on the table, spun for a dramatic length of time, then came to rest between Sigma Nu and Delta Kappa Epsilon.

Tails.

◎

I MANAGED TO see Vivian for a half hour that afternoon. After the usual complement of urgent kisses I said, "I'm hopeful. About us, I mean. About our future."

"Really?"

"Really. I have the feeling things are going to work out."

"Oh, darling," she said.

◎

THE FOLLOWING SATURDAY dawned bright and clear. By arrangement we met on the handball court, but this time we played only half a dozen games before calling it a day. And after we had toweled off and put on shirts, we went to a different bar and had but a single beer apiece.

"Wednesday or Thursday night," he said. "Wednesday I'll be playing poker. It's my regular game and it'll last until two or three in the morning. It always does, and I'll make certain that this is no exception. On Thursday, my wife and I are invited to a dinner party and we'll be playing bridge afterward. That won't last past midnight, so Wednesday would be better—"

"Wednesday's fine with me."

"She lives alone and she's almost always home by ten. As a matter of fact she rarely leaves the house. I don't blame her, it's a beautiful house." He pursed his lips. "But forget that. The earlier in the evening you do the job, the better it is for me—in case doctors really can determine time of death—"

"I'll call the police."

"How's that?"

"After she's dead I'll give the police an anonymous phone call, tip them off. That way they'll discover the body while you're still at the poker game. That lets you out completely."

He nodded approval. "That's damned intelligent," he said. "You know something? I'm thrilled you and I ran into each other. I don't know your name and I don't want to know your name, but I sure like your style. Wednesday night?"

"Wednesday night," I agreed. "You'll hear it on the news Thursday morning, and by then your troubles will be over."

"Fantastic," he said. "Oh, one other thing." He flashed the shark's smile. "If she suffers," he said, "that's perfectly all right with me."

SHE DIDN'T SUFFER.

I did it with a knife. I told her I was a burglar and that she wouldn't be hurt if she cooperated. It was not the first lie I ever told in my life. She cooperated, and when her attention was elsewhere I stabbed her in the heart. She died with an expression of extreme puzzlement on her none-too-pretty face, but she didn't suffer, and that's something.

Once she was dead I went on playing the part of the burglar. I ransacked the house, throwing books from their shelves and turning drawers over and generally making a dreadful mess. I found quite a bit of jewelry, which I ultimately put down a sewer, and I found several hundred dollars in cash, which I did not.

After I'd dropped the knife down another sewer and the white cotton gloves down yet a third sewer, I called the police. I said I'd heard sounds of a struggle coming from a particular house, and I supplied the address. I said that two men had rushed from the house and had driven away in a dark car. No, I could not identify the car further. No, I had not seen the license plate. No, I did not care to give my name.

THE FOLLOWING DAY I spoke to Vivian briefly on the telephone. "Things are going well," I said.

"I'm so glad, darling."

"Things are going to work out for us," I said.

"You're wonderful. You know that, don't you? Absolutely wonderful."

◎

ON SATURDAY WE played a mere three games of handball. He won the first, as usual, but astonishingly I beat him in the second game, my first victory over him, and I went on to beat him again in the third. It was then that he suggested that we call it a day. Perhaps he simply felt off his game, or wanted to reduce the chances of someone's noticing the two of us together. On the other hand, he had said at our first meeting that he liked to win. Conversely, one might suppose that he didn't like to lose.

Over a couple of beers he said, "Well, you did it. I knew you'd do it and at the same time I couldn't actually believe you would. Know what I mean?"

"I think so."

"The police didn't even hassle me. They checked my alibi, of course—they're not idiots. But they didn't dig too deep because they seemed so certain it was a burglary. I'll tell you something, it was such a perfectly faked burglary that I even began to get the feeling that that was what happened. Just a coincidence, like. You chickened out and a burglar just happened to do the job."

"Maybe that's what happened," I suggested.

He looked at me, then grinned slyly. "You're one hell of a guy," he said. "Cool as a cucumber, aren't you? Tell me something. What was it like, killing her?"

"You'll find out soon enough."

"Hell of a guy. You realize something? You have the advantage over me. You know my name. From the newspapers. And I still don't know yours."

"You'll know it soon enough," I said with a smile. "From the newspapers."

"Fair enough."

I gave him a slip of paper. Like the one he'd given me, it had an address block-printed in pencil. "Wednesday would be ideal," I said. "If you don't mind missing your poker game."

"I wouldn't have to miss it, would I? I'd just get there late. The poker game gives me an excuse to get out of my house, but if I'm an hour late getting there my wife'll never know the difference. And even if she knew I wasn't where I was supposed to be, so what? What's she gonna do, divorce me and cut herself out of my money? Not likely."

"I'll be having dinner with a client," I said. "Then he and I will be going directly to a business meeting. I'll be tied up until fairly late in the evening—eleven o'clock, maybe midnight."

"I'd like to do it around eight," he said. "That's when I normally leave for the poker game. I can do it and be drawing to an inside straight by nine o'clock. How does that sound?"

I allowed that it sounded good to me.

"I guess I'll make it another fake burglary," he said. "Ransack the place, use a knife. Let them think it's the same crazy burglar striking again. Or doesn't that sound good to you?"

"It might tend to link us," I said.

"Oh."

"Maybe you could make it look like a sex crime. Rape and murder. That way the police would never draw any connection between the two killings."

"Brilliant," he said. He really seemed to admire me now that I'd committed a murder and won two games of handball from him.

"You wouldn't actually have to rape her. Just rip her clothing and set the scene properly."

"Is she attractive?" I admitted that she was, after a fashion. "I've always sort of had fantasies about rape," he said, carefully avoiding my eyes as he spoke. "She'll be home at eight o'clock?"

"She'll be home."

"And alone?"

"Absolutely."

He folded the slip of paper, put it into his wallet, dropped bills from his wallet on the table, swallowed what remained of his beer, and got to his feet. "It's in the bag," he said. "Your troubles are over."

<hr>

"OUR TROUBLES ARE over," I told Vivian.

"Oh, darling," she said. "I can hardly believe it. You're the most wonderful man in the world."

"And a sensational handball player," I said.

<hr>

I LEFT MY house Wednesday night at half past seven. I drove a few blocks to a drugstore and bought a couple of magazines, then went to a men's shop next door and looked at sport shirts. The two shirts I liked weren't in stock in my size. The clerk offered to order them for me but I thought it over and told him not to bother. "I like them," I said, "but I'm not absolutely crazy about them."

I returned to my house. My handball partner's car was parked diagonally across the street. I parked my own car in the driveway and used my key to let myself in the front door. From the doorway I cleared my throat, and he spun around to face me, his eyes bulging out of his head.

I pointed to the body on the couch. "Is she dead?"

"Stone dead. She fought and I hit her too hard…" He flushed a deep red, then he blinked. "But what are you doing here? Don't you remember how we planned it? I don't understand why you came here tonight of all nights."

"I came here because I live here," I said. "George, I'd love to explain but there's no time. I wish there *were* time but there isn't."

I took the revolver from my pocket and shot him in the face.

"THE POLICE WERE very understanding," I told Vivian. "They seem to think the shock of his ex-wife's death unbalanced him. They theorize that he was driving by when he saw me leave my house. Maybe he saw Margaret at the door saying goodbye to me. He parked, perhaps with no clear intention, then went to the door. When she opened the door, he was overcome with desire. By the time I came back and let myself in and shot him it was too late. The damage had been done."

"Poor George."

"And poor Margaret."

She put her hand on mine. "They brought it on themselves," she said. "If George hadn't insisted on that vicious prenuptial agreement we could have had a properly civilized divorce like everybody else."

"And if Margaret had agreed to a properly civilized divorce she'd be alive today."

"We only did what we had to do," Vivian said. "It was a shame about his ex-wife, but I don't suppose there was any way around it."

"At least she didn't suffer."

"That's important," she said. "And you know what they say— you can't break an egg without making omelets."

"That's what they say," I agreed. We embraced, and some moments later we disembraced. "We'll have to give one another rather a wide berth for a month or two," I said. "After all, I killed your husband just as he finished killing my wife. If we should be seen in public, tongues would wag. In a month or so you'll sell your house and leave town. A few weeks after that I'll do the same. Then we can get married and live happily ever after, but in the meantime we'd best be very cautious."

"You're right," she said. "There was a movie like that, except nobody got killed in it. But there were these two people in a small town who were having an affair, and when they met in public they had to pretend they were strangers. I wish I could remember the title."

"*Strangers When We Meet?*"

"That sounds about right."

About Our Contributors:

Patricia Abbott: "The event that closes this story echoes one in my childhood when I found too excellent a hiding place behind the luggage in my grandmother's dusty closet. Hopefully, none of the stories I have since written has given a reader the fright my parents experienced on that day long ago."

Charles Ardai began his writing career at age thirteen, writing reviews of video games for magazines with names like *K-Power* and *Electronic Fun With Computers and Games*, so he comes by his familiarity with 1980s arcade games honestly. The Lexington Avenue pizza parlor in his story consumed many of his quarters, and though it's long gone, the Chinese restaurant next door is still serving the same lunch special it served in the eighties. If you listen closely while you eat your wonton soup, you can almost hear the ghosts of Pac-Men and Space Invaders marching in the distance.

S.A. Cosby is a fan of chess but could never master the game. He decided to focus his attentions on checkers, the unpretentious cousin of the game of kings. He didn't master that particular pastime either but has been endlessly fascinated by it nonetheless.

Jeffery Deaver doesn't hesitate to describe himself as a nerd when he was growing up. He was the sort of athlete about whom the captains of opposing teams plotted fiendishly to make sure he didn't end up on their side. No matter. He had a love of board games, which were not only more mentally challenging than softball or gridiron, but were considerably less physically dangerous. From Risk to chess to Clue to Monopoly and, yes, even Candyland, he would spend hour upon hour trying to best his opponents, and he did so without ever breaking a sweat...or bones.

Long before **Tod Goldberg** could read—owing to his profound dyslexia—he was creating elaborate fantasy worlds with his army men and Star Wars action figures, so when Dungeons & Dragons came along, he was already a practiced storyteller, ready to lead elves into battle. But by that same time, well, other things started to capture his interest, like girls and music and books about men with guns doing a little wrong or a little right. This story captures that time and a few of the stories he was reading about already, where bad stuff happened in small towns and where not everything is solved.

Jane Hamilton both loves and hates parlor games. *Psychiatrist,* she observes, is a perfectly horrible game, a game that is obvious if you know the conceit, and aggravating beyond reason for the single person who is It. Going nuts comes to mind, and so, a pleasurable entertainment for the polite people who are looking on.

James D.F. Hannah discovered gin rummy through Ernie Kovac's book, *How to Talk at Gin.* "I thought it'd be educational, but it's to gin rummy the way *Zen and the Art of Motorcycle Maintenance* is to small engine repair." Hannah did learn how to play the game eventually, and when not writing his Shamus-winning Henry Malone series (*She Talks to Angels, Behind the Wall Of Sleep*), he's probably losing at gin rummy to the app on his phone.

"Contraption." Isn't that a great word? **Gar Anthony Haywood** has always thought so. Contraptions are what the Little Rascals liked to build from lumberyard scrap, baling wire, the wheels taken off an old Radio Flyer wagon and a box of ten-penny nails. Contraptions are the machines of fantasy: cheap, complicated and intrinsically prone to failure. So is it any wonder Gar loved playing Mouse Trap as a boy more than any other board game? No. No, it is not.

Elaine Kagan says she doesn't like playing games, but if Mr. Block asks for a story about playing games, she writes one. She is still looking forward to a New York trip that includes a tuna melt at the Viand. On rye.

When asked what he wanted to be when he grew up, **Avri Klemer** always answered "a novelist," so imagine his surprise when his first published works were analog board games (about penguins and night clubs) rather than books. Avri argues with wife Johanna and daughter Lirit about whether there are more books or games on the shelves of their Brooklyn apartment. In either case, a genuine Hilinski Crokinole board hangs on their wall surveying more content than three people and a puppy could read and play in a lifetime.

Joe R. Lansdale recalls: "Games of marbles were really popular when I was a kid, but when I learned kids kept my marbles if I lost, I kept mine in my room and never played again. I bought several bags of them and they were shiny. I would take them out back and build a ring and shoot them at plastic army men. At some point the marbles disappeared. I must have lost a big game in my sleep."

Warren Moore's father often told him, "Son, if it won't make you any money, there's a good chance you know it." Over the decades, Moore has put that ability to use as a participant in the National Spelling Bee, captain of a state championship high school quiz team, Trivial Pursuit hustler, and occasional participant in barroom trivia competitions.

He makes a little money as an English professor at Newberry College, but otherwise, his father's prediction remains accurate.

In a world of chaos, **David Morrell** enjoys jigsaw puzzles and the satisfaction of combining the pieces into an ordered pattern (sort of like writing a story). He and his wife always have a jigsaw puzzle spread out on a table. Over the years, they realized that images by Steve Crisp (who also creates book covers) are their favorites. A puzzle that shows Steve in his workshop made them realize that he appears in many of his other puzzles. David began to imagine subliminal plots in the images, and that led him to write "The Puzzle Master." In no way is David suggesting that Steve is even remotely similar to the artist in the story.

When **Kevin Quigley** was growing up, board games got pretty competitive in his household. More than once, a game of Pictionary ruined a family reunion. Words were said. Sandwiches were thrown. Boggle was the kinder, gentler sport of the mind that functioned like a word scramble but made you shake the box so vigorously at first that most of your aggression went there. Unless someone, usually Kevin, made everyone use the challenge cube, which made the game infinitely harder. That is, if you weren't the sort of person who read the dictionary for fun. ("Why have friends when you can have books?" was a phrase that has come up in therapy more than once.)

Robert Silverberg has been a science-fiction writer since 1955 and has written a scad and a half of novels, such as *Dying Inside* and *Lord Valentine's Castle*, and three scads of short stories. In an earlier phase of his life he used to spend winters in the Caribbean, where he witnessed, but did not take part in, a turtle race somewhat like this one.

Wallace Stroby has never actually played the game he writes about in "Chance," for money or otherwise, and hopes to keep it that way.

There were often many spirited games of handball being played against the brick walls of Buffalo's P. S. 66, but **Lawrence Block** never participated, being endowed with neither the coordination nor the energy the game demanded. He went on to try golf and bowling and chess, with little to show for his efforts, before turning to writing—where, happily, his physical and mental shortcomings did not hold him back.